3 1994 01094 9482

SANTA ANA PUBLIC LIBRARY

D0768714

Get Your First Book Published

And Make it a Success

Jason Shinder

with Amy Holman
and Jeff Herman

*A recommended selection of
the AWP Writer's Bookshelf*

070.52 SHI
Shinder, Jason
Get your first book
    published
                          $15.99
CENTRAL   31994010949482

CAREER
PRESS
Franklin Lakes, NJ

Copyright © 2001 by Jason Shinder

All rights reserved under the Pan-American and International Copyright Conventions. This book may not be reproduced, in whole or in part, in any form or by any means electronic or mechanical, including photocopying, recording, or by any information storage and retrieval system now known or hereafter invented, without written permission from the publisher, The Career Press.

GET YOUR FIRST BOOK PUBLISHED
Cover design by Foster & Foster
Design by Eileen Munson
Typesetting by Stacey A. Farkas
Printed in the U.S.A. by Book-mart Press

To order this title, please call toll-free 1-800-CAREER-1 (NJ and Canada: 201-848-0310) to order using VISA or MasterCard, or for further information on books from Career Press.

The Career Press, Inc., 3 Tice Road, PO Box 687,
Franklin Lakes, NJ 07417
www.careerpress.com

Library of Congress Cataloging-in-Publication Data

Shinder, Jason, 1955-
     Get your first book published : and make it a success / by Jason Shinder with Amy Holman and Jeff Herman.
         p.   cm.
     Includes index.
     ISBN 1-56414-450X (pbk.)
     1. Authorship—Marketing. 2. Authors and publishers. I. Holman, Amy. II. Herman, Jeff, 1958- III. Title.

PN161 .S54 2000
070.52—dc21
                                                                                    00-057926

In memory of Allen Ginsberg
1926-1997

What lovest well remains, the rest is dross
What lovest well shall not bereft from thee
What lovest well is thy true history

—*Ezra Pound*
Pisan Cantos

*In an age defined by its modes of production,
where everybody tends to be a specialist of sorts,
the artist ideally is that rarity, a whole person
making a whole thing.*

—Stanley Kunitz

ACKNOWLEDGMENTS

Thanks to the people from the many organizations who responded to editorial questionnaires and/or phone interviews.

Although listings in this book were based on the questionnaires and phone interviews, two general resource books were also called upon, if necessary, to verify select information. These books were *Grants and Awards Available to Writers* (Editor, John Monroe; PEN, American Center) and *The Writer's Market* (Editor, Kristen C. Holm; *Writer's Digest*).

Thanks also to the many authors who contributed comments and advice regarding their first-book experiences. Special thanks to Terry McMillan, Nancy Means-Wright, Anna Monardo, and Sadi Ranson for their critical essays. And thanks to the Associated Writing Program and *Poets & Writers* for their help in securing and/or permitting the reprinting of select pieces.

Amy Holman, Director of Literary Horizons at *Poets & Writers, Inc.*, was very much a part of the book's development, especially in securing comments from authors and developing portions of the various listings.

Katie Adams, Elizabeth Wilson, Amanda White, and Johanna Haney created and researched a database of all the listings, and provided assistance on various other matters of research and technology. Without their hard work, responsibility, and quality of dedication, this book would not have been completed. Rodney Phillips, Director of the Berg Exhibition Room, Center for the Humanities at the New York Public Library, generously offered rare research and exhibition documents regarding the publishing information of the first books of our country's most distinguished authors. His many years of hard work on behalf of writers and books is of the highest quality and impact. Thanks also to editor Ruth Greenstein for her practical, important, and friendly advice introducing each part of the book.

Thanks to the publisher and editors at Career Press for their patience and critical input, especially Stacey A. Farkas, Editorial Director. Finally, thanks to Jeff Herman for his invaluable support and assistance, without whom this book would not have been possible.

CONTENTS

INTRODUCTION

Can a single volume enthusiastically reflect the richness, diversity, and extensive information and resources regarding the development of a first book?

Get Your First Book Published (previously *The First Book Market*), guest edited with Amy Holman and Jeff Herman, answers that question with great optimism and enthusiasm. Ms. Holman, Director of Literary Horizons at *Poets & Writers, Inc.*, and Mr. Herman, the editor of the highly regarded annual directory of agents and editors, *Writer's Guide to Book Editors, Publishers and Literary Agents*, offer this volume of new, invaluable information and advice.

There are dozens of obvious topics that a resource about first books needs to address: the awards for unpublished manuscripts, publishers favorable to first books, promotion of first books, first-hand accounts by writers on their first-book experiences, and a list of available resources. I'm pleased to say that *Get Your First Book Published* illuminates these matters and more. You'll find an extensive list of favorite first books by authors, a selection of classic American first book annotations, a section on resources on the Web, a suggested reading list, and more.

Tracking the information and resources available for *Get Your First Book Published* is always a rigorous experience, and would not be possible without the ongoing assistance of the book's editorial assistants, Katie Adams, Elizabeth Wilson, Amanda White and Johanna Haney. More than 350 general and specific literary arts magazines were surveyed to identify any and all information regarding first books. Many publishers and authors sent us information, or pointed us to publications or awards to review. Resources for first books on the Web has certainly become a critical factor, and our survey included online opportunities as well. What we realized, of course, was that it's a difficult task to keep up with what's out there, which only heightened the importance of our getting the best and most up-to-date information.

The research gathering and correspondences received during the preparation for this book has also been an instructive experience. At the risk of some oversimplification, it's become clear that writers move forward, and back and forth, through several levels of engagement—from contact, to participation, to commitment to ownership—at any point of which a first book might surface.

The first stage, *contact*, is that level where a writer first links up with his or her desire to write. Such an experience may happen very early on or later in life, say, upon hearing a poem or story read out loud in school or at a public reading. The second level, *participation*, is where the writer begins to identify his or her *need* to write by, for example, reading writers he or she loves, taking a writing workshop, attending readings on a regular basis, writing more regularly. The third level, *commitment*, is where a writer begins to identify him- or herself as a writer, in the role of a writer— where he or she begins to create the character and the environment he or she will need to write. At this level a writer might, for example, leave his or her job to finish or start a writing project, apply for awards and writing residencies, and/or enter a graduate writing program. The fourth level, *ownership*, is where a writer is struggling with the bone and flesh of his or her desire and the limits of his or her work in regards to content, context, structure, strategies, singularity, and joy. He or she is no longer participating in the literary community to ask permission to write, but instead for support to help stay the course already taken. At this level, the writer has usually moved a good deal from the *I* to the *We*. In other words, it is understood more fully that he or she is part of a much larger tradition and, therefore, hopefully can be seen as an essential contributor to writing and literature whatever level resources will allow. Finally, at this level, a writer usually has developed a small tribe of his or her own people, writers and others, to work through the many changes, challenges, opportunities, and joys that are always present.

I haven't read any biography, in fact, of any writer in which he or she didn't have some sort of community, some tribe, to work with—even if it was one person, even if there was a perceived and/or public need for utter privacy and/or isolation by the writer. In this light, who you have chosen to be in your tribe, and why, is critical and is not as accidental as we might believe. The question here is: Have you chosen people, teachers, and friends, only to keep you at a certain level, or have you been able to associate with people who might move you in other directions. Our partners, our literary and other friends, our community, at whatever level we choose to participate, is critical throughout these levels of engagement.

First books can change a writer's life. It did for Delmore Schwartz, James Baldwin, Alan Dugan, Amy Tan, Lucy Grealy, and hundreds of other authors, many of whom are noted in this book. For the most part, however, first books offer writers an opportunity to share their writing in public and, more important, move toward greater and greater ownership of their work. Over the last decade, there has been, in America at least, a sharp and glaring increase in the amount of first book publications and resources. At the same time, there has been a drop in the level upon which these books are observed by critics as the starting point of a writer's career. It is often the second or third book that critics now review to point the way toward the substance of a writer's themes and strategies. In light of this, several awards that once recognized first books now recognize second or third books, including, for example, the James Laughlin award of the Academy of American Poets. Yet with each change of a first book award's criteria to second or third books, a slew of new awards for first books appears.

The overall purpose of this book is to make sure all such changes and constants and additions regarding first book development is gathered together in one accessible and comprehensive format. It is the first book to focus exclusively on this subject. While the book shows writers the various and unique routes toward first-book publication, I also hope it reminds authors of the hard work, patience, faith, joy, and love writing and reading both requires and strengthens.

—Jason Shinder

USER'S GUIDE

Parts two, three, and four of this book regarding awards and publishers include listings of specific opportunities for your unpublished first book. Each listing includes basic information regarding the award and, wherever possible, information regarding previous winners, judges, and/or editorial comments from the publisher or award's administrators.

After you've identified an opportunity you want to pursue, send a self-addressed stamped envelope (SASE) to the address in the listing and carefully review all the submission requirements. Your chance to have your manuscript receive serious consideration, or any consideration, depends upon following any directions to the letter. In some cases, application forms need to be sent along with your manuscript. These forms will be sent to you with the information regarding submission requirements.

The listings in Chapter 2 and Chapter 3 are also arranged by award in the prize index and by their particular genre in the genre index. Many listings also let you know how long it will typically take for the organization to respond to your submission.

Please note: Listings are based on questionnaires and/or phone interviews. Listings are not advertisements. The results of contact with listed awards, contest, and publishers are not the responsibility of the editor.

Part 1

"What Lovest Well Remains": Writers on Their First Books

Introduction

—*Ruth Greenstein*

For most writers, the road to publishing that first book is long and far and full of rocks and ruts. Others get lucky and find their way with hardly a hitch. This part of *Get Your First Book Published* features real-life stories from contemporary writers of various stripes on their own first-book publication experience. While each of these writers has found his or her own road to publication, many offer the same admonitions on how to stay on that road until you reach your destination. Here, in short, is a listing of those suggestions that come up again and again:

Build up to the book

A writer's first book is almost never his or her first publication. Don't rush into trying to publish a whole book. Start slow. Take workshops. Get plenty of feedback on your work from peers and professionals. Self-publish. Publish small pieces in small magazines. (See Chapter 13 for the names of directories that list such magazines.) Keep an eye out for local magazines and journals that specialize in the subjects about which you write. Start your own small magazine.

WHAT YOU'VE HEARD IS TRUE

An M.F.A. Thesis is not a book

In most cases, especially for writers at the beginning of their careers, a thesis for a graduate writing program is simply a collection of their work to date. A book, on the other hand, is a meticulously arranged collection of a writer's very best work. The book as a whole is no different than its individual elements, in that each should reflect a single vision. As writer Nick Carbó reminds us in this section, do not make the mistake of assuming that your thesis is a publishable book.

—J.S. 📖

Gestate

Many writers warn that it is impossible to view their own work critically without some time and distance from it. Don't send out your work right after it's finished. "No wine before its time," says Ron Carlson, with homage to the ad writers at Gallo. Let your writing sit for a while. Then give it a fresh look and see if it still works.

Revise and retry

One of the wonderful things about the publishing business is that people and projects are constantly in flux. Take advantage of this. Get feedback on why your work has been rejected and revise it accordingly. Then go out and pursue new opportunities. For example, if your manuscript has been rejected by an editor at your favorite publishing house, chances are that by the time you've revised your work, that editor will be working elsewhere and may want to reconsider your project at his or her new house. Meanwhile, there will likely be a new editor at the original publisher whom you can also approach.

> ### WHAT YOU'VE HEARD IS TRUE
>
> Alan Dugan waited until he was 39 years old to submit his first book, *Poems*, for publication. When he finally did, it received the Yale Series of Younger Poets Award, the Pulitzer Prize, the National Book Award, the National Book Critics Circle Award, and the Prix de Rome.
>
> —J.S. 📖

Love the work

Don't lose sight of the goal, which must be the process of writing and the work itself, not the recognition that may or may not eventually come from it. Keep your focus there.

Network

Don't try to do it alone. Behind nearly every successful writer is a loyal peer support system that helped him or her get there. Talk to other writers and learn from their experiences as well as your own. Go to literary events and meet people in the business. Seek out editors who may be interested in your work.

Persevere

Learn to take rejections in stride. Consider each disappointment as one more stepping stone that leads to your goal. Don't pace yourself against other writers; remember that everyone finds his or her own road. Try out some of the suggestions from writers like Toi Derricotte for submitting and resubmitting your work. Create your own routines for keeping your writing in circulation.

Keep the faith

Be prepared for the long haul. If you're truly committed, the journey should not be a painful one. Consider the first-book experiences of writers like Anna Monardo and her 12-year journey into publication. Remember that for most writers, the old adage paraphrased by Carolyn Forche holds true: "It takes years to become an overnight success."

WHAT YOU'VE HEARD IS TRUE

Every return brings you closer to your goal

The return of your writing from an editor is not a rejection of you as a writer or as a person. It is information you can use in your pursuit of three objectives:

1. identifying how to make your writing as strong as possible;
2. identifying opportunities to build relationships with editors;
3. identifying opportunities to publish your work.

In this way, consider every return of your work as a cause for celebration. The sooner you receive such returns, the closer you will be to finding the appropriate place for your work.

William Kennedy's Pulitzer Prize-winning novel, Ironweed, *was rejected by more than 10 publishers before it found a home.*

—J.S.

Ruth Greenstein has been in the publishing business for nine years and has edited a wide range of fiction, nonfiction, and poetry. She has worked for Harcourt Brace & Company, The Ecco Press, and independently as an editor, writer, and publishing consultant.

WRITERS ON THEIR OWN FIRST BOOKS

"Write the Book You Want to Write, Not the One You Think Will Sell"

—Cathryn Alpert

Cathryn Alpert had the ideal first-book experience. "Before I was a third of the way into *Rocket City,* Greg Michalson of *The Missouri Review* and the fiction editor for MacMurray and Beck, asked to see it. His call came out of the blue and very early in the morning. I remember he woke me and I had no idea who he was, how he found me, or what he was talking about, as I'd never heard of MacMurray and Beck and had never sent any work to *The Missouri Review*. I had been published twice in *Puerto Del Sol,* which he mentioned, but I failed to see the connection," Ms. Alpert says. "I am not much of a morning person." In fact, she would not have sent her completed manuscript if he had not sent a follow-up letter. Two weeks after she did, Michalson called to offer to publish *Rocket City.* Ms. Alpert secured Felicia Eth to be her agent, "whom I'd once seen give an excellent and very savvy talk about book publishing. She negotiated the terms of the contract with MacMurray and Beck, and upon the book's publication, brought it to the attention of Marty Asher at Vintage, who purchased the paperback rights."

Vintage sent Ms. Alpert on a national book tour, garnering serious publicity for *Rocket City.* Between the hardcover and paperback editions, she'd recorded an interview and read excerpts from the novel for Kay Bonetti of the American Audio Prose Library and gave about 20 readings and book signings throughout her home state of California. The hardcover edition was chosen for Barnes & Noble's Discover Great New Writers Series, but it was the national book tour afforded by Vintage that gave her the sense that her book was actually being read.

Ms. Alpert had heard horror tales about the fate of "mid-listed" writers in the big houses and although she did not have any knowledge of working with any kind of publisher to begin with, she's glad she started small. "MacMurray and Beck put everything it had behind *Rocket City.* Both Greg Michalson and Fred Ramey, the editor in chief, spent hours on the phone with me, discussing everything from commas to semicolons to how I envisioned the cover. They were both wonderful—patient and nurturing—and two of the best editors I've ever had. I wouldn't trade that experience for anything."

Ms. Alpert's beginning as a writer can be traced back to her reading and rereading *Stuart Little,* E.B. White's first book for children. "Stuart Little was my first picaresque hero, whose story of longing and differentness [sic] simply broke my heart." *Sense and Sensibility,* by Jane Austen, is her favorite 19th-century first novel, if only for its intelligence, which includes "Austen's wit, social acuity, sparkling language and innate sensitivity to nuance." Amy Tan's *The Joy Luck Club* is "as perfect a first book as has ever been written." Ms. Alpert lists some other firsts, including David Bowman's *Let the Dog Drive* and Laurie Hendrie's *Stygo,* among others.

The nonfiction firsts are *Girl Interrupted,* by Susanna Kaysen, "for its lyrical lack of sentimentality," *Reeling and Writhing,* by Candida Lawrence, "for its understated humor," and Michael Harrington's *The Other America,* "a book about poverty in America that controverted 12 years of programming by my white, upper-middle-class, Nixon-adoring parents."

She says, "write the book you want to write, not the book you think will sell," because "dedicated and committed publishers, both large and small, remain. Find an agent with whom you have rapport. Can you call your agent at home on a Sunday or does the thought of such an intrusion make you break out in hives? Your agent should be your partner. Find one who makes you feel comfortable." She says not to resist changes suggested by your editor because "editors exist in the world to make you look good. Although the changes suggested for *Rocket City* were minor, they were crucial to the betterment of the novel."

"Don't be wary of small publishing houses. The downside is money. They don't pay much in the way of advances, and often don't have the budget to support such luxuries as book tours and trips to the ABA. The upside is the individual attention they can give you, especially if they're a new house and only releasing one or two titles a season." But she warns writers not to get hung up on publication, either. "Losing sight of the goal—which is writing—is the quickest way to box in your imagination. Write well, and the rest will follow."

Cathryn Alpert's first novel is Rocket City *published by MacMurray and Beck and reprinted by them in 1996. She is a "recovering academic" with a Ph.D. in theatre and lives with her family in Aptos, California.*

📖

"They Make You Think You Have a Book When You Graduate"

—Nick Carbó

Nick Carbó, a Filipino-American poet, whose first book, *El Grupo McDonalds,* was published by Tia Chucha Press in Chicago, recommends three first books: *White Elephants,* by Reetika Vazrani, Beacon Press, 1996; *Likely,* by Lisa Coffman, Kent State University Press, 1997; and *Ismaila Eclipse,* by Khaled Mattawa, Sheep Meadow Press, 1995. These poets won prizes and fellowships, and Mr. Carbó suggests that if you look at how the poems in these books are ordered, that will help you put together your own poetry collections.

"It just took me so long," he says when asked about the publication of his first book. "For those who go through MFA programs, they make you think you have a book when you graduate—with your thesis—but most of the poems aren't really finished. In the two years it took me to put together a manuscript, only 10 poems from the thesis survived. Most I wrote after. It was four years after graduating that the book was accepted."

Mr. Carbó says to send to publishers and competitions. "Of course that's a lot of rejections in four years. The publisher that finally accepted me, Luis Rodriguez at Tia Chucha, publishes a lot of ethnic writers, including Elizabeth Alexander, so I definitely had a better chance. You can't send blindly." The anthology of Filipino and Filipino-American poetry Mr. Carbó edited, *Returning a Borrowed Tongue,* was accepted by Coffee House Press around the same time as *El Grupo McDonalds,* so he had the good fortune of two books coming out the same year. "It's dry for a while and it suddenly rains," he says.

Nick Carbó recently edited the anthology Returning a Borrowed Tongue: Filipino/Filipina Poetry *(Coffee House Press). He teaches at The New School for Social Research in New York City.*

"Write Only What You Love"

—Ron Carlson

Ron Carlson's favorite first book is F. Scott Fitzgerald's *This Side of Paradise*, "not because the novel is so 'young' and dear and tender toward its confused protagonist Amory Blaine, but because it, more than any other first book I know, reveals so dearly how it was constructed, pasted together, stitched, and ironed," he says, revealing the editorial eye of one who teaches creative writing. "It's some kind of fresh, untutored, or barely tutored, scrapbook with just a nod at narrative. Sophomoric and self-conscious half the time, lyric and uninhibited others, the novel ultimately carries, despite Fitzgerald's efforts in the final pages to make it important. I read it when I was 19 and I moved my bed over by the window. If I had waited a year, the answer to this question would have been different."

Mr. Carlson's advice is not limited to writers of first books, but can be applied to every process of writing. "Keep your head down; stay in the room; write only what you love; don't write it for other people; if someone else could write the book you're working on, let them."

"I wrote my first novel, *Betrayed by F. Scott Fitzgerald*, because I was young and because I wanted to; I was not in a program or school. I had too great affection for many curiosities I'd come across and I wrote a book to claim them," he says, adding, "I'm from Utah and no one had asked me to please write a book. When I had most of a draft, I looked in the *Literary Market Place* in the library for publishers and came across W.W. Norton in New York City."

He ran his finger down the list of editors, "until I was halfway past the presidents and chairman and vice presidents to the editors and then to the name, Carol Houck Smith, and it looked like a good name, a person at that place in the list who might not be too busy."

The sequence of events that followed Mr. Carlson's query, in which he admitted that much of the novel was set in Utah, has comic twists worthy of his own fiction. "She wrote back that she would read the book, to send it, and then a month later she wrote back that Norton wanted to publish the book. We spoke on the telephone and at the end of the call, I had to ask her to send back the two-page synopsis of the last section of the book, because I had neglected to keep a copy. I didn't know then that they had decided to publish the book whether I could finish it or not. We've laughed about that many times since," he says, "but there is a nice part two-thirds through where Larry is walking through town in the twilight and I guess the book could've ended there."

Still in Utah in 1977 when the novel came out, he received a call from Carol Houck Smith with the report that the daily *New York Times* had reviewed the book and that she had good news and bad news. "I asked for the good news and it was good news indeed, as she read the review and it was the perfect review. I was thrilled. 'Your picture is in the paper too by the review,' she said, and I asked her how I looked. She said I looked good.

"The bad news was simply that it was a blackout in New York, the paper never hit the streets. So my picture and that review of *Betrayed by F. Scott Fitzgerald,* my first novel, published when I was 29, is in a collector's edition of that famous paper—an irony I now appreciate."

Mr. Carlson's advance back then "was minuscule, but what it has meant since to me and to my career is immeasurable. Carol and I have worked on all five of my books," he says, stating that *Betrayed...* is still in print. His latest collection of stories, *The Hotel Eden,* was published in 1997. And like his favorite first book, "it is a book I see now that is a bit of a scrapbook, but it's a good story, and even though I've evolved as a writer in the years since, I'm sticking to it."

Ron Carlson's latest book is a collection of stories, The Hotel Eden *(W. W. Norton, 1997). He directs the writing program at Arizona State University.*

"An Editor Is Not God"

—Toi Derricotte

Toi Derricotte sent her first book, *The Empress of the Death House,* Lotus Press, 1978, out to African-American publishing houses, "since several of the poems were about race," and they'd be more open to publishing her work at that time. "I got a letter from Broadside Press saying that the editor, Dudley Randall, was interested but not publishing books at this time. He recommended Naomi Long Madgett at Lotus Press and she accepted my book, *The Empress of the Death House,* shortly after I sent it.

"I had been writing seriously, often several hours a day seven days a week, for about 10 years when my first book was published. I did not get much guidance. I am scrupulous and like to turn over finished manuscripts to my publishers. I didn't take any money at all on the sale. And now that I think about it, I have never been sent any money from sales of the book, though it's in third or fourth printing, I think. I don't keep up with money matters concerning poetry book sales, especially since most poets don't make that much on sales. However, I am delighted that the publisher has kept my book in print for almost 20 years!"

Ms. Derricotte named three books that most impressed her when she began writing seriously and she still thinks they are wonderful: *A Street in Bronzeville,* by Gwendolyn Brooks; *Howl,* by Allen Ginsberg; and *Colossus,* by Sylvia Plath. Her advice to writers refers to the build-up to a book, publishing the poems in magazines. She says to make a list of the magazines you want to be published by and rotate poems to all those magazines until all poems have been read by all magazines. "Remember if you like a certain editor's taste, that editor may be one likely to like your taste. Wait until you have enough poems to send out several to each of those magazines on your list at the same time."

"So you won't be disappointed, count on one acceptance out of 14 or 15 tries." Ms. Derricotte offers a method by which to handle responses to these mailings. "Use a post office box so that you can go pick up your news of acceptances and/or rejections when you're in the right mood. When you get poems back, repackage them—have an envelope ready to go—and send them out quickly to another magazine on your list. In this way, editors get accustomed to your work and name. If you get a personal note from an editor, however brief, keep sending to that editor, even if it takes 80 tries.

"Remember," she concludes, "an editor is not God, only a person with a certain viewpoint, certain taste; therefore, don't let rejection slips stop you from writing or sending out."

Toi Derricotte's most recent book is The Black Notebooks *(W. W. Norton, 1997).*

"Learn From the Insights of Another Writer"

—John Haines

In his favorite first book, poet and creative nonfiction writer John Haines, who lives in, and writes often about Alaska, was "deeply impressed by a novel, *The Sleepwalkers,* by the German writer Hermann Broch. I have forgotten how I first came upon Broch's novel, but I read it in the standard translation by Willa and Edwin Muir early in the 1980s. I read it slowly, a chapter or two a day, absorbing page by page and episode by episode the three interconnected sections of the book, in which the various characters mingled, then separated, to meet again at a later time in greatly changed circumstances brought on by the First World War as it affected Prussian and Austrian empires, challenging and altering all traditional values in the general upheaval of the age." Mr. Haines praises the novel as a first book and also recognizes Broch's succeeding works as "distinctive and individual, each of them in its own way attempting to define some aspect of this modern period." He even reread *The Sleepwalkers,* aloud, to a close friend, with renewed insight and admiration.

"I remember quite vividly that when copies of my first book, *Winter News,* arrived in the mail in the spring of 1966, I was afraid to open it, fearful of what I might find there: mistakes, bad lines, poems I no longer liked, etc.," Mr. Haines says, a bit shy about recalling the publication of his first book. "I had similar reactions when a magazine arrived with a poem of mine featured. I read nearly everything else in the journal before I turned to my own work. I'm not sure why I reacted this way, and I don't know if it is common with other writers. I've long since put that sort of thing behind me, yet I still feel a certain hesitation when I turn to, say, a poem of mine in *The New Criterion,* [even though] I'm naturally eager to see it there, [and] pleased that the editors thought enough of the poem to publish it."

Mr. Haines also speaks on the favorable reaction to his first collection of poems, published when he was 42, since "it had its source in a part of the country, remote from the major literary activities in cities like New York. I have to say I feel quite fortunate in having that early reception, with all the invitations to read that followed, the correspondence with other poets; the request for poems from many editors. Meanwhile, I had begun work on an entirely new collection of poems, one that would take me a long way from the setting in that first slim book."

Mr. Haines speaks about the critical aspect of being a writer, how one eagerly reads reviews and comments made of one's work, especially in the case of a first book. "We want to know what others think of the work, whether they like it, whether they understand what it is one is trying to do. And I know it can be disappointing, sometimes irritating, when we feel that the reviewer has somehow misread the work, failed to appreciate just what it was one intended in a particular poem or essay. I recall reacting with a mixture of amusement and resentment in the case of a well-known university poet condescending to a remark on what he called 'Mr. Haines's few artful but subdued triumphs,' etc. I have since had the occasion to review a book by this same poet, in which I was tempted to, as we say, 'get even'!

Well that's the literary life, isn't it? But in this case I tried to be fair, while also being honest about some fairly serious flaws I found in the poems.

"I think it's important not to take this sort of thing too seriously," Mr. Haines continues in his advice to writers. "Especially in the case of a first book, and to see if there is not something to be learned from a critic's remarks. After all, he or she might be of some help in achieving a firmer grasp on verse technique, a deeper insight on whatever it is one is attempting to say. There have been examples of writers who have refused to read a review of their book, and there may be some wisdom in that—a refusal to allow the potential distraction from one's real work. Finally, this is a matter of individual disposition, ideally tempered by an honest desire to learn, if possible, from the insights of another writer."

John Haines's recent books include the collection of essays, Fables and Distances *(Graywolf) and the poetry book,* A Guide to the Fourchambered Heart *(Larkspur Press). He lives in Anchorage, Alaska.*

"A Novel Can Be Workshopped to Death"

—Shelby Hearon

In 1967, Shelby Hearon sent her first novel, *Armadillo in the Grass,* over the transom without a name, without knowing writers or editors, to Knopf because they had beautiful books. In her letter she said that if they didn't love this to send it back to her and she would send it elsewhere. Judith Jones, her current editor, took it. Her first reader read it, then the second reader, and then, Judith. "That was back when they had first readers," Ms. Hearon says.

And while it's amazing to have one's first novel accepted by a big house on the first try, Ms. Hearon is quick to say that she worked on that novel for five years and didn't show it to anybody, and still never shows her novels to anybody until they are finished. Her advice to novelists is the advice she gives to people she's taught—"you have to learn to tell if it's good. A novel can be workshopped to death."

Three first novels sprung to Ms. Hearon's mind as her favorites: *Mysteries of Pittsburgh,* by Michael Chabon; *The Movie Goer,* by Walker Percy; and *Mona in the Promised Land,* by Gish Jen.

Shelby Hearon's latest novel, Footprints, *was published by Knopf. She lives in Burlington, Vermont.*

"Who Wrote This Way Before?"

—Gail Mazur

Gail Mazur is limiting her choices to the "most astonishing first books that had an enormous impact on me." Ms. Mazur imagines the debut of Elizabeth Bishop's *North & South.* "To guess what it must've been like to have opened this book in 1946, by a new poet, with 'The Map,' 'The Man-Moth,' 'The Weed,' 'Cirque d' Hiver,' 'Roosters,' 'The Fish'—well, why guess, read it, and read Randall Jarrell's piece on Bishop. These early poems were 'echt-Bishop': lucent, lucid, luscious! And this poet, who would become known for, among more significant attributes, perhaps, the economy of her output, continued until her death in 1979 to write brilliant poems, always, it seems to me, at the top of her form."

James Tate's *The Lost Pilot* is her second choice. "At 23, Tate's poems already had the bravura, zany lyricism, courage, and poignancy that was to grow steadily in the following decades. These poems certainly triggered poems in me, for which I am still grateful."

Ms. Mazur will never forget the feeling she had when she read Frank Bidart's *Golden State* in manuscript form in the early '70s, that this would be the new American voice in poetry. "Who wrote this way before Bidart?" she asks. "Twenty-odd years later, a body of work, an individual, unmistakable voice, at the center of our senses of poetry at the end of the century."

Gail Mazur's first book of poetry, Nightfire, *was published by David R. Godine in 1978. Her most recent collection,* The Common, *is with the University of Chicago Press, 1995. She teaches at Emerson's Creative Writing Program and is the founder and director of the Blacksmith House Poetry Center in Cambridge, Massachusetts.*

"Worldly Matters and Matters of Art Are Different"

—Robert Pinsky

The United States Poet Laureate, Robert Pinsky, is glad his first manuscript did not get published as his first book, although he tried. When the second manuscript was taken, he was 34, and he "felt extremely old with a much-delayed first book." He'd been publishing a lot in little magazines since he was very young, and he just swept a lot of them into the manuscript, *Sadness & Happiness,* "and now I just wish they were swept out to sea."

Naturally, age influences Mr. Pinsky's interest in other poets' first books, and he separates his favorites into past and present. "Historically, *Prufrock and Other Observations* [T.S. Eliot], because he was so young, and *A Boy's Will* [Robert Frost], because he was so old." He also cites William Carlos Williams's first book, "because of its saucy address to the readers on the cover." Mr. Pinsky also likes Anne Winter's *The Key to the City,* which came late, and had seven poems about New York City that are the best. When he taught Mark Halliday's *Little Star* at Berkeley, the students liked it so much, "I was sure *Little Star* would become a best-seller." Carl Phillips's *In the Blood* was written and published while he was in the Boston University Creative Writing Program, and it was followed by an even better book.

Mr. Pinsky's advice to writers is "to remember that everyone is different, there's no one manner in which first books come." And on the line of perseverance, to remember the importance of acceptance of a different pace for each poet. "Worldly matters touch art, but are not necessarily matters of art," Mr. Pinsky says. "With the publication and reception of the first book, one cares so much, so it's hard." It's important not to confuse the two realms. "Worldly matters and matters of art are different."

Robert Pinsky's latest books include The Figured Wheel: New and Selected Poems *(Farrar, Straus, & Giroux, 1996) and an award-winning translation of Dante's* Inferno. *He teaches at Boston University.*

"I Laugh at an Advance"

—Terese Svoboda

"After graduating from Columbia, I worked on my poetry for 10 years and won a first-book contest with the University of Georgia. No editorial guidance was offered, but workshops contributed a lot in the shaping of individual poems. No advance. My first book of prose took 15 years to write, ditto about the workshops, but in particular an exhilarating experience with Gordon Lish taught me that I might as well write the way I pleased since goddamn nobody would ever publish it. It won the Bobst Prize, the Great Lakes New Writers Award, and was runner-up for the Paterson Prize." *Cannibal* was published in 1995 with NYU Press. "It went through three agents, a hundred rejections—13 alone in the form that won the prizes. No advance. I laugh at an advance."

"Whereas a first book of poetry is regarded as a poet's first mewlings, the first book of prose must soar impossible heights, as reflected in the bidding wars. The prose writer is like a film director; if he hasn't scored a sell-out by the third time, he's out. The poet is just beginning to be recognized by the third book." However, Ms. Svoboda knows that poets can also be selected by big houses after publishing with smaller presses because they work so hard promoting their own work.

Thus, her advice to writers is threefold and simple—perseverance, constant review of your own work, and belief in your own voice. "By the way, NYU's prize is the only one that offers cash, a fabulous cocktail party, lots of photographers, and a catered dinner party for intimate friends and family after the awards ceremony. They really make a big deal out of a first book. The Great Lakes New Writers Award is another stroke of genius in that the award is a reading series throughout the Great Lakes region, giving the writer a chance to tap a new audience and gain experience reading in public."

Terese Svoboda's favorite first books include Anne Caston's book, *Flying Out with the Wounded* and David Rivard's *Torque.* Her own first book of poetry, *All Aberration,* was published in 1985.

Terese Svoboda's most recent books include the novel Cannibal *(NYU Press) and the poetry book* Mere Mortals *(University of Georgia Press). She teaches at Williams College.*

📖

"Small Presses Are the Way to Go"

—Karen Tei Yamashita

Karen Tei Yamashita has no idea what her favorite first books are because she doesn't ever pay attention to whether a book is the author's first or second or fifth. She has an inch stack of rejection letters for her own first effort, *Through the Arc of the Rain Forest,* eventually published by Coffee House Press. "I took a one-day class at UCLA on how to publish it and wrote a note to Alan Lau, who wrote back one of his funny postcards suggesting three publishers interested in Asian-American writers. I wasn't sure about that because the book is not necessarily about Asian-Americans, but I went ahead and sent queries. The University of Washington didn't want fiction, Graywolf looked at it, but Coffee House took it." It took Allen Kornblum of Coffee House to recognize what Ms. Yamashita was doing with the novel, which is slipped between the genres.

"I knew nothing about the business, but I learned very quickly. Sue Ostfield, the publicist, was marvelous, and walked me through the process. Allen has a great love of the publishing business." She says that she didn't meet them in person until the ABA book fair held that year in Las Vegas. "A strange place for a book fair. I enter this huge hall and the small presses are all in one row. I have a great respect for the independent presses. I don't want any to die and it's sad that the NEA didn't come through."

Ms. Yamashita says that small presses are the best options for literature, except that they are overloaded. Every year Coffee House's submissions get more overwhelming. "I believe they are the way to go. Small presses have small staffs who know you, who've all read your book and believe in you. I think, unless you have a blockbuster and can get an agent, they are the best way. Not a lot of money, but nobody's looking to make a lot with a first book."

Ms. Yamashita mentions a detail that often comes into play with small presses: The publishers are willing to consider the author's input when it comes to the cover design. "Allen called me and asked me if I had any idea of color for the cover. I thought that was strange, but he said that people have strong associations with color, some can be bad. I told him that my husband was an artist," she laughs. "I couldn't see his face because this was the telephone but he probably thought, 'oh no.' But he asked me to send him a sample—and that's the cover of the book. That can happen at a small press."

All of Karen Tei Yamashita's books are published with Coffee House Press. Through the Arc of the Rain Forest was published in 1990 and Tropic of Orange in 1997. She teaches at UC Santa Cruz.

Part
2

First Light:
Awards for
Unpublished
First-Book
Manuscripts

Introduction

—*Ruth Greenstein*

The many organizations that sponsor literary contests and awards are an excellent venue for writers seeking recognition and publication for a first-book manuscript. But before sending out your manuscript, there are a number of questions you can ask yourself to help ensure that your work is in suitable shape and that you are sending it to the most appropriate and promising places.

Have I received several professional opinions on the quality of my manuscript?

Family and friends are often good sounding boards, but only a professional such as a writing teacher, an editor, or a published writer can give you the kind of knowing critique that will help you produce a publishable work. If you are not sure of where to find such professionals, Part 7 of this book will help steer you in the right direction.

Have I prepared my manuscript in a suitable format?

One of the hazards of home computing is that it enables people to do too much with the format of their work. I recommend that writers avoid using fancy typography. A clean-looking page in a plain and readable typeface such as Courier, Times Roman, or a classic book font will let your words be seen without distracting your readers. Be sure your manuscript is properly paginated and cleanly photocopied, and that it includes appropriate front and back matter, if necessary.

Have I determined which types of contests and awards are the most suitable for my work?

This is where *Get Your First Book Published* comes in. The listings that follow are divided into two categories: Awards Exclusively for Unpublished First-Book Manuscripts and Awards Favorable to Unpublished First-Book Manuscripts. Awards for longer manuscripts such as novels and works of nonfiction can be found in these sections, while awards for shorter works that lend themselves to the chapbook format can be found in Chapter 5.

Have I done enough research?

Once you've read through the listings and noted which awards seem suitable for your work, request the guidelines for each award that interests you and review them carefully. Then have a look at the books published by past winners, and find out what you can about the writers who are judging the awards. Does the style and quality of your work seem consistent with the work written by past winners? If it differs dramatically from that of previous winners, you may want to focus your efforts (and dollars) elsewhere.

WHAT YOU'VE HEARD IS TRUE

There is life after 40

A woman once approached me after a reading and, within a few moments of conversation, she told me that her husband was very depressed. "Why?" I asked.

She said, "He just turned 40." I said, "My father is 50 and he's not depressed. What's so depressing about turning 40?" She then told me that he had been a finalist for the Yale Series of Younger Poets Award, but now that he was 40 he could no longer apply.

It was clear to me that by pursuing only one path to publication, the man had set himself up for trouble. In addition, the path he chose was an extremely difficult one. The odds of being chosen from hundreds, sometimes thousands, of applicants by one or more judges with their own particular aesthetics are always slim. The healthiest attitude is to expect *not* to win, and to be surprised if you do. And never assume that submitting your work to one award—or to awards only—is a good way to get your book published.

—J.S. 📖

To how many places should I send my work?

The awards game is a game of odds: The more places you send your work, the greater your chances are of winning. However, there is no point in sending your work to places that are not appropriate, nor in submitting your work to several places when the guidelines require that your submission be exclusive. So after carefully researching each award that interests you and ruling out those that don't fit, I would recommend you send your work to every place that remains on your list—or as many of them as time and money allow.

In general, after heeding the advice of peers and mentors, guidelines and guidebooks, the best way to learn is by doing. So, send out your manuscript, hope for the best, remember that the decisions of judges are subjective, and don't let yourself be discouraged by rejection.

Winning an Award:
Does It Change Your Life?

—Nancy Means Wright

For most writers, winning a prestigious contest seems a fantasy, a panacea, a way out of anonymity. We know the odds: Literary competitions like the AWP Award Series or the National Poetry Series can receive up to 1,000 manuscripts, asking fees that range from $10 to $30—and the fruits of our time and money will most likely be a form letter of rejection. Still, there is something in us that loves a contest, and we rush to apply. Someone, we reason, has to win—and for a time at least, rise like a fragile balloon into the public eye.

Who are these winners, and how did they do it? How has the prize altered their lives and work? Is it really the panacea it seems? What did they do after the initial euphoria paled, after the champagne and the congratulatory calls—that moment of "apotheosis," as Sondra Spatt Olsen, winner of the 1991 Iowa Short Fiction prize for *Traps,* terms it? To answer these questions, I interviewed nine poets and writers, whose wins date from 1981 to 1994.

Most of these winners had been submitting for months, even years. Six months before her novel, *Cannibal,* won the '93 Bobst prize, Terese Svoboda had thought of "giving up fiction entirely, because I hadn't had any interest in a story of mine for six years." Sondra Olsen admits to dark night fantasies that "maybe I'm too New York, too old, too out of touch with what's going on." David Rivard was twice a nonwinning contest finalist before taking the '87 Starrett Poetry prize for *Torque.* "On the one hand, it was great to be getting closer to publishing a book—in another sense enormously frustrating. When you're getting close you end up feeling, well, okay, your work is as good as the ones who get published. But why were they chosen, and why not you?"

But ultimately he was chosen, and although "no planes pulled banners across the sky," the prize, he allows, "is a boost in confidence, and it guarantees a certain amount of attention. It probably gets new poems past the screeners, and read seriously."

For others, too, the win had positive results. Terese Svoboda was approached by a "prestigious agent"; for Sondra Olsen there were magazine solicitations, readings in bookstores and colleges. Annabel Thomas, who won the Iowa in '81 for *The Phototropic Woman,* and then an Ernest Hemingway Foundation Special Citation in '82, found herself a sudden celebrity: her original, mythic stories adapted for theater, her book in demand for college lit classes. Moreover, the award offered a chance to get out of a small farm community in Ohio and meet other writers—in her day there were few MFA programs.

For some winners, though, the results were bittersweet. Lamar Herrin had already published three novels with major publishers before he won the '91 AWP for a novel, *The Lies Boys Tell.* He entered the contest because W.W. Norton, a commercial firm, would publish the winning manuscript. "But I don't think they publicized it at all. They said they'd set up readings—but even after a long, rave review in the *Times,* and a film option, they didn't do it." When Alan Hewat was awarded the '86 Hemingway Foundation award for his "ragtime" novel, *Lady's Time,* submitted by Harper & Row's Ted Solataroff, there was only a brief notice in the *Times.* And when Harper sent him to New Orleans, where the novel was set, "it wasn't even in the bookstores. This was a literary novel by an unknown." Though it earned back its $10,000 advance, went into paperback, and was optioned for film, the book was ultimately remaindered.

More harrowing still, the contest brought on a "writing block" for Elizabeth Inness-Brown, whose collection, *Satin Palms,* was published by Fiction International as the result of an '81 AWP competition. Because the publisher was a "one-man operation," there was limited distribution of the 1,000 copies printed. Although the collection was subsequently awarded the St. Lawrence Short Fiction prize, the then 27-year-old felt she "had to produce a novel, had to top what I'd already done."

For the next five years she couldn't write; she felt "tremendous guilt. Like other women in our culture I thought: Was it just luck? Am I really any good on my own or because a mentor was always there in the wings?"

For most of the nine writers, though, the win has led to new openings in their work, an opportunity to take more risks. In rethinking *Torque,* David Rivard had come to see "an ongoing betrayal" of the voice of his Massachusetts Catholic, working-class background. "But I now [feel I've] reached a point where I could begin to explore other ways of writing, other forms, altering my sense of the subject I was dealing with." Terese Svoboda, who had concentrated on poetry and translations, is now moving deeper into prose, and Sondra Olsen is working on linked stories that for the first time will touch on her childhood, on "recovered memories" of an extended family lost in the Holocaust. And poet Allison Joseph, winner of the '92 Ampersand Press Women Poets Series prize, and then the Ploughshares/Zacharis Award for her coming-of-age collection, *What: Keeps Us Here,* is writing poems on darker themes: "dealing more directly with racism than I'd allowed myself to do before."

And so, with the contest behind them, the winners write on and market their work—often fruitfully. Graywolf Press has just published *Wise Poison,* a second collection by David Rivard, which won the '96 James Laughlin Award from the Academy of American Poets. University of Georgia Press has issued *Mere Mortals,* a second collection by Terese Svoboda; and Allison Joseph has now had manuscripts accepted, almost simultaneously, by the University of Pittsburgh Press and by Carnegie Mellon. Elizabeth Inness-Brown placed a second book of stories on her own after an agent had given up: In '92 *Here* was accepted by Louisiana State University Press. In '94 Annabel Thomas won the Helicon Nine Willa Cather Fiction prize after entering *Knucklebones,* a book of stories, in two other contests. Finding a home for a novel, though, seemed a dead end. A self-styled recluse and "second generation hillbilly," Thomas was approached by agents after the Iowa win, but found them "turned off" by her Appalachian settings and dialect.

Because "agents want novels," Inness-Brown and Olsen have been stretching themselves to be more commercial—"to prove to myself I can do it," says Inness-Brown. But the process can be harrowing, according to Olsen, for a writer whose method of revision is to "cut it, make it tighter, smaller." Inness-Brown is just finishing that first novel for her agent in the wings, but Olsen has a completed work, "a comedy of manners" set in academe, that agents inform her is "hard to place. They want the big seller—maybe their jobs depend on it," says Olsen, who describes her work as "subtle, low-key." Alan Hewat had "a rush from agents" when a story came out in *Esquire*, "but when they saw my nonsensational-type fiction, they got sort of demure. The obvious subtext was 'This is not a blockbuster.'" Terese Svoboda, who calls her work "idiosyncratic," had found—and lost—two agents before signing up with a third. Lamar Herrin, whose earlier novels were placed by his agent (who failed to sell *The Lies Boys Tell* before the author entered the AWP), admits that these days "it would be harder to get an agent for a literary novel—much harder." "Driven to write," Herrin still has four orphan novels in his desk.

How, then, I asked, do these writers, after that moment in the sun, deal with rejections? How do they dredge up the courage to resubmit? "You get used to them," Herrin allows, but he only revises after he hears the same complaint, "rejection after rejection. Then I'll give thought to it." Terese Svoboda tends to work quickly; at first she is "terribly satisfied. I think it's the best thing anyone has ever written. And almost without exception I have got the book back 10 minutes, it seems, after I've sent it out. Then I always reexamine it and make changes."

One could conceivably send the same work to a contest over and over again, Annabel Thomas observes, "but it pays to improve it." She lets a new manuscript rest for a while before she begins her process of "re-visioning." While the work "cools off," she studies the stories of other authors, learning from them techniques she had hoped to accomplish in hers. "When I finally take it up again, I can see its flaws."

For writers of collections, rejection seems a process of reorganizing: "taking out a story, adding a story, trying to package it differently, giving it a different title or spin," advises Elizabeth Inness-Brown, who continually "revamped" her work after *Here* was rejected "everywhere in the first round of submissions." "Of course the frustration of not winning the contest," says Sondra Olsen, "is that you are left clueless about what went wrong." In resubmitting her latest collection for the

Heinz she reversed the order of her first and last stories "to amazingly different effect. Who knows if this is a real improvement or just wishful thinking? Without critical feedback, it's like reading entrails." Allison Joseph agrees that "rejections are frustrating—it's difficult to publish a second book," but feels that "if the writing is important enough, you'll come back to it." She would "love" to publish with a feminist or African American press, "but presses once committed to these writers are losing their funding. They can't publish more than one book every two years. I don't know when," she says, "or if, it will happen to me again."

"You simply get the rejections and go on," says Terese Svoboda, who, as a sometime judge, finds many manuscripts "worthy of publication, but with nothing particularly driving them." Svoboda would go the contest route "at any time," and so would David Rivard, along with poet Belle Waring, a staff nurse who had published "only a few poems" before winning the '89 AWP for *Refuge*. Both poets had a positive experience with the University of Pittsburgh Press, a series publisher. But Rivard "worries" about contests that are "one-shot deals," that publish a single book but can't promote it or keep it in print. He worries that contests are an inadequate response to the trade presses "having by and large abandoned poetry." He worries about the screeners, "their lack of experience at judging the work of others." The final judging, he argues, "is only as good as the judge himself," and "judges seem to be drawn from a fairly small pool." He worries, too, that despite the large number of contests, "the dominant aesthetic simply reinforces itself, is not reinventing itself. Would a Muriel Rukeyser or George Oppen win a prize these days?"

"You realize there are so many different voices," says Allison Joseph, who has served as both final and preliminary judge for AWP contests. "It's practically impossible to choose one, I keep on reading and listening for something that appeals to me. But what appeals to me may not be what appeals to the final judge. So there's a very big chance element to contests."

With contests publishing one out of 1,000, and talented writers dropping through the holes—how, then, I asked, do these immensely talented, largely unagented writers survive?

Through connections with other writers, some suggest; through endorsements of their work, and recommendations: Poets David Wojahn and Alice Fulton gave Rivard and Waring, respectively, a leg up onto the faculty at Vermont College's M.F.A. program. "Ultimately the prize meant job offers that would otherwise have been out of reach, since to that point I had no real teaching experience," says Waring, who now combines nursing with teaching writing to patients at a Washington, D.C. children's hospital; her second collection of poems, *Dark Blonde,* is forthcoming from Sarabande Books. Sondra Olsen and Terese Svoboda belong to city writers' groups; Alan Hewat has an agent patiently awaiting a novel—although "it's a couple of years since I've had time or energy," says Hewat, who at 55, with a new baby, combines work as a rural Vermont mail carrier with freelance editing. Annabel Thomas, who tried teaching but found it "pumped the creative fountains dry," helps with her husband's veterinary practice. And with her children and grandchildren, has "other people's lives to watch, and write about."

Others, though, appear to thrive in academe. Inness-Brown has a "really great teaching job" at St. Michael's College (Vermont), for which she gives the AWP prize credit. Rivard is a part-time lecturer at Tufts; Joseph teaches poetry writing at Southern Illinois University in Carbondale, where she lives with her husband, poet Jon Tribble. She finds that talking about the writing process with her students "helps when I return to my own writing." Lamar Herrin, who passed through careers in pro baseball and the movies (he appeared in *Flaming Star* with Elvis Presley) to ultimately write, has tenure at Cornell. He likes teaching, but finds "teaching energy similar to writing energy: You come away a bit drained. So you've got to figure ways to do two things."

But mostly these writers survive through the act of writing itself. "It's not attention and awards that sustain you," says Rivard, "the work itself sustains." And Terese Svoboda adds, "The world measures success by money, and most writers can't. It seems to me the point of it all is not the book party and certainly not the royalty statement, but the wonderful moment when the story or poem comes together." Inness-Brown tells her students "to focus on the writing first, and publishing after"; and then to "always keep something in the mail." The key to success, she insists, "is persistence, making a job of it, making it methodical."

For Annabel Thomas, survival means "detaching" a submission from her ego, sending it out "as unemotionally as if I were playing Ping-Pong—for fun, not to win. Otherwise it's easy to take each returned manuscript as an announcement that I'm a failure, and so I find myself hurtling into a depression that will dry up the creative juices." She would agree with Sondra Olsen, who feels that too close an attachment "can be counter-productive to one's stamina and productivity." So Thomas just keeps "re-writing and sending out." Without the contests, she allows, "my work would be mustering in some basement or periodical nobody reads any more. Out of the contests came readings, friendships with other writers and overworked editors of literary journals who took time to write a line or two on a rejected manuscript."

And so the contest survives, and the numbers of applicants proliferate. The country is "flooded with good writing," claims Lamar Herrin, who to date has only entered one contest, but sees the publishing of serious fiction "increasingly being left to regional and university presses." It's up to them, he says, and often through contests, "to take up the slack that's being created by commercial houses."

"It would be a cold world out there without them," agrees Terese Svoboda, to whom any university press with a deadline is a "contest." For Svoboda, who is "always" circulating a new collection, the contest offers above all a time frame in which "to get something organized," and get it out. She figures the period of gestation—the time it takes to get a book published—to be about five years. "So staying at it is the most important aspect. You're always learning, trying something new. You're always getting bored with what you've just finished. You're always trying to make it better."

Winning a contest then, these nine interviewees might conclude, is no panacea: There will always be disappointments, there will always be rejections—those nagging self-doubts. But there will be moments of intense gratification as well. Most would agree with Elizabeth Inness-Brown that the true reward comes when one has a book that one "can be proud of," that one can "show to people."

The contest, it would seem, in spite of the cost, in spite of the odds, is a reasonable gamble.

Nancy Means Wright is the author of six books, including the recent Mad Search *(St. Martin's Press). Her fiction, nonfiction, and writing for young adults have appeared in leading magazines nationwide. She is currently a lecturer at Marist College.*

Awards Exclusively for Unpublished First-Book Manuscripts

Name of Prize: Alabama State Council on the Arts Fiction Fellowships
Prize: $10,000
Open to: Alabama residents
Contact: Randy Shoults
        Alabama State Council on the Arts
        201 Monroe Street
        Montgomery AL 36130
Categories: Novel-length fiction, short story.
Description: Fellowships of $5,000-$10,000 available to Alabama residents (minimum residence of two years required) for previously published or unpublished works of fiction to encourage writers to set time aside and explore their creativity. The award is based on the quality of work submitted, career status, and achievement.

Name of Prize: Arizona Commission on the Arts Grants in Creative Writing
Prize: $7,500
Open to: Arizona residents
Contact: Jill Bernstein, Literature-Director
        Arizona Commission on the Arts
        417 West Roosevelt
        Phoenix, AZ 85003
Categories: Fiction, poetry.
Description: Arizona residents over the age of 18, who are not students, are eligible for fellowship awards of $5,000-$7,500 in the category of fiction and poetry. Category alternates each year. Send postcard for complete guidelines and deadline or visit the Web site at *az.arts.asu.edu/artscomm*, or e-mail to general@ArizonaArts.org.

Name of Prize: Artist Trust GAP (Grants for Artists' Projects) in Fiction
Prize: $1,200
Open to: Washington State residents
Contact: Program Director
Artist Trust
1402 Third Avenue, Suite 404
Seattle, WA 98101-2118
Categories: Novel-length fiction, short story.
Description: The Selection Committee may award any amount up to $1,200 for the Artist Trust GAP Projects. The specific definition of Arts Projects is purposefully left flexible so that the writer's request can be determined by his/her own ideas, visions, and needs, and so that the Selection Committee for each round has the freedom to select recipients without restrictions. Send SASE for guidelines and application forms.

Name of Prize: AWP Award Series in Poetry, Fiction, Creative Nonfiction, and the AWP/Thomas Dunne Books Novel Award *$20 fee*
Prize: Varies; see description
Open to: All authors writing original works in English.
Contact: Katherine Perry, AWP Writing Programs
Tallwood House
Mail Stop 1E3
George Mason University
Fairfax, VA 22030
Categories: Poetry, fiction, creative nonfiction.
Description: The AWP Award Series is an annual competition for the publication of excellent new book-length works of poetry, fiction, creative nonfiction, and the novel. Winners in the Award Series receive a $2,000 case honorarium plus publication of their book by University of Pittsburgh Press, University of Massachusetts Press, or University of Georgia Press. The winner of the AWP/Thomas Dunne Books Novel Award receives a $10,000 case advance and publication of their novel by St. Martin's Press.

Name of Prize: California Arts Council's Fellowships
Prize: $5,000
Open to: California residents
Contact: Artists Fellowship Program Administrator
California Arts Council
1300 1st Street, Suite 930
Sacramento, CA 95814
Categories: Fiction.

Description: Fellowships of $5,000 each are given in recognition of outstanding artistic achievement to exemplary California artists every year. Categories change in a four year cycle and alternate among visual arts, performing arts, media/news, and literature. Applicants must be legal residents of California for one year prior to the application deadline. Send SASE for complete guidelines.

Name of Prize: Connecticut Commission on the Arts Fiction Fellowships
Prize: $2,500
Open to: Connecticut residents
Contact: Linda Dente, Program Director
      Artist Fellowships
      Connecticut Commission on the Arts
      One Financial Plaza
      Hartford, CT 06103
Categories: Fiction.
Description: In even-numbered years, grants of $2,500 to $5,000 are made to Connecticut writers who have resided in the state for at least one year for new work or work-in-progress. Write for complete guidelines.

Name of Prize: Delaware Individual Artist Fellowships for Fiction
Prize: $5,000
Open to: Delaware residents
Contact: Fellowship Coordinator
      Delaware Division of the Arts
      State Office Building
      820 North French Street
      Wilmington, DE 19801
Categories: Novel-length fiction, short story.
Description: Fellowships of $2,000 to emerging professional writers and $5,000 to established professional writers are available to Delaware residents. Winners are chosen by an out-of-state panel of judges. Applicants must be Delaware residents for at least one year, 18 years of age or older, and cannot be enrolled in a degree-granting program. Send SASE for full guidelines, or visit the Web site at *www.dca.net/artsdel.*

Name of Prize: District of Columbia City Arts Projects
Prize: Varies; see description.
Open to: District of Columbia residents
Contact: Pamela G. Holt, Executive Director
　　　　D.C. Commission on the Arts & Humanities
　　　　Stables Art Center
　　　　410 Eighth Street NW
　　　　Fifth Floor
　　　　Washington DC 20004
Categories: Fiction.
Description: The District of Columbia City Arts Projects are awarded to individual writers of literature by the D.C. Commission on the Arts and Humanities; prizes range from $1,000 to $4,500. According to the commission, the "D.C. Commission on the Arts and Humanities is the official arts agency of the District of Columbia. Commission grant programs support and promote stability, vitality, and diversity of artistic expression in the District. The City Arts projects offer funds for programs that encourage the growth of quality arts activities throughout the city, support local artists, and make arts experiences accessible to District residents. Projects must provide exposure to the arts and arts experiences to the broader community or to persons traditionally undeserved or separated from the mainstream due to geographic location, economic constraints, or disability." Send SASE for complete guidelines and required application form.

Name of Prize: District of Columbia Grants-In-Aid Program
Prize: Varies
Open to: District of Columbia residents
Contact: Pamela G. Holt, Executive Director
　　　　D.C. Commission on the Arts & Humanities
　　　　Stables Art Center
　　　　410 Eighth Street NW
　　　　Fifth Floor
　　　　Washington DC 20004
Categories: Fiction.
Description: Grants-In-Aid Fellowships are awarded to writers by the D.C. Commission on the Arts and Humanities, which "supports and promotes stability, vitality, and diversity of artistic expression in the District." In order to "demonstrate artistic merit, applicants are required to submit work samples no more than two years old." For literature, up to three representative samples are required. "Work samples must be labeled with applicant's name, title, and date of work." Send SASE for complete guidelines and required application forms.

Name of Prize: Electronic Arts Grants Program
Prize: $500
Open to: New York State residents
Contact: Electronic Arts Grants Program Director
       Experimental Television Center
       109 Lower Fairfield Road
       Newark Valley, NY 13811
Categories: Novel-length fiction, short story, nonfiction, poetry, drama, screenplay, children's literature, religion, women, Gay/Lesbian, journalism.
Description: The Electronic Arts Grants Program annually awards approximately 25 grants of up to $500 to New York State artists involved in the creation of audio, video, or computer-generated time-based works. Funds must be used to assist in the completion of work that is currently in progress. Eligible forms include film; audio and video as single or multiple-channel presentations; computer-based moving-imagery and sound works; installations and performances; and works for CD-ROM, multimedia technologies, and the Internet. Work must be innovative, creative, and approach the various media as art forms; all genres are eligible, including experimental, narrative, and documentary work. Send SASE for complete guidelines.

Name of Prize: Illinois Artists' Fellowships for Poetry
Prize: Varies
Open to: Illinois residents
Contact: Richard Gage, Communication Arts Program
       Illinois Arts Council
       James R. Thompson Center
       100 West Randolph, Suite 10-500
       Chicago, IL 60601
Categories: Poetry.
Description: In odd-numbered years, fellowships are available to poets. According to the council, "The awards are given to creative individuals in recognition of their outstanding work and commitment within the arts." The amount of the fellowships vary from year to year. Send SASE for complete guidelines.

Name of Prize: Illinois Writers Inc. Annual Chapbook Contest
Prize: Publication
Open to: Open competition
Contact: Jim Elledge
       Illinois Writers Inc.
       Illinois State University
       English Department 4240
       Normal, IL 61790-4240

Categories: Short story, poetry.
Description: The genre for this award alternates yearly: poetry in even-numbered years, and fiction in odd-numbered years. Send SASE for complete guidelines.

Name of Prize: Illinois Arts Council Special Assistance Grants for Poetry
Prize: $1,500
Open to: Illinois residents
Contact: Richard Gage
    Communication Arts Program
    Illinois Arts Council
    James R. Thompson Center
    100 West Randolph, Suite 10-500
    Chicago, IL 60601
Categories: Poetry.
Description: These awards vary according to annual budget. They are open-deadline, project specific grants with a $1,500 maximum request, which must be matched one-to-one with either cash or in-kind contributions. Send SASE for guidelines and application forms.

Name of Prize: Illinois Arts Council Special Assistance Grants for Fiction
Prize: $1,500
Open to: Illinois residents
Contact: Richard Gage
    Communication Arts Program
    Illinois Arts Council
    James R. Thompson Center
    100 West Randolph, Suite 10-500
    Chicago, IL 60601
Categories: Fiction.
Description: These awards vary according to annual budget. They are open-deadline, project specific grants with a $1,500 maximum request, which must be matched one-to-one with either cash or in-kind contributions. Send SASE for guidelines and application forms.

Name of Prize: Jenny McKean Moore Fund for Writers in Washington
Prize: $48,000
Open to: Open competition
Contact: Faye Moskowitz, Department Chair
    George Washington University
    Department of English
    Washington, DC 20052

Categories: Varies.
Description: The Jenny McKean Moore Fund for Writers in Washington and George Washington University jointly engage a writer for the Jenny McKean Moore appointment. The creative writer will teach two semesters at George Washington University. A salary of $48,000 is provided. The Visiting Lecturer will reside in the District of Columbia during the academic year. Enclose an SASE for guidelines; prepare a resume and writing sample to accompany the application.

Name of Prize: Kentucky Artists' Fellowships in Poetry
Prize: $5,000
Open to: Kentucky residents
Contact: Lori Meadows
       Kentucky Arts Council
       Old Capitol Annex
       300 W. Broadway
       Frankfort, KY 40601
Categories: Poetry.
Description: In even-numbered years, Kentucky writers of poetry may win awards up to $5,000 to assist in the continued development of their creative work. Send SASE for application forms and guidelines.

Name of Prize: Kentucky Artists' Fellowships in Fiction
Prize: $5,000
Open to: Kentucky Residents
Contact: Lori Meadows
       Kentucky Arts Council
       Old Capitol Annex
       300 W. Broadway
       Frankfort, KY 40601
Categories: Fiction.
Description: In even-numbered years, Kentucky writers of fiction may win awards up to $5,000 to assist in the continued development of their creative work. Send SASE for application forms and guidelines.

Name of Prize: Larry Neal Writers' Competition for Poetry
Prize: $500
Open to: District of Columbia Writers
Contact: Larry Neal Writers' Competition Director
       District of Columbia Commission on the Arts and Humanities
       410 8th Street NW, 5th Floor
       Washington, DC 20004

Categories: Poetry.
Description: $500 awards are given to residents of the District of Columbia. Send SASE for complete guidelines, application forms, and deadlines.

Name of Prize: Louisiana State Fellowships for Poetry
Prize: $5,000
Open to: Louisiana residents
Contact: Louisiana Division of the Arts
PO Box 44247
Baton Rouge, LA 70804
Categories: Poetry.
Description: This fellowship is offered to poets who are Louisiana residents (two years prior to application required). Send SASE for required application forms and guidelines, e-mail to arts@crt.state.la.us, or the Web site at *www.crt.state.la.us/arts*.

Name of Prize: Louisiana State Fellowships for Fiction
Prize: $5,000
Open to: Louisiana residents
Contact: Louisiana Division of the Arts
PO Box 44247
Baton Rouge, LA 70804
Categories: Fiction.
Description: This fellowship is offered to writers of fiction who are Louisiana residents (two years prior to application required). Send SASE for required application forms and guidelines, e-mail them at arts@crt.state.la.us, or visit the Web site at *www.crt.state.la.us/arts*.

Name of Prize: Maine Arts Commission Individual Artist Fellowships in Literature
Prize: $3,000
Open to: Maine residents
Contact: Kathy Ann Jones, Associate for Contemporary Arts
Maine Arts Commission
25 State House Station
Augusta, ME 04333-0025
Categories: Fiction.
Description: Individual Artist Fellowships for Writers, established in 1987, are offered every two years by the Maine Arts Commission. Guidelines and application forms may be obtained through the Maine Arts Commission Web site at: *www.mainearts.com* or e-mail to kathy.jones@state.us.me.

Name of Prize: Maine Community Foundation Writing Awards in Poetry
Prize: $1,000
Open to: Maine residents
Contact: Contest Director
Maine Community Foundation
210 Main Street
PO Box 148
Ellsworth, ME 04605
Categories: Poetry.
Description: The Maine Community Foundation Writing Awards in Poetry is given in odd-numbered years. Established in 1995, the fellowship honors the late Maine resident and author Martin Dibner. One grant ranging from $500 to $1,000 is awarded to a poet so that he/she can attend a writing workshop and complete a writing project. Poets who are residents of Maine should submit a one-page summary of their project, an income and expense budget for the project, a resume including published works, and no more than 10 pages of poetry. Send SASE for complete guidelines.

Name of Prize: Maryland State Individual Artist Award for Fiction
Prize: $6,000
Open to: Maryland residents
Contact: James Backas
Maryland State Arts Council
601 North Howard Street
1st Floor
Baltimore, MD 21201
Categories: Fiction.
Description: Individual Artist Awards for Fiction are available in the amounts of $1,000; $3,000; and $6,000 in odd-numbered years to Maryland residents over the age of 18 who are not students. The awards are chosen solely on excellence of previous work. Send SASE for guidelines and applications.

Name of Prize: Massachusetts Artist Grants in Poetry
Prize: $7,500
Open to: Massachusetts residents
Contact: Artist Grants Program Director
Massachusetts Cultural Council
120 Boylston Street, Suite 1000
Boston, MA 02116
Categories: Poetry.
Description: Guidelines available on the Massachusetts Cultural Council Web site *(www.massculturalcouncil.org)*. Awards of $7,500 are available to eligible writers,

and finalists will receive $1,000. Writers must be 18 years or older, not students, and have lived in Massachusetts for two consecutive years prior to application.

————

Name of Prize: Massachusetts Artist Grants in Fiction
Prize: $7,500
Open to: Massachusetts residents
Contact: Artist Grants Program Director
        Massachusetts Cultural Council
        120 Boylston Street, Suite 1000
        Boston, MA 02116
Categories: Fiction.
Description: Guidelines available on the Massachusetts Cultural Council Web site *(www.massculturalcouncil.org)*. Awards of $7,500 are available to eligible writers, and finalists will receive $1,000. Writers must be 18 years or older, not students, and have lived in Massachusetts for two consecutive years prior to application.

————

Name of Prize: Mississippi Arts Fellowships in Literary Arts for Poetry
Prize: $5,000
Open to: Mississippi residents
Contact: Fellowship Director
        Mississippi Arts Commission
        239 North Lamar Street, Suite 207
        Jackson, MS 39201
Categories: Poetry.
Description: In odd-numbered years, poets and fiction writers vie for $5,000 fellowships. Send SASE for guidelines.

————

Name of Prize: Mississippi Arts Fellowships in Literary Arts for Fiction
Prize: $5,000
Open to: Mississippi residents
Contact: Fellowship Director
        Mississippi Arts Commission
        239 North Lamar Street, Suite 207
        Jackson, MS 39201
Categories: Fiction.
Description: In odd-numbered years, poets and fiction writers vie for $5,000 fellowships. Send SASE for guidelines.

————

Name of Prize: Montana Arts Individual Artists Fellowships
Prize: $2,000
Open to: Montana residents
Contact: Arlyrm Fishbany
        Montana Arts Council
        316 North Park Avenue, Suite 252
        Helena, MT 59620
Categories: Fiction.
Description: Up to four $2,000 Literature Fellowships are made available annually to Montana residents. To apply, you must be at least 18 years old and not a student seeking a degree. Send SASE for complete guidelines and application forms.

Name of Prize: NCWN Harperprints Poetry Chapbook Competition
Prize: $200
Open to: North Carolina residents
Contact: NCWN Award Director
        North Carolina Writers' Network
        PO Box 954
        Carrboro, NC 27510
Categories: Poetry.
Description: The NCWN Harperprints Poetry Chapbook Competition is open to poets who have not published a full-length book of poetry (48 pages). The winner receives $200, a public reading and reception, plus 50 complimentary copies of the 500 print-run chapbook. The entry fee is $10 for NCWN members and $12 for nonmembers. Send SASE for complete guidelines.

Name of Prize: Nebraska Arts Individual Artist Fellowships in Poetry
Prize: $4,000
Open to: Nebraska residents
Contact: Suzanne Wise
        Nebraska Arts Council
        3838 Davenport Street
        Omaha, NE 68131-2329
Categories: Poetry.
Description: Biennial awards (literary awards alternate with performing arts awards) are given to minimum two-year residents of Nebraska, who are at least 18 years of age, to help support the contributions made by Nebraska artists to the quality of life in the state. Master Awards range between $3,000 and $4,000; Merit Awards range between $1,000 and $2,000, depending on funds available. The applicant cannot be enrolled in an undergraduate, graduate, or certificate-granting program in English, creative writing, literature, or any other related field. Send SASE for guidelines.

Name of Prize: Nebraska Arts Individual Artist Fellowships in Fiction
Prize: $5,000
Open to: Nebraska residents
Contact: Suzanne Wise
        Nebraska Arts Council
        3838 Davenport Street
        Omaha, NE 68131-2329
Categories: Fiction.
Description: Awards are given every third year; literary awards alternate with per-forming arts and visual arts awards. They are given to minimum two-year residents of Nebraska, who are at least 18 years of age, to help support the contributions made by Nebraska artists to the quality of life in the state. Distinguished Achievement Awards are $5,000; Merit Awards range between $1,000 and $2,000, depending on funds available. The applicant cannot be enrolled in an undergraduate, graduate, or certificate-granting program in English, creative writing, literature, or any other related field. Send SASE for guidelines.

Name of Prize: Nevada Arts Council's Artists' Fellowships for Literary Arts
Prize: $5,000
Open to: Nevada residents
Contact: Sharon Rosse
        Nevada Arts Council
        602 Curry Street
        Carson City, NV 89703
Categories: Fiction.
Description: The Nevada Arts Council offers two fellowships in literary arts to Nevada residents. Send for complete guidelines and application forms.

Name of Prize: Nevada Arts Council Arts-in-Education Special Project Grants for Schools and Organizations
Prize: $2,500
Open to: Nevada residents
Contact: Laura Rawlings
        Nevada Arts Council
        602 Curry Street
        Carson City, NV 89703
Categories: Fiction.
Description: Nevada Arts Council Arts-in-Education Special Project Grants for Schools and Organizations offer varying amounts of money (up to $2,500) to be awarded as Special Project Grants. The grants are available each year to residents (for at least one year) of Nevada. Send SASE for complete guidelines.

Name of Prize: New England/New York Award
Prize: $1,000
Open to: Poets living in New England and New York
Contact: Contest Director
Alice James Books
NE/NY Contest
98 Main Street
Farmington, ME 04938
Categories: Poetry.
Description: The New England/New York Award offers a prize of $1,000 and publication, as well as a runner-up prize of $500 and publication for a manuscript of poetry 50-70 pages long. Winners become members of the Alice James Poetry Cooperative and help judge future contests. Poets must live in New England or New York. There is a $20 processing fee. Please send an SASE or visit the Web site at *www.unf.maine.edu/-ajb* for complete guidelines.

Name of Prize: New Hampshire State Artist Fellowships in Literature
Prize: $3,000
Open to: New Hampshire residents
Contact: Audrey V. Sylvester, Artist Services Coordinator
New Hampshire State Council on the Arts
40 North Main Street
Concord, NH 03301-4974
Categories: Fiction.
Description: The New Hampshire State Council on the Arts offers Artist Fellowships in Literature to New Hampshire residents of at least one year who are not enrolled as full-time students to recognize artistic excellence and professional commitment. To request guidelines, call 603/271-2789.

Name of Prize: New Jersey Council on the Arts Fellowship in Prose
Prize: $10,000
Open to: New Jersey residents
Contact: Fellowship Director
New Jersey Fellowships, c/o MA2ZF
22 Light Street
Baltimore, MD 21202
Categories: Fiction.
Description: The New Jersey State Council on the Arts offers fellowships in fiction writing up to $12,000. The fellowships are offered annually to enable artists and writers to continue producing new work. Persons eligible for the fellowships are artists who are permanent residents of the state of New Jersey (all awards are subject to verification of New Jersey residency) and artists who have not received

a fellowship since fiscal year 1995 (recipients may not re-apply for four years). Fellowships may not provide funding for scholarships or academic study in pursuit of any college degree. Send SASE for complete guidelines and application forms.

Name of Prize: New Jersey Council on the Arts N.J. Writers Project
Prize: Varies
Open to: New Jersey residents
Contact: Art Education Programs
New Jersey State Council on the Arts
PO Box 306
Trenton, NJ 08625
Categories: Novel-length fiction, short story, drama, poetry, nonfiction, residential/colony.
Description: The New Jersey Council on the Arts N.J. Writers Project, cosponsored by Playwrights Theatre of N.J., offers prosewriters, playwrights, and poets short-term residences in New Jersey schools each year. The council funds pay for a portion of the artists' fees. Please contact the NJSCA Arts Education Program to receive a copy of the guidelines and application form.

Name of Prize: New Rivers Press Minnesota Voices Project in Poetry
Prize: $500
Open to: Minnesota residents
Contact: Minnesota Voices Project Director
New Rivers Press
420 North 5th Street, Suite 938
Minneapolis, MN 55401
Categories: Poetry.
Description: New Rivers Press will publish a collection of poetry (between 40-60 pages), and $500 will be awarded to two winners. Writers must be residents of Minnesota and must not have been published yet by a commercial publishing house. No author who has had more than two books published (not including chapbooks) by small independent presses is eligible. Send SASE for guidelines, application, and deadlines, or visit the Web site at *www.mtn.org/newrivpr*.

Name of Prize: New York Foundation's Fellowships in Fiction
Prize: $7,000
Open to: New York (non-student) residents
Contact: Artists' Fellowships Department
NYFA
155 Avenue of the Americas, 14th Floor
New York, NY 10013

Categories: Fiction.
Description: New York State writers with a minimum residence of two years are invited to apply for this fellowship. The writer will be judged on the excellence of his/her recent work. The award of $7,000 includes an agreement to perform a mutually agreed-upon public service during the grant period. Send SASE for complete guidelines and application.

Name of Prize: North Carolina Arts Council Fellowships in Fiction
Prize: $8,000
Open to: North Carolina residents
Contact: Deborah McGill, Literature/Public Media Director
North Carolina Arts Council
Department of Cultural Resources
Raleigh, NC 27699-4632
Categories: Fiction.
Description: North Carolina Arts Council offers fellowships in fiction for up to $8,000 for current North Carolina residents. You must have lived in the state for at least a year to apply. Write or call for complete guidelines and application forms (no SASE is needed). Reach them at 919/733-2111, ext. 22, fax 919/733-4834, or e-mail to debbie.mcgill@ncmail.net. You can also visit the Web site at *www.ncarts.org.*

Name of Prize: North Carolina Arts Council Fellowships in Poetry
Prize: $8,000
Open to: North Carolina residents
Contact: Deborah McGill, Literature/Public Media Director
North Carolina Arts Council
Department of Cultural Resources
Raleigh, NC 27699-4632
Categories: Fiction.
Description: North Carolina Arts Council offers fellowships in poetry for up to $8,000 for current North Carolina residents. You must have lived in the state for at least a year to apply. Write or call for complete guidelines and application forms (no SASE is needed). Reach them at 919/733-2111 x22, fax 919/733-4834, or e-mail to debbie.mcgill@ncmail.net. You can also visit the Web site at *www.ncarts.org.*

Name of Prize: Oregon Arts Commission Individual Artists Fellowships for Fiction
Prize: $3,000
Open to: Oregon residents
Contact: Michael Faison, Assistant Director
        Oregon Arts Commission
        775 Summer Street SE
        Salem, OR 97310
Categories: Fiction.
Description: Oregon residents may apply for fellowships in fiction from the Oregon Arts Commission. The fellowships are designed to assist writers in furthering their careers and are given every two years. Applicants must have lived in Oregon for at least one year. Send name and address for complete guidelines and application forms, or e-mail to Oregon.artsComm@state.or.us. Get complete guidelines and application forms at *www.das.state.or.us/oac* or *art.econ.state.or.us.*

—————

Name of Prize: Oregon Arts Commission Individual Artists Fellowships for Poetry
Prize: $3,000
Open to: Oregon residents
Contact: Michael Faison, Assistant Director
        Oregon Arts Commission
        775 Summer Street SE
        Salem, OR 97310
Categories: Poetry.
Description: Oregon residents may apply for fellowships in poetry from the Oregon Arts Commission. The fellowships are designed to assist writers in furthering their careers and are given every two years. Applicants must have lived in Oregon for at least one year. Send name and address for complete guidelines and application forms, or e-mail to Oregon.artsComm@state.or.us. Their home page also has complete guidelines and application form at *www.das.state.or.us/oac/*or *art.coon.state.or.us.*

—————

Name of Prize: Oregon Literary Fellowships for Writers in Fiction

Prize: $3,000
Open to: Oregon residents
Contact: Kristy Athens
        Literary Arts, Inc.
        720 S.W. Washington Street, Suite 700
        Portland, OR 97205
Categories: Fiction.
Description: The Oregon Literature Advisory Council of Literary Arts, Inc. offers the Oregon Literary Fellowships for Writers in Fiction. Publication is not necessary to be eligible for this fellowship. According to the council, "the intention of the

fellowship is to help those in need of funds to initiate, develop, or complete a literary project in fiction." This award offers writers a cash award of $500 to $3,000. All work submitted is judged by an out-of-state panel. Send SASE for guidelines and application forms, or visit the Web site at *www.literary-arts.org*.

Name of Prize: Peninsula Community Foundation Literature Program in Poetry
Prize: $5,000
Open to: Pennsylvania residents
Contact: Literature Program in Poetry Director
Literature Program
Pennsylvania Council on the Arts
216 Finance Building
Harrisburg, PA 17120
Categories: Poetry.
Description: The $5,000 fellowship is awarded to a poet on the basis of the artistic quality of his/her work. This award is offered biennially (in odd-numbered years) to allow poets to set aside time for creative work. Applicants must be Pennsylvania residents. Send SASE before August 1 for complete guidelines and application forms.

Name of Prize: Pennsylvania Council on the Arts Fellowships
Prize: $5,000
Open to: Pennsylvania (non-student) residents
Contact: Arts Fellowships Director
Pennsylvania Council on the Arts
216 Finance Building
Harrisburg, PA 17120
Categories: Fiction.
Description: Fellowships of up to $5,000 are offered to Pennsylvania residents with established careers as writers. Write for guidelines.

Name of Prize: Pew Fellowships in the Arts for Poets
Prize: $50,000
Open to: See description
Contact: Melissa Franklin, Director
Pew Fellowships in the Arts
University of the Arts
250 South Broad Street, Suite 1003
Philadelphia, PA 19102

Categories: Poetry.
Description: The Pew Fellowships in the Arts provides financial support directly to artists so that they may have the opportunity to dedicate themselves wholly to the development of their artwork for up to two years. A goal of the Pew Fellowships in the Arts is to provide such support at a critical juncture in an artist's career, when a concentration on artistic development and exploration is most likely to contribute to personal and professional growth. Applicants must be 25 years or older and Pennsylvania residents of Bucks, Chester, Delaware, Montgomery, or Philadelphia county for two years or longer. Twelve fellowships of $50,000 are awarded each year. Call (215) 875-2285 or write for application and guidelines (applications are available in mid-September) or visit *www.pewarts.org*.

Name of Prize: Rhode Island Fellowships for Literature
Prize: $5,000
Open to: Rhode Island (non-student) residents
Contact: Randall Rosenbaum, Exec. Director
Rhode Island State Council on the Arts
95 Cedar Street
Suite 103
Providence, RI 02903-1034
Categories: Fiction.
Description: Fellowships are given to encourage Rhode Island writers to achieve specific goals in their careers. Grants of $5,000 and $1,000 are given to Rhode Island residents who are over 18 years of age and are not undergraduate or graduate students. Finalists are chosen by a panel of state or regional writers, and the winner is selected by an out-of-state judge. Please send SASE for complete guidelines and application forms, e-mail to info@risca.state.ri.us, or visit the Web site at *www.risca.state.ri.us*.

Name of Prize: South Carolina Project Grants for Fiction Writers
Prize: $7,500
Open to: South Carolina residents
Contact: Project Grants Director
South Carolina Arts Commission
1800 Gervals Street
Columbia, SC 29201
Categories: Fiction.
Description: A chance for South Carolina writers of proven professional ability or exceptional promise to win $7,500 in matching funds for research, travel to conferences or abroad, and/or completion of a manuscript. Send SASE for guidelines.

Name of Prize: South Dakota Touring Artists Programs for Fiction Writers
Prize: Varies
Open to: South Dakota writers
Contact: Jocelyn Hanson, Assistant Director
  South Dakota Arts Council
  800 Governors Drive
  Pierre, SD 57501-2294
Categories: Novel-length fiction, short story, residency/colony.
Description: Grants are made available to tour writers through South Dakota cities. Please send SASE for application forms and guidelines.

Name of Prize: Tennessee Arts Commission Fiction Writing Fellowships
Prize: $2,500
Open to: Tennessee residents
Contact: Alice Swanson
  Tennessee Arts Commission
  401 Charlotte Avenue
  Nashville, TN 37243-0780
Categories: Fiction.
Description: The Tennessee Arts Commission offers Fiction Writing Fellowships to Tennessee residents in the amount of $2,500. Special emphasis is given to emerging writers and the fellowship alternates literary categories each year. Send request for complete guidelines and application forms.

Name of Prize: Utah Arts Council Publication Prize
Prize: $5,000
Open to: Utah residents
Contact: G. Barnes, Literary Coordinator
  Utah Arts Council
  17 East South Temple Street
  Salt Lake City, UT 84102-1177
Categories: Fiction.
Description: The Publication Prize offers one prize of $5,000 to one of the book-length first-place winners of the Utah's Original Writing Competition in the following categories: autobiography/biography, fiction novel, short story collections, or the young adult book. Applicant must be a resident of Utah. This prize is designed specifically to expedite publication and to ensure a high-quality presentation and wide publicity for the chosen work. The prize money may be used only to assist a reputable publisher with the production and distribution of the work. Any eligible manuscript accepted for publication during the year before the prize is awarded cannot be considered for the prize. Send SASE for complete guidelines and application forms.

Name of Prize: Vermont Arts Council Opportunity Grants
Prize: $5,000
Open to: Vermont residents
Contact: Michele Bailey, Director of Artist Programs
Vermont Arts Council
136 State Street, Drawer 33
Montpelier, VT 05633-6001
Categories: Fiction.
Description: Opportunity Grants (ranging from $250 to $5000 - all grants require a 1:1 non-federal cash match) are available to artists, organizations, communities, and schools for 1) projects and programs, 2) artist development, and 3) organization and community technical assistance. The Council welcomes request for support of new projects as well as to continue existing programs. Application fees are $10 for individual artists and $20 for organizations/schools/municipalities. Vermont Arts Council members do not pay an application fee. There are four deadlines a year. These Grants are open to artists who have been residents of Vermont for a minimum of one year prior to the application deadline, and are residents at the time the award is granted. Please call 802/828-3291 for guidelines or e-mail to info@arts.vca.state.vt.us. Visit the Web site at *www.state.vt.us/vermont-arts*.

Name of Prize: Walter Rumsey Marvin Grant
Prize: $1,000
Open to: Ohio residents; see description
Contact: Linda R. Hengst, Director
Ohio Library Association
65 South Front Street, Suite 1105
Columbus, OH 43205
Categories: Novel-length fiction, short story, nonfiction.
Description: Applicants born in Ohio, or who have lived there for at least five years, are 30 years of age or younger, and have not published a book may apply for this $1,000 grant, which is given annually. Writer may submit up to six pieces of prose no more than 60 pages and no less than 10. Send SASE for complete guidelines and application forms, or e-mail to ohioana@winslo.state.oh.us.

Name of Prize: West Virginia Literature Fellowships in Fiction
Prize: $3,500
Open to: West Virginia residents
Contact: Tod Ralstin, Fellowship Awards
West Virginia Commission on the Arts Cultural Center
1900 Kanawha Boulevard East
Charleston, WV 25305-0300
Categories: Varies.

Description: The West Virginia Literature awards cycle every three years. Playwrights; poets; and writers of fiction, nonfiction, and children's literature are offered the fellowships. Suggestions by the Commission on how the writer should use the award money are given, but its really up to the winner on how he/she chooses to utilize the funds. Send SASE for guidelines.

Name of Prize: Wisconsin Institute for Creative Writing Fellowships
Prize: $20,000
Open to: See description.
Contact: Wisconsin Institute for Creative Writing Director
　　　Wisconsin Institute for Creative Writing
　　　University of Wisconsin
　　　Department of English
　　　600 North Park Street
　　　Madison, WI 53706
Categories: Fiction, novel and short story, poetry, residency/colony.
Description: Poets and fiction writers who have completed an M.A., M.F.A., or equivalent degree in creative writing, and have yet to publish a book, may apply for residency at the Wisconsin Institute for Creative Writing and receive a $20,000 stipend. This fellowship is open annually to two writers who are working on their first book of poetry or fiction. Fellows will be required to teach one introductory class in creative writing and give public readings of their works-in-progress. Send SASE for complete guidelines and application forms.

Name of Prize: Wyoming Arts Council Annual Creative Writing Fellowships
Prize: $2,500
Open to: Wyoming residents
Contact: Mike Shay, Literary Coordinator
　　　Wyoming Arts Council
　　　2320 Capitol Avenue
　　　Cheyenne, WY 82002
Categories: Varies.
Description: The Wyoming Arts Council annually offers Creative Writing Fellowships to writers who are residents of Wyoming and are more than 18 years of age. The work may be in any literary genre, fiction, nonfiction, poetry, and drama. Send SASE for complete guidelines and application forms.

Awards Exclusively for Unpublished
First-Book Manuscripts by Size of Prize

Award Name	Prize
Pew Fellowships in the Arts for Poets	$50,000
Jenny McKean Moore Fund for Creative Writing Fellowships	$48,000
Wisconsin Institute for Creative Writing Fellowships	$20,000
Alabama State Council on the Arts Fiction Fellowships	$10,000
AWP/Thomas Dunne Books Novel Award	$10,000
North Carolina Arts Council Fellowships in Fiction	$8,000
North Carolina Arts Council Fellowships in Poetry	$8,000
Arizona Commission on the Arts Grants in Creative Writing	$7,500
Massachusetts Artist Grants in Fiction	$7,500
Massachusetts Artist Grants in Poetry	$7,500
South Carolina Project Grants for Fiction Writers	$7,500
New York Foundation's Fellowships in Fiction	$7,000
Maryland State Individual Artist Award for Fiction	$6,000
California Arts Council's Fellowships	$5,000
Delaware Individual Artist Fellowships for Fiction	$5,000
Kentucky Artists' Fellowships in Fiction	$5,000
Kentucky Artists' Fellowships in Poetry	$5,000
Louisiana State Fellowships for Poetry	$5,000
Louisiana State Fellowship for Fiction	$5,000
Mississippi Arts Fellowships in Literary Arts for Fiction	$5,000
Mississippi Arts Fellowships in Literary Arts for Poetry	$5,000
Nebraska Arts Individual Artist Fellowships in Fiction	$5,000
Nevada Arts Council's Artists' Fellowships for Literary Arts	$5,000
Peninsula Community Foundation Literature Program in Poetry	$5,000
Pennsylvania Council on the Arts Fellowships	$5,000
Rhode Island Fellowships for Literature	$5,000
Utah Arts Council Publication Prize	$5,000
Vermont Arts Council Opportunity Grants	$5,000
District of Columbia City Arts Projects	$4,500
Nebraska Arts Individual Artist Fellowships in Poetry	$4,000
West Virginia Literature Fellowships in Fiction	$3,500

Maine Arts Commission Individual Artist Fellowships in Literature	$3,000
New Hampshire State Artist Fellowships in Literature	$3,000
Oregon Arts Commission Individual Artists Fellowships for Fiction	$3,000
Oregon Arts Commission Individual Artists Fellowships for Poetry	$3,000
Oregon Literary Fellowships for Writers in Fiction	$3,000
Connecticut Commission on the Arts Fiction Fellowships	$2,500
Nevada Arts Council Arts-in-Education Special Project Grants for Schools and Organizations	$2,500
Tennessee Arts Commission Fiction Writing Fellowships	$2,500
Wyoming Arts Council Annual Creative Writing Fellowships	$2,500
AWP Award Series in Poetry, Fiction, and Creative Nonfiction	$2,000
Montana Arts Individual Artists Fellowships	$2,000
Illinois Arts Council Special Assistance Grants for Poetry	$1,500
Illinois Arts Council Special Assistance Grants for Fiction	$1,500
New England/New York Award	$1,500
Artist Trust GAP (Grants for Artists' Projects) in Fiction	$1,200
Maine Community Foundation Writing Awards in Poetry	$1,000
Walter Rumsey Marvin Grant	$1,000
Electronic Arts Grants Program	$500
Larry Neal Writers' Competition for Poetry	$500
New Rivers Press Minnesota Voices Project in Poetry	$500
NCWN Harperprints Poetry Chapbook Competition	$200
Illinois Writer's Inc. Annual Chapbook Contest	Publication
District of Columbia Grants-in-Aid Program	Varies
Illinois Artists' Fellowships for Poetry	Varies
New Jersey Council on the Arts Fellowship in Prose	Varies
New Jersey Council on the Arts N.J. Writers Project	Varies
South Dakota Touring Artists Programs for Fiction Writers	Varies

Awards Exclusively for Unpublished First-Book Manuscripts by Genre

Fiction

AWP Award Series
Wisconsin Institute for Creative Writing Fellowships
Alabama State Council on the Arts Fiction Fellowships
Arizona Commission on the Arts Grants in Creative Writing
California Arts Council's Fellowships
Connecticut Commission on the Arts Fiction Fellowships
Delaware Individual Artist Fellowships for Fiction
District of Columbia City Arts Projects
District of Columbia Grants-in-Aid Program
Illinois Arts Council Special Assistance Grants for Fiction
Kentucky Artists' Fellowships in Fiction
Louisiana State Fellowships for Fiction
Maine Arts Commission Individual Artist Fellowships in Literature
Maryland State Individual Artist Award for Fiction
Massachusetts Artist Grants in Fiction
Mississippi Arts Fellowships in Literary Arts for Fiction
Montana Arts Individual Artists Fellowships
Nebraska Arts Individual Artist Fellowships in Fiction
Nevada Arts Council Arts-in-Education Special Project Grants for Schools and
    Organizations
Nevada Arts Council's Artists' Fellowships for Literary Arts
New Hampshire State Artist Fellowships in Literature
New Jersey Council on the Arts N.J. Writer's Projects
New Jersey Council on the Arts Fellowship in Prose
New York Foundation's Fellowships in Fiction
Electronic Arts Grants Program
North Carolina Arts Council Fellowships in Fiction
Walter Rumsey Marvin Grant
Oregon Arts Commission Individual Artists Fellowships for Fiction
Oregon Literary Fellowships for Writers in Fiction
Pennsylvania Council on the Arts Fellowships
Rhode Island Fellowships for Literature
South Carolina Project Grants for Fiction Writers
South Dakota Touring Artists Programs for Fiction Writers
Tennessee Arts Commission Fiction Writing Fellowships
Utah Arts Council Publication Prize
Vermont Arts Council Opportunity Grants

Artist Trust GAP (Grants for Artists' Projects) in Fiction
Jenny McKean Moore Fund for Writers in Washington
West Virginia Literature Fellowships in Fiction
Wisconsin Institute for Creative Writing Fellowships
Wyoming Arts Council Annual Creative Writing Fellowships

Short Story (Fiction)

AWP Award Series
Wisconsin Institute for Creative Writing Fellowships
Alabama State Council on the Arts Fiction Fellowships
Delaware Individual Artist Fellowships for Fiction
Illinois Writers Inc. Annual Chapbook Contest
New Jersey Council on the Arts N.J. Writer's Projects
Electronic Arts Grants Program
Walter Rumsey Marvin Grant
South Dakota Touring Artists Programs for Fiction Writers
Artist Trust GAP (Grants for Artists' Projects) in Fiction

Poetry

AWP Award Series
Wisconsin Institute for Creative Writing Fellowships
Arizona Commission on the Arts Grants in Creative Writing
Larry Neal Writers' Competition for Poetry
Illinois Artists' Fellowships for Poetry
Illinois Writers Inc. Annual Chapbook Contest
Illinois Arts Council Special Assistance Grants for Poetry
Kentucky Artists' Fellowships in Poetry
Louisiana State Fellowships for Poetry
Maine Community Foundation Writing Awards in Poetry
Massachusetts Artist Grants in Poetry
New Rivers Press Minnesota Voices Project in Poetry
Mississippi Arts Fellowships in Literary Arts for Poetry
Mississippi Arts Fellowships in Literary Arts for Fiction
Nebraska Arts Individual Artist Fellowships in Poetry
New Jersey Council on the Arts N.J. Writer's Projects
New England/New York Award
Electronic Arts Grants Program
NCWN Harperprints Poetry Chapbook Competition
North Carolina Arts Council Fellowships in Poetry
Oregon Arts Commission Individual Artists Fellowships for Poetry
Peninsula Community Foundation Literature Program in Poetry
Pew Fellowships in the Arts for Poets

Nonfiction

AWP Award Series
New Jersey Council on the Arts N.J. Writer's Projects
Electronic Arts Grants Program
Walter Rumsey Marvin Grant

Drama

New Jersey Council on the Arts N.J. Writer's Projects
Electronic Arts Grants Program

Residential/Colony

New Jersey Council on the Arts N.J. Writer's Projects
South Dakota Touring Artists Programs for Fiction Writers

Screenplay

Electronic Arts Grants Program

Children's Literature

Electronic Arts Grants Program

Religion

Electronic Arts Grants Program

Gay/Lesbian

Electronic Arts Grants Program

Journalism

Electronic Arts Grants Program

Awards Favorable to Unpublished First-Book Manuscripts

Name of Prize: 96 Inc. Bruce Rossley Literary Awards
Prize: $1,000
Open to: Open competition
Contact: Vera Gold, Director
96 Inc.
PO Box 15559
Boston, MA 02225
Categories: Novel-length fiction and short story, nonfiction, poetry.
Description: *96 Inc.*, a literary magazine and resource center in Boston, presents cash prizes to writers of merit whose works are of outstanding merit but with limited public recognition. Writers may be nominated by anyone with a letter of recommendation and supporting documents (six copies of published and/or unpublished manuscripts that are up to 20 pages in length). The writer is expected to be accomplished in teaching and community service, as well as written work. Write and send SASE for guidelines and recommendation forms.

Name of Prize: ALA: Gay/Lesbian and Bisexual Book Award in Literature
Prize: Varies
Open to: Open competition
Contact: Faye Chadwell, Chairperson
Collection Development
University of Oregon Library
1299 University of Oregon
Eugene, OR 97403-1299
Categories: Fiction, novel, poetry, drama, Gay/Lesbian.
Description: A cash honorarium and a commemorative plaque are given "to authors of fiction, drama, and poetry books of exceptional merit relating to Gay/Lesbian experience." The donor for this award is the Gay/Lesbian and Bisexual Task Force. For more information and complete guidelines, please send an SASE.

Name of Prize: Arizona Authors' Association's Annual Literary Contest
Prize: Publication
Open to: Open competition
Contact: Iva Martin
   Arizona Authors' Association
   3509 East Shea, Suite 117
   Phoenix, AZ 85028-3339
Categories: Novel-length fiction and short story, poetry.
Description: The Arizona Author's Association Annual National Literary Contest is open to poets, fiction writers, and nonfiction writers. The cash award varies; however, the winning manuscripts will be published in the *Arizona Literary Magazine*. Previously unpublished poems, short stories, and essays are all accepted. Send SASE for complete guidelines, or call 602/867-9001 for more information.

Name of Prize: AWP Thomas Dunne Books Novel Award
Prize: $10,000
Open to: Open competition
Contact: Katherine Perry, AWP Writing Programs
   Tallwood House
   Mail Stop 1E3
   George Mason University
   Fairfax, VA 22030
Categories: Novel-length fiction.
Description: For the AWP Thomas Dunne Books Novel Award, Thomas Dunne Books will offer to enter into an agreement with the winner. The agreement provides for an advance against earnings of $10,000 (payable $5,000 on signing and $5,000 on publication), with all other terms of the offer to be determined by Thomas Dunne Books in its discretion. The submission must be at least 60,000 words. Send one copy of each manuscript entered, prepared according to manuscript formatting guidelines. Multiple entries must be accompanied by separate entry fees and separate cover sheet. Send SASE for specific guidelines, visit the Web site at *www.awpwriter.org,* or e-mail to awp@gmu.edu.

Prize: Bellwether Prize
Prize: $25,000
Open to: Open competition
Contact: Prize Director
   National Writers' United Service Organization
   113 University Place, 6th Floor
   New York, NY 10003
Categories: Novel-length fiction.

Description: A prize of $25,000 and publication by HarperCollins is given annually for an unpublished novel. Established and funded by Barbara Kingsolver, the prize is given for a literary novel whose content addresses issues of social justice and the impact of culture and politics on human relationships. U.S. citizens who have some previous publications but have not published a novel that sold more than 10,000 copies are eligible. Submit an unpublished novel of at least 200 pages with entry fee. Send SASE for required application and complete guidelines.

Name of Prize: Best First Private Eye Novel Contest
Prize: $10,000
Open to: Writers unpublished in the genre
Contact: Private Eye Contest Director
St. Martin's Press
175 Fifth Avenue
New York, NY 10010
Categories: Novel-length fiction.
Description: Writers of the traditional private eye novel compete for this $10,000 prize (advance against royalties) and publication. Only authors who have not previously published a novel in this particular genre (and have no novel in this genre under contract for publication) are eligible. Send SASE for full details and entry forms. Please do not send manuscripts.

Name of Prize: Bottom Dog Press' Midwest First Novel Contest
Prize: $200
Open to: Midwestern writers
Contact: Midwest First Novel Contest Director
Bottom Dog Press
c/o Firelands College
Huron, OH 44839
Categories: Novel-length fiction.
Description: Bottom Dog Press will offer $200, 30 copies, and 10 percent royalties on the winning novel in the Midwest First Novel Contest. The story must be set in the Midwest and be less than 62,000 words. Author must have lived in the Midwest for at least two years, and the novel must be the first novel published by the author. Send SASE for complete guidelines.

Name of Prize: BRIO (Bronx Recognizes Its Own) Excellence in Arts Awards
Prize: $1,500
Open to: Bronx residents
Contact: BRIO
       Bronx Council on the Arts
       1738 Hone Avenue
       Bronx, NY 10461-1486
Categories: Novel-length fiction and short story; nonfiction; drama; poetry; screen-play.
Description: The BRIO (Bronx Recognizes Its Own) Excellence in Arts Awards are offered for published or unpublished works created within five years of application date to support the artistic development and contributions of Bronx literary artists. Awardees are required to perform a public service activity within the Bronx. Applications are available mid-December. Be sure to send your artistic resume. For an application, call the Bronx Council on the Arts at 718/931-9500; fax: 718/409-6445. You can e-mail to bronxart@artswire.org or visit the Web site at *www.bronxarts.org.*

Name of Prize: Chapter One Fiction Competition and Reading Series
Prize: $200
Open to: New York City residents over 18 years old
Contact: Leslie Shipmen
       The Bronx Writers' Center
       2521 Glebe Ave.
       Bronx, NY 10461
Categories: Novel-length fiction.
Description: The Chapter One Fiction Competition and Reading Series, held by the Bronx Writers' Center, a program of the Bronx Council on the Arts, seeks first chapters from published or unpublished novels, or works in progress. Writers must live in one of the five boroughs. No more than four selections will be made. Each one of the winners will receive a $200 honorarium and be invited to read the winning selection. For more information, including submission guidelines and deadlines, please contact the Center by mail, phone 718/409-1265, fax 718/409-1351, e-mail to wtrsctr@artswire.org, or visit the Web site at *www.bronxarts.org.*

Name of Prize: Chicano/Latino Literary Contest for Fiction
Prize: $1,000
Open to: U.S. citizens/Permanent residents
Contact: Alejandro Morales, Director
        University of California at Irvine
        Department of Spanish and Portuguese
        322 Humanities Hall
        Irvine, CA 92697-5275
Categories: Novel-length fiction, short story.
Description: The Department of Spanish and Portuguese at the University of California, Irvine invites submissions for the annual Chicano/Latino Literary Contest. Winners are given a first-place prize of $1,000 and publication of the collection if not under previous contract, and transportation to Irvine to receive the award. A second-place prize of $500 and a third-place prize of $250 are also offered. The manuscript must be unpublished and submitted in triplicate. Author must be a citizen or permanent resident of the United States. The manuscript's first page should bear the title Chicano/Latino Literary Contest, the writer's full name, address, telephone number, indication of citizenship or residence, if work is contracted to a publisher, and a social security number. Send SASE for complete guidelines

---

Name of Prize: Chinook Literary Prize
Prize: $10,000
Open to: Open competition
Contact: Chinook Literary Prize, Editor
        Sasquatch Books
        615 Second Avenue, Suite 206
        Seattle, WA 98104-2200
Categories: Novel-length fiction, nonfiction.
Description: The Sasquatch Books offers the Chinook Literary Prize. Winner will receive an advance of $10,000 against royalties, and publication will be given for a book-length manuscript of fiction or nonfiction on the theme of the Pacific Northwest by any writer. The Chinook Literary Prize is offered annually by Sasquatch Books, a regional publisher based in Seattle. Send SASE from complete guidelines and information.

Name of Prize: CNW/FFWA Florida State Writing Competition
Prize: $100
Open to: Open competition
Contact: Dana K. Cassell, Executive Director
Florida Freelance Writers Association
PO Box A
North Stratford, NH 03590
Categories: Novel-length fiction, short story, poetry, drama, nonfiction, children's literature, journalism.
Description: CNW/FFWA Florida State Writing Competition accepts short fiction, a chapter from a fiction novel, nonfiction previously published, a feature article, essay or column, poetry, and juvenile literature; there is no page limit. Send SASE for complete guidelines, or print out the guidelines and entry form from the Web site at *www.writers-editors.com.* A list of previous year's winners is also posted at the site. Applicants can also e-mail to contest@writers-editors.com.

Name of Prize: Constance Salto: The Sydney Taylor Manuscript Award
Prize: $5,000
Open to: New York State residents
Contact: Program Manager
Constance Saltonstall Foundation Arts Colony
120 Brindley Street
Ithaca, NY 14850
Categories: Fiction, novel, and short story.
Description: The Constance Saltonstall Foundation, in Ithaca, New York, will award grants of $5000 to fiction writers living in central and western counties of New York State. The competition is open to painters, photographers, and writers of fiction, poetry, and creative nonfiction. Please send SASE for an application and information or e-mail to *www.saltonstall.com.*

Name of Prize: Coretta Scott King Awards in Fiction
Prize: $250
Open to: African-American authors and illustrators
Contact: Coretta Scott King Awards Director
American Library Association
50 East Huron Street
Chicago, IL 60611
Categories: Novel-length fiction, short story.
Description: This distinguished award offers $250 and a set of encyclopedias to both an African-American author and an illustrator whose works promote understanding and appreciation of culture and contributions of all people. The donors of this

award are Johnsen Publishing Company and Encyclopedia Britannica. Send SASE for complete guidelines.

_____

Name of Prize: Dana Award for the Novel
Prize: $1,000
Open to: Open competition
Contact: Mary Elizabeth Parker, Chair
Dana Awards in Poetry and the Novel
7207 Townsend Forest Court
Browns Summit, NC 27214
Categories: Novel-length fiction.
Description: The Dana Award for the Novel is $1,000 for the first 50 pages of a novel (not under contract to any publisher). Send first 50 pages only. No children's or young adult themes are accepted. Send SASE for complete guidelines, visit the Web site at *danaawards.home.pipeline.com*, or e-mail to danaawards@pipeline.com.

_____

Name of Prize: Deep South Writers Conference Literary Contest for Fantasy/Science Fiction
Prize: $500
Open to: Open competition
Contact: David Thibodaux, Contest Clerk
The Deep South Writers Conference
c/o English Department
Box 44691
University of Southwestern Louisiana
Lafayette, LA 70504-4691
Categories: Novel-length fiction, short story.
Description: The Literary Contest for Fantasy and Science Fiction, given by The Deep South Writers Conference, offers a minimum of $500 annually to novel and short story writers. Send SASE for complete guidelines and application forms.

_____

Name of Prize: Deep South Writers Conference Literary Contest for Fiction
Prize: $500
Open to: Open competition
Contact: David Thibodaux, Contest Clerk
The Deep South Writers Conference
c/o English Department
Box 44691
University of Southwestern Louisiana
Lafayette, LA 70504-4691

Categories: Novel-length fiction, short story.
Description: The Literary Contest for Fiction, given by The Deep South Writers Conference, offers a minimum of $500 annually to novel and short story writers. Send SASE for complete guidelines and application forms.

Name of Prize: Deep South Writers Conference Literary Contest for Juvenile Fiction
Prize: $500
Open to: Open competition
Contact: David Thibodaux, Contest Clerk
      The Deep South Writers Conference
      c/o English Department
      Box 44691
      University of Southwestern Louisiana
      Lafayette, LA 70504-4691
Categories: Novel-length fiction, short story, children's literature.
Description: The Literary Contest for Juvenile Fiction, given by The Deep South Writers Conference, offers a minimum of $500 annually to juvenile fiction writers. Send SASE for complete guidelines and application forms.

Name of Prize: Delacourt Press Prize for a First Young Adult Novel
Prize: $7,500
Open to: Open competition
Contact: Delacourt Press Prize Director
      Bantam Doubleday Dell
      Books for Young Readers
      1540 Broadway
      New York, NY 10036
Categories: Novel-length fiction, children's literature.
Description: This contest offers a book contract for a hardcover and a paperback edition, a $1,500 cash prize, and a $6,000 advance against royalties. Submissions should consist of a book-length manuscript (100 to 224 typewritten pages), with a contemporary setting, that will be suitable for ages 12 to 18. Write for complete submission guidelines. This prize is available to American and Canadian writers who have not previously published a young adult novel. Send SASE for complete guidelines.

Name of Prize: Eaton Literary Associates Awards for Book-Length Work
Prize: $2,500
Open to: Open competition
Contact: Richard Lawrence
        Eaton Literary Associates
        Literary Awards for Book-Length Work
        PO Box 49795
        Sarasota, FL 34230-6795
Categories: Novel-length fiction, nonfiction.
Description: The Eaton Literary Associates sponsors the Literary Awards for a Book-Length Work, open to unpublished fiction or nonfiction works of more than 10,000 words. Send SASE for complete guidelines. An SASE must be included (with adequate postage) for the manuscript's return. Please e-mail to eatonliterary@aol.com for information about the awards program and instructions for e-mailing manuscripts.

Name of Prize: Evergreen Chronicles Novella Contest for Emerging Writers
Prize: $500
Open to: Open competition
Contact: Brendan Kramp, Managing Editor
        Evergreen Chronicles Novella Contest
        PO Box 8939
        Minneapolis, MN 55408-0939
Categories: Novel-length fiction, Gay/Lesbian.
Description: The Evergreen Chronicles Novella Contest is for emerging writers, sponsored by *The Evergreen Chronicles* with a grant from the Jerome Foundation. Published winners will appear in a special issue of *Evergreen*. Evergreen will submit first- and second-prize manuscripts to a publisher for possible publication in a separate volume. The novella shall be an original work of prose fiction, no less than 15,000 words and no more than 30,000 words. The contest is open to writers who have had no more than one novel or novella published. Each novella must in some way speak to the gay, lesbian, bisexual, or transgender experience. Send SASE for complete guidelines or e-mail to evergchron@aol.com.

Name of Prize: Fannie Lou Hamer Award
Prize: $500
Open to: Women writers
Contact: Susan P. Liner
        Money for Women/Barbara Denting Memorial Fund
        PO Box 630125
        Bronx, NY 10463

Categories: Novel-length fiction, short story, nonfiction, poetry, women, Gay/Lesbian.
Description: The Money for Women/Barbara Deming Memorial Fund, Inc. gives small grants to individual feminists in the arts, in art, fiction (prose), nonfiction (prose), and poetry whose work addresses women's concerns and/or speaks for peace and justice from a feminist perspective. In addition to these grants, the Fund occasionally offers two special awards: 1) The 'Gerty, Gerty, Gerty in the Arts, Arts, Arts' for outstanding work by a lesbian, and 2) The 'Fannie Lou Hamer Award' for work that combats racism and celebrates women of color. No special application need be made for either grant; recipients will be chosen from all proposals. The Fund does not give educational assistance, monies for personal study or loans, monies for dissertation or research projects, grant for group projects, business ventures or emergency funds for hardships." Send SASE for complete guidelines.

Name of Prize: Fine Arts Work Center in Provincetown Writers' Fellowships
Prize: $3,150
Open to: Open competition
Contact: Writers' Fellowships Coordinator
Fine Arts Work Center
Writers' Fellowships
24 Pearl Street
Provincetown, MA 02657
Categories: Novel-length fiction, short story, poetry, residency/colony.
Description: The Fine Arts Work Center in Provincetown offers Writers' Fellowships to emerging writers and artists who reside at the Center for seven uninterrupted months. The fellowships provide living/working space and a $450 stipend a month (for a total of $3,150) and run from October 1 to May 1. There is also a summer program of writing and visual arts workshop available. Send SASE for complete guidelines and required application form.

Name of Prize: Gavel Awards
Prize: Varies
Open to: Open competition
Contact: Howard Kaplan
Gavel Awards
American Bar Association
Division of Public Education
541 North Fairbanks Court
Chicago, IL 60611-3314
Categories: Novel-length fiction, short story, poetry, drama, screenplay, nonfiction.
Description: According to the American Bar Association, "each year, the American Bar Association presents these prestigious Gavel Awards to recognize products in

media and the arts published or presented during the preceding year that have been exemplary in helping to foster public understanding of the law and the American legal system." Newspaper articles, magazine articles, books (fiction and non-fiction), theatrical productions, television programs, radio programs, and films and videos are all eligible. The prize is an inscribed Silver Gavel, a Certificate of Merit, and incorporation into the American Bar Association Gavel Awards Archives. Send SASE for further guidelines and required application form.

Name of Prize: Gerty, Gerty, Gerty in the Arts, Arts, Arts Award
Prize: $1,000
Open to: Lesbian writers
Contact: Susan P. Liner
       Money for Women/Barbara Deming Memorial Fund
       PO Box 630125
       Bronx, NY 10463
Categories: Novel-length fiction, short story, nonfiction, poetry, women, Gay/Lesbian.
Description: The Money for Women/Barbara Deming Memorial Fund, Inc. gives small grants to individual feminists in the arts, in art, fiction (prose), nonfiction (prose), and poetry whose work addresses women's concerns and/or speaks for peace and justice from a feminist perspective. In addition to these grants, the Fund occasionally offers two special awards: 1) The 'Gerty, Gerty, Gerty in the Arts, Arts, Arts' for outstanding work by a lesbian, and 2) The 'Fannie Lou Hamer Award' for work that combats racism and celebrates women of color. No special application need be made for either grant; recipients will be chosen from all proposals. The Fund does not give educational assistance, monies for personal study or loans, monies for dissertation or research projects, grant for group projects, business ventures, or emergency funds for hardships. Send SASE for complete guidelines.

Name of Prize: Glimmer Train, Fiction Open
Prize: $2000 and publication
Open to: All writers
Contact: Glimmer Train, Fiction Open
       710 SW Madison Street, Suite 504
       Portland, Oregon 97205
Categories: Fiction.
Description: Open to all themes, all story lengths, and all writers. First-place winner receives $2,000 and publication in *Glimmer Train Stories*, and 20 copies of that issue. Second- and third-place winners receive $1,000 and $600, respectively. Please staple all pages together. Cover letter is optional. The first page of your unpublished story must include your name, address, and phone number. Keep a copy of your story; materials will not be returned. Please be sure the address and phone

number on your check are correct; winners will be contacted at this address, so please keep us advised of changes. Include SASE marked "List of winning FIC- TION OPEN entries, please" if you would like to receive that. Postmark deadline is May 1-June 30; notification of winners by October 15. Please mark envelope: "FICTION OPEN."

- - - - -

Name of Prize: Glimmer Train, Poetry Open
Prize: $500 and publication
Open to: All poets
Contact: Glimmer Train, Poetry Open
710 SW Madison Street, Suite 504
Portland, Oregon 97205
Categories: Poetry.
Description: Open to all themes, all lengths, all forms, and all poets. First-place winner receives $500, publication in *Glimmer Train Stories*, and 20 copies of that issue. Second- and third-place winners receive $250 and $100, respectively. In- clude name, address, and phone number on each poem. Keep a copy of your work; materials will not be returned. Reading fee is $10 for up to three unpublished poems. Please staple poems longer than one page. Be sure the address and phone number on your check are correct; winners will be contacted at this address, so please keep us advised of changes. Include SASE marked "List of winning PO- ETRY OPEN entries, please" if you would like to receive that. April contest: Postmark between April 1-April 30. Winners will be telephoned by September 1. October contest: Postmark between October 1-October 31. Winners will tele- phoned by March 1.

- - - - -

Name of Prize: Glimmer Train Short Story Award for New Writers
Prize: $1000
Open to: See description
Contact: Glimmer Train Press, Inc.
710 SW Madison Street, Suite 504
Portland, Oregon 97205
Categories: Fiction, short story.
Description: This competition is open to writers whose fiction hasn't appeared in a nationally distributed publication with a circulation of more than 5,000. Manu- scripts should be typed, double-spaced, and have a 1,200 to 8,000 word limit. Our issues have no themes, but we do not accept children's stories or nonfiction. Please include your name, address, and telephone number on the first page of the manu- script. The first-place winner receives $,1200, publication in *Glimmer Train Sto- ries,* and 20 copies of that issue. Second- and third-place winners receive $500 and $300, respectively. Send SASE for complete guidelines and deadline information.

- - - - -

Name of Prize: Glimmer Train, Very Short Fiction Award
Prize: $1200 and publication
Open to: All published and unpublished writers
Contact: Glimmer Train, Very Short Fiction Awards
        710 SW Madison Street, Suite 504
        Portland, Oregon 97205
Categories: Fiction, very short fiction.
Description: This competition is held twice yearly, in the winter and summer. Story length must not exceed 2000 words; word count needs to appear on first page of story. Must be typed, double-spaced, and not previously published. First-place winner receives $1200, publication in *Glimmer Train Stories*, and 20 copies of that issue. Second- and third-place winners receive $500 and $300, respectively. Applicants should staple all pages together. Cover letter is optional. First page of story must include word count and your name, address, and phone number. Keep a copy of your work; materials will not be returned. Reading fee is $10 per story. Be sure the address on your check is correct; winners will be contacted at this address, so please keep us advised of changes. Please write "Very Short Fiction Award" on the envelope and send it to the address listed. Include SASE marked "List of winning VSF entries, please" if you would like to receive the list of contest winners. Winter dates: Postmark deadline is January 31. Winners will be telephoned by April 1. Summer dates: Postmark deadline is July 31. Winners will be telephoned by October 1.

_____

Name of Prize: Great Lakes New Writer Awards for Fiction
Prize: $300
Open to: Publisher submission *only*
Contact: Mark Andrew Clark, Director
        GLCA New Writer Awards
        The Philadelphia Center
        North American Building
        121 South Broad Street, 7th Floor
        Philadelphia, PA 19107-4577
Categories: Novel-length fiction.
Description: A New Writer Award in fiction is given for the best first book of fiction published in the year preceding the award. Winner must visit Great Lakes College Association member colleges as arranged, receiving at least a $300 stipend, room and board, and transportation costs for each. Author receives recognition and participates in each college's activities. Send SASE for guidelines.

_____

Name of Prize: Hackney Literary Award for a Novel
Prize: $5,000
Open to: Open competition
Contact: Myra Crawford
    Hackney Literary Award
    Birmingham-Southern College
    Box 549003
    Birmingham, AL 35254
Categories: Novel-length fiction.
Description: The Hackney Literary Award annually offers a $5,000 prize for the best unpublished novel submitted. There is no length restriction. No submissions will be accepted prior to June 1. Send SASE for complete guidelines.

Name of Prize: Heekin Foundation James Fellowships for a Novel-in-Progress
Prize: $3,000
Open to: Open competition
Contact: Sarah Heekin Redfield
    Heekin Group Foundation
    PO Box 1534
    Sisters, OK 97759
Categories: Novel-length fiction.
Description: Unpublished writers or writers just beginning their careers are eligible for the $3,000 fellowship for a novel-in-progress offered by The Heekin Foundation. Two fellowships are given each year. Submit the first 50 to 75 pages of the work-in-progress. Only writers who have never published a novel are eligible. Publication occurring after entry (but before winning) will not disqualify the candidate. Send SASE for complete guidelines or e-mail to *hgfhl@aol.com*.

Name of Prize: Hurston/Wright Awards
Prize: $1,000
Open to: See description
Contact: Writing Program Secretary
    Hurston/Wright Awards
    Virginia Commonwealth University
    Department of English
    PO Box 842005
    Richmond, VA 23284-2005
Categories: Novel-length fiction, short story.
Description: The Zora Neale Hurston/Richard Wright Awards have been established by novelist Marita Golden to honor excellence in fiction writing by students of African descent enrolled full-time as graduate or undergraduate students in any college or university in the United States. The first-place award of $1,000 and

publication in *The New Virginia Review* along with a second-place award of $500 will be presented each spring to the writers of the best previously unpublished short story or novel excerpt. Send SASE for complete guidelines.

Name of Prize: Ian St. James Annual Awards
Prize: Varies
Open to: Unpublished authors
Contact: Merric Davidson
　　　PO Box 60
　　　Cranbrook, Kent
　　　TN17 2ZR, England
Categories: Novel-length fiction
Description: The Annual Ian St. James Awards are open to writers who have not published a novel or novella. The top 10 stories of up to 3,000 words and the top 10 stories of more than 3,000 words will be published in an anthology. Prizes range from 500 British Pounds to 5,000 British Pounds. For complete rules and entry form, write with international reply coupon (IRC).

Name of Prize: ICS Books, Inc. Outdoor Adventure Tale
Prize: $2,000
Open to: Open competition
Contact: Contest Director
　　　ICS Books, Inc.
　　　Outdoor Adventure Tale
　　　PO Box 10767
　　　1370 East 86th Place
　　　Merrillville, IN 46410
Categories: Novel-length fiction, short story, nonfiction.
Description: ICS Books, Inc. Outdoor Adventure Tale offers a first prize of $2,000 and a second prize of $500 for an outdoor adventure that exaggerates within moderation. Send SASE for complete guidelines and application form.

Name of Prize: International Quarterly Crossing Boundaries Writing Awards
Prize: $500
Open to: Open competition
Contact: Van K. Brock, Editor
　　　International Quarterly Crossing Boundaries Writing Awards
　　　PO Box 10521
　　　Tallahassee FL 32302-0521
Categories: Fiction, novel and short story; poetry; commercial nonfiction; translation.
Description: The International Quarterly Crossing Boundaries Writing Awards offers four prizes of $500 each plus publication in the *International Quarterly* in four

categories: poetry, fiction, nonfiction, and "crossing boundaries." The "crossing boundaries" category includes "atypical work and innovative or experimental writing." Entries in poetry, nonfiction, and fiction may also be recommended by the judges for the "crossing boundaries" category. Manuscripts may be written in English or in English translations from any other language. The maximum length for fiction and nonfiction manuscripts is 5,000 words. Up to five poems may be submitted for the entry fee. Send SASE for complete guidelines.

Name of Prize: Jack Kerouac Annual Literary Prize in Fiction
Prize: $500
Open to: Open competition
Contact: Contest Director
The Jack Kerouac Literary Prize
PO Box 8788
Lowell, MA 01853-8788
Categories: Novel-length fiction, short story.
Description: The Jack Kerouac Literary Prize is sponsored by Lowell Celebrates Kerouac! (a non-profit organization), and the Estate of Jack and Stella (Sampas) Kerouac. Experienced and emerging writers are invited to submit written works for this prize, which will consist of a $500 honorarium and the invitation to present the winning manuscript at a public reading during the annual Lowell Celebrates Kerouac! Festival. Writers should submit one typed, double-spaced copy of their manuscript. Each entry must not exceed 30 pages excerpted from a novel, or a maximum of three short stories with a combined length of 30 pages or less.

Name of Prize: James Jones First Novel Fellowship
Prize: $5,000
Open to: Unpublished American novelists
Contact: James Jones Society Chairperson
The James Jones Society
Department of English
Wilkes University
Wilkes-Barre, PA 18766
Categories: Novel-length fiction.
Description: The James Jones First Novel Fellowship will be awarded to an American author of a first novel in progress. Novellas (up to 150 pages) and collections of closely linked short stories may also be considered for the competition. The award is intended to honor the spirit of unblinking honesty, determination, and insight into modern culture exemplified by the late James Jones, author of *From Here to Eternity* and other prose narratives of distinction. Jones was himself the recipient of aid from many supporters as a young writer, and his family, friends, and admirers have established this award of $5,000 to continue this tradition in his

name. The competition is open to all American writers who have not previously published novels. Manuscripts may be submitted for publication simultaneously, but the Society must be notified of acceptance elsewhere. Send SASE for more information, visit *wilkes1.wilkes.edu/~ english/jones.html,* or e-mail to english@wilkes.edu.

_____

Name of Prize: James D. Phelan Literary Award
Prize: $2,000
Open to: Native-born Californians, ages 20-35
Contact: Awards Coordinator
Phelan Literary Awards
Intersection for the Arts
446 Valencia Street
San Francisco, CA 94103
Categories: Novel-length fiction and short story; nonfiction; poetry; drama; screenplay.
Description: The James D. Phelan Award, sponsored by the San Francisco Foundation/Intersection of the Arts, is open to native-born Californians, 20-35 years of age. The award is offered annually for an unpublished work-in-progress to bring about a further development of native talent in California. Send SASE for complete guidelines.

_____

Name of Prize: Kate Snow Writing Contest for a Short Story
Prize: $300
Open to: See description
Contact: Contest Director
Kate Snow Writing Contest for an Adult Short Story
Willamette Writers
9045 SW Barbur Blvd., Suite 5A
Portland, OR 97219
Categories: Novel-length fiction, short story.
Description: The Kate Snow Writing Contest for a Short Story offers a $300 first-place prize, a $150 second-place prize, and a $50 third-place prize for the best short story submitted. Writers should submit one complete genre short story or novel excerpt intended for an adult audience. Genres may include mainstream, literary, horror, romance, fantasy, science fiction, western, or detective, but are not limited to these. Maximum word length is 2500 words. Fees for each category, per entry. Kate Snow was the founder of Willamette Writers, and the purpose of this annual contest, named in her honor, is to help writers reach professional goals in writing, and to honor the best struggling writers in a broad array of categories. Send SASE for complete guidelines.

_____

Name of Prize: Kenneth Patchen Competition for Fiction
Prize: $500
Open to: Open competition
Contact: Contest Director
        Kenneth Patchen Competition
        Pig Iron Press
        PO Box 237
        Youngstown, OH 44501
Categories: Novel-length fiction, short story.
Description: The Kenneth Patchen Competition for Fiction (either novel or short story) offers a $500 cash award, plus publication and royalties, for a book-length unpublished novel. The winner will also receive 20 copies of the 800 paperback copies published. Send SASE for brochure and list of previous winners.

Name of Prize: Leeway Grants to Emerging and Established Women Artists
Prize: $50,000
Open to: Women writers
Contact: Program Coordinator
        The Leeway Foundation
        123 South Broad Street, Suite 2040
        Philadelphia, PA 19109
Categories: Novel-length fiction, short story, poetry, women.
Description: Leeway Grants are awarded in a selected visual or literary arts discipline each year to women who are residents of Bucks, Chester, Delaware, Montgomery, or Philadelphia county in Pennsylvania and are 20 years old or older. Write for complete guidelines, e-mail to info@leeway.org, or visit the Web site at *www.leeway.org.*

Name of Prize: Mammoth Books Literary Book Publication Series
Prize: $750
Open to: Open competition
Contact: Antonio Vallone, Publisher/Editor
        Mammoth Books Press Inc.
        7 South Juniata Street
        DuBois, PA 15801
Categories: Novel-length fiction, short story, nonfiction, poetry, translation.
Description: Mammoth Books invites submissions to its literary book publication series. There are two contests offered each year: prose (creative nonfiction and fiction) and poetry. In prose, literary nonfiction, short stories, and novels are acceptable. In poetry, a single long poem or collection are acceptable, but not anthologies. First-place winners in each category will receive $750 and a standard

royalty contract. All finalists will be considered for publication. Send SASE for complete guidelines or e-mail to mammothbooks@hotmail.com.

Name of Prize: Marguerite de Angeli Contest
Prize: $5,000
Open to: Open competition
Contact: Marguerite de Angeli Contest Director
        Bantam Doubleday Dell
        Books for Young Readers
        1540 Broadway
        New York, NY 10036
Categories: Novel-length fiction, children's literature.
Description: Marguerite de Angeli (1889-1987), for whom the contest is named, told simple stories about the lives and dreams of active, impulsive, and inquisitive children, whose adventures often brought them into contact with persons of other races and cultures. She showed all children that they are important parts of a diverse, larger society. The contest offers a book contract for a hardcover and a paperback edition, and consists of $1,500 cash and a $3,500 advance against royalties. Manuscripts should be between 40 and 144 typewritten pages of contemporary or historical fiction set in North America, for readers aged 7-10. Write for complete submission guidelines. This prize is available to American and Canadian writers who have not previously published a novel for middle grade readers.

Name of Prize: Mary Roberts Rinehart Fund for Fiction
Prize: $2,500
Open to: Unpublished writers—nomination only
Contact: William Miller
        English Department
        Attn: Mary Roberts Rinehart Fund
        George Mason University
        MSN 3E4 4400 University Drive
        Fairfax, VA 22030
Categories: Novel-length fiction, short story.
Description: Three grants each year are given to writers who need financial assistance, not otherwise available, to complete their work. Nominations can come from writing program faculty, sponsoring writer, agent, or editor. Grants are from $2,000 to $2,500 each. Send a nominating letter and 30 pages or less of the candidate's prose. Please send SASE for complete guidelines.

Name of Prize: Mid-List Press First Series Award for Creative Nonfiction
Prize: $1,000 $30 fee
Open to: Open Competition
Contact: Awards Director
       First Series Award for Creative Nonfiction
       Mid-List Press
       4324 12th Avenue South
       Minneapolis, MN 55407-3218
Categories: Nonfiction.
Description: Mid-List Press First Series Award for Creative Nonfiction is open to any writer who has never published a book of creative nonfiction. "Creative nonfiction" includes (but is not limited to) memoir, autobiography, nature writing, travel writing, personal essay, literary journalism, social commentary, and cross-disciplinary work. Eligible writers may submit either a collection of essays or a single book-length work. Manuscripts must be at least 50,000 words in length. Send SASE for complete guidelines or visit the Web site *www.midlist.org*.

Name of Prize: Mid-List Press First Series Award for the Novel
Prize: $1,000
Open to: Open competition
Contact: Award Director
       Mid-List Press
       4324 12th Avenue South
       Minneapolis, MN 55407-3218
Categories: Fiction, novel.
Description: The Mid-List Press First Series Award for a Novel is open to any writer who has never published a novel. There are no genre restrictions, but manuscripts must be at least 50,000 words in length. Send SASE for complete guidelines or visit the Web site at *www.midlist.org*.

Name of Prize: Milkweed National Fiction Prize
Prize: $5,000
Open to: Open competition
Contact: Elisabeth Fitz, First Reader
       Milkweed Editions
       430 First Avenue North, Suite 668
       Minneapolis, MN 55401
Categories: Novel-length fiction, short story.
Description: Milkweed Editions is looking for fiction manuscripts (novels, novellas, and short story collections) of high literary quality that embody humane values and contribute to cultural understanding. Milkweed Editions will award the National Fiction Prize to the best work of fiction Milkweed accepts for publication

during each calendar year by a writer not previously published by Milkweed Editions. Before submitting a manuscript, please send SASE for fiction guidelines or visit the Web site at *www.milkweed.org.*

Name of Prize: New Writing Award
Prize: $3,000
Open to: Open competition
Contact: Contest Director
New Writing
New Writing Award
PO Box 1812
Amherst, NY 14226-7812
Categories: Novel-length fiction, short story, nonfiction, poetry, screenplay, drama.
Description: The New Writing Award is annually sponsored by New Writing Literary Agency, The Book Doctor, and *New Writing Magazine* for unpublished work to award the best of new writing. The contest accepts short stories, poems, plays, novels, essays, films, and emerging forms. The monetary award is up to $3,000 in cash and prizes, and possible publication. Send SASE for complete guidelines and application forms, e-mail to awards@uewwfiting.com, or visit the Web site at *members.aol.com/newwriting/contest~html.*

Name of Prize: New York University Press Prize in Fiction
Prize: $1,000
Open to: Open competition
Contact: Prize Coordinator
New York University Press
Prizes in Fiction
838 Broadway
New York, NY 10003-4812
Categories: Novel-length fiction.
Description: This award is given to writers who have been insufficiently recognized in their careers. Submit one typewritten copy of a book-length manuscript; a one-page letter of recommendation on letterhead from a qualified reader such as a teacher, agent, or editor; and a cover sheet with the writer's name, address, and telephone number. Send SASE for complete guidelines and rules or visit the Web site at *www.nyupress.nyu.edu.*

Name of Prize: North American Native Authors First Book Award for a Prose Collection
Prize: $500
Open to: Native Americans
Contact: North American Native Authors Awards Director
    The Greenfield Review Literary Center
    PO Box 308
    Greenfield Center
    New York, NY 12633
Categories: Novel-length fiction, short story, poetry.
Description: The contest is open to North American Native writers of American Indian, Inuit, Aleut and Metis ancestry who have not published a book. All of North America, including Mexico and Central America, is included. Manuscripts must be bilingual or entirely in English. Send SASE for guidelines and application forms.

Name of Prize: NWA Novel Writing Contest
Prize: $500
Open to: Open competition
Contact: Sandy Whelchel
    National Writers Association
    Book Manuscript Contest
    3140 S. Peoria Street, 295
    Aurora, CO 80014-3155
Categories: Novel-length fiction.
Description: The NWA Novel Writing Contest is offered to writers with unpublished novels in any genre. The first prize is $500, second prize $300, and third prize $100. No more than 90,000 words can be submitted. The NWA also offers critiques of submitted material for an additional reading fee. Send SASE for complete guidelines and required application forms.

Name of Prize: Omaha Prize
Prize: $1,000
Open to: Open competition
Contact: Greg Kosmicki, Editor/Publisher
    The Backwaters Press
    3502 N. 52nd Street
    Omaha, NE 68104-3506
Categories: Novel-length fiction.
Description: The Backwaters Press offers the Omaha Prize for novel manuscripts between 180 and 300 pages of original fiction in English (no translations). Authors name on cover letter only. Sections of the novel may have been previously published

in magazines, but the complete manuscript may not have been previously published. Simultaneous submissions are acceptable; state in cover letter and inform The Backwaters Press immediately if manuscript is accepted for publication elsewhere. Send SASE for return of manuscript. Winner announced in November/ December *Poets & Writers*. All entrants receive a copy of prize-winning book. Send SASE for complete guidelines.

Name of Prize: Ommation Press Book Contest
Prize: Publication
Open to: Open competition
Contact: Effie Mihopoulos
        Ommation Press Book Contest
        5548 North Sawyer
        Chicago, IL 60625
Categories: Novel-length fiction, short story, poetry.
Description: The Ommation Press Book Contest is offered to poets and fiction writers for an unpublished book-length manuscript of fiction or poetry. The prize for the winning manuscript is publication and 100 copies of the book. Applicants may enter more than one manuscript, but a separate entry fee must be included with each manuscript submission. The entry fee includes a free copy of a book by a former winner—publisher's choice; if you enter a second manuscript or entered the contest in the past, please specify so that you will be mailed a different book. Manuscripts should be no longer than 60 pages. Simultaneous submission are acceptable, but please note this in the manuscript or in cover letter. SASE for complete guidelines.

Name of Prize: Opus Magnum Discovery Awards in Fiction
Prize: Varies
Open to: Open competition
Contact: Carlos de Abreu
        Christopher Columbus Society
        433 North Camden Drive, Suite 600
        Beverly Hills, CA 90210
Categories: Novel-length fiction, screenplay/teleplay.
Description: Each month, awards are given for unpublished works of genre fiction (Action, Thriller, Suspense, Science Fiction), to discover new authors with books/ manuscripts that can be optioned for features or television movies. First-prize manuscript is published by Custos Morum Publishers with option moneys to winner (up to $10,000); second and third prizes are $500 each. The work is judged by entertainment industry story analysts and producers. Send SASE for complete guidelines.

Name of Prize: PEN Fund for Writers and Editors with AIDS
Prize: $1,000
Open to: Writers and editors with AIDS
Contact: PEN Writers Fund Coordinator
       PEN American Center
       568 Broadway
       New York, NY 10012
Categories: Novel-length fiction, short story, nonfiction, poetry, drama, screenplay, women, Gay/Lesbian, religion, journalism, children's literature, translation.
Description: PEN American Center offers grants of up to $1,000 to professional writers and editors with AIDS who are experiencing serious financial difficulty due to HIV or AIDS-related illness. Funds cannot be used to finance writing or research time, publication or professional development of any kind. Send SASE for complete guidelines and application forms. E-mail to pen@pen.org or visit the Web site at *www.pen.org*.

Name of Prize: PEN/Norma Klein Award for Children's Fiction
Prize: $3,000
Open to: Authors of children's fiction
Contact: PEN/Norma Klein Award, Director
       PEN American Center
       568 Broadway
       New York, NY 10012
Categories: Novel-length fiction, children's literature.
Description: Offered biennially, PEN makes this award to a new author of children's (elementary to young adult) fiction of literary merit. The award judges will be looking for books that demonstrate the adventuresome and innovative spirit that characterizes the best of children's literature. Candidates may not nominate themselves. The judges (a panel of three distinguished children's book authors) welcome all nominations from authors and editors of children's books. Nominating letters should describe the author's work in some detail and how it promises to enrich American literature for children and include a list of the candidate's publications (either in the body of the letter or by enclosing a copy of the candidate's vita.) Please send SASE for complete guidelines.

Name of Prize: PEN Northwest Margery Davis Boyden Writing Residency
Prize: $1,200
Open to: Open competition
Contact: John Daniel
       PEN Northwest
       Boyden Writing Residency
       23030 West Sheffler Road
       Elmira, OR 97437

Categories: Novel-length fiction, short story, poetry, residency/colony.

Description: The PEN Northwest Margery Davis Boyden Writing Residency, sponsored and administered by PEN Northwest (a chapter of PEN America) and Frank and Bradley Boyden, the program founders and owners of the property, offers a seven-month writing residency in the wilderness of southern Oregon. The residency runs from April through October, and includes a house and a stipend of $1,200. The resident is asked to provide an hour a day of routine caretaking. All persons interested in the residency must send SASE for residency description and application guidelines. This is a unique residency in a backwoods location. The resident must be experienced in self-reliant living.

Name of Prize: Philip Roth Residence in Creative Writing
Prize: $1,000
Open to: Poets and writers at least 21 years of age
Contact: Cynthia Hogue, Director
Philip Roth Residence in Creative Writing
Bucknell University, Stadler Center for Poetry
Lewisburg, PA 17837
Categories: Fiction, novel and short story, poetry.

Description: The Residence at Bucknell University is intended to provide a young writer who has some record of accomplishment the opportunity to work for four months in an atmosphere conducive to writing, with all necessities provided. The residence provides a studio on campus, a fully equipped two-bedroom apartment, meals in the University Dining Services, and a stipend of $1,000. The period of the residence will begin on October 1 and last until mid-December, partially coinciding with the fall semester. In alternate years the residence will be awarded to a writer of fiction and a poet. You must be a U.S. citizen. Send SASE for complete guidelines, visit the Web site at *www.departments.bucknell.edu/stadlercenter/*, or e-mail to ciotola@bucknell.edu.

Name of Prize: Poets and Writers—Writers Exchange Program
Prize: $500
Open to: See description
Contact: Writers Exchange Program Director
Poets and Writers, Inc.
72 Spring Street
New York, NY 10012
Categories: Novel-length fiction, short story, poetry.

Description: The Writers Exchange Program gives writers an opportunity to share their work with other writers nationwide. Four poets and fiction writers will be chosen from two designated states. The Exchange Program will award a $500 honorarium to each writer and give the writer an opportunity to give readings and meet with the literary community in two states outside the writer's home. Winners must be available for a one-week tour on a schedule determined by Poets and Writers. All expenses and a per diem will be paid by Poets and Writers. Emerging writers from states designated by Poets and Writers are eligible for this program. Send SASE for complete guidelines, eligible states, and application forms.

Name of Prize: Quarter After Eight Prose Writing Contest
Prize: $500
Open to: Open competition
Contact: Prose Writing Contest Editor
      QAE
      Ellis Hall
      Ohio University
      Athens, OH 45701
Categories: Novel-length fiction, short story, poetry, nonfiction, drama.
Description: *Quarter After Eight*, a journal of prose and commentary, offers this prose writing contest. First-place prize is $500. Submit fiction, sudden fiction, prose, poetry, novel excerpts, drama, and essays less than 10,000 words in length. Send SASE for complete guidelines and rules.

Name of Prize: Rotten Romance
Prize: $10
Open to: See description
Contact: Contest Director
      Rotten Romance Contest
      PO Box 2907
      Decatur, IL 62524
Categories: Fiction, novel and short story.
Description: Here's your chance to write as terribly as you can. Just produce one sentence, of any length, as the worst opening sentence of the romance novel you plan to write someday. The worst entry will receive $10 and be published in a special flyer by Hutton Publications. You can order the flyer of previous winners for $1 + #10 typed SASE. The annual deadline is Valentine's Day. No entry fee; one entry per person; entry must be typed; envelopes must be typed. Submit with #10 typed SASE to Rotten Romance.

Name of Prize: Sandstone Prize in Short Fiction
Prize: $2,000
Open to: Open competition
Contact: Bill Roorbach, Fiction Editor
        Ohio State University Press
        1070 Carmack Road
        Columbus, OH 43210
Categories: Fiction, novel and short story.
Description: The Sandstone Prize in Short Fiction offers $2,000 and publication for an original collection of short fiction. The winner will also direct a workshop and give a reading at Ohio State University. The award is cosponsored by Ohio State University Press and the OSU Creative Writing Program. Submit a collection of short stories, novellas, or a combination of the two. Manuscripts should be 150 to 300 pages; individual novellas may not exceed 125 pages. Send SASE for complete guidelines.

Name of Prize: Scott Sommer Fiction Awards
Prize: $500
Open to: Open competition
Contact: Awards Coordinator
        Writers Voice of the West Side YMCA
        5 West 63rd Street
        New York, NY 10023
Categories: Novel-length fiction, short story.
Description: The honorarium is $500 and the prize is a reading at the Writer's Voice for published or unpublished writers who have not participated in the Writer's Voice. Submit 10 pages of fiction, double-spaced. Send SASE for entry form and guidelines.

Name of Prize: Shenango River Books Prose Chapbook Contest
Prize: $100
Open to: Open competition
Contact: Contest Director
        Shenango River Books Prose Chapbook Contest
        PO Box 631
        Sharon, PA 16146
Categories: Fiction, novel and short story; commercial nonfiction.
Description: The Shenango River Books Prose Chapbook Contest invites writers to submit 40 to 60 pages of prose (novella, short stories, or creative nonfiction). With the manuscript, submit a title page, a biography, and acknowledgments. The winner will receive publication, $100, and 100 copies. All entrants receive a copy of the winning book. Send SASE for complete guidelines.

Name of Prize: Southern Prize for Fiction and Poetry
Prize: $600
Open to: Open competition
Contact: The Southern Prize Director
        The Southern Anthology
        The Southern Prize
        2851 Johnson Street, #123
        Lafayette, LA 70503
Categories: Novel-length fiction, short story, poetry.
Description: The Southern Prize for Fiction and Poetry is offered annually by *The Southern Anthology*. The grand prize is $600 plus publication awarded to the best short story or novel excerpt submitted (7,500 words or less), or poem. Each short story applicant should submit one manuscript; poets may submit up to three poems. All manuscripts must be original and unpublished. Six finalist will be published in *The Southern Anthology*. No manuscripts are returned. Send SASE for complete guidelines.

———

Name of Prize: Southwest Writers Workshop Writing Contest
Prize: $1,000   *emailed*
Open to: Open competition
Contact: Contest Chair
        SWW Contest
        8200 Mountain Road N'E, Suite 106
        Albuquerque, NM 87110-7835
Categories: Novel-length fiction, short story, poetry, nonfiction, drama, journalism, screenplay, children's literature.
Description: The Southwest Writers Workshop Annual Contest includes novels, short stories, poetry, nonfiction (books and articles), screenplays, and children's literature. Every entry is critiqued by a professional. Send SASE for entry form and complete guidelines, e-mail to Swriters@aol.com, or visit the Web site at *www.southwestwriters.org*.

———

Name of Prize: St. Martin's Malice Domestic First Traditional Mystery Contest
Prize: $10,000
Open to: Writers unpublished in the genre
Contact: Malice Domestic Contest Director
        St. Martin's Press
        175 Fifth Avenue
        New York, NY 10010
Categories: Novel-length fiction.
Description: Writers of the traditional mystery novel compete for this $10,000 prize (advance against royalties) and publication. Only authors who have not previously

published a novel in this particular genre (and have no novel in this genre under contract for publication) are eligible. Send SASE for full details and entry forms.

Name of Prize: Summerfield G. Roberts Award for Fiction
Prize: $2,500
Open to: U.S. citizens
Contact: Summerfield G. Roberts Award, Director
        Sons of the Republic of Texas
        1717 8th Street
        Bay City ,TX 77414
Categories: Fiction, novel and short story.
Description: Manuscripts representing Texas from 1836-1846, written during the year preceding the award, will be considered for the $2,500 annual prize. Novel, short story or other fiction; poetry, biography; essay or other nonfiction that will encourage literary effort and research about historical events during the days of the Republic of Texas will be considered. Five non-returnable copies need to be submitted. Send SASE for guidelines.

Name of Prize: Sydney Taylor Manuscript Award
Prize: $1,000
Open to: Open competition
Contact: Paula Sandfelder
        Sydney Taylor Manuscript Award
        1327 Wyntercreek Lane
        Dunwoody, GA 30338
Categories: Fiction, novel, children's literature, religion.
Description: The Sydney Taylor Manuscript Award, sponsored by the Association of Jewish Libraries, offers a $1,000 cash prize to the winning author to encourage outstanding new books with Jewish themes (but with appeal to children everywhere) and to help launch new children's writers in their careers. The writer must have no previously published books. The material should be a work of fiction in English with universal appeal of Jewish content for readers aged 8-11. It should serve to deepen the understanding of Judaism for all children, Jewish and non-Jewish, and should reveal positive aspects of Jewish life. Send two copies of the manuscript, typed, doubled-spaced, between 64 to 200 pages. One submission per entrant only. Send #10 SASE for further guidelines and application forms.

Name of Prize: Tobias Wolff Award for Fiction
Prize: $1,000
Open to: Open competition
Contact: Fiction Award Director
        Tobias Wolff Award for Fiction
        Mail Stop 9053
        Western Washington University
        Bellingham, WA 98225
Categories: Novel-length fiction, short story.
Description: The Tobias Wolff Award for Fiction offers a first-place prize of $1000, a second- place prize of $250, and a third-place prize of $100 for the winning story or novel excerpt submitted on any subject or style. Submit a story or novel excerpt (maximum length of 10,000 words per story or chapter) that has not been previously published or has been accepted for publication. Stories/chapters may be under consideration elsewhere, but they should be withdrawn from the competition if they are accepted for publication. The author's name must not appear anywhere on the manuscript. Enclose with your story or chapter one 3 x 5" index card bearing the titles of stories/chapters submitted, word count for each story/chapter, author's name and address, phone number, fax number, and e-mail address if any. The entry fee is $10.00 for the first entry and $5.00 for each additional entry. Send SASE for complete guidelines and information. Visit the Web site at *www.edu/-bhreview*.

Name of Prize: University of Arizona Poetry Center Summer Residency
Prize: $500
Open to: Open competition
Contact: Frances Shoberg, Events Coordinator
        University of Arizona
        Poetry Center Residency Program
        1216 North Cherry Avenue
        Tucson, AZ 85719-4519
Categories: Novel-length fiction, short story, poetry, nonfiction, residency.
Description: The Poetry Center at the University of Arizona in Tucson offers a one-month residency between June 1 and August 31 to provide a writer with a place to create in a quiet neighborhood of a southwestern city. The guest cottage is an historic adobe located two houses from the nationally acclaimed collections of the University of Arizona Poetry Center. Applicants should send 10 pages of poetry or 20 pages of fiction or literary nonfiction (no name should appear on the work); SASE for reply, although the manuscripts will not be returned; $10 reading fee; a cover letter stating name, address, phone numbers, e-mail address, and title(s) of submitted work; and a one-page resume. Applicants must not have published more than one full-length book. (Self-published and chapbooks are

excluded.) Current University of Arizona students not eligible. Send SASE for complete application forms or visit *www.coh.arizona.edu/poetry*.

Name of Prize: Washington Prize for Fiction
Prize: $5,000
Open to: American and Canadian fiction writers
Contact: Larry Kaltman, Director
        Larry Kaltman Literary Agency
        Washington Prize for Fiction
        1301 South Scott St. #-424
        Arlington, VA 22204-4656
Categories: Novel-length fiction, short story.
Description: Submissions for the Washington Prize for Fiction should be previously unpublished manuscripts of novels, collections of short stories, or several novellas (at least 65,000 words). Multiple submissions are allowed, but a separate entry fee must accompany each submission. First prize is $5,000, second prize is $2,500, third prize is $1,000; and if desired, literary representation. Send SASE for guidelines.

Name of Prize: Whiting Writers Awards
Prize: $30,000
Open to: Emerging writers
Contact: Gerald Freund, Director
        Mrs. Giles Whiting Foundation Awards
        1133 Avenue of the Americas, 22nd Floor
        New York, NY 10036
Categories: Novel-length fiction, short story, poetry, nonfiction, drama.
Description: The Foundation gives annually $30,000 each to up to 10 writers of poetry, fiction, nonfiction, and plays. The awards place special emphasis on exceptionally promising emerging talent. This award is given to an author and/or playwright in recognition of the quality of the writer's accomplishment and promise for future work. Invited nominations only; applications not accepted.

Name of Prize: William Faulkner Creative Writing Competiton for a Novel
Prize: $7,500
Open to: Open competition
Contact: Fiction Prize Director
        Pirate's Alley Faulkner Society
        624 Pirate's Alley
        New Orleans, LA 70116
Categories: Novel-length fiction.
Description: This annual competition is open to unpublished original works by U.S. citizens. Novels (short story collections are not accepted) should be 50,000 words

or more. The award is $7,500, $2,500 of which is designated as an advance against royalties to encourage a publisher to print the winning book. Winner also receives a medal cast in gold. Send an SASE for an application and complete guidelines, or visit the Web site (preferred) at *www.wordsandmusic.org*.

Name of Prize: Writer's Digest Annual Writing Competition
Prize: $1,000
Open to: Open competition
Contact: Writing Competition
        Writer's Digest
        1507 Dana Avenue
        Cincinnati, OH 45207
Categories: Novel-length fiction, short story, nonfiction, poetry, drama, journalism, screenplay, children's literature.
Description: The Writer's Digest Annual Writing Competition offers more than $25,000 in prizes. The grand prize winner, judged as best overall from the 10 categories, will receive $1000 cash and an all-expense paid trip to New York City to meet with editors and agents. The first-, second-, and third-place winners in each category will receive $750, $350, and $250 respectively, as well as $100 worth of Writer's Digest Books. Additional cash awards and prizes for other winners. All entries must be original, unpublished, and unproduced. Winners will be notified by October 21 and winner's names will appear in the November issue of *Writer's Digest*. Send SASE for guidelines and entry form. Categories are personal essay, feature article, genre short story, mainstream/literary short story, rhyming poetry, non-rhyming poetry, stage play, TV/movie script, children's fiction, and inspirational. Visit the Web site at *www.writersdigest.com*.

Name of Prize: Writer's Film Project
Prize: $20,000
Open to: Open competition
Contact: Writer's Film Project Coordinator
        The Chesterfield Film Company
        8205 Santa Monica Blvd., #200
        Los Angeles, CA 90046
Categories: Novel-length fiction, short story, drama, screenplay.
Description: The Writer's Film Project (WFP) offers fiction, theater, and film writers the opportunity to begin a career in screenwriting. Send SASE for complete guidelines and deadline information.

Name of Prize: Writers at Work in Fiction
Prize: $1,500
Open to: Writers who have not published a book-length work
Contact: Fiction Fellowship Competition Director
　　　　　Writers at Work
　　　　　PO Box 1146
　　　　　Centerville, UT 84104-5146
Categories: Novel-length fiction, short story.
Description: First-place winner in genre receives $1,500 and publication in *Quarterly West*, as well as a featured reading and tuition (valued at $200) for the afternoon session at the annual Writers at Work summer conference in July, which features morning workshops in a variety of genres, afternoon panels/lectures, and access to writers, publishers, editors, and agents. Second place winners receive $500 and afternoon tuition. Send SASE for guidelines.

Name of Prize: Writers in Performance Contest for Novel Excerpt
Prize: Varies
Open to: Open competition
Contact: Contest Director
　　　　　Seattle Writers Association
　　　　　PO Box 33265
　　　　　Seattle, WA 98133
Categories: Novel-length fiction.
Description: Writers in Performance Contest accepts up to 2,000 words of a novel excerpt. When submitting, please do not place your name on the entry. Send SASE for manuscript return. All entrants will get free admission to the contest's reading and awards ceremony. Prizes include cash, anthology, publicity, and public performance. Send SASE for complete guidelines.

Name of Prize: Writers of the Future Contest in Fantasy
Prize: $1,000
Open to: Unpublished writers
Contact: Contest Administrator
　　　　　L. Ron Hubbard Writers of the Future Contest
　　　　　PO Box 1630
　　　　　Los Angeles, CA 90078
Categories: Novel-length fiction, short story.
Description: Entrants may not have published a novel, or more than three short stories, or more than one novella. Winners are published in major anthology and brought to a five-day writing workshop. Send SASE for rules.

Name of Prize: Writers of the Future Contest in Science Fiction
Prize: $1,000
Open to: Unpublished writers
Contact: Contest Administrator
      L. Ron Hubbard Writers of the Future Contest
      PO Box 1630
      Los Angeles, CA 90078
Categories: Novel-length fiction, short story.
Description: Entrants may not have published a novel, or more than three short stories, or more than one novella. Winners are published in major anthology and brought to a five-day writing workshop. Send SASE for rules.

Name of Prize: Yaddo Residencies
Prize: Varies
Open to: Open competition
Contact: Admissions Committee
      Yaddo
      PO Box 395
      Sarasota Springs, NY 12866
Categories: Novel-length fiction, short story, poetry, nonfiction, drama, children's literature, screenplay, journalism, translation.
Description: Yaddo offers professional published and unpublished writers who show artistic merit and promise one to two months residencies at Yaddo (a working community for writers, visual artists, and composers). Applicants must send samples of work, with application forms and letters of recommendation. Awards include room, board, and studio space. Send large SASE for complete guidelines and application forms, or e-mail to yaddo@yaddo.org.

Awards Favorable to Unpublished First-Book Manuscripts by Size of Prize

Award Name	Prize
Leeway Grants to Emerging and Established Women Artists	$50,000
Whiting Writers Awards	$30,000
Bellwether Prize	$25,000
Writer's Film Project	$20,000
AWP Thomas Dunne Books Novel Award	$10,000

Best First Private Eye Novel Contest	$10,000
Chinook Literary Prize	$10,000
St. Martin's Malice Domestic First Traditional Mystery Contest	$10,000
Delacourt Press Prize for a First Young Adult Novel	$7,500
William Faulkner Creative Writing Competition for a Novel	$7,500
Constance Salto: The Sydney Taylor Manuscript Award	$5,000
Hackney Literary Award for a Novel	$5,000
James Jones First Novel Fellowship	$5,000
Marguerite de Angeli Contest	$5,000
Milkweed National Fiction Prize	$5,000
Washington Prize for Fiction	$5,000
Fine Arts Work Center in Provincetown Writers' Fellowship	$3,150
Heekin Foundation James Fellowships for a Novel-in-Progress	$3,000
New Writing Award	$3000
PEN/Norma Klein Award for Children's Fiction	$3,000
Eaton Literary Associates Awards for Book-Length Work	$2,500
Mary Roberts Rhinehart Fund for Fiction	$2,500
Summerfield G. Roberts Award for Fiction	$2,500
ICS Books, Inc. Outdoor Adventure Tale	$2,000
James D. Phelan Literary Award	$2,000
Glimmer Train, Fiction Open	$2,000/ Publication
Sandstone Prize in Short Fiction	$2,000/ Publication
BRIO (Bronx Recognizes Its Own) Excellence in the Arts Award	$1,500
Writers at Work in Fiction	$1,500
PEN Northwest Margery Davis Boyden Writing Residency	$1,200
Glimmer Train, Very Short Fiction Award	$1,200/ Publication
Chicano/Latino Literary Contest for Fiction	$1,000/ Publication
Dana Award for the Novel	$1,000
Gerty, Gerty, Gerty in the Arts, Arts, Arts Award	$1,000
Glimmer Train Short Story Award for New Writers	$1,000
Hurston/Wright Awards	$1,000
Mid-List Press First Series Award for Creative Nonfiction	$1,000
Mid-List Press First Series Award for the Novel	$1,000
New York University Press Prize in Fiction	$1,000
96 Inc. Bruce Rossley Literary Award	$1,000

Omaha Prize	$1,000
PEN Fund for Writers and Editors with AIDS	$1,000
Philip Roth Residence in Creative Writing	$1,000
Southwest Writers Workshop Writing Contest	$1,000
Sydney Taylor Manuscript Award	$1,000
Tobias Wolff Award for Fiction	$1,000
Writer's Digest Annual Writing Competition	$1,000
Writers of the Future Contest in Fantasy	$1,000
Writers of the Future Contest in Science Fiction	$1,000
Mammoth Books Literary Book Publication Series	$750
Southern Prize for Fiction and Poetry	$600/ Publication
Deep South Writers Conference Literary Contest for Fantasy/Science Fiction	$500
Deep South Writers Conference Literary Contest for Fiction	$500
Deep South Writers Conference Literary Contest for Juvenile Fiction	$500
Evergreen Chronicles Novella Contest for Emerging Writers	$500
Fannie Lou Hamer Award	$500
Kenneth Patchen Competition for Fiction	$500
North American Native Authors First Book Award for a Prose Collection	$500
NWA Novel Writing Contest	$500
Poets and Writers—Writers Exchange Program	$500
Quarter After Eight Prose Writing Contest	$500
University of Arizona Poetry Center Summer Residency	$500
Jack Kerouac Annual Literary Book Publication Series	$500/ Reading
Scott Sommer Fiction Awards	$500/ Reading
Glimmer Train, Poetry Open	$500/ Publication
International Quarterly Crossing Boundaries Writing Awards	$500/ Publication
Great Lakes New Writer Awards for Fiction	$300
Kate Snow Writing Contest for a Short Story	$300
Coretta Scott King Awards in Fiction	$250
Bottom Dog Press' Midwest First Novel Contest	$200
Chapter One Fiction Competition and Reading Series	$200
CNW/FFWA Florida State Writing Competition	$100
Shenango River Books Prose Chapbook Contest	$100
Southern Prize for Fiction and Poetry	$100

Rotten Romance	$10
Arizona Authors' Association's Annual Literary Contest	Publication
Ommation Press Book Contest	Publication
ALA: Gay/Lesbian and Bisexual Book Award in Literature	Varies
Gavel Awards	Varies
Ian St. James Annual Awards	Varies
Opus Magnum Discovery Awards in Fiction	Varies
Writers in Performance Contest for Novel Excerpt	Varies
Yaddo Residencies	Varies

Awards Favorable to Unpublished First-Book Manuscripts by Genre

Children's Literature

CNW/FFWA Florida State Writing Competition
Deep South Writers Conference Literary Contest for Juvenile Fiction
Marguerite de Angeli Contest
PEN Fund for Writers and Editors with AIDS
PEN/Norma Klein Award for Children's Fiction
Southwest Writers Workshop Writing Contest
Writer's Digest Annual Writing Competition
Yaddo Residencies

Fiction

ALA: Gay/Lesbian and Bisexual Book Award in Literature
AWP Thomas Dunne Books Novel Award
BRIO (Bronx Recognizes Its Own) Excellence in Arts Award
Chapter One Fiction Competition and Reading Series
Chicano/Latino Literary Contest for Fiction
Chinook Literary Prize
CNW/FFWA Florida State Writing Competition
Coretta Scott King Awards in Fiction
Deep South Writers Conference Literary Contest for Fantasy/Science Fiction
Deep South Writers Conference Literary Contest for Fiction
Deep South Writers Conference Literary Contest for Juvenile Fiction
Eaton Literary Associates Awards for Book-Length Work
Fannie Lou Hamer Award
Fine Arts Work Center in Provincetown Writers' Fellowships
Gavel Awards
Gerty, Gerty, Gerty in the Arts, Arts, Arts Award

Glimmer Train Fiction Open
Glimmer Train, Very Short Fiction Award
Hackney Literary Award for a Novel
International Quarterly Crossing Boundaries Writing Award
Jack Kerouac Annual Literary Prize in Fiction
James D. Phelan Literary Award
Mammoth Books Literary Book Publication Series
Marguerite de Angeli Contest
Omaha Prize
Ommation Press Book Contest
Opus Magnum Discovery Awards in Fiction
PEN Fund for Writers and Editors with AIDS
PEN Northwest Margery Davis Boyden Writing Residency
PEN/Norma Klein Award for Children's Fiction
Philip Roth Residence in Creative Writing
Poets and Writers—Writers Exchange Program
Quarter After Eight Prose Writing Contest
Rotten Romance
Sandstone Prize in Short Fiction
Scott Sommer Fiction Awards
Shenango River Books Prose Chapbook Contest
Southern Prize for Fiction and Poetry
Southwest Writers Workshop Writing Contest
Summerfield G. Roberts Award for Fiction
Tobias Wolff Award for Fiction
University of Arizona Poetry Center Summer Residency
Washington Prize for Fiction
Whiting Writers Awards
William Faulkner Creative Writing Competition for a Novel
Writer's Digest Annual Writing Competition
Writers in Performance Contest for Novel Excerpt
Yaddo Residencies

Nonfiction

BRIO (Bronx Recognizes Its Own) Excellence in Arts Award
Chinook Literary Prize
CNW/FFWA Florida State Writing Competition
Eaton Literary Associates Awards for Book-Length Work
Fannie Lou Hamer Award
Gavel Awards
Gerty, Gerty, Gerty in the Arts, Arts, Arts Award
ICS Books, Inc. Outdoor Adventure Tale
International Quarterly Crossing Boundaries Writing Awards

James D. Phelan Literary Award
Mammoth Books Literary Book Publication Series
PEN Fund for Writers and Editors with AIDS
Quarter After Eight Prose Writing Contest
Shenango River Books Prose Chapbook Contest
Southwest Writers Workshop Writing Contest
University of Arizona Poetry Center Summer Residency
Whiting Writers Awards
Writer's Digest Annual Writing Competition
Yaddo Residencies

Screenplays
BRIO (Bronx Recognizes Its Own) Excellence in Arts Award
Gavel Awards
Opus Magnum Discovery Awards in Fiction
PEN Fund for Writers and Editors with AIDS
Southwest Writers Workshop Writing Contest
Writer's Digest Annual Writing Competition
Yaddo Residencies

Short Fiction
BRIO (Bronx Recognizes Its Own) Excellence in Arts Award
Chicano/Latino Literary Contest for Fiction
CNW/FFWA Florida State Writing Competition
Coretta Scott King Awards in Fiction
Deep South Writers Conference Literary Contest for Fantasy/Science Fiction
Deep South Writers Conference Literary Contest for Fiction
Deep South Writers Conference Literary Contest for Juvenile Fiction
Fannie Lou Hamer Award
Fine Arts Work Center in Provincetown Writers' Fellowships
Gavel Awards
Gerty, Gerty, Gerty in the Arts, Arts, Arts Award
Glimmer Train, Very Short Fiction Award
ICS Books, Inc. Outdoor Adventure Tale
International Quarterly Crossing Boundaries Writing Awards
Jack Kerouac Annual Literary Prize in Fiction
James D. Phelan Literary Award
Mammoth Books Literary Book Publication Series
Ommation Press Book Contest
PEN Fund for Writers and Editors with AIDS
PEN Northwest Margery Davis Boyden Writing Residency
Philip Roth Residence in Creative Writing
Poets and Writers—Writers Exchange Program

Quarter After Eight Prose Writing Contest
Rotten Romance
Sandstone Prize in Short Fiction
Scott Sommer Fiction Awards
Shenango River Books Prose Chapbook Contest
Shenango River Books Prose Chapbook Contest
Southern Prize for Fiction and Poetry
Southwest Writers Workshop Writing Contest
Summerfield G. Roberts Award for Fiction
Tobias Wolff Award for Fiction
University of Arizona Poetry Center Summer Residency
Washington Prize for Fiction
Whiting Writers Awards
Writer's Digest Annual Writing Competition
Yaddo Residencies

Poetry
ALA: Gay/Lesbian and Bisexual Book Award in Literature
BRIO (Bronx Recognizes Its Own) Excellence in Arts Award
CNW/FFWA Florida State Writing Competition
Fannie Lou Hamer Award
Fine Arts Work Center in Provincetown Writers' Fellowships
Gavel Awards
Gerty, Gerty, Gerty in the Arts, Arts, Arts Award
Glimmer Train, Poetry Open
International Quarterly Crossing Boundaries Writing Awards
James D. Phelan Literary Award
Mammoth Books Literary Book Publication Series
Ommation Press Book Contest
PEN Fund for Writers and Editors with AIDS
PEN Northwest Margery Davis Boyden Writing Residency
Philip Roth Residence in Creative Writing
Poets and Writers—Writers Exchange Program
Quarter After Eight Prose Writing Contest
Southern Prize for Fiction and Poetry
Southwest Writers Workshop Writing Contest
University of Arizona Poetry Center Summer Residency
Writer's Digest Annual Writing Competition

Drama
ALA: Gay/Lesbian and Bisexual Book Award in Literature
BRIO (Bronx Recognizes Its Own) Excellence in Arts Award
CNW/FFWA Florida State Writing Competition

Gavel Awards
PEN Fund for Writers and Editors with AIDS
Quarter After Eight Prose Writing Contest
Southwest Writers Workshop Writing Contest
Writer's Digest Annual Writing Competition
Yaddo Residencies

Translation
International Quarterly Crossing Boundaries Writing Awards
Mammoth Books Literary Book Publication Series
PEN Fund for Writers and Editors with AIDS
Yaddo Residencies

First Book American Classics

Edgar Allan Poe

Tamerlane and Other Poems. By a Bostonian
Boston: Calvin F. S. Thomas, Printer, 1827

The publication of *Tamerlane* was an obscure event from an obscure period in Poe's life. When the young man's career at the University of Virginia closed in December 1826, with debts and dissipations, Mr. Allan failed to understand how his own attitude might have contributed to his foster son's excesses, nor did he help him find suitable work. After three months in Richmond, Poe ran away from home. He went to Boston, drawn perhaps by the accident that his parents had been performing there when he was born. Little is known of his first two months in Boston. Possibly he tried to follow in his parents' footsteps and obtain work in the theater. On May 26, 1827, he enlisted in the U. S. Army as Private Edgar A. Perry. By August he had arranged for the publication of *Tamerlane* with Calvin Thomas, a 19-year-old printer. Not many copies were printed, perhaps as few as 40, perhaps as many as 200. Certainly, the book dropped quickly out of sight.

A 40-page pamphlet, *Tamerlane* was originally covered in paper wrappers. It was discovered in Maine by Andrew McCance, another Boston bookseller. Mr. McCance sold it to the collector W. T. H. Howe for $3,700 in 1938. Howe's library was purchased by Albert A. Berg in 1941. In 1990, at the sale of the library of collector H. Bradley Martin, a copy (with wrappers) of the pamphlet sold for $150,000.

Nathaniel Hawthorne

Fanshawe, a Tale
Boston: Marsh & Capen, 1828

When Hawthorne entered Bowdoin in 1821, it was a small college of 114 students on the edge of the Maine wilderness. There, in his senior year, 1824-1825, he may have begun *Fanshawe*. There, too, he observed incidents and personalities that he used in the novel to illustrate those ideas of good and evil that he was to develop so forcefully in later work. Hawthorne paid $100 for the publication of the novel, and the greatest return on his investment was the interest *Fanshawe* aroused in Samuel Griswold Goodrich, the Boston publisher. For the next 14 years, Goodrich provided an outlet for Hawthorne's stories in his annual, *The Token*, and in the *New England Magazine*, to which he introduced Hawthorne. He also employed Hawthorne to compile *Peter Barley's Universal History*, a compendium for children, for him in 1837. Though Goodrich was tardy in paying for such hack work as the latter, his interest kept Hawthorne writing.

Walt Whitman

Franklin Evans; or The Inebriate. A Tale of the Times
In the *New World*, Vol. 2, No. 10, Extra Series No. 34, November, 1842

The first 40 years of Walt Whitman's life are intimately associated with Brooklyn. Of English and Dutch blood, Whitman (1819-1892) was born on a farm on Long Island and brought to the city as a child. There he attended school until he was 11 or 13. His first real job was as a printer's devil, and for the next three decades he was primarily associated with newspapers and magazines as printer or editor, in Brooklyn, New York, or New Orleans.

While working as a compositor for the *New World* in 1842, he produced *Franklin Evans; or The Inebriate* for an extra issue of the paper. Influenced by the melodramatic and sentimental side of Dickens, this "original temperance novel" gave no promise of what would follow. It was *Leaves of Grass*, first published in 1855 in Brooklyn, that brought Whitman fame, first in England and later in America, and made him a subject of violent controversy during the latter part of his life. He died, an enigmatic idol, in his shrine in Camden, New Jersey.

Henry David Thoreau

A Week on the Concord and Merrimack Rivers
Boston and Cambridge: James Munroe; New York:
George E Putnam; Philadelphia: Lindsay and Blackiston;
London: John Chapman, 1849

Thoreau and his brother John, his devoted companion, spent the first half of September, 1839 in a dory equipped with sails on the Concord and Merrimack Rivers. Ten years later, Thoreau published an account of this expedition, into which he fitted sections dealing with his reading and his philosophy taken from the journals that he had kept since he was at Harvard. He could not find a publisher for *A Week on the Concord and Merrimack Rivers*, so he paid for publication himself.

Despite the outlets suggested by the imprint, the book was a failure. Of the 1,000 copies printed, Munroe sold 219; another 75 were given away; and 706 were returned to Thoreau in 1853. "I have now a library of nearly 900 volumes," he wrote in his journal, "over 700 of which I wrote myself."

Louisa May Alcott

Flower Fables
Boston: George W. Briggs, 1855

Louisa May Alcott (1832-1888) was the second of the four daughters of Amos Bronson Alcott, who was called the most transcendental of the Transcendentalists, a lovable, gifted, and entirely impractical man. Something of the poverty and struggles of the Alcotts, but softened and idealized, can be found in her *Little Women*. The privations of her early life— which even included a stint of democratic service—were brightened by the interest taken in her by such friends of her father's as Theodore Parker, Thoreau, and Emerson. The little fairy stories that make up *Flower Fables* were written when its author was 16 to entertain Emerson's daughter Ellen, to whom Alcott later dedicated the book.

Flower Fables waited six years for publication. It was brought out in time for Christmas 1854, in an edition of 1,600 copies that was paid for by a friend, the appropriately named Miss Wealthy Stevens. Though the author received only $32—not the "money and fame" that she confided to her journal, she hoped for—she was delighted with what she called her "first born."

Mark Twain

*The Celebrated Jumping Frog of Calaveras County,
    and Other Sketches*
New York: C. H. Webb, 1867

The actual event upon which this story and the beginning of Clemens's fame are based occurred in 1849 and had been written up briefly in a California newspaper as early as 1853. Clemens remembered that he had told the anecdote, which he had jotted down in his notebook, to Atremus Ward, the professional humorist, and that Ward had urged him to write it out and send it to G. W. Carleton, the New York publisher. Carleton turned the manuscript over to a magazine called the *Saturday Press*, which published "Jim Smiley and His Jumping Frog" in its final issue, November 18, 1865. Charles Henry Webb, whom Clemens had known first in San Francisco, brought out the story with other newspaper sketches by the humorist. Clemens was already using the pseudonym Mark Twain, which he had derived from the Mississippi River term for two fathoms. He got a 10 percent royalty on his first book.

The Jumping Frog himself is celebrated among book collectors for the numerous positions he assumes on the front cover.

Edith Wharton

Verses
Newport, RI: C. E. Hammett, Jr., 1878
The Pierpont Morgan Library. Gift of Mr. Louis S. Auchincloss,
    1986
Novelist Edith Wharton's (1862-1937) first publication is a thin book of delicate poetry, looking for all the world like the product of a debutante daughter of Longfellow. It was printed in haste and in few copies

(only nine are now known to exist), as a gift for the 16-year-old Edith Newbold Jones of 14 West 23rd Street, New York City. The poems included in it had been written by young Miss Jones in her fourteenth and fifteenth years, and were full of the weather and flowers.

Miss Jones, like her first book, was a product of Old New York wealth, gentility, and repression. Born in the enclave of New York's fashionable and aristocratic society, she was baptized at Grace Church, spent summers in elegant Newport, Rhode Island, and came out into society at a Fifth Avenue mansion near 42nd Street. Although her first book was published when she was 16, Edith Wharton would have to wait 20 years until she could "come out" into literary society with *The Greater Inclination*, a book of short stories published in 1899 by Scribner's. In the ensuing years, she published some of the finest novels of the century, including *House of Mirth* (1905), *Ethan Frome* (1911), *The Custom of the Country* (1913), and *The Age of Innocence* (1920). Each of these novels was first published in a printing of more than 40,000 copies, testifying to the remarkable popularity of her work.

A woman of accomplishment in other areas as well, Edith Wharton introduced Henry James to the charms of the automobile and Paris on a three-week trip, or "motor flight," in 1907.

Part
3

Less Is
Often More:
Book and
Chapbook
Awards for
Poetry

What is a Chapbook?

—Ruth Greenstein

A chapbook is a short, booklet-style publication of a work that can be encapsulated in a short form. Chapbooks are well known in the worlds of poetry and small press publishing. Many chapbooks are only 24 to 28 pages, and are printed in runs of no more than 500 copies. While chapbooks are unlikely to make their way into the neighborhood superstore in the same way that full-sized books might, for many authors—Ezra Pound, A. R. Ammons, and Denis Johnson, to name a few—they offer an excellent opportunity for getting your work into print.

You may want to set aside a period of time, two years or so, for submitting your work to first-book contests and publishers, after which, if you have had no luck, you could pursue the chapbook option.

Bear in mind, however, that in some cases, publishing a chapbook will disqualify you from later submitting your work for certain first-book awards. For example, chapbooks that are more than 24 pages long or are printed in editions of more than 500 copies are considered to be first books by certain contests. So if you have published a chapbook and want to submit your work for first-book awards, it is critical that you review the guidelines for each award you are considering to find out if any such restrictions apply.

When considering the chapbook option, it's up to you to weigh the pros and cons. While you do not want to jeopardize your chances of entering first-book competitions, you may also feel that publishing a chapbook at this point in your career is your best opportunity for publication.

Book and Chapbook
Awards for Poetry

Name of Prize: Agnes Lynch Starrett Prize
Prize: $5,000
Open to: Poets without a published book
Contact: Agnes Lynch Starrett, Prize Administrator
University of Pittsburgh Press
3347 Forbes Avenue
Pittsburgh, PA 15261
Categories: Poetry
Description: Poets who have not yet published a full-length book of poetry may submit manuscripts (between 48-100 pages) to be considered for the $5,000 prize and publication by the University of Pittsburgh Press. Writers must send SASE for current guidelines, or visit the Web site at *www.pitt.edu/~press*.

Name of Prize: Aldrich Museum Emerging Poets Reading Competition
Prize: Varies
Open to: Open competition
Contact: Poetry Committee
Aldrich Museum
258 Main Street
Ridgefield, CT 06877
Categories: Poetry
Description: The Aldrich Museum Emerging Poets Reading Competition sponsored by the Aldrich Museum seeks four poets to read at an established contemporary arts museum series in the Fall. Only poets who have not yet published a full-length book may enter. Send SASE for complete guidelines and application forms.

Name of Prize: Alice James Books Beatrice Hawley Award
Prize: Varies
Open to: Open competition
Contact: Beatrice Hawley Award Director
    Alice James Books
    University of Maine at Farmington
    98 Main Street
    Farmington, ME 04938
Categories: Poetry
Description: The Beatrice Hawley Award offers publication for a first book of poetry by Alice James Books. Because Alice James Books is a non-profit press, it does not pay the author royalties; however, the author will receive 100 free copies of his/her book. Submit two copies of 60-70 pages of the manuscript, including a table of contents and acknowledgments. The poet's name, address, and phone number should appear on the title page. A business-sized SASE is required for return of manuscript and another SASE for notification. Please send SASE for complete guidelines.

Name of Prize: Anamnesis Press Poetry Chapbook Award
Prize: $1,000
Open to: Open competition
Contact: Keith Allen Daniels
    Anamnesis Press
    PO Box 51115
    Palo Alto, CA 94303
Categories: Poetry
Description: The Anamnesis Press offers the annual Anamnesis Poetry Chapbook Award. Winner will receive $1,000 and 20 copies of the chapbook published by Anamnesis Press. Submit 20 to 30 pages of poetry. Send SASE for complete guidelines and information, visit the Web site at *ourworld.compuserve.com/homepages/anamnesis/contest.htm*, or e-mail to anamnesis@compuserve.com

Name of Prize: Anhinga Prize for Poetry
Prize: $2,000
Open to: Open competition
Contact: Awards Director, Anhinga Prize for Poetry
    Anhinga Press
    PO Box 10595
    Tallahassee, FL 32302
Categories: Poetry
Description: This award is designed for poets trying to publish a first or second book. Offered annually for a book-length collection of poetry by an author who has not

published more than one book. Besides the $2,000 cash award, the winning manuscript is published by Anhinga Press. Send SASE for guidelines, visit the Web site at *www.anlainga.org*, e-mail to info@anhinga.org.

Name of Prize: APR/Honickman First Book Prize
Prize: $3,000
Open to: Poet's first book of poetry
Contact: Contest Manager
The American Poetry Review
1721 Walnut Street
Philadelphia, PA 19103
Categories: Poetry
Description: The APR/Honickman First Book Prize annually offers a first-place prize of $3,000 and publication for a book of poetry, with national bookstore distribution. Send SASE for complete guidelines and applications before submitting manuscript.

Name of Prize: AWP Award Series for Poetry
Prize: $2,000
Open to: Open Competition
Contact: Katherine Perry
AWP Award Series in Poetry
George Mason University
Tallwood House
Mail Stop 1E3
Fairfax, VA 22030
Categories: Poetry
Description: AWP, in conjunction with university and independent presses, publishes a number of book-length manuscripts from published or unpublished writers in poetry. AWP also circulates finalist manuscripts among publishers. Write for guidelines and deadline information, or visit the Web site at *awpwriter.org*.

Name of Prize: Bacchae Press' Annual Chapbook Contest
Prize: Publication
Open to: Open competition
Contact: Annual Chapbook Contest Editor
Bacchae Press
c/o Brown Financial Group
No. 10 Sixth Street
Astoria, OR 97103
Categories: Poetry

Description: The Bacchae Press' annual Chapbook Contest offers the winner publication plus 25 copies of professionally printed chapbook. Send 16-24 pages of poetry, biography, and acknowledgments. Send SASE for complete guidelines.

Name of Prize: Bakeless Literary Publication Prize in Poetry
Prize: Varies
Open to: Open competition
Contact: Inn Pounds
        Bread Loaf Writers' Conference
        Middlebury College
        Middlebury, VT 05753
Categories: Poetry
Description: Named for Middlebury College supporter Katherine Bakeless Nason, this competition is designed for emerging writers with an unpublished first book of poetry. The winner will have his/her work published by Middlebury College University Press of New England and be given a fellowship to attend the Breadloaf Writers' Conference. Send SASE for compete guidelines, or e-mail to Bakeless@Middlebury.edu.

Name of Prize: Barnard New Women Poets Prize for Women
Prize: $1,500
Open to: Women poets
Contact: Barnard New Women Poets Prize Coordinator
        Barnard College
        3009 Broadway
        New York, NY 10027-6598
Categories: Poetry, women
Description: An honorarium of $1,500 and publication by Beacon Press is offered to a woman poet for a book-length manuscript of poems. To be eligible, the poet must not have yet published a book, although published chapbooks or similar works of fewer than 500 copies are permitted. Send SASE for guidelines and deadline information.

Name of Prize: Bernard F. Coiners Prize for Poetry
Prize: $1,000
Open to: Open competition
Contact: Richard Howard, Poetry Editor
        Paris Review
        541 East 72nd Street, Box 5
        New York, NY 10021
Categories: Poetry

Description: The editors of the *Paris Review* seek the best unpublished poem (must be more than 200 lines). Prize is $1,000 plus publication in the *Paris Review*. Send SASE for guidelines.

———

Name of Prize: ByLine Chapbook Competition
Prize: $200
Open to: Open competition
Contact: ByLine Chapbook Competition
      ByLine Magazine
      PO Box 130596
      Edmond, OK 73013-0001
Categories: Poetry
Description: The ByLine Chapbook Competition offers 50 beautifully published chapbooks for author's personal use, plus $200 cash award. Submit 24 to 30 original poems, maximum 39 lines each including title and stanza breaks. Style and subject are open. We suggest (but do not require) that the poems be centered on a theme. Send SASE for complete guidelines, or visit the Web site at *www.bylinemag.com*.

———

Name of Prize: Cactus Alley Annual Poetry Contest
Prize: Varies
Open to: Open competition
Contact: Contest Director
      Cactus Alley Awards
      UTSA:ECPC, 6900 North Loop, 1604
      West San Antonio, TX 78249
Categories: Poetry
Description: The Cactus Alley Annual Poetry Contest offers cash prizes and publication in *Cactus Alley*, the literary journal of UT-San Antonio, to the winner of this contest. Send SASE for complete guidelines.

———

Name of Prize: Center for Book Arts Poetry Chapbook 2000 Competition
Prize: $1,000
Open to: Open competition
Contact: Poetry Chapbook Prize Director
      Center for Book Arts
      28 West 27th Street, Third Floor
      New York, NY 10001
Catergories: Poetry
Description: The winning poet receives a $500 prize and a $500 reading honorarium, as well as the publication of a letter-press printed, limited-edition poetry chapbook. The winning manuscript will be designed and printed by artists at the Center for

Book Arts in New York City. Send SASE for complete guidelines, visit the Web site at *www.centerforbookarts.org*, or e-mail to info@centefforbookarts.org.

Name of Prize: Center Press Masters Literary Awards
Prize: $1,000
Open to: Open competition
Contact: Gabriella Stone
　　　　Center Press
　　　　Masters Literary Awards
　　　　PO Box 16452
　　　　Encino, CA 91416-6452
Categories: Poetry
Description: The Masters Literary Awards, sponsored by Center Press, are offered annually and quarterly for both published work (published within the preceding two years) and unpublished fiction, poetry, and nonfiction. Send SASE for complete guidelines.

Name of Prize: Chelsea Award for Poetry
Prize: $1,000
Open to: Open competition
Contact: Richard Foerster, Editor
　　　　Chelsea Award Competition
　　　　PO Box 1040
　　　　York Beach, ME 03910
Categories: Poetry
Description: Chelsea awards a cash prize for previously unpublished poetry. They will choose the best group of four to six poems (500 lines or less). The winner will be published in *Chelsea*. Send SASE for guidelines, or e-mail ChelseaMag@aol.com.

Name of Prize: Cleveland State University Poetry Center Prize
Prize: $1,000
Open to: Open competition
Contact: Rita Grabowski, Coordinator
　　　　Poetry Center Prize
　　　　Cleveland State University, English Department
　　　　Rhodes Tower, Room 1815
　　　　Poetry Center, 1983 East 24th Street
　　　　Cleveland, OH 44115-2440
Categories: Poetry
Description: Offered annually, The Cleveland State University Poetry Center Prize awards $1,000 plus publication in the CSU Poetry Series for a volume of original

poetry. The manuscript should be between 50 and 100 pages, with the poet's name, address, and telephone number appearing on the cover sheet only. One or more runners-up to the finalist manuscript may also be published in the CSU Series for standard royalty (no cash prize). Open to many kinds of form, length, subject matter, style, and purpose. No light verse, devotional verse, or verse in which rhyme and meter seem to be of major importance. Send SASE for complete guidelines, visit the Web site at *www.ims.csuohio.edu/poetry/poetrycenter.html*, or e-mail requests to poetrycenter ~ opmail.csuohio.edu.

Name of Prize: Colorado Prize
Prize: $1,500
Open to: Open competition
Contact: Colorado Prize Director
      c/o Colorado Review
      Department of English
      Colorado State University
      Fort Collins, CO 80523
Categories: Poetry
Description: The Colorado Prize offers a $1,500 honorarium and publication by the Center for Literary Publishing/University Press of Colorado for a book-length collection of poems. Manuscript may consist of poems that have been published, but the manuscript as a whole must not have been previously published. Send an SASE for complete guidelines.

Name of Prize: Crab Orchard Review Award Series
Prize: $3,000
Open to: U.S. poets
Contact: Jon Tribble
      Crab Orchard Review
      Department of English
      Southern Illinois University
      Carbondale, IL 62901-4503
Categories: Poetry
Description: A first-place prize of $3,000 and a second prize of $1,000 are given for two unpublished collections of poems by U.S. poets. The winning manuscripts will be published by the Southern Illinois University Press, which cosponsors the award with the *Crab Orchard Review*. Each winner will also give a reading at Southern Illinois University at Carbondale. Submit a manuscript of 50 to 70 pages with entry fee. All entrants receive a one-year subscription to the *Crab Orchard Review*. Send an SASE for complete guidelines, or visit the Web site at *www.siu.edu/ ~ crborchd*.

Name of Prize: CWA Writing Competition for Poetry
Prize: $250
Open to: Open competition
Contact: CWA Writing Competition for Poetry Director
The Community Writers Association
CWA Writing Competition for Poetry
PO Box 12
Newport, RI 02840-0001
Categories: Poetry
Description: CWA Writing Competition for Poetry, sponsored by The Community of Writers Association, annually offers $250 plus full tuition to the annual Newport Writers Conference. Poems of any length and style are eligible. Send SASE for complete guidelines.

Name of Prize: Dead Metaphor Press Chapbook Contest
Prize: Varies
Open to: Open competition
Contact: Richard Wilmarth, Publisher
Dead Metaphor Press
PO Box 2076
Boulder, CO 80306-2076
Categories: Poetry
Description: Contestants must submit 24 pages of poetry, along with a biography, acknowledgments, and an SASE. There are no restrictions in regard to subject, matter, and style. Winner will receive 10 percent of the press run. Press run will be determined by the number of submissions received. Publication will take place one year after winning manuscript is selected. Winning manuscript will be assigned an ISBN number and listed in *Books in Print*. Book will be distributed by Small Press Distribution. Send SASE for guidelines and deadline information, or e-mail to DmetaphorP@aol.com.

Name of Prize: Devil's Millhopper Press Annual Poetry Chapbook Contest
Prize: $50
Open to: Open competition
Contact: Editors
Annual Chapbook Contest
TDM Press
USC-Aiken
171 University Parkway
Aiken, SC 29801-6309
Categories: Poetry
Description: The Devil's Miilhopper Press Annual Poetry Chapbook Contest offers $50, Publication, and 50 copies to the best chapbook of poetry received. Manuscripts

must include title page, contents page, list of acknowledgments, and no more than 24 pages of poetry. Previously published poems may be included (author must possess right to reprint) and simultaneous submissions are acceptable. Send SASE for complete guidelines.

———

Name of Prize: Discovery/The Nation Poetry Contest/Joan Leiman Jacobson Prizes
Prize: $300
Open to: See description
Contact: Contest Director
　　　　Discovery/The Nation Poetry Contest
　　　　The Unterberg Poetry Center of the 92nd St. Y
　　　　1395 Lexington Avenue
　　　　New York, NY 10128
Categories: Poetry
Description: Discovery/The Nation Poetry Contest/Joan Leiman Jacobson Poetry prizes offer four cash awards of $300, a reading at the Poetry Center of the 92nd Street Y in New York City, and publication in *The Nation* to poets who have not published a book-length manuscript of poetry (chapbooks included). All manuscripts must be original, written in English, not more than 500 lines or 10 typed pages long, and photocopied four times. Send for complete guidelines and application forms, or call 212/415-5759.

———

Name of Prize: Emporia State Bluestem Award
Prize: $1,000
Open to: U.S. and international poets
Contact: Bluestem Poetry Awards
　　　　Emporia State University
　　　　English Department
　　　　Box 4019
　　　　Emporia, KS 66801-5087
Categories: Poetry
Description: A $1,000 cash award plus publication for a book-length collection of poems, at least 48 typed pages long, is offered in the Bluestem Award sponsored by Emporia State University. Manuscripts may include poems previously published in periodicals or anthologies but not in a full-length single volume. Send SASE for complete guidelines, or call 316/341-5216 for further information.

———

Name of Prize: Felix Pollak Prize in Poetry
Prize: $1,000
Open to: Open competition
Contact: Ronald Wallace, Contest Director
University of Wisconsin Press
2537 Daniels Street
Madison, WI 53718-6772
Categories: Poetry
Description: The Felix Pollak Prize in Poetry offers a cash prize of $1,000 and publication by the University of Wisconsin Press for the best book-length manuscripts (50-80 pages) of original poetry. The poet's name, address, and telephone number should appear on the title page. The manuscript must be previously unpublished in book form. Poems published in journals, chapbooks, and anthologies may be included but must be acknowledged. No changes in the manuscript will be considered between submission and acceptance. Send SASE for complete guidelines and application forms.

Name of Prize: Field Poetry Prize
Prize: $1,000
Open to: Open competition
Contact: Contest Director
Oberlin College Press
10 N. Professor Street
Oberlin, OH 44074
Categories: Poetry
Description: The Field Poetry Prize offers the winning manuscript, a book-length collection of poems, publication in the Field Poetry Series. The winning author also receives an award of $1,000. The contest is open to all poets, those who have published in book form as well as those who have not. Previously unpublished manuscripts of poetry in English between 50 to 80 pages in length will be considered. Send SASE for guidelines, or visit the Web site at *www.oberlin.edu/ocpress/Main*.

Name of Prize: Firewheel Editions Annual Chapbook Competition
Prize: Publication
Open to: Open competition
Contact: Annual Chapbook Competition
Firewheel Editions
1133 Melissa Lane
Garland, TX 75040
Categories: Poetry, short fiction, nonfiction.
Description: Firewheel Editions Annual Chapbook Competition is open to manuscripts in all genres and will publish one winner in a chapbook of up to 24 pages.

All entries must include the author's name, an SASE, and either a phone number or an e-mail address. Winner will receive 25 copies of the chapbook and standard royalties. Send SASE for complete guidelines.

Name of Prize: Four Way Book Intro Series in Poetry
Prize: $2,000
Open to: U.S. poets
Contact: Contest Director
Four Way Books
PO Box 535
Village Station
New York, NY 10014
Categories: Poetry
Description: The Four Way Book Intro Series in Poetry competition offers a $2,000 prize consisting of a $1,500 honorarium and $500 for a promotional tour. The prize varies from year to year. The competition is open to U.S. poets who have not published a full-length collection. Send SASE for guidelines and entry form, or visit the Web site at *www.gypsyfish.com/fourway*.

Name of Prize: Frank Cat Press Poetry Chapbook Contest
Prize: Varies
Open to: Open contest
Contact: Contest Director
The Frank Cat Press
1008 Ouray Avenue
Grand Junction, CO 81501
Categories: Poetry
Description: The Frank Cat Press Poetry Chapbook Contest offers the winner of the competition cash, copies, and publication of the winner's chapbook. Submit 20-24 pages including title page, table of contents, and acknowledgments. Send SASE for complete guidelines.

Name of Prize: Frank O'Hara Award Chapbook Competition
Prize: $500
Open to: Gay, lesbian, or bisexual writers
Contact: Jim Elledge
Campus Box 4240
English Department
Illinois State University
Normal, IL 61790-4240
Categories: Poetry, Gay/Lesbian.

Description: The Frank O'Hara Award Chapbook Competition is open to emerging or established gay, lesbian, transgender, or bisexual writers. The winner receives $500, publication of his/her chapbook, and 25 free copies. Poetry submitted can be traditional, postmodern, or free verse; prose poems or cross-genre texts will be accepted. Submitted manuscript may have been previously published in journals or anthologies. The winner will be responsible for obtaining reprint permissions of his/her work. Submissions are limited to 20 pages of the writer's text plus four pages of front matter (title page, dedication, acknowledgments, if applicable, and epigraph). Send SASE for complete guideline

Name of Prize: Garden Street Press Poetry Prize
Prize: Publication
Open to: Open competition
Contact: Contest Director
Garden Street Press
PO Box 1231
Truro, MA 02666
Categories: Poetry.
Description: The Garden Street Press Poetry Prize offers the winner of a book-length (48 to 68 pages in length) poetry collection 100 copies and publication by Garden Street Press. Submit original manuscript with a brief biography and SASE for announcement of winners. Send SASE for complete guidelines.

Name of Prize: Genesis Award for Poetry
Prize: Varies
Open to: African-American authors
Contact: Genesis Award for Poetry Director
American Library Association
Social Responsibilities Round Table
50 East Huron Street
Chicago, IL 60611
Categories: Poetry.
Description: The Genesis Plaque is given to recognize the talents of African-American authors in the beginning of their careers with no more than three published books. It is presented by the Coretta Scott King Award Task Force. For more information and complete guidelines, please send an SASE.

Name of Prize: Gerald Cable Book Award
Prize: $1,000
Open to: Open competition
Contact: Rodger Moody, Editor
    Silverfish Review Press
    PO Box 3541
    Eugene, OR 97403
Categories: Poetry.
Description: A prize of $1,000 and publication by Silverfish Review Press is given annually for a poetry manuscript by a poet who has not published a full-length collection. Submit a manuscript of at least 48 pages. Send SASE for complete guidelines, or e-mail to sfrpress@aol.com

Name of Prize: Great Lakes College Association New Writers Awards—Poetry
Prize: Varies
Open to: Nomination from publishers
Contact: Mark Andrew Clark, Director
    Great Lakes Colleges Association
    New Writers Awards
    North American Building
    121 South Broad Street
    Philadelphia, PA 19107-4577
Categories: Poetry.
Description: The New Writers Awards are given annually for a first book of poetry. Winners read at several of the GLCA's 12 member colleges, each of which pays an honorarium plus travel expenses. Publishers are limited to one entry in each category (fiction and poetry) and must submit four copies of each book. Galleys are accepted. Send SASE for complete guidelines.

Name of Prize: Grolier Poetry Prize
Prize: $200
Open to: Open competition
Contact: Grolier Poetry Prize
    Grolier Poetry Book Shop, Inc.
    6 Plympton Street
    Cambridge, MA 02138
Categories: Poetry.
Description: The Grolier Poetry Prize is sponsored by The Grolier Poetry Book Shop and The Ellen LaForge Memorial Poetry Foundation to encourage and recognize developing writers. Poems must be unpublished work. The prize is open to all poets who have not published a vanity, small press, trade, or chapbook of poetry. The prize honorarium of $200 is given to two winning poets. The winning

poets will have four poems each published in the *Grolier Poetry Annual*. Seven runners-up will each have two poems published. Send SASE for complete guidelines.

Name of Prize: Guggenheim Fellowship for Poetry
Prize: $25,000
Open to: U.S. and Canadian permanent residents/citizens
Contact: Director
        John Simon Guggenheim Memorial Foundation
        90 Park Avenue
        New York, NY 10016
Categories: Poetry.
Description: Applicants should have demonstrated exceptional creative ability in the arts or ability for productive scholarship. More than 140 awards, averaging more than $25,000 each, are available in this competition. Creative works in any of the arts and scholarly research in any field are considered. These prestigious fellowships are for accomplished U.S. and Canadian citizens or permanent residents. Send SASE for guidelines.

Name of Prize: Heaven Bone Press International Chapbook Competition
Prize: $100
Open to: Open competition
Contact: International Chapbook Competition Director
        Heaven Bone Press
        Attn: Steve Hirsch
        PO Box 486
        Chester, NY 10918
Categories: Poetry.
Description: Applicants should submit a single original, unpublished poetry manuscript with a title, comprised of no more than 30 pages, including graphics and front and back matter, along with your check or money order made out to Heaven Bone Press in the amount of $10 as a reading fee. Include a cover letter indicating any previous publication credits for any published poems. All entrants will receive a copy of the winning chapbook with their returned materials. The winning chapbook will be advertised and promoted nationally and the poet will get at least one New York area reading engagement. The winner will also receive 30 copies of his/her chapbook as part of the prize. Send SASE for complete guidelines.

Name of Prize: Honickman First Book Award
Prize: $1,000
Open to: Poets who have not published a book
Contact: Award Director
        American Poetry Review
        1721 Walnut Street
        Philadelphia, PA 19103
Categories: Poetry.
Description: A prize of $1,000 and publication in *The American Poetry Review* is given annually for a book-length volume of poetry by a poet who has never published a book of poetry. The winning book will be distributed by Copper Canyon Press through Consortium. Submit a collection of at least 48 pages with entry fee. Send SASE for complete guidelines.

Name of Prize: Jack Kerouac Annual Literary Prize in Poetry
Prize: $500
Open to: Open competition
Contact: Contest Director
        The Jack Kerouac Literary Prize
        PO Box 8788
        Lowell, MA 01853-8788
Categories: Poetry.
Description: The Jack Kerouac Literary Prize is sponsored by Lowell Celebrates Kerouac! (a non-profit organization), and the Estate of Jack and Stella (Sampas) Kerouac. Experienced and emerging writers are invited to submit written works in competition for the Annual Jack Kerouac Literary Prize. This prize will consist of a $500 honorarium and the invitation to present the prize manuscript at a public reading during the annual Lowell Celebrates Kerouac! Festival. Send SASE for complete guidelines.

Name of Prize: Jane Kenyon Chapbook Award
Prize: $300
Open to: U.S. residents
Contact: Contest Director
        Alice James Books
        98 Main Street
        Farmington, ME 04938
Categories: Poetry.
Description: The Jane Kenyon Chapbook Award Series is a biannual contest sponsored by Alice James Books and the Jane Kenyon Memorial Fund. Winner receives publication and $300. Submit two copies of a typed 24-32 page manuscript. Manuscripts must have a table of contents and acknowledgments page. Please

send an SASE, or visit the Web site at *www.umf.maine.edu/-ajb* for complete guidelines.

Name of Prize: John Train Humor Prize for Poetry
Prize: $1,500
Open to: Open competition
Contact: John Train Humor Prize, Director
      Paris Review
      541 East 72nd Street
      New York, NY 10021
Categories: Poetry.
Description: The editors of the *Paris Review* look for the best unpublished work of humorous poetry (fewer than 10,000 words). SASE for complete guidelines.

Name of Prize: Kate Tufts Discovery Award
Prize: $5,000
Open to: Open competition
Contact: Kate Tufts Poetry Award Director
      The Claremont Graduate School
      740 North College Avenue
      Claremont, CA 91711
Categories: Poetry.
Description: The Kate Tufts Discovery Award was established in 1993 and is presented annually for a first or very early work by a poet. Submitted work must be either a book published during the previous year or a book-length (unpublished) manuscript completed within the year; however, the unpublished writer must provide evidence that he/she has previously been published in a legitimate book, magazine, or literary journal. The winner will be required to spend, within six months of the award presentation, at least one week in residence at The Claremont Graduate School's Humanities Center for letters or poetry readings in Claremont and greater Los Angeles. Send SASE for complete guidelines and required entry form.

Name of Prize: Kathryn A. Morton Prize in Poetry
Prize: $2,000
Open to: Open competition
Contact: Kathryn A. Morton Prize in Poetry Director
      Sarabande Books, Inc.
      PO Box 4999
      Louisville, KY 40204
Categories: Poetry.

Description: The Kathryn A. Morton Prize in Poetry is sponsored annually by Sarabande Books for an unpublished full-length volume of poetry (minimum of 48 pages). The winning author will receive $2,000 and publication by Sarabande Books. Send SASE for required entry form and guidelines, or visit the Web site *www.Sarabande.org*.

Name of Prize: Kenneth Patchen Competition for Poetry
Prize: $500
Open to: Open competition
Contact: Contest Director
　　　　Pig Iron Press
　　　　PO Box 237
　　　　Youngstown, OH 44501
Categories: Poetry.
Description: The Kenneth Patchen Competition for Poetry offers a $500 cash award plus publication and royalties for a book-length poetry collection. The winner will also receive 20 copies of the 800 paperback copies published. Send SASE for complete guidelines and deadline information.

Name of Prize: Kingsley Tufts Poetry Award
Prize: $50,000
Open to: Open competition
Contact: Kingsley Tufts Poetry Award Director
　　　　The Claremont Graduate School
　　　　740 North College Avenue
　　　　Claremont, CA 91711
Categories: Poetry.
Description: The Kingsley Tufts Award was established in 1992 by Kate Tufts to honor her late husband, poet and writer Kingsley Tufts. It is presented annually for a work by an emerging poet who is past the very beginning but has not yet reached the acknowledged pinnacle of his/her career. Submitted work must be either a book published during the previous year or a book-length (unpublished) manuscript completed within the year. Send SASE for complete guidelines and required entry form.

Name of Prize: La Jolla Poets Press National Poetry Book Series Contest
Prize: $500
Open to: U.S. citizens
Contact: Kathleen Iddings, Editor
　　　　La Jolla Poets Press
　　　　PO Box 8638
　　　　La Jolla, CA 92038

Categories: Poetry.
Description: The La Jolla Poets Press National Poetry Book Series Contest awards a cash prize of $500 plus publication. Send a poetry manuscript of 60 to 70 pages, a biography, and a cover letter. Send SASE for complete guidelines.

Name of Prize: Larry Levis Missouri Review Editors' Prize Award for Poetry
Prize: $1,500
Open to: Open competition
Contact: Speer Morgan
        Missouri Review
        University of Missouri
        1507 Hillcrest Hall, UMC
        Columbia, MO 65211
Categories: Poetry.
Description: The *Missouri Review* offers a $1,500 award for unpublished poetry plus publication. Submit a group of poems or a long poem, but no more than 10 pages in length. Send an SASE for complete guidelines.

Name of Prize: Ledge Annum Poetry Chapbook Contest
Prize: $500
Open to: Open competition
Contact: Tim Monaghan, Editor & Publisher
        The Ledge
        Ledge Annual Poetry Chapbook Contest
        PO Box 310010
        Jamaica, NY 11431
Categories: Poetry.
Description: Ledge Annual Poetry Chapbook Contest offers the winner $500 and 50 copies of a typeset, perfect-bound, and professionally printed chapbook. Submit 16-28 pages of poetry with title page, biography, and acknowledgments, if any. Simultaneous submissions are acceptable and poets may enter as many manuscripts as they wish. There are no restrictions on form or content; excellence is the only criterion. Send SASE for complete guidelines.

Name of Prize: Lena-Miles Wever Todd Poetry Series
Prize: $1,000
Open to: U.S. and Canadian poets
Contact: Kevin Prefer
        Pleiades Press
        Department of English
        Central Missouri State University
        Warrensburg, MI 64093

Categories: Poetry.
Description: The Lena-Miles Wever Todd Poetry Series is open to any poet from the U.S. or Canada. Submit a 48-100 page poetry manuscript; the winning manuscript will be published in trade paperback edition by Pleiades Press and distributed by LSU Press. The winning poet will receive $1,000. Send an SASE for complete guidelines.

Name of Prize: Marianne Moore Poetry Prize
Prize: $1,000
Open to: Open competition
Contact: Literary Prize Coordinator
Helicon Nine Editions
3607 Pennsylvania
Kansas City, MO 64111
Categories: Poetry.
Description: The cash award of $1,000 plus publication by participating presses is offered for an unpublished poetry manuscript (at least 50 pages). Poetry published in magazines, journals, or anthologies may be included. The contest is open to poets residing in the United States, its territories, and Canada only. Send an SASE for complete guidelines.

Name of Prize: Mary Roberts Rinehart Fund for Poetry
Prize: $2,500
Open to: Unpublished writers—nomination only
Contact: William Miller
English Department
Attn: Mary Roberts Rinehart Fund
George Mason University
MSN 3E4 4400 University Drive
Fairfax, VA 22030-4444
Categories: Poetry.
Description: Three grants each year are given to writers who need financial assistance, not otherwise available, to complete their work. Nominations can come from writing program faculty, sponsoring writer, agent, or editor. Grants are from $2,000 to $2,500 each. Send a nominating letter and 30 pages or less of the candidate's poetry. Please send SASE for complete guidelines.

Name of Prize: Maryland Poetry Review's Chapbook Contest
Prize: $125
Open to: Open competition
Contact: Contest Director
Maryland Poetry Review
Chapbook Contest
Drawer H
Baltimore, MD 21228
Categories: Poetry.
Description: The Maryland Poetry Review's Chapbook Contest offers the winner of this contest $125, publication, and 50 copies of the published chapbook. Send SASE for complete guidelines.

Name of Prize: May Swenson Poetry Award
Prize: $1,000
Open to: Open competition
Contact: Poetry Competition
May Swenson Poetry Award
Utah State University Press
7800 Old Main Hill
Logan, UT 84322-7800
Categories: Poetry.
Description: This competition honors May Swenson as one of America's most provocative, insouciant, and vital poets. The winning manuscript will receive a $1,000 award, publication, and royalties. Submitted collections must be original poetry in English, 50 to 100 pages; there are no restrictions on form or subject. Send SASE for complete guidelines and deadline information.

Name of Prize: Mid-List Press First Series Award for Poetry
Prize: $500
Open to: Open competition
Contact: Mid-List Press
4324 12th Avenue South
Minneapolis, MN 55407-3218
Categories: Poetry.
Description: Mid-List Press First Series Award for Poetry is open to any writer who has never published a book of poetry. (A chapbook is not considered a book of poetry.) Manuscripts must be 60 pages in length, numbered, and single-spaced. Send SASE for complete guidelines, or visit the Web site at *www.midlist.org*.

Name of Prize: Naomi Long Madgett Poetry Award
Prize: $500
Open to: African-American poets
Contact: Constance Withers
      Lotus Press, Inc
      PO Box 21607
      Detroit, MI 48221
Categories: Poetry
Description: The Naomi Long Madgett Poetry Award offers a cash prize of $500 plus publication by Lotus Press, Inc. for an outstanding volume of poems (between 60 and 100 pages) by an African-American poet. Send SASE for complete guidelines.

Name of Prize: National Looking Glass Poetry Chapbook Competition
Prize: $100
Open to: Open competition
Contact: Jennifer Bosveld, Editor
      National Looking Glass Poetry Chapbook Competition
      Pudding Magazine: The International Journal of Applied Poetry
      60 North Main Street
      Johnstown, OH 43031
Categories: Poetry.
Description: *Pudding Magazine: The International Journal of Applied Poetry* annually sponsors the National Looking Glass Poetry Chapbook Competitions "to publish a collection of poems that represents our magazine's editorial slant: popular culture, social justice, etc. Poems might have a theme or not. We recommend subject matter in the area of social justice, ecology and human impact, human relations, popular culture and artistic work transformed out of a therapeutic process." The manuscript should be between 10 and 40 pages in length, although 24-28 pages is preferred. The winner is awarded $100, has the work published, and receives 20 copies, plus wholesale rights. Send SASE for complete guidelines, or visit the Web site at *www.puddlnghouse.com*.

Name of Prize: National Poetry Series
Prize: $1,000
Open to: U.S. citizens
Contact: The Coordinator
      National Poetry Series
      PO Box G
      Hopewell, NJ 08525
Categories: Poetry.
Description: The National Poetry Series was established in 1978 to ensure the publication of five books of poetry each year. Winning manuscripts are selected by

means of an annual open competition. Each winning poet receives a $1000 cash award in addition to having his/her manuscript published by a participating trade, university, or small press publisher. All manuscripts must be previously unpublished, although some or all of the individual poems may have appeared in periodicals. Send SASE for complete guidelines and application forms.

Name of Prize: New Issues Press Poetry Prize
Prize: $1,000
Open to: Open competition
Contact: Herbert Scott, Editor
New Issues Press
Poetry Prize
Department of English
Western Michigan University
Kalamazoo, MI 49008-5092
Categories: Poetry.
Description: New Issues Press Poetry Prize offers $1,000 and publication for a first book of poems in their annual contest. The winning entry will be published as part of the New Issues Press Poetry Series, which annually publishes three to six first books of poetry with forewords written by nationally known writers or poets. Poets who have not previously published a collection of poems of more than 48 pages in an edition of 500 or more copies are eligible. Send SASE for complete guidelines, or visit the Web site at *www.wmich.edu/english/fac/nipps*.

Name of Prize: New Rivers Press Minnesota Voices Project in Poetry
Prize: $500
Open to: Minnesota residents
Contact: Minnesota Voices Project Director
New Rivers Press
420 North 5th Street, Suite 938
Minneapolis, MN 55401
Categories: Poetry.
Description: New Rivers Press will publish a collection of poetry (between 40-60 pages), and $500 will be awarded to two winners. Writers must be residents of Minnesota and must not have been published yet by a commercial publishing house. No author who has had more than two books published (not including chapbooks) by small independent presses are eligible. Send SASE for guidelines and application, or visit the Web site at *www.mtn.org/newrivpr*.

Name of Prize: New York University Press Prize in Poetry
Prize: $1,000
Open to: First-time authors
Contact: Prize Coordinator
New York University Press
Prizes for Poetry
838 Broadway
New York, NY 10003-4812
Categories: Poetry.
Description: Formerly the Mamdouha S. Bobst Literary Awards for Emerging Writers, the awards now recognize first-time authors or authors whose work remains unrecognized relative to the quality and ambition of their writing. Send SASE for complete guidelines, or visit the Web site at *www.nyupress.nyu.edu* for more information.

Name of Prize: NFSPS Poetry Manuscript Competition
Prize: $1,000
Open to: Open competition
Contact: Amy Zook, Chair
NFSPS Poetry Manuscript Contest
3520 State Route 56
Mechanicsburg, OH 43044
Categories: Poetry.
Description: The National Federation of State Poetry Societies (NFSPS) sponsors this competition. Winner of the best manuscript of poetry will receive $1000 plus publication. Manuscripts should be between 35 and 60 pages in length. A second-place prize of $500 will also be awarded. Send SASE for complete guidelines.

Name of Prize: Nicholas Roerich Poetry Prize
Prize: $1,000
Open to: Poets who have not published a book-length volume
Contact: Roerich Coordinator
Story Line Press
Three Oaks Farm
PO Box 1240
Ashland, OR 97520-0055
Categories: Poetry.
Description: Any writer who has not published a full-length collection of poetry (48 pages or more) in English is eligible for the Nicholas Roerich Poetry Prize, which offers a cash award of $1,000, publication by Story Line Press, and a reading upon publication at the Nicholas Roerich Museum in New York. Send SASE for complete guidelines.

Name of Prize: North American Native Authors First Book Award for Poetry
Prize: $500
Open to: Native Americans
Contact: North American Native Authors Awards Director
    The Greenfield Review Literary Center
    PO Box 308
    Greenfield Center
    New York, NY 12633
Categories: Poetry.
Description: This competition offers an award of publication plus $500 for a first collection of poetry. The contest is open to North American Native writers of American Indian, Inuit, Aleut and Metis ancestry who have not published a book. All of North America, including Mexico and Central America is included. Manuscript must be bilingual or entirely in English. Send SASE for guidelines and application forms.

———

Name of Prize: Ohio State University Press and The Journal Poetry Award
Prize: $1,500
Open to: Open competition
Contact: David Citino, Poetry Editor
    The Ohio State University Press
    1070 Carmack Road
    Columbus, OH 43210
Categories: Poetry.
Description: The Journal and The Ohio State University Press Poetry Award offers $1,500 plus publication for the best collection of original, unpublished poetry submitted. Send SASE for complete guidelines.

———

Name of Prize: Pablo Neruda Prize for Poetry
Prize: $2,000
Open to: Open competition
Contact: Nimrod Prize Competition
    Nimrod/Hardman Prize
    Nimrod International Journal
    University of Tulsa
    600 South College
    Tulsa, OK 74104
Categories: Poetry.
Description: The magazine offers $2,000 for first-place and $1,000 for the second-place. This prize is sponsored by the Tulsa Philanthropist Ruth Hardman, the Arts and Humanities Council of Tulsa, and the council's literary magazine *Nimrod: International Journal of Prose and Poetry*. The winning pieces will be

published and winners are flown to Tulsa for Nimrod's annual October awards dinner and writers' workshop. Send SASE for guidelines, or visit the Web site at *www.utulsa.edu/NIMROD*.

Name of Prize: Painted Bride Quarterly Annual Poetry Chapbook Contest
Prize: $250
Open to: Open competition
Contact: Annual Poetry Chapbook Contest
PBQ
c/o Painted Bride Art Center
230 Vine Street
Philadelphia, PA 19106
Categories: Poetry.
Description: The Painted Bride Quarterly Annual Chapbook Poetry contest offers a first-place prize of $250, a second-place prize of $150, a third-place prize of $50, and publication for all in *PBQ*. Send SASE for complete guidelines.

Name of Prize: Panhandler Poetry Chapbook Competition
Prize: $100
Open to: Open competition
Contact: Laurie O'Brien, Editor
The Panhandler Poetry Chapbook Competition
Panhandler Magazine
English Department
University of West Florida
Pensacola, FL 32514-5751
Categories: Poetry.
Description: The Panhandler Poetry Chapter Competition, annually sponsored by *The Panhandler Magazine,* offers a cash prize of $100, plus publication and 50 copies of the winning books to two winners for unpublished poetry chapbooks. The submitted material should be between 24 to 30 pages. Send SASE for complete guidelines and application forms.

Name of Prize: Pavement Saw Press Chapbook Contest
Prize: $500
Open to: Open competition
Contact: David Baratier, Editor
Pavement Saw Press
Chapbook Contest
PO Box 6291
Columbus, OH 43206

Categories: Poetry.
Description: Pavement Saw Press (a nonprofit press) offers an annual Poetry Chapbook Contest and awards $500 and 25 copies of the winning chapbook for the finest collection of poetry received. Submit up to 32 pages of poetry. Send SASE for complete guidelines and deadline information.

Name of Prize: Pearl Poetry Prize
Prize: $500
Open to: Open competition
Contact: Contest Director
      Pearl Poetry Prize
      3030 E. Second Street
      Long Beach, CA 90803
Categories: Poetry.
Description: The Pearl Poetry Prize is for a chapbook of original poetry. Winner receives $500, publication, and 50 copies of the manuscript. Manuscripts should include a title page with the author's name, address, phone number, and acknowledgments of previously published poems. Submit 20-24 pages of poetry and SASE for reply or return of manuscript. Send SASE for complete guidelines.

Name of Prize: Peregrine Smith Poetry Competition
Prize: $500
Open to: Open competition
Contact: Peregrine Smith Poetry Competition Director
      Gibbs Smith, Publisher
      PO Box 667
      Layton, UT 84041
Categories: Poetry
Description: A $500 cash award plus publication by Gibbs Smith, Publisher is offered for the best book-length manuscript of poems (48 to 64 pages long). Send SASE for complete guidelines and application forms.

Name of Prize: Poets Out Loud Prize
Prize: $1,000
Open to: Open competition
Contact: Elisabeth Frost
      Fordham University at Lincoln Center
      Room 924
      113 West 60 Street
      New York, NY 10023

Categories: Poetry.
Description: A prize of $1,000 and publication by Fordham University Press will be given for a book-length collection of poetry in the Poets Out Loud Prize. Submit an unpublished manuscript. Send SASE for complete guidelines, or visit the Web site at *www.fordham.edu/english/pol.*

Name of Prize: Quarterly Review of Literature Poetry Series
Prize: $1,000
Open to: Open competition
Contact: Theodore and Renee Weiss; QRL Awards
  Quarterly Review of Literature Poetry Series
  26 Haslet Avenue
  Princeton, NJ 08540
Categories: Poetry, drama.
Description: The Quarterly Review of Literature Poetry Series offers a $1,000 cash prize, plus publication and 100 copies of the book to five winners for a book of miscellaneous poems, a poetic play, a long poem, or poetry translation of 60 to 100 pages. Send SASE for complete guidelines and application forms.

Name of Prize: Red Hen Press Poetry Book Award
Prize: $1,000
Open to: Open competition
Contact: Poetry Book Award, Editor
  Red Hen Press
  PO Box 902582
  Palmdale, CA 93590-2582
Categories: Poetry.
Description: The Red Hen Press sponsors the Poetry Book Award. Winner will receive $1,000 and publication by Red Hen Press for an original, full-length poetry manuscript. Red Hen Press is an independent publisher of poetry, fiction, and literary nonfiction founded in 1993. Send SASE for complete guidelines and information.

Name of Prize: Richard A. Seffron Memorial Award
Prize: Publication
Open to: Poets 30 years of age or younger
Contact: Leonard Chino, Editor
  Pygmy Forest Press
  2434 C Street
  Eureka, CA 95501
Categories: Poetry.

Description: The Richard A. Seffron Memorial Award invites poets 30 years of age or younger to submit 8 to 12 pages of poetry for an initial response. No prize money is offered in this contest; however, the winner will receive 40 percent of a press run of at least 200 copies. Ten to 15 finalists will be advised to send their entire manuscript. Send SASE for complete guidelines.

Name of Prize: Richard Phillips Poetry Prize
Prize: $1,000
Open to: Open competition
Contact: Richard Phillips Poetry Prize Director
 The Phillips Publishing Company
 PO Box 121
 Watts, OK 74964
Categories: Poetry.
Description: The Richard Phillips Poetry Prize, sponsored by Phillips Publishing Company, is offered annually to give a modest financial reward to emerging poets who have not yet established themselves sufficiently to generate appropriate compensation for their work. Send SASE for complete guidelines.

Name of Prize: Richard Wilbur Award
Prize: $1,000
Open to: Open competition
Contact: Richard Wilbur Award
 Department of English
 University of Evansville
 1800 Lincoln Avenue
 Evansville, IN 47722
Categories: Poetry.
Description: The Richard Wilbur Award for an original, unpublished poetry collection is open to all American poets. Manuscripts of 50 to 100 typed pages may be submitted bound, unbound or clipped, accompanied by two title pages: one with the title of the collection, the author's name, address, and telephone number, and one only with the title. Manuscripts will not be returned. In addition to the prize money, the winning manuscript will be published by the University of Evansville press. Send SASE for complete guidelines and rules.

Name of Prize: Riverstone Chapbook Contest
Prize: $100
Open to: Open competition
Contact: Riverstone Chapbook Contest Director
 Riverstone, A Press for Poetry
 7571 East Visao Drive
 Scottsdale, AZ 85262

Categories: Poetry.
Description: The Riverstone Chapbook Contest winner receives publication, a cash award of $100, and 50 free copies of the chapbook. Applicants should submit one chapbook manuscript of 20-24 pages, including poems in their proposed arrangement, title page, contents, and acknowledgments. All styles welcome. Multiple entries and simultaneous submissions are accepted. The reading fee of $8 should be included with the submission. Every entrant will receive a copy of the winning chapbook. These are the complete guidelines. Sample of the chapbook is available for $5.

***

Name of Prize: Salmon Run Press National Poetry Book Award
Prize: $1,000
Open to: Open competition
Contact: Poetry Awards Coordinator
Salmon Run Press
National Poetry Book Award
PO Box 672130
Chugiak, AK 99567-2130
Categories: Poetry.
Description: Salmon Run Press Poetry Book Award offers a $1,000 cash prize and publication for a poetry book-length manuscript (from 48 to 96 pages) on any subject or style. The winning book will be nationally distributed by Salmon Run Press. Send SASE for complete guidelines.

***

Name of Prize: Samuel French Morse Poetry Prize
Prize: $1,000
Open to: U.S. citizens and residents
Contact: Professor Guy Rotella, Editor
Morse Poetry Prize
Northeastern University
English Department
406 Holmes Hall
Boston, MA 02115
Categories: Poetry.
Description: The Samuel French Morse Poetry Prize is open to authors of a book-length manuscript of a first or second book. There is a cash award of $1,000 and the winning manuscript will be published by the Northeastern University Press. Send SASE for complete guidelines and application forms, or visit the Web site at *www.casdn.neu.edu/~english/morse.htm.*

***

Name of Prize: Silverfish Review Gerald Cable Poetry Book Contest
Prize: $1,000
Open to: Open competition
Contact: Gerald Cable Poetry Book Contest Director
Silverfish Review Press
PO Box 3541
Eugene, OR 97403
Categories: Poetry.
Description: The Silverfish Review Gerald Cable Poetry Book Contest (formally known as the Silverfish Review Poetry Chapbook Contest) will give a cash award of $1,000 and a press run of 1,000 copies. The work should be a book-length manuscript (64-80 pages long). Send SASE for complete guidelines, or e-mail to SFRpress@aol.com.

―――――

Name of Prize: Slapering Hol Press Chapbook Competition
Prize: $500
Open to: Unpublished poets
Contact: Stephanie Strickland
The Hudson Valley Writers' Center
300 Riverside Drive
Sleepy Hollow, NY 10591
Categories: Poetry.
Description: The Slapering Hol Press Chapbook Competition is open to poets who have not yet published a book or chapbook. Please send 24 pages of poems with acknowledgments, SASE, and reading fee. Manuscripts should be anonymous with second title page containing name, address, and telephone number. Send SASE for complete guidelines.

―――――

Name of Prize: Slipstream Annual Poetry Chapbook Contest
Prize: $1,000
Open to: Open competition
Contact: Dan Sicoli, Co-editor
Slipstream Annual Poetry Chapbook Contest
Department D
Box 2071
Niagara Falls, NY 14301
Categories: Poetry.
Description: Slipstream Annual Poetry Chapbook Contest offers $1,000, plus publication by Slipstream Publications, and 50 copies of the chapbook, to the winning manuscript. Send up to 40 pages of poetry. Published poems with acknowledgments are also accepted. Send SASE for complete guidelines and application forms, or visit the Web site at *www.slipstreampress.org.*

―――――

Name of Prize: Soundpost Press Chapbook Contest
Prize: $500
Open to: Open competition
Contact: Chapbook Contest Director
Soundpost Press Chapbook Contest
Soundpost Press
632 N. 23rd Street
La Crosse, WI 54601
Categories: Poetry.
Description: The Annual Soundpost Press Chapbook Contest awards the winner $500 against royalties. Manuscript should be 18 pages or less. Soundpost Press will publish a handsomely designed chapbook with a hand-printed cover. Send SASE for complete guidelines and information.

Name of Prize: Southwest Writers Workshop Writing Contest
Prize: $1,000
Open to: Open competition
Contact: Contest Chair
SWW Contest
8200 Mountain Road NE, Suite 106
Albuquerque, NM 87110-7835
Categories: Poetry.
Description: The Southwest Writers Workshop Annual Contest includes novels, short stories, poetry, nonfiction (books and articles), screenplays, and children's literature. Every entry is critiqued by a professional. Send SASE for entry form and complete guidelines, or visit the Web site at *www.southwestwriters.org*, or e-mail to SWriters@aol.com.

Name of Prize: Sow's Ear Chapbook Competition
Prize: $1000
Open to: Open Competition
Contact: Managing Editor
The Sow's Ear Poetry Review
Chapbook Contest
19535 Pleasant View Drive
Abingdon, VA 24211-6827
Categories: Poetry.
Description: The Sow's Ear Chapbook Competition offers a cash award of $1,000 plus 25 copies for first place, $200 for second place, and $100 for third place for the best chapbook of poetry (22-26 pages in length). The winning manuscript will be published by Sow's Ear Press and distributed to subscribers. Send SASE for complete guidelines, or e-mail to richman@preferred.com.

Name of Prize: Stan and Tom Wick Poetry Prize
Prize: $2,000
Open to: Open competition
Contact: Maggie Anderson, Director
Stan and Tom Wick Poetry Prize
Department of English
PO Box 5190
Kent, OH 44242-0001
Categories: Poetry.
Description: The Stan and Tom Wick Poetry Prize is given to a poet who has not yet published a full-length collection of poems. The winner receives $2,000 plus publication by the Kent State University Press. Manuscripts should be between 48 and 68 pages long. Include a separate cover sheet with your name, address, telephone number, and title of the manuscript. Send SASE for complete information.

Name of Prize: Taproot Writer's Annual Writing Contest in Poetry
Prize: Publication
Open to: Open competition
Contact: Contest Director
Taproot Writer's Annual Writing Contest
PO Box 204
Ambridge, PA 15003
Categories: Poetry
Description: Taproot Writer's Workshop Inc. is accepting entries for its Annual Poetry Writing Contest. Submissions will be judged by a panel from the English Department of a university in Pennsylvania. First-place winner will receive cash prizes, publication, and a biography in *Taproot Literary Review*. Send SASE for complete guidelines, or e-mail to taproot10@aol.com.

Name of Prize: Tennessee Annual Chapbook Prize
Prize: Varies
Open to: Open Competition
Contact: Gaylord Brewer, Editor
Poems & Plays
English Department
Middle Tennessee State University
Murfreesboro, TN 37132
Categories: Poetry.
Description: The Tennessee Annual Chapbook Prize will publish the winning entry as an interior chapbook in *Poems & Plays*. Author will receive 50 copies. Manuscripts of poems or short plays are eligible. Send SASE for complete guidelines.

Name of Prize: Tennessee Arts Commission Poetry Writing Fellowships
Prize: $2,500
Open to: Tennessee residents
Contact: Alice Swanson
Tennessee Arts Commission
401 Charlotte Avenue
Nashville, TN 37243-0780
Categories: Poetry.
Description: The Tennessee Arts Commission offers Poetry Writing Fellowships to Tennessee residents in the amount of $2,500. Special emphasis is given to emerging writers and the fellowship alternates literary categories each year. Send request for complete guidelines and application forms.

Name of Prize: Tom McAfee Discovery Feature in Poetry
Prize: $250
Open to: Unpublished poets
Contact: Speer Morgan
Missouri Review
University of Missouri
1507 Hillcrest Hall, UMC
Columbia, MO 65211
Categories: Poetry.
Description: The Tom McAfee Discovery Feature in Poetry is offered once or twice a year, at the discretion of the editors, to an outstanding new poet who has not yet published a book. Awards are made from regular submissions. Send SASE for complete information.

Name of Prize: Transcontinental Poetry Award
Prize: $1,000
Open to: Unpublished volume authors
Contact: Contest Director
Pavement Saw Press
Transcontinental Poetry Award
PO Box 6291
Columbus, OH 43206
Categories: Poetry.
Description: Each year Pavement Saw Press will seek to publish at least one book of poetry and/or prose poems from manuscripts received during this competition. Selection is made anonymously through a competition that is open to anyone who has not previously published a volume of poetry or prose. The author receives $1,000 and a percentage of the press run. All poems must be original, all prose

must be original, fiction or translations are not allowed. Send SASE for complete guidelines and information.

Name of Prize: T.S. Eliot Prize for Poetry
Prize: $2,000
Open to: Open competition
Contact: Contest Director
Truman State University Press
100 East Normal Street
Kirksville, MO 63501-4221
Categories: Poetry.
Description: Truman State University sponsors the T.S. Eliot Prize. This annual international poetry competition for a book-length collection of poetry offers $2,000 and publication of the winning collection. Poets who have yet to publish a book are welcome, as are poets who have published several books. Send a typed or printed manuscript (or clear photocopy) of 60-100 pages. Poems must be original work, not translations, and in English. Send SASE for complete guidelines, visit the Web site at *www2.truman.edu/tsup*, or e-mail to tsup@tmman.edu.

Name of Prize: University of Georgia Press Contemporary Poetry Series
Prize: Publication
Open to: Open competition
Contact: Contemporary Poetry Series Director
University of Georgia Press
330 Research Drive, Suite B-100
Athens, GA 30602-4901
Categories: Poetry.
Description: The University of Georgia Press Contemporary Poetry Series invites poets who have never had a book of poems published to submit their book-length poetry manuscripts. The winning poet is awarded publication by the University of Georgia Press plus a standard royalty contract. Send SASE for complete guidelines. Guidelines are also available on the Web site *www.uga.edu/ugapress*.

Name of Prize: Utah's Original Writing Competition in Poetry
Prize: $300
Open to: Utah residents
Contact: G. Barnes, Literary Coordinator
Utah Arts Council
617 East South Temple Street
Salt Lake City, UT 84102-1177

Categories: Poetry.
Description: The Utah's Original Writing Competition in Poetry offers a first-place cash award of $300 and a second-place cash award of $200 for the best unpublished collection of poetry written by a Utah resident. No part of the collection may have been published in book form or accepted for book publication at time of entry. Send SASE for complete guidelines and application forms.

Name of Prize: Van Lier Fellowship and Residency
Prize: $7,000
Open to: New York City residents ages 18-30
Contact: Leslie Shipmen
        The Bronx Writers' Center
        2321 Glebe Avenue
        Bronx, NY 10461
Categories: Poetry.
Description: Writers of fiction, poetry, plays, and screenplays who are residents of New York City and between the ages of 18 and 30 are invited to apply for the Van Lier Fellowship and Residency Program. Created to provide career-launching opportunities for young writers, the Van Lier Fellowship and Residency Program will award three recipients with a nine-month residency. Each fellowship carries a $7,000 stipend. Fellows will be required to design and implement a public service project during their residency at The Bronx Writers' Center. For more information, including submission guidelines and deadlines, or to request an application, please contact them by mail, or phone 718/409-1265, or fax 718/409-1351. Applicants can also e-mail to wtrsctr@artswire.org, or visit the Web site at *www.bronxarts.org.*

Name of Prize: Vassar Miller Prize in Poetry
Prize: $1,000
Open to: Open competition
Contact: Dr. Scott Cairns, Series Editor
        c/o English Department
        Tare Hall 107
        University of Missouri
        Columbia, MO 65211
Categories: Poetry.
Description: The Vassar Miller Prize in Poetry is offered annually for an unpublished poetry manuscript (50 to 80 pages). The winner will receive $1,000 plus publication by UNT Press. Send an SASE for complete guidelines.

Name of Prize: Walden Residency Program for Poets
Prize: Varies
Open to: Oregon residents
Contact: Brooke Friendly
　　　　　Extended Campus Programs
　　　　　Oregon
　　　　　1250 Sisldyou Blvd.
　　　　　Ashland, OR 97250
Categories: Poetry.
Description: The Walden Residency Program offers a quiet workspace (for six to eight weeks) to Oregon poets who are working on a project. This fellowship offers a cabin in Southern Oregon and utilities. Send SASE for complete guidelines and application forms, or e-mail to friendly@sou.edu.

Name of Prize: Wallace E. Sterner Fellowships for Poetry
Prize: Varies
Open to: Open competition
Contact: Gay Pierce
　　　　　Stanford University
　　　　　Creative Writing Center
　　　　　Department of English
　　　　　Stanford, CA 94305-2087
Categories: Poetry
Description: Ten fellowships are given in writing annually, five in fiction writing and five in poetry to writers, published or not, who are considered promising. Residence at the University and instruction and criticism by the staff of the Writing Program are provided. A stipend of $15,000 is provided annually, as well as tuition. It is a two-year fellowship. Send SASE for details.

Name of Prize: The Walt Whitman Award
Prize: $5,000
Open to: United States citizens who have never published a book
Contact: Academy of American Poets
　　　　　584 Broadway, Suite 1208
　　　　　New York, NY 10012-3250
Categories: Poetry.
Description: The Walt Whitman Award brings first-book publication, a cash prize of $5,000, and a one-month residency at the Vermont Studio Center to an American who has never before published a book of poetry. The winning manuscript, chosen by an eminent poet, is published by Louisiana State University Press. The Academy purchases more than 8,000 copies of the book for distribution to its members. The award was established in 1975 to encourage the work of emerging poets and to

enable the publication of a poet's first book. The award is now given in memory of Eric Mathieu King, a businessman who believed that poetry has an indispensable role to play in society as a direct, intimate means of communication. Please send SASE for complete guidelines, or visit *www.poets.org.*

Name of Prize: West Virginia Literature Fellowships in Poetry
Prize: $3,500
Open to: West Virginia residents
Contact: Tod Ralstin, Fellowship Awards
    West Virginia Commission on the Arts
    Cultural Center
    1900 Kanawha Boulevard East
    Charleston, WV 25305-0300
Categories: Poetry.
Description: The West Virginia Literature awards cycle every three years. Send SASE for guidelines and deadline information.

Name of Prize: Whiskey Island Magazine Annual Poetry Contest
Prize: $1,200
Open to: Open competition
Contact: Contest Director
    Whiskey Island Contest-AP
    Department of English
    Cleveland State University
    Cleveland, OH 44115
Categories: Poetry.
Description: The Whiskey Island Magazine Annual Poetry Contest offers up to $1,200 in cash prizes. Send SASE for complete guidelines, visit the Web site at *www.csuohio.edu/whiskyisland,* or e-mail whiskeyisland@popmail.csuohlo.edu.

Name of Prize: White Pine Press Poetry Prize
Prize: $1,000
Open to: U.S. citizens
Contact: Contest Director
    White Pine Press
    Poetry Prize
    PO Box 236
    Buffalo, NY 14201
Categories: Poetry.
Description: The White Pine Press Poetry Prize, annually sponsored by White Pine Press, offers a cash award of $1,000 plus publication for a book-length collection of

poetry (up to 100 pages in length), written by a U.S. poet. Applicants should submit an original typed manuscript. Poems may have been previously published in periodicals or in limited-edition chapbooks. Send SASE for complete guidelines, visit the Web site at *whitepine.org*, or e-mail wpine@whitepine.org.

Name of Prize: Wick Poetry Program
Prize: Publication
Open to: Ohio residents
Contact: Maggie Anderson
    Department of English
    Kent State University
    PO Box 5190
    Kent, OH 44242
Categories: Poetry.
Description: The Kent State University Press and The Wick Poetry Program announce the Chapbook Competitions for Ohio poets. Two to four chapbooks will be selected for publication during the spring in editions of 750 copies. Manuscripts of 15 to 25 pages of poetry should be submitted. Send SASE for complete guidelines, or visit the Web site at *www.kent.edu:80/english/wick/WickPoetry.htm*.

Name of Prize: William and Kingman Page Poetry Book Award
Prize: $1,000
Open to: Open competition
Contact: Roy Zarucchi, Editor
    Potato Eyes Foundation
    Book Award
    PO Box 76
    Troy, ME 04987
Categories: Poetry.
Description: The William and Kingman Page Poetry Book Award, sponsored by The Potato Eyes Foundation (publishers of *Potato Eyes,* a biannual journal established in 1988), offers a cash prize of $1,000 plus 25 copies of the winning book, in lieu of royalties. Send SASE for complete guidelines, or e-mail to potatoeyes@uninets.net.

Name of Prize: Wisconsin Artist Fellowship Awards
Prize: $8,000
Open to: Wisconsin residents (not full-time students)
Contact: Fellowship Coordinator
    Wisconsin Arts Board
    First Floor
    101 East Wilson Street
    Madison, WI 53702

Categories: Poetry.
Description: Artist Fellowship Awards are intended to reward outstanding, professionally active Wisconsin artists by supporting their continued development, enabling them to create new work, complete work in progress, or pursue activities which contribute to their artistic growth. Currently, 10 to 12 artists are selected each year to receive an $8,000 Fellowship. Send SASE for guidelines, or visit the Web site at *www.arts.state.wi.us*.

Name of Prize: Women-In-Literature, Inc. Poetry Manuscript Contest
Prize: $600
Open to: Women writers
Contact: Contest Director
　　　　Women-in-Literature, Inc.
　　　　PO Box 60550
　　　　Reno, NV 89506-0550
Categories: Poetry.
Description: Women-in-Literature, Inc. Poetry Manuscript Contest will give the winner $600 and publication of an original, unpublished manuscript. Poets who have published one previous book or only chapbooks are also eligible. Send SASE for complete guidelines.

Name of Prize: Writer's Digest Annual Writing Competition
Prize: $1,000
Open to: Open competition
Contact: Terri Boes
　　　　Writer's Digest
　　　　1507 Dma Avenue
　　　　Cincinnati, OH 45207
Categories: Poetry.
Description: The Writer's Digest Annual Writing Competition offers more than $25,000 in prizes. The grand-prize winner, judged as best overall from the ten categories, will receive $1000 cash and an all-expense paid trip to New York City to meet with editors and agents. Send SASE for guidelines, or visit their Web site at *www.writersdigest.com*.

Name of Prize: Writers at Work in Poetry
Prize: $1,500
Open to: Writers who have not published book-length work
Contact: Poetry Fellowship Competition Director
　　　　Writers at Work
　　　　PO Box 1146
　　　　Centerville, UT 84104-5146

Categories: Poetry.
Description: First-place winner in this genre receives $1,500 and publication in *Quarterly West*, as well as a featured reading and tuition (valued at $200) for the afternoon session at the annual Writers at Work summer conference in July, which features morning workshops in a variety of genres, afternoon panels/lectures, and access to writers, publishers, editors, and agents. Second-place winners receive $500, and afternoon tuition. Send SASE for guidelines, or visit the Web site at *www.iki-env.com/watw.html*.

Name of Prize: WWPH 2000 Poetry Competition
Prize: Publication
Open to: Poets residing in the Washington, D.C. area
Contact: Poetry Competition Director
Washington Writers' Publishing House (WWPH)
WWPH 2000 Poetry Competition
4100 Blackthorn Street
Chevy Chase, MD 20815
Categories: Poetry.
Description: The Washington Writers' Publishing House Poetry Competition annually offers poets residing within 60 miles of Washington, D.C. (including Baltimore) a prize of publication, 50 copies of the winning manuscript, and membership in Washington Writers' Publishing House (a nonprofit cooperative press, which has published 48 volumes of poetry since its founding in 1975). Applicants should submit three copies of a book-length poetry manuscript (between 50 and 60 pages). Send SASE for complete guidelines.

Name of Prize: Wyoming Arts Literary Fellowships in Poetry
Prize: $2,500
Open to: Wyoming residents (non-student)
Contact: Guy Lebeda, Literature Coordinator
Wyoming Council on the Arts
2320 Capitol Avenue
Cheyenne, WY 82002
Categories: Poetry.
Description: Up to four fellowships are offered each year to honor the most outstanding published or unpublished works by Wyoming resident writers over 18 years of age. Send SASE for guidelines.

Name of Prize: Yachats Literary Festival Chapbook Competition
Prize: $600
Open to: Unpublished poets over the age of 50
Contact: Frena Gray-Davidson, Director
        Chapbook Competition
        Yachats Literary Festival
        124 N.E. California Street
        Yachats, OR 97498
Categories: Poetry.
Description: The Yachats Literary Festival Chapbook Competition, sponsored by the Yachats Literary Festival, offers a cash award of $600 plus publication for an unpublished poet over the age of 50. Submit a collection of unpublished poems that is "sufficient to make a chapbook" (approximately 32 pages). Send SASE for complete guidelines.

Name of Prize: Yale Series of Younger Poets
Prize: Varies
Open to: American writers 40 years old and younger
Contact: Richard Miller, Editor
        Yale University Press
        PO Box 209040
        New Haven, CT 06520-9040
Categories: Poetry.
Description: The Yale Series of Younger Poets offers American poets under the age of 40, who have not yet published a manuscript of poetry, publication of their manuscript (48-64 pages) by Yale University Press and the standard royalties. Send SASE for complete guidelines and application forms, or e-mail to richard.miller@yale.edu.

Awards for Poetry by Size of Prize

Award Name	Prize
Kingsley Tufts Poetry Award	$50,000
Guggenheim Fellowship for Poetry	$25,000
Wisconsin Artist Fellowship Awards	$8,000
Van Lier Fellowship and Residency	$7,000
Agnes Lynch Starrett Prize	$5,000
Kate Tufts Discovery Award	$5,000
The Walt Whitman Award	$5,000
West Virginia Literature Fellowships in Poetry	$3,500

APR/Honickman First Book Prize	$3,000
Crab Orchard Review Award Series	$3,000
Mary Roberts Rinehart Fund for Poetry	$2,500
Tennessee Arts Commission Poetry Writing Fellowships	$2,500
Wyoming Arts Literary Fellowships in Poetry	$2,500
Anhinga Prize for Poetry	$2,000
AWP Award Series for Poetry	$2,000
Four Way Book Intro Series in Poetry	$2,000
Kathryn A. Morton Prize in Poetry	$2,000
Pablo Neruda Prize for Poetry	$2,000
Stan and Tom Wick Poetry Prize	$2,000
T.S. Eliot Prize for Poetry	$2,000
Barnard New Women Poets Prize for Women	$1,500
Colorado Prize	$1,500
John Train Humor Prize for Poetry	$1,500
Larry Levis Missouri Review Editors' Prize Award for Poetry	$1,500
Ohio State University Press and The Journal Poetry Award	$1,500
Writers at Work in Poetry	$1,500
Whiskey Island Magazine Annual Poetry Contest	$1,200
Anamnesis Press Poetry Chapbook Award	$1,000
Bernard F. Coiners Prize for Poetry	$1,000
Center for Book Arts Poetry Chapbook 2000 Competition	$1,000
Center Press Masters Literary Awards	$1,000
Chelsea Award for Poetry	$1,000
Cleveland State University Poetry Center Prize	$1,000
Emporia State Bluestem Award	$1,000
Felix Pollak Prize in Poetry	$1,000
Field Poetry Prize	$1,000
Gerald Cable Book Award	$1,000
Honickman First Book Award	$1,000
Lena-Miles Wever Todd Poetry Series	$1,000
Marianne Moore Poetry Prize	$1,000
May Swenson Poetry Award	$1,000
National Poetry Series	$1,000
New Issues Press Poetry Prize	$1,000
New York University Press Prize in Poetry	$1,000
NFSPS Poetry Manuscript Competition	$1,000
Nicholas Roerich Poetry Prize	$1,000
Poets Out Loud Prize	$1,000
Quarterly Review of Literature Poetry Series	$1,000
Red Hen Press Poetry Book Award	$1,000
Richard Phillips Poetry Prize	$1,000
Richard Wilbur Award	$1,000

Salmon Run Press National Poetry Book Award	$1,000
Samuel French Morse Poetry Prize	$1,000
Silverfish Review Gerald Cable Poetry Book Contest	$1,000
Slipstream Annual Poetry Chapbook Contest	$1,000
Southwest Writers Workshop Writing Contest	$1,000
Sow's Ear Chapbook Competition	$1,000
Transcontinental Poetry Award	$1,000
Vassar Miller Prize in Poetry	$1,000
White Pine Press Poetry Prize	$1,000
William and Kingman Page Poetry Book Award	$1,000
Writer's Digest Annual Writing Competition	$1,000
Women-In-Literature, Inc. Poetry Manuscript Contest	$600
Yachats Literary Festival Chapbook Competition	$600
Frank O'Hara Award Chapbook Competition	$500
Jack Kerouac Annual Literary Prize in Poetry	$500
Kenneth Patchen Competition for Poetry	$500
La Jolla Poets Press National Poetry Book Series Contest	$500
Ledge Annum Poetry Chapbook Contest	$500
Mid-List Press First Series Award for Poetry	$500
Naomi Long Madgett Poetry Award	$500
New Rivers Press Minnesota Voices Project in Poetry	$500
North American Native Authors First Book Award for Poetry	$500
Pavement Saw Press Chapbook Contest	$500
Pearl Poetry Prize	$500
Peregrine Smith Poetry Competition	$500
Slapering Hol Press Chapbook Competition	$500
Soundpost Press Chapbook Contest	$500
Discovery/The Nation Poetry Contest/Joan Leiman Jacobson Prizes	$300
Jane Kenyon Chapbook Award	$300
Utah's Original Writing Competition in Poetry	$300
CWA Writing Competition for Poetry	$250
Painted Bride Quarterly Annual Poetry Chapbook Contest	$250
Tom McAfee Discovery Feature in Poetry	$250
ByLine Chapbook Competition	$200
Grolier Poetry Prize	$200
Maryland Poetry Review's Chapbook Contest	$125
Heaven Bone Press International Chapbook Competition	$100
National Looking Glass Poetry Chapbook Competition	$100
Panhandler Poetry Chapbook Competition	$100
Riverstone Chapbook Contest	$100
Devil's Millhopper Press Annual Poetry Chapbook Contest	$50
Bacchae Press' Annual Chapbook Contest	Publication
Firewheel Editions Annual Chapbook Competition	Publication

Garden Street Press Poetry Prize	Publication
Richard A. Seffron Memorial Award	Publication
Taproot Writer's Annual Writing Contest in Poetry	Publication
University of Georgia Press Contemporary Poetry Series	Publication
Wick Poetry Program	Publication
WWPH 2000 Poetry Competition	Publication
Aldrich Museum Emerging Poets Reading Competition	Varies
Alice James Books Beatrice Hawley Award	Varies
Bakeless Literary Publication Prize in Poetry	Varies
Cactus Alley Annual Poetry Contest	Varies
Dead Metaphor Press Chapbook Contest	Varies
Frank Cat Press Poetry Chapbook Contest	Varies
Genesis Award for Poetry	Varies
Great Lakes College Association New Writers Awards—Poetry	Varies
Tennessee Annual Chapbook Prize	Varies
Walden Residency Program for Poets	Varies
Wallace E. Sterner Fellowships for Poetry	Varies
Yale Series of Younger Poets	Varies

Part
4

More
Light:
Publishers

Introduction

—*Ruth Greenstein*

There are thousands of publishers in the United States, from huge corporate media giants to university presses to small family-style operations. Some are only looking to publish blockbuster books with the widest possible appeal, while others specialize in books aimed at very narrow markets. One of the primary jobs of a literary agent is to match the right publisher and editor with the right book project. If you are working without an agent, you will need to become familiar with these various kinds of publishers to determine where your work is most likely to be well received. Here are some questions to ask yourself in your search to locate publishers who will consider your work.

Have I familiarized myself with the field?

The library, the bookstore, and your own bookshelves are the best places to begin. Look at books by writers you admire and whose work seems similar to your own. Who published their first books? Then read the listings here as well as those found in other reference guides (see the Resources section of this book) to find out more about the publishers that interest you. Request catalogs from publishers of interest to look more closely at what they do.

What kind of publisher is the best for me?

That depends on the type of book you have written and the kind of readers you hope to attract. Is it a specialized book that will only appeal to gardeners, mutual fund investors, gay men, parents of children with learning disabilities? If so, a specialized publisher may be your best bet. If you've written a novel with broad appeal, a large or small general publisher is probably the right place to begin.

What is an unsolicited manuscript?

Many publishers use the term "unsolicited" to refer to manuscripts that are sent to them unagented. Such manuscripts are generally given the lowest priority and are read by junior staff if and when time allows. More generally, an unsolicited manuscript can be any project a publisher receives—agented or not—beforehand, without having expressed interest in it.

What is a simultaneous or multiple submission?

Most agents and writers send out manuscripts to several publishers simultaneously. As with awards, this is the best way to maximize your time and your chances of finding a publisher. However, when a writer or agent has a special relationship with a publisher and has reason to believe the publisher is very likely to be interested in the work, a submission may be made exclusively to one publishing house.

How should I approach the publisher?

Find out exactly how the publisher wants to be approached and, if possible, an appropriate contact name. Staff changes at publishing houses happen fast and frequently, so

---

WHAT YOU'VE HEARD IS TRUE

Less is more

There are several reasons why it is often more effective to submit a portion of your manuscript rather than the entire work. First, the fewer pages an editor has to read, the more likely it is that he or she will be able to finish them. Second, it is easiest to showcase your best writing by selecting a particularly compelling section of your work. Finally, submitting a portion of your manuscript is a good way to spark an editor's curiosity and to make him or her hungry for more.

Lucy Grealy's forthcoming first novel was accepted for publication on the basis of the quality of her previous work, plus one chapter of her novel.

—J.S. 📖

be sure your contact information is current. Most publishers are extremely busy and cannot spend time answering questions by phone. If you need to request information by phone, be succinct. The first step in approaching a publisher is usually to write a brief query letter. There is an art to writing a compelling letter about yourself and your work, without which you may never receive the kind of serious consideration you are looking for. So take the time to write your best letter, and if possible, have a professional look at it before you send it out.

How should I follow up on my submission?

Most publishers need at least two or three months to evaluate and respond to a submission. Give them the time they need. If you haven't received an answer after several months, follow up with a brief letter, fax, or phone call. Don't be a pest. The surest way to put off a publisher is to phone every week to check on the status of your manuscript.

What should I do when my manuscript has been returned?

Most publishers do not have time to respond to projects they are not interested in with more than a form letter. If you are fortunate enough to receive a rejection letter that addresses the particulars of your project, send a thank-you note to the person who wrote to you and give serious consideration to what he or she has said. Has he or

WHAT YOU'VE HEARD IS TRUE
A good critique is as good as publication
Well, maybe not exactly. But having an editor give your manuscript serious and thorough consideration points you in the right direction. Sometimes the best way to approach a publisher is to seek editorial advice rather than publication. Perhaps a published writer you know can ask his or her editor to take a serious look at your work.

Jill Bialosky submitted her first collection of poems to Harry Ford at Knopf not for publication, but to seek his advice about the quality of the poems and his suggestions about where they might be published.

—J.S.

she suggested that you approach a different kind of publisher, or that you need to revise your manuscript? If so, you may want to redirect your efforts accordingly. Again, bear in mind that rejections are an inevitable part of the submissions process, and are often invaluable in helping you reach your goal.

Chronology of a First Book, 1981-1993

—Anna Monardo

I spent 10 years writing my first novel, *The Courtyard of Dreams*. When the book was published in August 1993 by Doubleday, many good things happened. It was reviewed well. There were three foreign sales. Most of the first printing was sold. Then, after the book had been on the market for 15 months, I got word from my agent that it was being remaindered. What did this mean? It meant that my baby would show up on the discount tables of bookstores for a while, and then disappear. The novel would no longer be in print; it could not be ordered. Remaindering meant it was time for me to come to terms with what had not happened—no extra printings, no paperback sale. Secretly, I had always hoped the novel would give me a chance to meet Johnny Carson. Remaindering meant it was time to move on. Before I could do that, though, I had to figure out exactly what I'd been doing during the decade it took me to give birth to this book. I sketched the following chronology:

July 1981. I spend a month in New Jersey. I am living in a damp cottage near a gritty beach. At night, from the back porch, I see the A&P parking lot stretched out flat and soulless. From the front porch, I see the thinnest slice of ocean. But there's the smell of salt water every morning and the feel of sand when I walk barefoot in the home. That's all it takes—I begin thinking wildly, obsessively, of summers I spent on a beach with my relatives in southern Italy. Giulia, the young American girl who will be my main character, appears on the pages of my sandy legal pad. Giulia is talking to her young cousin Lina, and Lina is talking to me, telling the story of a time when Giulia was in Italy. Every sunset they talk about Italy. I take notes. New Jersey disappears.

September 1981. Back home in New York City, I have a few note-books full of Giulia and the Italian beach. I'm caught in an extended "hallucination." When I walk down Broadway, the fruit stands remind me of markets in Calabria. And the fat old buildings on West End Avenue remind me of Rome. Parallel to my life—and more compelling—is Giulia's life. I am in a workshop at this time, and I try to manipulate my notes into a short story. People in the workshop see right through it. "This is a novel, isn't it?" Oh God, now what? I know nothing about writing a novel.

October 1981. My grandmother, whom I am very close to, is dying. One of the last times I see her she says to me, slowly, "You know what I want? I want to write the story of my life." The story I've begun is not her life, and it's not my life, but, whatever it is, I have no way out now. My grandmother has just told me that a story's urgency never fades; with time it gets sharper.

Spring 1982. I have a chance to hear Gail Hochman, an agent, give a talk about how to find an agent. She's young, energetic, warm; she suggests you look for an agent who is, above all, enthusiastic, someone with a particular interest in your kind of book. "Me, for example," she says, "I love Italy." I am thrilled. And terrified. I've been paralyzed by shyness about approaching editors, agents, and established writers when I go to hear them speak. This time, though, I will have to do it. At the end of Gail's talk, I introduce myself and tell her I'm writing a novel set in Italy. "Great," she says. "Whenever you're ready, let me see it."

May 1982. My workshop ends. I decide I've had enough workshopping for a while. All I want is to sit and get this novel done. What I need is space. I move to a big apartment in Brooklyn.

March 1984. I move out of Brooklyn.

Summer 1984. It has been almost three years. I have arranged my world to have time for "the n-word." I want a published novel, of course, but more than that, the material is important to me: a young woman's separation from her family, and an Italian immigrant family's separation from their culture. I work night shifts as a *Time* proofreader. Social life? Less is not more. For all this commitment, I have very little to show—only messy piles of notes, lists, scenes, dialogues. So far I see the book in three parts: Part One is Giulia's childhood in Ohio. In Part Two she's 17, goes to Italy, some big stuff (still not sure what) happens. Part Three is 10 years later and we see the consequences of the big stuff that happened when she was 17. I'm still on Part One. Lina, the young cousin, is still the Nick Carraway-like, involved-uninvolved narrator. I've shown Gail a few batches of pages. She's interested in reading more. I'm encouraged. But also sad and afraid Here's this wonderful agent, yet I can't come up with a finished novel. What if she loses interest, what if I blow it?

March 1985. I spend a month in northern California, at the Djerassi Foundation, a relatively new artists' colony. No one I know has ever heard of it, but I'm desperate to make headway on this novel. I go there, half afraid it will be a Moonie ranch. It is not. It is heaven. I have a room with a view of the hills (there is even a view from my shower). I don't have to do anything but write all day and show up for dinner at 6:00. I get to the end of Part One. I plunge into Part Two, which takes place in Italy. It's clear to me that I need a stretch of time in Rome. One day, I stand in the hills and vow to the cows grazing in the fields of the Djerassi Foundation that I will go to Italy.

September-December 1985. I live in Rome. I have my uncle's Olivetti manual. But now that I'm in Italy there seems little point to sitting inside writing about Italy. Rome is a city for walking. I am in love with this city. I walk and take notes. One hot afternoon I step off a busy street, into a monastery, and find myself in a courtyard. It is small, quiet, ancient, and perfect. It comes to me this way: To be a woman in an Italian family is to live in a courtyard, an enclosed world—it is safety, confinement, beauty, deprivation, fulfillment, wretched, wonderful, inescapable. I can't stop writing about courtyards. By the time I leave Rome I haven't finished the novel, but I do have my central metaphor. This will organize everything.

April 1987. I've been working on the novel for six years. I've been to Italy and back and still don't have a finished manuscript. I've been trying to give Part One a dramatic focus, but Lina, the narrator, is like a wind-up doll, going over and over the same scenes. When I sit to work I can barely look at the pages. I can't write unless I have a box of Dutch Mill doughnuts (the ones in the blue box) next to me. Usually I have powdered sugar or cinnamon. On very bad days, chocolate-dipped.

Something is not happening. Writing is not fun any more. The story is lead. The day before my thirty-first birthday, I sit at the desk and think, Is there any way on God's good earth for Lina to tell this story and make it halfway interesting? Wait a minute. Why is Lina telling this story? It's Giulia's story. Giulia has to speak. This thought is light and heavy at the same time; it comes to me with the unmistakable weight and flight of truth. This is it. I write on a sheet of paper: Giulia must tell her own story.

Why did I waste so much time with Lina? Years later I will realize that the Lina drafts were crucial. The novel deals with autobiographical issues, and writing the story through Lina's eyes has helped me to make Giulia a character who is different from me. But I don't understand this yet. Feeling completely defeated, I put the whole manuscript in a drawer and lock it. I don't have to write.

I get a job teaching English as a Second Language, I read *War and Peace*, I prepare to be audited by the IRS in June. I am not writing; I am living in the world. I'm not happy, but I'm not tortured.

November 1987. On a train going to a friend's for Thanksgiving, I hear an older Giulia begin talking about when she was young, living in Rome. I take notes. At home, I write scenes. This feels good, but I refuse to consider I may be working on the you-know-what again. It is not long, though, before Giulia is telling the story of her childhood. And I am writing Part One. Again.

But I am smarter this time. I find a group of writers. We meet monthly; this gives me deadlines. We read each other's work and talk. Writing begins to feel more like a way of life, a good thing, and less like prison.

December 1987. I get a Christmas card—simple, elegant, no return address, signed Gail. I get tears in my eyes. She still believes in me. Strengthened by this, I set a deadline. I will get her a manuscript in six months. I make and break many deadlines, but through spring, summer, and fall, Gail's Christmas card is on my desk. It gives me courage. It gives me hope.

December 1988. I'm talking with a friend in the copy room at *Time*. She is saying she wishes she were organized enough to send Christmas cards. She mentions a woman from a different department of the magazine who last year sent cards to everyone, even people in our department. I say, "She didn't send me a Christmas card."

"Of course she did. At first I wasn't sure who it was from. There was no return address, no note. She just wrote her name."

The woman's name is Gail.

June 1989. I get together Part One, Part Two, and a summary of Part Three, all written in Giulia's voice. I send this to Gail Hochman, who writes back, "I think you cover way too much ground." She suggests I cut Part One, make Part Two the body of the novel, skip Part Three. I do it.

November 1989. The novel is condensed; Gail has a completed manuscript. She sends it to three or four editors, who all reject it. A few say, "This seems kind of Young Adult." I am upset, not because I have anything against YA novels, but because I didn't mean to write one. I've failed to do what I set out to do.

January 1990. At the Virginia Center for the Creative Arts (another heaven-sent haven, more cows; do all artists' colonies have cows?), I begin the novel again. This time Giulia is 28 and very depressed, so depressed there is no mistaking this for a YA novel. She's in mid-crisis, which forces her to look back over her childhood, Italy, the whole shebang. When Gail sees this new rough draft, she says, "You have a lot of work to do here."

"I'll be done in a few months."

"It may take longer," she warns. I try to ignore that.

February 1991. Fourteen months after I began the new draft, I am finished. The manuscript is 660 pages. It takes an entire weekend to print out. At one point, my super knocks on my door and asks if everything is alright.

June 10, 1991. I come home from teaching. There is a message from Gail. Sit down, she says. I have news. Deb Futter, a great young editor, has accepted the manuscript. We all agree the novel is too long. But the next morning I wake up happy, thinking, I don't have to write that novel anymore! This happiness is completely false.

July 10, 1991. Lunch with Deb. We agree on which parts of the manuscript need to be cut. A cinch, I say.

August 14, 1991. I sign the contract at Gail's office. That week, half my advance arrives in the mail—a check for real money, for words I wrote myself. Problem is, I wrote way too many words. And what if I can't pull this unruly thing together? That night I have a horrific dream. I wake, sit bolt upright in the dark. I am still not done rewriting. I am Sisyphus. I have been put on this earth to do nothing but write and rewrite this one novel. Mountains will crumble. Oceans will dry up. Children will grow old. But I will never be released from this task.

August-December 1991. I cut and revise. I cry daily.

December 1991. The manuscript has been to Weight Watchers, lost 200+ pages. I deliver it to Deb. This is the first Christmas in nine years that I am not writing the novel. My family rejoices.

January 1992. Deb and I meet for the first of many working sessions in her office at Doubleday. In the lobby of the building is a newsstand that sells penny candy. I fill up my purse. Upstairs, I dump small Mounds bars and Hershey's kisses onto Deb's round glass-top work table. There's lots of work ahead. We go over this and that. Then Deb says, "I have a really wild idea. Tell me what you think. It occurred to me, Chapter 1 begins with this woman who's 28, depressed. I've read this kind of story before. Chapter

2, on the other hand, starts with the childhood scenes, and they seem fresh. So I'm thinking, Why not start with Chapter 2?" I am thinking, I just spent three months writing Chapter 1.

I feel sick to my stomach; it's not the chocolate. "But if we cut Chapter 1, we'll have to cut all the chapters of Giulia at twenty-eight."

Deb's eyes widen. "Good idea!" she says. "Excellent!"

She made me say it. What's worse, I know she is right—the new material is not strong enough yet. I also see two years of work pass before my eyes.

April 1992. I deliver the newest condensed version to Deb. She accepts it. We have several glasses of wine. They taste good.

August 1992. Deb calls. Time to write catalog copy. It's a sales tool, and it's important. Years of work and thousands of sheets of paper reduced to three paragraphs that describe the novel and make it a must-buy. This is exciting—the book is more real now—but it's in other people's hands, becoming a thing outside of me. I feel nervous. Or sad. Or something.

November 1992. Several afternoons Deb and I meet over her glasstop table to line edit. More candy.

January 1993. A few people read the edited, cut-down story. Two readers tell me, "I couldn't put it down. I spent the whole weekend reading it." This equation—10 years to write equals one weekend to read—is, I tell myself, better than its converse.

February 1993. Loose galleys are in. I'm to read them and make corrections. Last chance for changes. No more "work-in-progress." When I release the galleys, the novel will be done. I have two problems: (1) I am afraid it is not perfect yet; and (2) I do not want to read this novel again. I can't look at it any more. A sunny cold Sunday afternoon; my friends go ice skating and I cannot go. Poor me.

By nighttime, though, I've reached the middle—Giulia is in Italy, in love. I have the music on—Italian pop I listened to all the years

I was writing; schmaltzy music, but it always had the power to transport me. It's just me and the music and this story and we're lost in the night, like so many nights and weekends and years we spent together. I realize that during all those years I was doing exactly what I wanted to do.

July 1993. Deb calls me. "Come down to my office as soon as you can." When I get there, she puts a copy of *The Courtyard of Dreams* in my hands. I cry.

October 1994. I get the letter from Doubleday informing me that the book is being remaindered. I have a month to send in my order to buy copies at discount. "Buy as many as you can afford," Gail tells me, "as many as you have room for."

I've needed a table in the hallway—you know, a place to put mail, to plop down my purse when I come in the door. I order 200 copies of my novel. They arrive in little boxes of 10. Twenty boxes, as neat and manageable as Legos. Piled up against the wall in the hallway, covered with a bright cloth, the boxes of my novel make a perfect narrow table. Having them there makes my day-to-day life better, a little easier.

PUBLISHERS FAVORABLE TO UNPUBLISHED FIRST-BOOK MANUSCRIPTS

ALFRED A. KNOPF
Address: 201 East 50th Street, New York, NY 10022
Phone: (212) 751-2600
Category: Fiction and Nonfiction
General Information: Publishes hardcover and paperback originals. Royalties and advances vary. Publishes book one year after acceptance of manuscript. Accepts simultaneous submissions if informed. Reports in three months on manuscript. Knopf publishes 200 titles each year and won three Pulitzer Prizes in 1995. Recent titles include *I Was Amelia Earhart*, Jane Mendelsohn.

ALYSON PUBLICATIONS
Contact: Julie K. Trevelyan
Address: PO Box 4371, Los Angeles, CA 90078-4371
Phone: (213) 871-1225
Fax: (213) 467-6805
Category: Fiction and Nonfiction
Publisher's Notes on First Books: Published five first books out of 35 total books last year. Publish two first books in 1997, as well as six in 1998, and six in 1999. First-book titles include *Lucy on the West Coast*, Mary Beth Caschetta, 1996; *Fast Ride With the Top Dawn*, Harper Gray, 1996; and *Dancing with Two Dogs and Mozart*, Michael Freiberg, 1996. "Our first books sell moderately. Some of the benefits to publishing first books are giving new authors publishing recognition, exposing readers to their work, and possibly discovering a very good writer we can publish again in the future. The difficulties we encounter are dealing with new authors who are not familiar with the publishing procedures, in addition to the unknown selling strength of the author."

Advice to new authors: "Send us an original, dynamite proposal—typed and double-spaced. Don't forget to include SASE. Please do not call us."

ARCADE PUBLISHING
Contact: Richard Seaver
Address: 141 Fifth Ave., New York, NY 10010
Phone: (212) 353-8148
Category: Fiction, Nonfiction, and Poetry
Publisher's Notes on First Books: Arcade Publishing published 10 to 12 first books, out of 40 total books, last year. Accepts agented submissions only. Recent first-book titles include *The Secret Diary of Anne Bolan*, Robin Maxwell, 1997; and *Elvis in the Twilight Memory*, June Juanico, 1996.
General Information: Publishes hardcover originals, trade paperback originals, and reprints. Pays royalty on retail price. Offers $1,000 to $100,000 advance. Publishes book 18 months after acceptance. Reports in three months on queries. "We do not publish poetry as a rule; since our inception we have published only a few volumes of poetry." Recent fiction titles include *Trying to Save Piggy Sneed*, John Irving.

AVON BOOKS
Contact: Alice Webster-Williams
Address: 1350 Avenue of the Americas, New York, NY 10019
Phone: (212) 261-6800
Fax: (212) 261-6895
Category: Fiction and Nonfiction
General Information: Publishes trade and mass market paperback originals and reprints. Royalty and advance negotiable. Publishes manuscript two years after acceptance. Accepts simultaneous submissions. Reports in three months on manuscript. Avon Books publishes 400 titles each year. Send SASE for guidelines. Recent titles include *Memoir from Antproof Case*, Mark Helprin.

BALLANTINE BOOKS,
DIVISION OF RANDOM HOUSE, INC.
Address: 201 East 50th Street, New York, NY 10022
Phone: (212) 572-4910
Fax: (212) 572-2676
Category: Nonfiction and Fiction
General Information: Receives 3,000 submissions per year. Pays royalty on retail price. Accepts simultaneous submissions. Reports in two months on manuscript submission. Publishes 120 titles each year. Book catalog free. Send SASE for manuscript guidelines. Recent fiction titles include *Weighed in the Balance*, Anne Perry.

BEACON PRESS
Contact: Amy Caldweil
Address: 25 Beacon Street, Boston, MA 02108-2800
Phone: (617) 742-2800
Category: Fiction, Nonfiction, and Poetry
Publisher's Notes on First Books: Beacon Press publishes nonfiction, political, anthropology, and gender studies. Also publishes historical, religious, and spirituality subjects if book is an academic treatment of these subjects. Does not accept unsolicited manuscript submissions. Beacon publishes approximately 60 books per year. Recent first-book titles include *Here and No Where Else: Late Seasons of a Farm and Its Family,* Jane Brox; *The Very Rich Hours,* Emily Hiestand; and *The Power of Their Ideas*, Deborah Myer. New authors are generally referred to the press from other Beacon writers or agents.
General Information: Receives 6,000 manuscript submissions and query submissions each year. Letter of query (with SASE) and sample chapter should precede manuscript. Responds to mansucript and query submissions in six to eight weeks. Returns manuscript with SASE. Manuscript should be on 81/2 x 11-inch paper, single-sided, typed, double-spaced, letter-quality.

BLUE STAR PRODUCTIONS
A DIVISION OF BOOKWORLD, INC.
Contact: Barbara DeBolt
Address: 9666 E. Riggs Rd., #194, Sun Lakes, AZ 85248
Phone: (602) 895-7995
Fax: (602) 895-6991
Category: Fiction and Nonfiction
General Information: Publishes trade and mass market paperback originals. Receives 500 queries and 400-500 manuscript submissions per year. Pays 10 percent royalty on either wholesale or retail price. Reports in one month on queries, two months on proposals, six months on manuscript submissions. Publishes 10 to 12 titles per year. Book catalog free. Send #10 SASE for manuscript guidelines. Know our no-advance policy beforehand and know our guidelines. No response ever comes without SASE. No phone queries. "We have absolutely restricted our needs to those manuscript submissions whose focus is metaphysical, urology, time travel, and North American." Recent fiction includes *Dance on the Water*, Laura Leffers.

BRANDEN PUBLISHING CO., INC.
Contact: Adolf Caso
Address: 17 Station Street, Box 843, Brookline Village, MA 02147
Phone: (617) 734-2045
Fax: (617) 734-2046
Category: Fiction and Nonfiction
General Information: Publishes hardcover and trade paperback originals, reprints, and software. Receives 1,000 submissions each year. Pays 5 to 10 percent royalty on net. Offers $1,000 maximum advance. Publishes book 10 months after acceptance. Reports in one month. Publishes 15 titles per year. Average first print run for a first book is 3,000 copies. Branden publishes manuscripts that are determined to have a significant impact on modern society. "Our audience is a well-read general public of professionals, college students, and some high school students. If I were a writer trying to market a book today, I would thoroughly investigate the number of potential readers. We like books by or about women." Recent fiction titles include *The Straw Obelisk*, Adolf Caso. Recent nonfiction titles include *From Trial Court*, Diane Wakowski.

BROOKLINE BOOKS
Contact: Sadi Ranson
Address: PO Box 1047, Cambridge, MA 02238
Phone: (617) 888-0360
Fax: (617) 868-1772
Category: Fiction and Nonfiction
Publisher's Notes on First Books: Brookline Books published five to six first books, out of 20 total titles, last year. We will not read any manuscript submissions that do not include return postage. Also, we are not open to publishing science fiction, horror, or pornography—though we are open to anything else. Recent first-book titles include *Silk*, Grace Dane Mazur, 1996; and *Urban Oracle*, Mayar Santos Febref, 1997. "Publishing first books gives us the opportunity to provide a fresh perspective and new language. It is difficult dealing with the unknown element in a person and in a new manuscript. You have to push first books harder than work written by someone previously published and sold."

Advice to new authors: "Call for a catalog and push your own work. New authors have to push their own work."

CALYX BOOKS
Contact: Margarita Donnelly
Address: PO Box B, Coravallis, OR 97339
Category: Women's Fiction, Nonfiction, and Poetry
Publisher's Notes on First Books: Calyx Books only publishes first books. Last year they published three first books. Recent first book titles include *Into the Forest*, Gene Heglend. The average first print run for first books is 1,500 copies for poetry, and usually 5,000 copies for fiction. "Publishing first books and discovering emerging writers is our mission."
General Information: Receives 400 manuscript submissions and query submissions each year. Letter of query should precede manuscript submission. Responds to queries in one month. Responds to manuscript submissions in one year. Accepts simultaneous submissions. Offers advances; pays royalties.

Advice to new authors: "Find out our deadlines, accept that we are slow, and be patient."

———

CENTER PRESS
Contact: Gabriella Stone
Address: PO Box 16452, Encino, CA 91416-6452
Category: Fiction, Nonfiction, and Poetry
Publisher's Notes on First Books: The Center Press is no longer accepting unsolicited manuscripts.
General Information: Publishes hardcover and trade paperback originals. Receives 600 queries and 300 manuscripts per year. Pays 10 to 30 percent royalty on wholesale price or makes outright purchase of $500 to $5,000. Publishes book 10 months after acceptance. Accepts simultaneous submissions. Reports in three months on manuscript submission. Publishes four to six titles per year. Offers $200 to $2,000 advance. Send a #10 SASE for manuscript guidelines. "Our readers are typically well educated, tending to be urban, creative, middle income (mostly), eclectic, and well intended."

———

CHAMPION BOOKS
Contact: Rebecca Rush
Address: PO Box 636, Lemont, IL 60439
Phone: (800) 280-1135
Category: Fiction, Nonfiction, Poetry, and Short Fiction

Publisher's Notes on First Books: All titles are first books. Champion publishes approximately five titles each year. Recent first-book titles include *Warning This is Not a Book*, Pete Babones; *Simple Shrine*, Jim Vetrer; and *My Gradual Demise & Honeysuckle*, Douglas A. Martin.

General Information: Imprint is the New Shoes Series. Publishes trade paperback originals. Pays eight to 10 percent royalty on retail price. Publishes book five months after acceptance of manuscript. Accepts simultaneous submissions. Reports in four months on manuscript submissions. Send an SASE for book catalog and manuscript guidelines. Submissions may include ethnic, feminist, gay/lesbian, literary, poetry, and short story collections. Any finished or unfinished fiction work will be considered. "We are seeking work that applies to or deals with contemporary American society with an emphasis on counterculture and alternative lifestyles." Average first print run is 500 copies.

Advice to new authors: "Do a lot of self-promotion. It's best if authors have heavily promoted their own writing in the form of publishing chapbooks, self-publication, and doing a lot of readings."

CHRONICLE BOOKS
Address: 85 Second Street, San Francisco, CA 94105
Phone: (415) 777-7240
Category: Fiction, Nonfiction, and Short Fiction
General Information: Twenty percent of books from first-time authors. Publishes book 18 months after acceptance. Accepts simultaneous submissions and reports in three months on queries for nonfiction. For fiction and short fiction, send complete manuscript—do not query. Nonfiction submissions may include coffee-table books, cookbooks, regional California, architecture, art ands design, gardening, gifts, health, nature, nostalgia, photography, recreation, and travel. Fiction submissions may include novels, novellas, and short story collections. Submissions may also include children's books. Recent titles: *Lat'arilla: The Mexican Grill*, Reed Hearon (cookbook); and *The Lies of the Saints*, Erin McGraw (short story collection).

CLEIS PRESS
Contact: Frederique Delacoste
Address: PO Box 14684, San Francisco, CA 94114
Fax: (415) 575-4705
Category: Proactive Fiction and Nonfiction books by women (and a few men)

Publisher's Notes on First Books: Cleis Press published six first books, out of 15 total titles, last year. Recent book titles include *Memory Mumble*, Achy Obejas. Niche books (lesbian, gay, Hispanic, African-American), sell much better than general fiction. Authors must believe in what we do. We are known for doing risky books.

General Information: Receives 300 manuscripts and query submissions each year. Responds to queries in four to six weeks. Responds to mansucript submissions in four weeks. Manuscripts should be on 81/2 × 11-inch paper, typed, double-spaced. Pays royalties.

Advice to new authors: Have enough experience as a writer; develop your craft. Be clear and have a function for your work. Also, have a sense of who we are.

CONFLUENCE PRESS INC.
Address: Lewis-Clark State College, 500 Eighth Ave., Lewiston, ID 83501-1698
Phone: (208) 799-2336
Fax: (208) 799-2324
Category: Fiction, Nonfiction, Poetry, and Short Fiction
General Information: Receives 500 queries and 150 manuscripts each year. Pays 10 to 15 percent royalty on net sales price. Offers $100 to $2,000 advance. Publishes book 18 months after acceptance. Accepts simultaneous submissions. Reports in one month on proposals, two months on queries, and three months on manuscripts. Publishes an average of four to five titles each year. Book catalog and manuscript guidelines free upon request. Nonfiction submissions may include reference books and bibliographies. Fiction submissions may include ethnic, literary, mainstream/contemporary, and short story collections. Send six sample poems for poetry submissions. Recent titles include *Even in Quiet Places*, William Stafford; and *Cheerleaders Groin Gomorrah*, John Rember.

COPPER CANYON PRESS
Address: PO Box 271, Port Townsend, WA 98368
Phone: (360) 385-4925
Category: Poetry
Publisher's Notes on First Books: Copper Canyon published two first books, out of 10 to 12 total books, last year. Recent first-book titles include *Country of Air*, Richard Jones, 1996; *Leaving a Shadow*, Heather Allen, 1996; *Infanta*, Erin Belieu, 1995; *Terra Firma*, Thomas Centolena, 1992; and *The Island*, Michael White, 1992. The average first print run for first books is approximately 3,000 copies.
General Information: Receives 1,500 queries and 500 manuscripts each year (95% of books from unagented authors). Publishes book 18 months after acceptance. Reports in one month on manuscripts. Manuscript guidelines and book catalog free

on request. Query must be accompanied by five to seven sample poems. Recent poetry titles include *Collected Poems*, Hayden Carruth.

Advice to new authors: "In some ways it is easier to see first books because our culture is predicated on the next new thing. We are always looking for new authors. The best thing an author can do is to be familiar with Copper Canyon's work. Know our books. What we publish is governed by individual taste. It also helps to have an understanding of the classics, as well as to be published in journals and magazines—already have your name out there."

COUNTERPOINT
Contact: Jack Shoemaker
Address: 1627 1ˢᵗ St., NW, Suite 850, Washington, DC 20006
Fax: (202) 887-0562
Category: Fiction, Nonfiction, and Short Fiction
General Information: Publishes hardcover and trade paperback originals and reprints. Receives 10 queries per week and 250 manuscripts each year. Pays 7 percent to 15 percent royalties on retail price. Publishes book 18 months after acceptance. Accepts simultaneous submissions. Reports in two months on manuscripts. Publishes an average of 20 to 25 titles each year. Nonfiction submissions may include biography, coffee table, and gift books. Agented submissions only for nonfiction. Recent nonfiction titles include *The Invention of Television*, David E. Fisher and Marshall John Fisher. Fiction submissions may include historical, humor, literary mainstream/contemporary, religious, and short story collections. Agented submissions only. Recent fiction titles include *Women in Their Bed*, Gina Berriault (short stories).

DANCING JESTER PRESS
Contact: Glenda Daniel
Address: 3411 Garth Rd., Suite 208, Baytown, TX 77521
Phone: (281) 427-9560
Category: Fiction, Nonfiction, Poetry, and Short Fiction
General Information: Publishes hardcover and trade paperback originals and reprints. 100 percent of books from unagented authors. Pays 4 to 12 percent royalties on retail price or makes outright purchase. Does not pay advances. Publishes book 18 months after acceptance. Accepts simultaneous submissions. Reports in three months on proposals, six months on manuscripts. Publishes an average of 16 titles each year. Also sponsors the "One Night in Paris Should Be Enough" prize. Nonfiction submissions may include autobiography, children's/juvenile, coffee table, cookbooks, how-to, humor, illustrated, multimedia, reference, self-help, and textbooks. Fiction submissions may include adventure, erotica, ethnic, experimental,

feminist, gay/lesbian, historical, humor, juvenile, mainstream/contemporary, mystery picture books, plays, short story collections, suspense, thrillers, westerns, and young adult. Send complete manuscript when submitting poetry. Recent fiction titles include *Twin Blue Slipper of Swan Lake*, Lillian Cagle (children's mysteryseries). Recent poetry titles include *Sex Lives of Animals*, Jason Love (annotated limericks).

DANTE UNIVERSITY OF AMERICA PRESS, INC.

Contact: Adolf Caso
Address: PO Box 843, Brookline Village, MA 02147-0843
Fax: (617) 734-2046
Category: Fiction, Nonfiction, and Poetry
General Information: Publishes hardcover and trade paperback originals and reprints. Receives 50 submissions each year. 50 percent of books published from unagented authors. Average print run for a first book is 3,000 copies. Pays royalties. Advances are negotiable. Publishes book 10 months after acceptance of manuscript. Query with an SASE. Reports in two months on manuscripts. Publishes an average of five titles each year. Nonfiction submissions may include biography, reference, reprints, and translations from Italian and Latin. Fiction submissions may include translations from Italian and Latin. Send query with an SASE. "There is a chance that we would use Renaissance poetry translations." Recent fiction titles include *Rogue Angel*, Carol Damioll. Recent poetry titles include: *Italy Poetry 1950-1990*.

DAVID R. GODINE, PUBLISHER

Contact: Lissa Warren
Address: PO Box 9103, Lincoln, MA 01773
Phone: (617) 259-0700
Fax: (617) 259-9198
Category: Fiction and Nonfiction
Publisher's Notes on First Books: David R. Godine published two first books, out of 25 total books, in 1996. They do not accept unsolicited manuscripts. Manuscripts must be submitted through an agent. Recent first-book titles include *Little Orion*, Marly Youmam, 1995; *The Empty Creel*, Geraldine Pope, 1995; and *Eliza's Carousel Lion*, Lynn Strough, 1994. Of the three books above (two children's books and one novel), they sold 2,000 to 3,000 copies of each (3,000 for *Little Orion*). Returns were high for both children's books.

Advice to new authors: "We find new authors via suggestions from authors we have previously published. Have your agent contact us, or have a published author who knows your work write us on your behalf."

THE ECCO PRESS
Contact: Daniel Halpern
Address: 100 W. Broad Street, Hopewell, NJ 08525
Phone: (609) 466-4748
Fax: (609) 466-4706
Category: Fiction, Nonfiction, and Poetry
Publisher's Notes on First Books: Ecco Press published five to 10 first books, out of a total of 60 books, last year. Recent first book titles include: *One Day as a Tiger*, Anne Haverty, 1997; *The Killer*, Patricia Melo, 1997. The average first print run for first books is 5,000 to 7,500 copies.
General Information: Publishes hardcover and trade paperback originals, reprints, and trade paperback reprints. Receives 1,200 queries each year. Publishes book one year after acceptance of manuscript. Reports in two months on queries.

Advice to new authors: "Writer should be published in journals and/or participate in a writing program. Somehow they need to show us that they are committed writers, that this is a career."

EIGHTH MOUNTAIN PRESS
Contact: Ruth Gundle
Address: 624 SE 29th Ave., Portland, OR 97214
Phone: (503) 233-3936
Category: Fiction, Nonfiction, and Poetry by women
Publisher's Notes on First Books: Eighth Mountain published one first book (a second edition), out of two total books published, last year. Recent first book titles include *A Journal of One's Own: Uncommon Advice for the Independent Woman Traveler*, Thalia Zepatos. The average final print run for all books ranges from 15,000 to 35,000 copies (nonfiction selling more).
General Information: Eighth Mountain has an annual contest for book-length poetry manuscripts. Contest prize is $1,000 cash and publication in the prize series. Receives 500 to 1,000 manuscripts and query submissions each year. Letter of query should precede manuscript submission. Responds to queries in two to eight weeks. Responds to manuscript submissions in one to four months. Does not accept simultaneous submissions. Has an average overall marketing budget of $5,000 to $6,000. Has an average per-book marketing budget of $2,000 to $3,000. Pays royalties.

Advice to new authors: "Submit a query that is as clear as possible and a manuscript that fits what Eighth Mountain is doing. Eighth Mountain Press publishes high-quality feminist literature written by women, in beautifully designed and produced editions."

FABER & FABER, INC.
Address: 53 Shore Rd., Winchester, MA 01890
Phone: (617) 721-1427
Category: Fiction and Nonfiction
Publisher's Notes on First Books: Faber and Faber, Inc. published two first books, out of 30 total books, last year. Recent first-book titles include *A Child Out of Alcatraz*, Tara Ison, 1997; and *Offseason*, Niomi Haloch, 1997.
General Information: Publishes hardcover and trade paperback originals. Receives 1,200 submissions each year. Twenty-five percent of all books by unagented authors. Pays royalty on retail price. Advance varies. Publishes book one year after acceptance of manuscript. Accepts simultaneous submissions. Reports in three months on queries. Send a #10 SASE for guidelines. Nonfiction submissions may include anthologies, biographies, contemporary culture, screenplays and film, history and natural history, cooking, and popular science. Faber and Faber, Inc. is not open to mysteries, thrillers, or children's fiction. Recent nonfiction tides include *Uncommon Voyage: Parenting a Special Needs Child in the World of Alternative Medicine*, Laura Shapiro Kramer. Recent fiction titles include *Empire Under Glass*, Julian Anderson.

Advice to new authors: "Please send us quality literary fiction that is unique."

FIREBRAND BOOKS
Contact: Nancy K. Bereano
Address: 141 The Commons, Ithaca, NY 14850
Phone: (607) 272-0000
Category: Publishes Lesbian and Feminist Fiction, Nonfiction, Poetry, Erotica, News, and Political Subjects.
General Information: Receives 500 manuscripts and query submissions per year. Fifty percent of books published from first-time authors and 90 percent from unagented authors. Book catalog free upon request. Responds to queries in two weeks. Responds to manuscripts submissions in two months. Accepts simultaneous submissions (with notification only). No handwritten submissions except from institutionalized women. Pays royalties. Firebrand Books publishes eight to 10 books per year. Recent first-book titles include *Stone Butch Blues*, Leslie Feinberg. Other titles include *S/HE*, Minnie Bruce Pratt; *Good Enough to Eat*, Leslea Newman; *The Women Who Hate Me*, Dorothy Allison; *Presenting. Sister NoBlues*, Hattie Gossett; and *A Burst of Light*, Audre Lorde.

FOUR WALLS EIGHT WINDOWS
Contact: John Oakes
Address: 39 West 14th Street, #503, New York, NY 10011
Phone: (212) 206-8965
Category: Fiction, Nonfiction, and Poetry
Publisher's Notes on First Books: Four Walls Eight Windows published three first books, out of 18 total books, last year. Recent first-book titles include *Slaughtermatic*, Steve Aylett, 1998; *Simple Annals*, Robert Howard Allen, 1997; and *The Renunciation*, Edgardo Rodriguez Julia, 1997. The average first print run for first books is 3,000 to 5,000 copies.
General Information: Does not accept unsolicited manuscripts. However, 50 percent of books published come from unagented authors. Receives 2,000 manuscripts and query submissions per year. Letter of query (with SASE) should precede manuscript submission. Responds to queries in three weeks. Responds to manuscript submissions in three months. Accepts simultaneous submissions. Pays ad vances. Other recent titles include *Bike Cult*, David Perry and *Ribo Punic*, Paul Di Filippo.

Advice to new authors: "We are always looking for good strong fiction. We often write to people we read. Be familiar with our list and have a reason for publishing the thing you submit."

———

FREDERIC C. BEIL, PUBLISHER, INC.
Contact: Mary Ann Bowman
Address: 609 Whitaker Street, Savannah, GA 31401
Phone: (912) 233-2446
Fax: (912) 233-2446
Category: Fiction and Nonfiction
Publisher's Notes on First Books: Frederic C. Beil published four first books, out of nine total book, in 1996. They were scheduled to publish five more in 1997. Recent first-book titles include *The Red Blackboard: An American Teacher in China*, Ruth Koenig, 1997; *A Buffer's Life: Scenes From the Other Side of the Silver Salver*, Christopher Allen, with Kimberly K. Allen, 1997; and *A Master of the Century Past*, Robert S. Metzger, 1997.
General Information: Does not accept unsolicited manuscripts. Publishes hardcover originals and reprints. Receives 700 queries and nine manuscripts each year. Pays 71/2 percent royalty on retail price. Publishes book 20 months after acceptance. Reports in one month on queries. Book catalog free on request. Submissions may include biography, general trade, illustrated book, juvenile, and reference. Subjects may include art, architecture, history, language/literature, and book arts. Recent fiction titles include *A Woman of Means*, Peter Taylor.

———

GRAYWOLF PRESS
Contact: Jeffrey Shotts
Address: 240 University Avenue, Suite 203, St. Paul, MN 55114
Phone: (612) 641-0077
Fax: (612) 641-0036
Category: Fiction, Nonfiction, and Poetry
Publisher's Notes on First Books: Graywolf Press published four first books, out of 16 total books, in 1996. They were scheduled to publish three to four each year for the next three years. While they do not accept unsolicited manuscripts, they do accept unsolicited queries. Recent first-book titles include *Wild Kingdom*, Vijay Seshadri, 1996; *Jack & Rochelle Sutton*, Edited by Lauren Sutton, 1996; *Rainey Lake*, Mary F. Rockcastle, 1996; and *The Apprentice*, Louis Libbey. The average first print run is approximately 4,000 copies.

Advice to new authors: "Sometimes we seek out new authors—those who seem promising—in journals and magazines. It is important that you are familiar with the press. Create a really professional query and sample of your writing. Read other Graywolf books. There is a real rush to be published. Slow down and be clear—be professional."

HANGING LOOSE PRESS
Contact: Bob Hershon
Address: 231 Wyckoff, Brooklyn, NY 11217
Phone: (212) 206-8465
Category: Fiction, Poetry, and Short Fiction
Publisher's Notes on First Books: Hanging Loose Press published one first book, out of six total books, last year. Recent first-book titles include *Familiar*, Carole Bernstein; and *American Guise*, Elinor Nauen. The average first print run for first books is 1,200 to 1,500 copies.
General Information: "We have a habit of keeping all of our books in print—eventually they do find their audience. We are committed to certain people—as well as staying open to new writers."

Advice to new authors: "Work hard on your book. We read manuscripts by invitation and we request manuscripts from writers we read in magazines. The best way to be considered for publication is to first send work to the magazine and let us get to know your work through that."

HARD PRESS INC.
Contact: Jonathan Gains
Address: PO Box 184, West Stockbridge, MA 01266
Phone: (413) 232-4690
Category: Fiction, Poetry, and Short Fiction
Publisher's Notes on First Books: Hard Press Inc. published four first books last year and is scheduled to publish five this year. Recent first-book titles include *Little Men*, Kevin Killian, 1996 (won the PEN Oakland Award); *Solow*, Lynn.Crawford, 1995; and *The Geographics*, Albert Mobilio, 1995.

Advice to new authors: "Anything that has a niche market (African-American, Hispanic, lesbian, and gay), is easier to sell and market. First, find yourself an editor who is not your friend and who is willing to work on your manuscript. Also, a phone call is good. Read what we publish and see if your work fits or is close/similar to what we publish. Finally, your synopsis and cover letter should be clear and engaging as only 10 percent of received manuscripts are completely read."

MILKWEED EDITIONS
Address: 430 First Ave. N., Suite 400, Minneapolis, MN 55401-1743
Phone: (612) 332-3192
Fax: (612) 332-6248
Category: Children's, Fiction, Nonfiction, and Poetry
Publisher's Notes on First Books: Milkweed Editions publishes an average of five to six first books, out of 12 to 15 total books, each year. Recent first-book titles include *Confidence of the Heart*, David Schweidel; *The Tree of Red Stars*, Tessa Bridal; *Rescuing Little Roundhead*, Syl Jones; and *Homestead*, Annick Smith.
General Information: Pays 71/2 percent royalty on list price. Advance varies. Publishes work one year after acceptance. Accepts simultaneous submissions. Send SASE for manuscript guidelines. Reports in six months on manuscripts. Returns unsolicited manuscript if SASE provided. No longer accepting children's biographies.

Advice to new authors: "We are looking for unpublished authors. Thirty percent of books published are from first-time authors. We find them in magazines, journals, through other writers, writing programs, our own unsolicited manuscripts, and agents. Read our catalog. Understand what we publish. If it seems to be a good fit, send the manuscript with an intelligent letter explaining why this book should be published."

NAIAD PRESS, INC.
Contact: Barbara Grier
Address: PO Box 10543, Tallahasse, FL 32302
Phone: (904) 539-5965
Category: Lesbian Fiction, Nonfiction, Erotica, Academic, and Historical Subjects
Publisher's Notes on First Books: Naiad published nine first books, out of 30 total books, last year. Recent first-book titles include *Dream Lover*, Lynn Denison; *The Color of Winter*, Lisa Shapiro; and *First Impressions*, Kate Calloway. The average first print run for first books is approximately 6,000 copies in the first year and approximately 12,000 in the second year. "Being a lesbian press we have a very specific audience."
General Information: One of the largest and oldest lesbian presses in the country (their 25th anniversary was in January 1998). Receives 1,100 query and manuscript submissions each year. Letter of query should precede manuscript submission. Does not accept simultaneous submissions. Fiction manuscript should not exceed 50,000 words. Responds to manuscript submissions in three to six months. Manuscripts should be on 8 1/2 x 11-inch paper, typed, double-spaced, consecutively numbered pages with 1" top and bottom margins. Has an average annual marketing budget of $200,000. Pays royalties.

Advice to new authors: "Send one page, with three paragraphs, about the book. Make it simple. Also send a brief history and explanation of why you can write."

NEW VICTORIA PUBLISHERS
Contact: Beth Dingham
Address: PO Box 27, Norwich, VT 0S05S
Phone: (802) 649-5297
Fax: (802) 649-5297
Category: Lesbian Biography, Fiction, History, Nonfiction, and Poetry
Publisher's Notes on First Books: New Victoria published five first books, out of eight books total, last year. Recent first-book titles include *No Daughter of the South*, Cynthia Webb; and *Orlando's Sleep*, Jennifer Spry. The average first print run for first books is 4,000 to 5,000 copies (mysteries sell much better and therefore have a larger first print run).
General Information: Receives 150 to 200 manuscripts and query submissions each year. Letter of query should precede manuscript submission. Responds to queries in two weeks. Responds to manuscript submissions in one month. Prefers not to receive simultaneous submissions. Pays royalties. "If you want a response, always send an SASE."

Advice to new authors: "First books tend to pile up on our desk. Be active in promoting your own work. Be daring and adventurous in your work. Don't be too subtle, and try to successfully write tension."

OWL CREEK PRESS

Address: 1620 North 45th Street, Seattle, WA 98103
Phone: (360) 387-6101
Category: Fiction, Poetry, and Short Fiction
Publisher's Notes on First Books: Owl Creek Press published four first books last year. Recent first-book titles include *Broken Darlings*, Ellen Watson. The average first print run for first books is approximately 1,000 copies and 500 copies for chapbooks: "We are totally nonprofit so the benefit of publishing first books is that everyone we publish is totally dedicated."

Advice to new authors: "We do accept unsolicited manuscripts, but poetry manuscripts must come through our contest (The Owl Creek Poetry Prize)."

PRESS GANG PUBLISHERS

Contact: Barbara Kuhne
Address: 603 Powell Street, Vancouver, British Columbia, V6A 1H2 Canada
Phone: (604) 876-7892
Category: Feminist and Lesbian Fiction, Nonfiction, Erotica, and Political Subjects
General Information: Receives 150-200 submissions and manuscript queries per year. Book catalog free upon request. Letter of query (with SASE) should precede manuscript submission. Responds to queries in two months. Responds to manuscript submissions in three to four months. Accepts simultaneous submissions. Publishes approximately five total titles each year. Manuscripts should be double-spaced. Prefers letter-quality submissions. Pays royalties. U.S. writers should send postal coupons, not U.S. stamps on SASE. "We give priority to Canadian women's writing."

SEVEN STORIES PRESS

Contact: Daniel Simon
Address: 140 Watts Street, New York, NY 10013
Phone: (212) 226-8760
Fax: (212) 226-1411
Category: Fiction and Nonfiction
Publisher's Notes on First Books: Seven Stories Press published five first books, out of 25 total books, last year.

General Information: Does not accept unsolicited manuscripts. Publishes hardcover and trade paperback originals. Pays 7 to 15 percent royalty on retail price, Publishes book one to three years after acceptance. Accepts simultaneous submissions. Reports in three months on manuscripts. Book catalog and manuscript guidelines free upon request. Recent titles include *Parable of the Sower*, Octavia E. Butler (feminist fiction). Audience is well educated, progressive, and mainstream.

Advice to new authors: "Publish anywhere you can. Read the books we publish. Submit manuscript only when you feel your own work resonates with a publisher's list."

ST. MARTIN'S PRESS
Contact: Calvert Morgan
Address: 175 Fifth Ave., New York, NY 10010
Phone: (212) 674-5151
Fax: (212) 674-9314
Category: Fiction and Nonfiction
Publisher's Notes on First Books: St. Martin's Press publishes approximately 150 first books, out of 600 total books, each year. "St. Martin's finds that we can support authors early in their career who, even if not with their first title, have success in their future. The most difficult thing about publishing first books is convincing retailers to give space to unknown writers—finding publicity for first-time novelists."

Advice to new authors: "Write a smart, concise cover letter."

W. W. NORTON
Contact: Jill Bialosky
Address: 500 Fifth Ave., New York, NY 10110
Phone: (212) 354-5500
Fax: (212) 869-0856
Category: Fiction, Nonfiction, and Poetry
Publisher's Notes on First Books: W. W. Norton published one first book last year. Recent first-book titles include *Piaceso Effects*, Jeanie Marie Beaumont.
General Information: General trade publisher of fiction and nonfiction, educational, and professional books. Subjects include biography, history, music, psychology, and literary fiction. Do not submit juvenile or young adult, religious, occult or paranormal, genre fiction (formula romances, science fiction, or westerns), or arts and crafts manuscripts. Send query with an outline, the first three chapters, and an SASE.

Advice to new authors: "Be published in distinguished literary journals."

WHITE PINE PRESS
Contact: Bree Bishop
Address: 10 Village Square, Fredonia, NY 14063
Phone: (716) 672-5743
Category: Fiction
Publisher's Notes on First Books: White Pine Press published one first book last
   year through the White Pine Press New American Voices Series. Recent first-
   book titles include *Where This Lake Is*, Jeff Lodge.

Advice to new authors: Do a standard query along with a biography and sample
writing (two to three chapters). The White Pine Press New American Voices
Series was established in 1996 in response to dramatic changes in the book industry that made it more difficult for first-time novelists to find a publisher. We
believe that our literary heritage must continue to grow and that it must be vast
enough to encompass the tremendous variety of writing from the Americas. Readers must be given the opportunity to hear vibrant, new voices. It is the intent of the
series to present first novels that not only entertain but also offer insights into our
world and ourselves.

Publishers Favorable to Unpublished First-Book Manuscripts

By Genre

Children's Literature
Milkweed Editions

Fiction
Alfred A. Knopf
Alyson Publications
Arcade Publishing
Avon Books
Ballantine Books (a Division of Random House Inc.)
Beacon Press
Blue Star Productions (a Division of Bookworld, Inc.)
Branden Publishing Co., Inc.
Brookline Books
Calyx Books

Center Press
Champion Books
Chronicle Books
Cleis Press
Confluence Press Inc.
Counterpoint
Dancing Jester Press
Dante University of America Press, Inc.
David R. Godine, Publisher
The Ecco Press
Eighth Mountain Press
Faber & Faber, Inc.
Firebrand Books
Four Walls Eight Windows
Frederic C. Beil, Publisher, Inc.
Graywolf Press
Hanging Loose Press
Hard Press Inc.
Milkweed Editions
Naiad Press, Inc.
New Victoria Publishers
Owl Creek Press
Press Gang Publishers
Seven Stories Press
St. Martin's Press
W.W. Norton
White Pine Press

Nonfiction
Alfred A. Knopf
Alyson Publications
Arcade Publishing
Avon Books
Ballantine Books (a Division of Random House)
Beacon Press
Blue Star Productions (a Division of Bookworld, Inc.)
Branden Publishing Co., Inc.
Brookline Books
Calyx Books
Center Press
Champion Books

Chronicle Books
Cleis Press
Confluence Press Inc.
Counterpoint
Dancing Jester Press
Dante University of America Press, Inc.
David R. Godine, Publisher
The Ecco Press
Eighth Mountain Press
Faber & Faber, Inc.
Firebrand Books
Four Walls Eight Windows
Frederic C. Beil, Publisher, Inc.
Graywolf Press
Milkweed Editions
Naiad Press, Inc.
New Victoria Publishers
Press Gang Publishers
Seven Stories Press
St. Martin's Press
W.W. Norton

Poetry
Arcade Publishing
Beacon Press
Calyx Books
Center Press
Champion Books
Confluence Press Inc.
Copper Canyon Press
Dancing Jester Press
Dante University of America Press, Inc.
The Ecco Press
Eighth Mountain Press
Firebrand Books
Four Walls Eight Windows
Graywolf Press
Hanging Loose Press
Hard Press Inc.
Milkweed Editions
New Victoria Publishers
Owl Creek Press

Press Gang Publishers
W.W. Norton

Short Fiction
Champion Books
Chronicle Books
Confluence Press Inc.
Counterpoint
Dancing Jester Press
Hanging Loose Press
Hard Press Inc.
Owl Creek Press

FIRST BOOK AMERICAN CLASSICS

Emily Dickinson

Poems
Boston: Roberts Brothers, 1890

The poems of Emily Elizabeth Dickinson (1830-1886) suggest hidden meanings that are never boldly revealed, and her life, appropriately, holds at its heart a mystery that has never been plucked out. Her world was Amherst, Massachusetts, where her father, who dominated his family, was a man of considerable importance. She was well educated for her time and locality, and for the first 24 years of her life enjoyed the usual social activity of a small college town.

In 1854, she visited Washington and Philadelphia, where she may possibly have fallen in love with a married man. Certainly thereafter she drifted further and further into seclusion. Her time was occupied with family duties and with the writing of poetry. Although she wrote hundreds of poems, she published only a handful during her lifetime. The first collection of them was brought out after her death, by two friends, Mabel Loomis Todd and Thomas Wentworth Higginson, to whom she had shown them. Although this and the second volume they edited finally brought Dickinson the public she had never known during her lifetime, Higginson's editing seriously misrepresented her art: In an effort to tame what he considered to be unorthodoxies of rhyme, meter, and even language, Higginson had altered Dickinson's texts.

Jack London

The Son of the Wolf. Tales of the Far North
Boston: Houghton Mifflin, 1900

No other American man of letters crowded into 40 years so much adventure and activity as Jack London (1876-1916). The illegitimate son of an Irish astrologer named Chaney, the boy received his early education primarily on the waterfront of Oakland, California. At age 16, he owned his own sloop and was the hard-drinking Prince of the Oyster Pirates, a dangerous profession. On his seventeenth birthday, he signed on to a sealer as an able-bodied seaman for a year's cruise in the North Pacific. Ashore again, he took to the road as a hobo and toured the eastern states.

Thirty days in a New York State jail gave London time to realize that he was too smart to spend his life that way. He returned to Oakland, went to high school, and read widely, especially in the socialist philosophers. In August 1896, he entered the University of California—and left it five months later.

Next he went to the Klondike in the Gold Rush of 1897, and nearly died of scurvy. Unable to find work on his return to California, he turned to writing. *The Son of the Wolf*, drawn from his Alaskan experiences, was published within two years and thereafter he had no trouble selling as much as he could write—50 volumes in 18 years. The brutality of his material, the vividness of his stories, the socialist dream he followed, won him wide popularity. He is said to have earned more than $1 million, all of which he spent.

Always restless, London visited Europe and was a correspondent for the Russo-Japanese and the Mexican wars. His first marriage ended in divorce. With his second wife he traveled in the West Indies and the South Pacific Islands. He then settled in California, where he poured money and energy into his ranch. His health began to crack, and in November 1916, he died of an overdose of morphine.

Theodore Dreiser

Sister Carrie
New York: Doubleday, Page, 1900

Long before his death, Theodore Dreiser (1871-1945) had become one of the legendary figures of American letters and a center of controversy.

Born in Indiana of German parents, he was brought up in an atmosphere of religious intolerance. The future novelist attended Indiana University for a year and then went into business in Chicago. When he was 21, he decided to become a journalist and worked, off and on, on newspapers and magazines in Chicago, St. Louis, New York, and Philadelphia from 1892-1934.

The struggle that Dreiser waged for acceptance of his realistic depiction of life began with his first book, *Sister Carrie*. Declined by Harper's, the manuscript was accepted by Doubleday, Page. Mrs. Doubleday is said to have insisted that it not be published, and Dreiser to have demanded that the firm honor its contract. The book was published, in an edition of some 1,000 copies: 129 were sent out for review, 465 were sold, and 423 copies were remaindered.

Dreiser's fight for freedom of expression and of opinion did not end with *Sister Carrie*. In 1914 *The Genius* and in 1925 *An American Tragedy* met with attack and censorship. Dreiser's pro-Russian and anti-British point of view was also subject to intense criticism. Nevertheless, his insistence upon independence for the writer was an important factor in the development of 20th-century literature.

Willa Cather

April Twilights
Boston: Richard G. Badger, The Gorham Press, 1903

Cather published her first poem, a derivative effort entitled "Shakespeare," while she was a freshman at the University of Nebraska. The early and exploratory poetry of the young, star-struck devotee of literature included translations of Horace, Anacreon, and Heine. Some of her early work was published with the pseudonyms John Esten, John Charles Asten, or Clara Wood Shipman. These last names were used for poems published in *The Library*, a Pittsburgh literary magazine that Cather edited; the poems were perhaps written to fill white space in the magazine.

Most of the poems included in *April Twilights* were written from 1900 to 1902 when she was solidifying her relationship with Isabella McClung (from 1901 until her move to New York in 1906, Cather lived in the McClung household, discomforting Isabella's parents, brothers, and sisters). Although she began to come into her own as an authentic writer during this period, Cather found most of her early poetry (and her first stories) irredeemable, and republished little of it. She brought out a new edition of *April Twilights* in 1923, removing 13 poems from the original edition and adding 12 new ones. In fact, she so disliked her first book that at one point she bought up all the copies she could find and destroyed them. In 1925 she said, "I do not take myself seriously as a poet."

William Carlos Williams

Poems
Rutherford, N.J.: [Printed for the Author by Reid Howell], 1909
The Lily Library, Indiana University, Bloomington, Indiana

Poems is a delicate, pseudo-Victorian pamphlet, lovingly designed by William's beloved older brother Edgar. Its 22 pages were published locally by the job printer Reid Howell of Rutherford, N.J., a friend of William's father, and the first printing was a disaster, full of typographical and spelling errors. It was destroyed (except for two copies; one of them, annotated by Williams and his father, is now housed at the University of Pennsylvania).Williams later reminisced about this first printing and the Penn copy:

> The local journeymen must have a tough time of it, never having set up anything of the sort in their lives, because when I saw the first finished volume I nearly passed out. I've still got the thing in my trunk in the attic: about half errors—like the Passaic River in its relationship to the sewage of that time. I notice, by looking over the disastrous first issue (which never appeared), that it bears the markers of Pop's corrections and suggestions all over it— changes most of which I adopted. Poor Pop, how he must have suffered.

The second printing sold for 25 cents (only four of the 100 copies printed were sold at Garrison's stationary store in Rutherford). Williams gave nine or 10 copies to friends and relatives; the rest were stored by the stationer and "inadvertently burned after they had reposed 10 years or more on a rafter under the eaves of his old chicken coop." As of 1968, only nine copies had been located by Williams's bibliographer, Emily Mitchell Wallace. In publishing his first volume himself, Williams joined a long list of self-publishers, which included his friend Ezra Pound, who had published his own first book, *A Lume Spento*, in Venice the previous year. The original printer's estimate for *Poems* was $32.45. Williams also paid Elkin Matthews for the publication in London of his second volume, *The Tempers* (1913), which was introduced by Pound with this prophetic line: "God forbid that I should introduce Mr. Williams as a cosmic force."

Gertrude Stein

Three Lives. Stories of the Good, Melanctha, and the Gentle Lena
New York: The Grafton Press, 1909

Gertrude Stein (1874-1946), the most controversial writer of her generation, was born in Pennsylvania and grew up in California. During her youth in San Francisco, Stein read voraciously in Mechanics Library's collection of 17th- and 18th-century English literature. (As for the dawning 20th-century literature, Gertrude Stein helped invent it.) At Radcliffe, which she left in 1897 without taking a degree, she studied psychology with William James. She next studied medicine for four years at Johns Hopkins, again without taking a degree. Her distaste for examinations may not be without bearing upon the state of mind that produced her mature literary style.

Gertrude Stein really found herself when in 1903 she went with Alice B. Toklas to live in Paris. There she made friends, enemies, and disciples among artists and literary men, natives and expatriates. Her collection of paintings by contemporary artists who were not yet popular with collectors was astutely gathered. Young American writers, including Hemingway, were inspired by her encouragement. Except for a lecture tour of the United States in 1934, she remained in France, even during the dangerous days of World War II.

In writing *Three Lives*, the most traditional of her books, Stein said she was influenced by Flaubert a little, and "because the realism of the people who did realism before was a realism of trying to make people real. I was not interested in making people real, but in the essence, or as a painter would call it a value. One cannot live without the other...the Cezanne thing I put into words came in *Three Lives*." *Three Lives* does not look much like anything else Gertrude Stein wrote. She financed its publication herself, and it was very much just the beginning. Her writing has been hailed as fundamental to an understanding of advanced contemporary art, praised as a fertilizing influence on more intelligent writers, and denounced as a racket. *Three Lives*, her first book, presents the reader with no problem in communication.

Robert Frost

A Boy's Will
London: David Nutt, 1913

The 39-year-old Robert Frost's first book, *A Boy's Will* (1913), was not published in New York, but in England, and by the first publisher he approached. The first copy from the press of David Nutt was spirited off by Ezra Pound, who used it to advance Frost's career, writing a long and positive review of the book for Harriet Monroe's *Poetry* magazine, and passing the book and a copy of his review on to Yeats, who was later to entertain the two with stories by candlelight.

A Boy's Will was actually Frost's second publication; it had been preceded by a 20-page pamphlet, *Twilight*, containing five poems, which Frost had printed in 1894 by a job printer in Lawrence, Massachusetts. Only two copies were printed: Frost destroyed one of them after his marriage proposal had been rebuffed by his eventual wife, Elinor White. The surviving copy, originally given to Mrs. Frost, is now owned by the Clifton Waller Barrett Library of the University of Virginia.

Frost chose to reprint only one of the five poems, "The Butterfly," 20 years later in *A Boy's Will*. Probably a little more than 1,000 copies were printed of *A Boy's Will*, but of the original first issue and first binding of pebbled clothe, there were less than 300 copies.

Part 5

"What Lovest Well Remains, What Lovest Well is Thy True History": More Writers on Their First Books

Faith and First Fiction

—Sadi Ranson

The offices of Conde Nast where I began my career in publishing have long, curving hallways, with offices off to the side, where editors sit fashionably dressed, moody, and always overworked. The usual hours, when I worked there at 17 years old, were something like 7:30 a.m. to late at night, depending on the day. Moments of respite came when we left at 5 p.m.

My first assignment was to read the "slush," the unsolicited manuscripts that hopeful writers had sent (kissing the envelope before popping it in the post box) addressed to the features editors.

I remember those summers, reading slush, trying to determine what was "good." It struck me then that almost everything had some redeeming quality. I was too much of a socialist in my youth, and I found the good in everything. So what if it wasn't original, it was well crafted, it was something new, and so on. To my knowledge, during my time there, we did not accept a single unsolicited manuscript. If memory serves, the manuscripts we did publish were always solicited or "agented," sent in by aggressive New York agents who pushed hard for their clients. As a young writer, it was depressing to think that a writer of talent would receive nothing more than a curt form letter in return for years of work. Still, I realize now that it is unreasonable, impossible, for every manuscript to get a personal response. This is the domain of M.F.A. programs in Creative Writing; this is the job of a teacher.

Years later, I read fiction for C. Michael Curtis at the *Atlantic Monthly.* On average, I suppose we received somewhere between 30 and 40 unsolicited manuscripts each day. If you factor in the agents, then there were more. The difference here was, it was my job to read a manuscript, and return it to the editor with a two-paragraph report detailing:

What is it about?

Should we/should we not publish it and why?

These reports, of which I kept copies, are brief and to the point. What I learned from C. Michael Curtis, and what I retain, is that if I am still thinking about a manuscript—its images, phrasing, characters, plot—if these are still with me a month from now, then indeed the manuscript merits serious consideration. Few were this affecting. But some were. And those that lodged in my temporal lobe, teasing me with their words, their snapshot images, were published.

Unlike so many publishers, the *Atlantic Monthly* does publish work that comes in over the transom—unsolicited—and often there were gems amongst this work. Writers who would later become well known: John Sayles, Joyce Carol Oates, E. S. Goldman, Tobias Wolff, and Heidi Jon Schmidt have all published at the *Atlantic Monthly*. These were "Atlantic Firsts." It is remarkable when one considers that the *Atlantic Monthly* receives some 15,000 manuscripts annually, all of which do get read.

Two years ago I started a publishing imprint that I named Lumen Editions. The name Lumen, a measure of light, derived from what I determined to be the mission of the house: to shed light on formerly unexplored corners of the world, to present things in a new way, to shine a brilliant light on new, younger, previously unpublished authors. To illuminate, and how brightly. This was not a philosophical ideal; we did not see it as a public service. But rather, as something that needed to be done.

We publish first fiction, first collections of short stories, and, yes, even poetry (gosh!). In the beginning, I was told this could never work. The naysayers who said, "it won't sell. Stories don't sell. Translations—who cares? And poetry?" Perhaps I was crazy, but it has served me well.

Presently, we publish between 10 and 15 new titles each year. At least three or four of these titles are by writers who have never been published, or have never been published in the English language. The media—the *New York Times Book Review,* the *Washington Post, Publishers Weekly,* all of the usual suspects—have given us tremendous support, allotting full-page reviews for our modest soft covers by first-time authors, and selecting one of them as among the best books of 1996. Three of our books went back to press within the first seven months of publication. We sold out our initial print run.

Those naysayers should sit back down and rethink their bleak vision of first fiction.

Publishing first fiction and succeeding is not about arrogance and being able to say "I told you so." It is about reading a book, having it affect you as an editor—so much so that you think about it for days, weeks, months after you first read it. Trust that instinct. Trust that if it impacted you, no matter how "unknown" the author, that this books merits being published. This is how I make publishing decisions. There's no science to it. It is instinctual, elemental, and pure. And in large part, it's about faith.

I once told someone that publishing is a ministry of sorts—the salaries are pitiful when one factors in the amount of time and work, yet it is a passion one cannot stay away from. Every project, every new book, becomes an obsessive love affair that you are determined to make work. You think about it late at night. You convince others of its worth. It often (though not always) changes your life. You hope it affects other readers the same way. You go to work, you read, you look for something good. Inspiring. The book that presents the elusive Other. Like a Jesuit or a nun, you wear too much black, you flog yourself, and you despair when a book doesn't make its mark and is instead pulled into the vortex of thousands of other books published each year. You pray. You keep your faith. You know there is undiscovered talent out there and you know that you will find it. The reward is in that First Fiction. It is the hope that we hold out that not all talent has been discovered—because we know there is more than this.

WRITERS ON THEIR OWN FIRST BOOKS

"Try Even Those Places You Are Doubtful About"

—Roberta Allen

Roberta Allen, whose new book, *Certain People,* was published in 1997 by Coffee House Press in their Coffee-To-Go Short Story Series, spent a year sending around her first story collection, *The Traveling Woman,* to small presses before it was accepted by Vehicle Editions, a one-woman press. She'd been aware of Vehicle for several years and submitted to them because they had beautiful books and had published Alex Katz and some poetry books. She was introduced to her Vehicle editor at a party for Gregory Corso's photographs. "She'd already decided to take my book but hadn't told me yet. When he introduced me, she had this big smile," Ms. Allen says, and adds, "She's the one who convinced me to put drawings in the book. I wasn't going to do it—this was my first literary experience and I wanted it to be pure." She laughs, "I drew 52 little drawings in one weekend and we used some of those. Now, I always include drawings." Ms. Allen says that the hardest part was organizing the stories: "It took me a year to find the sequence."

Ms. Allen advises writers to keep trying, since editors change. "Try even the places that you're doubtful about. It's important to keep the book around. There are certain times for certain books and this moment may not be your book's moment." Clarice LeSpector and Marguerite Duras are Ms. Allen's favorite authors, "but I don't know what was their first book or their tenth," she says.

Roberta Allen's first book was a collection of stories, The Traveling Woman *(Vehicle Editions). In addition* to Certain People, *her latest books include* Fast Fiction: Creating Fiction in Five Minutes *(Storyline Press). She teaches at NYU, The Writer's Voice, and The New School in New York City.*

"Spend All the Time You Can"

—Andrea Barrett

Andrea Barrett reveals that *Lucid Stars* really wasn't her first book. Largely self-taught, she'd spent seven years on a novel. "I couldn't write a sentence or a paragraph when I got started. I just kept scribbling and scribbling away," she says.

In 1984 or '85, she went to Bread Loaf Writer's Conference with "a story for class and a novel in my purse." Nicholas Delbanco asked her if she had anything else and out came the novel. He told her she was a pretty good writer but that she should throw it out and move on, because she'd been learning to write with that novel. "As a teacher, I realize how hard it is to say that," Ms. Barrett says. "But it was a relief to get rid of it and after that, *Lucid Stars* came quickly and happily."

Up at Bread Loaf, she'd met the literary agent, Wendy Well, who had asked Ms. Barrett to send something when she was finished. In 1987, *Lucid Stars* went to Jane Rosenman, who was then at Delacorte. The publisher was one of the first to start a paperback originals series, which they called Delta, and *Lucid Stars* was one of their launch books. So even though it was never in hardcover, "it had a little better chance," she says. "It was a pleasant experience, the book was pretty, and it had its little moment out in the world."

Ms. Barrett's all-time favorite first book is *Housekeeping,* by Marilyn Robinson. "*Learning By Heart,* by Margot Livesey really stuck with me." She also likes Brian Kitely's *Still Life With Insects* and Virginia Woolf's The *Voyage Out.* Kim Edward's collection of short stories, *Tales of the Fire King,* "is really strong. The stories are mature, assured, and finished," Ms. Barrett says, adding that many collections have only a handful of great stories because writers have rushed to get published. "But every story in Kim Edward's collection is great; the stories are devastating."

"It's hard advice, but spend all the time you can," Ms. Barrett says to the writers composing their novels and story collections. "It's easy to be frantic with the first book because it marks the transition between being known and being taken seriously. But, it's the last really secretive time with no one looking over your shoulder. As a teacher, it makes me sad to see them rushing," she says.

Andrea Barrett teaches in the M.F.A. Program for Writers at Warren Wilson College. Her first novel was Lucid Stars, *published with Delacorte in 1988, and her current collection of stories,* Ship Fever & Other Stories, *won the National Book Award in 1996.*

📖

"Wait Until the Last Minute"

—Sophie Cabot Black

Sophie Cabot Black's first book of poetry, *The Misunderstanding of Nature,* published by Graywolf, took a long while—two years—to be accepted, and in that time, she'd already started on her second book. She agonized over whether she should combine the two and decided she would. The agony was over how to make the arc work, since the first book had a distinct arc. Graywolf accepted the changed manuscript, which found its own structure—two-thirds of the old manuscript and one-half of the new that she'd already finished.

"I do believe in waiting and not worrying about the book not being taken. I know that's hard when you want to teach, but I'm glad I waited. I believe in waiting to the last minute to start, when the book has a strong, new, authoritative voice, a life without you," Ms. Cabot Black says. "When I teach first books, I choose breakthrough books that show the personality of the poet rather than just a collection of poems. Basically, keep putting the best poems in there."

Ms. Cabot Black took out 12 poems that were in the book originally and that had been published in magazines that she'd have loved to have listed in the beginning of the book, but they just didn't fit. Her favorite first books are *Sleeping with One Eye Open,* by Mark Strand; *The Lost*

Pilot, by James Tate; *The Colossus,* by Sylvia Plath; *Too Bright to See,* by Linda Gregg; and *Death of a Naturalist,* by Seamus Heaney.

Sophie Cabot Black's first collection of poems, The Misunderstanding of Nature, *received* The Norma Father Award *for a first book by the Poetry Society of America. She was recently a fellow at The Bunting Institute.*

"Read, Read, and Read"

—*T.C. Boyle*

The three best first novels that come to T. C. Boyle's mind, Thomas Pynchon's *V.*, John Fowles's *The Collector,* and Louise Erdrich's *Love Medicine,* certainly match the wild textures of his own fiction. "Read, read, and read," Mr. Boyle advises. "My first book was a collection of 17 stories, *Descent of Man.* All the stories had been published in magazines little and big. My agent, Georges Borchardt, who took me on the basis of these stories and a recommendation from one of his clients, sold the book to Peter Davison at Atlantic-Little, Brown. The first printing was 3,500. There was a second printing of 2,500. I was paid considerably less than $10,000. The year was 1979," Mr. Boyle says. After the success of two printings of his first book, Atlantic-Little, Brown & Co., as it was known then, published Mr. Boyle's first novel, *Water Music,* in 1982. "And for that, I was paid less than $10,000, but have recouped a bit of money since. Both books remain in print, both here and abroad."

T.C. Boyle's most recent novel is River Rock *(Viking, 1997). He teaches at the University of Southern California.*

"Do It"

—*Susan Cheever*

"Without question, my favorite first book is Genesis, God's first book," Susan Cheever says, laughing, while serious, having alighted upon a favorite book that is indeed that author's first. "Then, *War & Peace,* by Tolstoy," she adds, amazed and delighted to confirm that this epic was his first.

Ms. Cheever wrote her first book, *Looking For Work,* in France in 1978. "I never wanted to be a writer, it was my vow," she says. "I avoided it and at 35, I ended up at *Newsweek.* Then I quit and ran off to the south of France with somebody else's husband and sat down and wrote it. Nobody else spoke English." With all that pent-up energy and isolation writing in a French resort town in winter, Ms. Cheever wrote the book in a month, or two. It had been germinating without her knowing. "I felt so disoriented by it in those circumstances, I didn't believe I had written a novel," although she was in love with the story she wrote. "I went around counting the words in all the books to see if I had one," she says. They only had about 20 English books. Fortunately, they were mostly James M. Cain novels, which are short. "I was sophisticated in many ways, but innocent."

When asked what advice she'd give to writers approaching the publication of their first book, she says, "Duck." But, for those approaching the writing of their first books? "Do it."

Susan Cheever's nine books include Home Before Dark, Looking for Work, *and her forthcoming memoir,* Note Found in a Bottle: My Life as a Drinker. *All of her books have been published by Simon & Schuster. She teaches in the M.F.A. program at Bennington College.*

"A Worthy Book Will Eventually Find a Publisher"

—Stephen Dunn

Mr. Dunn's advice to writers is threefold. "One, try not to send out your manuscript as soon as you have enough poems for it to be considered a manuscript. Wait a while. As long as you can bear it. Your manuscript is likely to get better. Two, try not to get discouraged. I believe that a worthy book will eventually find a publisher. Three, write very good poems. Your poems, no one else's. Always be more concerned with furthering your work as opposed to furthering your reputation."

Mr. Dunn's experience with his first book, *Looking For Holes in the Ceiling,* best illustrates his advice. "It took me two years to realize that none of the poems I had written in graduate school (though I was a successful graduate student poet) should be in the manuscript. About three years of work went into the poems that eventually constituted the book.

It was rejected several times over a two-year period. It should have been. When finally I wrote a longish poem that became the book's centerpiece, the book was accepted by The University of Massachusetts Press. I believe I received a $500 advance. I was 35 when it was published in 1974."

Stephen Dunn's selected poems were published by W.W. Norton in 1996. He directs the writing program at Stockton State College.

"You Can't Just Sit Home"

—Elaine Equi

"Book contests have the function of independent films, today," says Elaine Equi, since they tend to support writers with a different view than the mainstream. The author of nine books of poetry, Ms. Equi says to try a lot of different things. Try contests and presses that don't have contests but who you think might like your work. Many think *Surface Tension* (Coffee House Press) is her first book since that brought her more widespread attention, but *Federal Woman,* in 1978, started the ball rolling.

A group of friends that were printers and visual artists interested in poetry, visual, and performing arts decided to put together chapbooks under the name Danaidus Press. They went around to readings in Chicago to hear what was being written. Ms. Equi had seen their chapbooks of Harry Crosby, which she loved, and, in turn, they liked her work. They told her they were tired of doing dead people, and asked her for *Federal Woman.*

"You can't just sit home and decide you have the gift of poetry," Ms. Equi says. "Get readings, be a known quantity. Build a resume with work in many different kinds of magazines, just get it out there and get your name around." She is sure that Allen Kornblum at Coffee House decided to look at her manuscript because he knew her name, not because he just started reading the poems. "Also, don't be afraid to change your manuscript, to polish and fine-tune the poems. It's one to two years between the time that Coffee House accepts my manuscript and publishes it, and in that time, the book will change."

She also recommends the wisdom of Harold Bloom in his book, *The Anxiety of Influence,* who states a case for all poems coming from other poems, "so poets shouldn't be worried that reading other poets will make them copy a style," Ms. Equi says.

Ms. Equi highly recommends the work of Lee Ann Brown, a poet in New York City, whose work has been published in magazines and who gives many readings. She's anticipating Brown's first book, which won a contest sponsored by Sun & Moon Press two years ago.

Elaine Equi's first book, Federal Woman, *was published by Danaidus Press. Her ninth collection,* Voice Over, *is from Coffee House Press.*

"The Most Deeply Private Joy"

—Carolyn Forche

A few of Carolyn Forche's list of impressive first books arrived on the scene without benefit of winning awards, including, *Disfortune,* by Joe Wenderoth; *The Tulip Sacrament,* by Annah Sobelman; and *Candy Necklace,* by Calvin Bendient, all recently published by Wesleyan. *Cities of Memory,* by Ellen Hinsey, which won the 1996 Yale Series of Younger Poets, and *The New Intimacy,* by Barbara Cully, which Ms. Forche selected for the National Poetry Series (Penguin, 1997) are the two standouts from award books. She was impressed, as well, by Ray DiPalma's National Poetry Series selection of *The Little Door,* by Jeff Clark (Sun & Moon, 1997) and remarks that a few of these writers are in their thirties and their manuscripts have made the rounds. "I'm reminded of the old adage: It takes years to become an overnight success."

Ms. Forche's first book, *Gathering the Tribes,* was the Yale Series of Younger Poets winner in 1975 when she was 25. "I had entered the manuscript in the previous year's competition, and when I received a handwritten, encouraging letter of rejection from the judge, Stanley Kunitz, I was naive enough to feel resigned rather than jubilant. I continued to revise the manuscript, but consigned it to a drawer. At the strong insistence of a friend, I typed a clean copy on my Smith Corona and sent it again on the deadline date. In the following months, I somehow forgot that I had entered, and so was worried when I received a telephone message from New

Haven, as I didn't know anyone there and associated Connecticut with insurance companies, that I very nearly did not return the call.

"Stanley Kunitz, who has perhaps done more for young poets than any other living poet, was immensely kind to me during the publication process, which I found interesting but also terrifying. I remember the day my Yale editor, Cathy Iino, accompanied me to a book-signing at the Grolier in Cambridge. Copies of the book were stacked in the windows. Inside, people were leafing through the book, people I didn't know— readers, most beloved of poets—but it was my first experience of having my poems read by people other than those to whom I had given them. Cathy Iino sensed my anguish, but told me that it was too late. I protested that I could buy all the copies and take them home. She laughed. "We'll print more."

"The most deeply private joy of my life had become, irrevocably, public."

Carolyn Forche's most recent book, The Angel of History, *was published by HarperCollins in 1994. She teaches at George Mason University.*

"A Pursuit of Art as Ruthless as the Pursuit of Experience"

—*Edward Hirsch*

"I, myself, have a sense of a book as a journey, a pilgrimage," says the poet, Edward Hirsch, whose first book, *For the Sleepwalkers,* also had a long journey to publication. His favorite first books are *White Buildings,* by Hart Crane, and *Harmonium,* by Wallace Stevens. "The process of the first book is long, moving through so many stages of progression and development," he says. "It covers a period of entire apprenticeship."

Mr. Hirsch first wrote poems in high school, but in 1976, at age 26, he wrote two poems that were better than any he'd written before, and that "sounded a note that I wanted to sound," he says. "Everything that went into *For the Sleepwalkers* came from that and stayed. It was the soil for the organic growth of poems that emerged in my thirties." A book should not be just the best hits, not just the best poems of poetic apprenticeship.

"The process of maturation is putting together the poems you like, but also, fused into a sum larger than its parts," he says, adding that Robert Frost said that if a book has 29 poems that the book, itself, is the thirtieth. "What one *wants* with a first book is a continual expansion and a radical coherence," he says.

Mr. Hirsch had a number of poems in magazines when, in 1978, he sent *For the Sleepwalkers* to Knopf, over the transom. Although it was easier back then to send an unsolicited manuscript of poetry to a major house, "it was not like it was wildly open," he contends. "They held it for a very long time, kept it for a year and a half, but they were enthusiastic about it. They reassured me many times that they wanted it. Alice Quinn was starting a poetry series there and said she wanted it. It was published as the fifth book of that series in 1981," he says. Knopf remains his publisher, although Alice Quinn moved on to edit poetry for the *New Yorker*. *For the Sleepwalkers* won both the Peter I. B. Lavan Younger Poet Prize from the Academy of American Poets and the Delmore Schwartz Award from New York University and was nominated for the National Book Critics Circle, an award Mr. Hirsch won for his second book, *Wild Gratitude.*

As for advice, Mr. Hirsch says, "Poetry comes out of poetry, not just from self-expression. Your experience in life is the gift of your material, but it's only a beginning. One needs to honor that material like your life because poetry is a vocation, a calling. Most books seem terrifically marred by inadequate means. What one wants from a first book is a pursuit of art as ruthless as the pursuit of experience, and intensity that shines."

Edward Hirsch teaches at the University of Houston. His first book, For The Sleepwalkers, *was published in 1981 with Knopf and reprinted in 1997 with Carnegie Mellon University Press. His newest collection,* The Lectures On Love, *is from Knopf in 1998.*

"The Importance of Friends to Support Both Art and Commerce"

—Marie Howe

Marie Howe's first book, *A Good Thief,* won the National Poetry series after being a finalist six times. She speaks of the great importance of a supportive network of friends—she had eight or nine—Tom Sleigh, Lucie Brock Broido, Stuart Dischell, among them. "We were all poets and part-time teachers in Cambridge," she says, so they used to call to remind each other of deadlines, as well as assist with the mailing of manuscripts when someone was too physically ill to follow through. "I'm a kind of tribal type, anyway," Ms. Howe says while making her point about the importance of writing friends to support both art and commerce.

"There were legendary stories we knew of writers always being runners-up in contests and we used to know all of them—you know, Denis Johnson for example, 13 times—and we would sit at cafe tables and repeat the eight names and numbers like mantras."

Ms. Howe has two things to share with writers approaching first-book publication. "The first thing that helped me was that I gave it to Tom Sleigh to read and he rearranged it from sections to an arc—didn't touch the poems, just the order—so that later I was sitting on the couch flipping through and sobbing because the book was suddenly revealed to me. I felt frightened and ashamed. Three places at once wanted it after that. I really think you go to the most exacting editor. It was like taking the cloth off the sculpture, undraping it, and I couldn't do it myself."

She laughs as she comes to the second helpful suggestion, as it eases the readers of manuscript competitions. She and Lucie Brock Broido decided to take the manuscripts out of the big black binders and go and have them made spiral bound. "It's such a pain to be eating and the pages flap closed in your lap. Spiral, you can open up and chew your sandwich at the same time."

Responding to the problem of a long wait to publication, Ms. Howe says that it really is better than publishing quickly. You keep writing more poems, changing that first book. "It's hard not to become attached, because it's like your union card," she says, but the farther away from it the better.

Her list of first books that "blew me away" are *Sweet Ruin,* by Tony Hoagland; *The Incognito Lounge,* by Denis Johnson; *Imaginary Timber,* by Jim Galvin; and *What A Kingdom It Was,* by Galway Kinnell. Galvin's book was important to her when she was first starting to write and Hoagland and Kinnell are "wholey, utterly original and necessary." She says that while always a fan of Kinnell's books, it was only last year that she got her hands on his first book and it riveted her. "I couldn't stop talking about it for four months. Everyone should read that as a book. It's deeply inspiring."

Marie Howe's most recent book is What the Living Do *(W.W. Norton, 1997). She teaches at Sarah Lawrence College.*

"First Book Is First World"

—Liam Rector

"My advice would fundamentally be what the actor, director, and *bon vivant*, Orson Welles said in the old Gallo wine ads: No Wine Before It's Time. First book is First World. First book is first child," Mr. Rector states. "Wait, the first book is and remains first-born. It should be more than a mere collection and more than an assemblage of greatest hits. First books should have found and executed their voice, their voices, amidst the inevitable historical boarding house exorcising of influences and homage."

But he warns the writer not to be, as he puts it, an ungrateful mutt. "A first book should have its own arc. Writers rightly have sentimentia about their first book, as one lives one's whole life with it—there staring, there voicing. Writers who denounce their first books as juvenilia came too quickly, and should be shot. Don't let this happen to you, lest you dwell in juvenilia as a Big Baby Sibling, an *idee fixe forever*," he says, emphasizing anew, "First Book is First World."

Mr. Rectors first collection of poetry, *The Sorrow of Architecture*, had a troubling start. He sent it to about 15 presses and it was accepted early on by a press that went under before it could publish the book. He started again. "When I received a letter of acceptance from Dragon Gate Press, an ambiguous letter which I didn't take to be an acceptance, I found out the book was also being considered as a finalist at Knopf. Knopf balked, and I went with Dragon Gate, a fine literary press by poet Gwen Head, run out of Port Townsend, Washington. *The Sorrow of Architecture* was beautifully designed by Scott Walker. I got my say on the cover photograph and the type size, and I was and remain happy with *The Sorrow Of Architecture* as First World."

The poet and director of Bennington Writer's Workshop, Liam Rector offers a partial list of 30 favorite books. *Pruffock,* by T.S. Eliot, *Howl,* by Allen Ginsberg, and *Open House*, by Theodore Roethke head the list. The first books of Donald Justice, Hedy Lamarr, Robinson Jeffers, Robert McDowell, Lucie Brock Broido, Linda Gregg, Mark Strand, David Huddle, and Ai also appear on this varied list.

Liam Rectors most recent book is American Prodigal *(Story Line Press). He is the founder and Director of the Writing Seminars at Bennington College.*

📖

"Literary Magazines Are the Lifeblood"

—*Scott Russell Sanders*

Although his very first book was about D. H. Lawrence and came from his doctoral dissertation, it is "really an anomaly because it's the only criticism book I've written out of 18." His start as a writer came with the publication in 1983 by William Morrow of *Wilderness Plots*, a collection of short stories that arose out of research he was doing for a novel. The novel was eventually published, but the collection came together first. "They were like outtakes on a film," Dr. Sanders says. "I had finished four unpublished books of fiction and after *Wilderness Plots* was published, the other three followed." The first helped him break loose and consider the possibility of publishing the others.

A few nonfiction pieces had been published before Dr. Sanders entered *Paradise Bombs* in the AWP Award for Creative Nonfiction. Because the submission is anonymous, his past publications were not of importance. "On the other hand, *Wilderness Plots* made it easier to get my other fiction published," including the novel it had interrupted. "Winning the AWP Award was very important in the sense that this new kind of writing that I had started in the last couple of years might be worth pursuing," he says. "The world took small notice of it. The essays reinforced one another and created a whole book." The AWP Award helped attract attention from magazine editors for more essays.

In offering advice to writers concerning the publication of their first books, Dr. Sanders recognizes two major paths. The first is contests, "which are fruitful if you win and does not require your having published anything beforehand." The second path is traditional. "I believe literary magazines are the lifeblood, and the best writers get their training by publishing in them and by gradually building a body of work. It's a worthy and viable way to publish that first book.

"The mistake is to put all your energy into getting that first book published," he says. "And the writer may be right in believing that it is utterly worthy. But even if you have no luck in getting it published, if you believe deeply enough in yourself to keep on writing that second and third and fourth book, you will grow as a writer." Instead of the book, "believe in your talent."

Scott Russell Sanders names Henry David Thoreau's *A Week on the Concord and Merrimack Rivers* and Walt Whitman's first poetry book *Leaves of Grass* as his favorite first books.

Scott Russell Sanders is Distinguished Professor of English at Indiana University. His first collection of stories, Wilderness Plots, *was published by William Morrow and his first collection of essays,* The Paradise of Bombs, *won the AWP Award in Creative Nonfiction. His latest book,* Writing From the Center, *won the 1996 Great Lakes Book Award.*

FAVORITE FIRST BOOKS OF WRITERS: A LISTING

Cathryn Alpert: *Girl Interrupted,* Susanna Kaysen; *Reeling and Writhing,* Candida Lawrence; *The Other America,* Michael Harrington

Andrea Barrett: *Housekeeping,* Marilyn Robinson; *Learning by Heart,* Margot Livesey; *The Voyage Out,* Virginia Woolf; *Tales of the Fire,* Kim Edward

Douglas Bauer: *Principles of American Nuclear Chemistry: A Novel,* Thomas McMahon; *A Bigamist's Daughter,* Alice McDermott; *Housekeeping,* Marilyn Robinson

Sven Birkerts: *Buddenbrookf,* Thomas Mann; *V,* Thomas Pynchon; *The Leopard,* Lampedusa

Sophie Cabot Black: *Sleeping With One Eye Open,* Mark Strand; *The Lost Pilot,* James Tate; *Colossus,* Sylvia Plath; *Too Bright to See,* Linda Gregg; *Death of a Naturalist,* Seamus Heaney

Laurel Blossom: *Dance Script With Electric Ballerina,* Alice Fulton; *The Ocean Inside Kenyi Takezo,* Rick Noguchi; *Out of Canaan,* Mary Stuart Hammond

T. C. Boyle: *V,* Thomas Pynchon; *The Collector,* John Fowles; *Love Medicine,* Louise Erdrich

Melanie Braverman: *Beginning with O,* Olga Brumas; *Maps to Anywhere,* Bernard Cooper; *The Virgin Suicides,* Jeffrey Eugendeis

Nick Carbó: *White Elephants,* Reetika Vazrani; *Likely,* Lisa Coffman; *Ismalia Eclipse,* Khaled Mattawa

Ron Carlson: *This Side of Paradise,* F. Scott Fitzgerald

Susan Cheever: Genesis; *War & Peace,* Tolstoy

Steven Cramer: *Lyrical Ballads,* William Wordsworth & Samuel Taylor Coleridge; *Some Trees,* John Ashbery; *Silence in the Snowy Fields,* Robert Bly; *Stop-Time,* Frank Conroy

Eric Darton: *Two Little Trains,* Margaret Wise Brown; *A Boy's Will,* Robert Frost; *In Our Time,* Ernest Hemingway; *Counter-Statement,* Kenneth Burke

Toi Derricotte: *A Street in Bronzeville,* Gwendolyn Brooks; *Howl,* Allen Ginsberg; *Colossus,* Sylvia Plath

Mark Dory: *Autobiography of a Face,* Lucy Grealy; *Refuge,* Terry Tempest Williams

Susan Dowd: *Here We Are In Paradise,* Tony Farley; *In The Garden of the North American Martyrs,* Tobias Wolff; *Same Place, Same Things,* Tim Gautreaux

Stephen Dunn: *Harmonium,* Wallace Stevens; *The Lost Pilot,* James Tate; *Heart's Needle,* W. D. Snodgrass

Thomas Sayers Ellis: *Death of a Naturalist,* Seamus Heaney; *Annotations,* John Keene; *Invisible Man,* Ralph Ellison

Elaine Equi: *The Anxiety of Influence,* Harold Bloom

Carolyn Forche: *Disfortune,* Joe Wenderoth; *The Tulip Sacrament,* Annah Sobolman; *Candy Necklace,* Calvin Bendient; *Cities of Memory,* Ellen Hinsey; *New Intimacy,* Barbara Cully; *The Little Door,* Jeff Clark

Lynn Freed: *Lost in Translation,* Eva Hoffman; *My Old Sweetheart,* Susana Moore

John Haines: *The Sleepwalkers,* Herman Broch

Shelby Hearon: *Mysteries of Pittsburgh,* Michael Chabon; The *Movie Goer,* Walker Percy

Amy Hempel: *Edisto,* Padgett Powell; *The Ice at the Bottom of the World,* Mark Richard

Robert Hershon: *Delores: The Alpine Years,* Pansy Maurer-Alvarez; *The Business of Fancy Dancing,* Sherman Aletie; *The Very Stuff,* Stephen Beal; *Air Pocket,* Kimiko Hahns

Edward Hirsch: *White Buildings,* Hart Crane; *Harmonium,* Wallace Stevens

Jane Hirshfield: *Views of Jeopardy,* Jack Gilbert; *North and South,* Elizabeth Bishop; *Leaves of Grass,* Walt Whitman

Tony Hoagland: *Airships,* Barry Hannah; *Keeping Still Mountain,* John Engel; *Incognito Lounge,* Denis Johnson

Marie Howe: *Incognito Lounge,* Denis Johnson; *Sweet Ruin,* Tony Hoagland; *Imaginary Timber,* Jim Galvin; *What A Kingdom It Was,* Galway Kinnel

David Lehman: *Meditations in An Emergency,* Frank O'Hara; *Some Trees,* John Ashbery; *Harmonium,* Wallace Stevens; *Ommateum,* A. R. Ammons; *Lucky Jim,* Kingsley Amis; *Ko, or A Season On Earth,* Kenneth Koch

Philip Levine: *Leaves of Grass,* Walt Whitman; *Harmonium,* Wallace Stevens

Carole Maso: *At The Bottom of The River,* Jamaica Kincaid; *The River,* Jayne Anne Philips

Uison Mattison: *Golden State,* Frank Bidart

Richard McCann: *After Leaving,* Jane Rhyes; *The Body and His Dangers,* Alan Barnet; *Tell Me a Riddle,* Tillie Olsen

Jill McCorkle: *The Heart is a Lonely Hunter,* Carson McCullers

Robert McDowell: *A Boy's Will,* Robert Frost; *Californians,* Robinson Jeffers; *The Sorrow of Architecture,* Liam Rector

N. Scott Momaday: *Blue Highways,* William Least Heat Moon

Carol Muske: *Letters from a Stranger,* Thomas James; *A Change of World,* Adrienne Rich; *Cooking for John,* Jon Anderson; *Presentation Piece,* Marilyn Hacker; *Winter Morning with Crow*, Clare Rossini

Robert Pinsky: *Prufrock & Other Observations,* T. S. Eliot; *Poems,* William Carlos Williams; *In The Blood,* Carl Phillips; *Little Star,* Mark Halliday; *The Key to the City,* Anne Winters

C. L. Rawlins: *Jacklight* (poetry), Louise Erdrich; *In The Wilderness: Coming of Age,* Kim Barnes; *Pleasure of Believing,* Anastasia Hobbet.

Liam Rector: *Prufrock & Other Observations,* T. S. Eliot; *Howl,* Allen Ginsberg; *Open House,* Theodore Roethke

Scott Russell Sanders: *A Week on the Concord and Merrimack Rivers,* Henry David Thoreau; *Leaves of Grass,* Walt Whitman

Gerald Stem: *Views of Jeopardy,* Jack Gilbert; *Poems,* Alan Dugan; *Vesper Sparrows,* Deborah Digges; *Catch 22,* Joseph Heller; *Too Bright to See,* Linda Gregg

David Trinidad: *Idols,* Dennis Cooper; *Howl,* Allen Ginsberg; *To Bedlam and Part Way Back,* Anne Sexton

Part
6

In Your Own Hands: Making Your First Book a Success

Introduction

—Ruth Greenstein

There comes a time for most writers when their work seems to be done: Their first book is in the final stages of production, and they don't quite know what to do with themselves. Instead of feeling relieved, they anxiously imagine all the things that might be going on—or going wrong—with their book. At the publishing house, the editor steps back as the publicist comes to the fore. Where does the author fit in?

After all the hard work that goes into writing a good book and getting it published, writers who then sit back and leave the rest to their publishers are doing themselves a great disservice. The fact is that most first books don't receive a lot of promotional attention from their publishers. Terry McMillan discovered this early on, and decided to take matters into her own hands. She made her first book a success, and so can you. Following are just a few of the things you can do.

Know your publisher's game plan

Find out as much as you can about your publisher's plans for your book. How many copies are they printing? How many do they hope to sell? Are they producing bound galleys? Do they have a budget for advertisements or a book tour? If not, negotiate. Are they willing to help you make arrangements and to split the expenses with you? Are you willing to cover certain expenses yourself?

Start early

Well before your book is published, you should develop an action plan and timetable for promoting it. (See the Promotional Action Plan Worksheet included in this section.) Set aside some money for your promotional activities. Will you need to hire someone to type mailing lists? Do you want to have postcards printed up, or to hire an outside publicist?

Prepare your pitch

How can you make your book stand out from the crowd? Is there an unusual story behind the writing of it? Is it topically related to a current events story? Is there something relevant in your own life story that may spark peoples' attention?

Summon your forces

What writers do you know or admire who might be willing to comment on your book? Do you have any media contacts who may be willing to help get the word out? Look at your resume—what schools and organizations have you been affiliated with that may help support your debut publishing "event"? What special interest groups might be interested in buying your book? Have you armed your publisher with this information?

Start locally

Talk to your local booksellers and librarians, and to organizations that sponsor literary events or that may be interested in you and your book. Let them know when your book is coming out. Find out if they'd like to host a reading, a talk, or a book party.

WHAT YOU'VE HEARD IS TRUE

It pays to invest

I cannot emphasize enough the importance of your investing in your work. Carole Maso recently purchased a full-page advertisement for her book *Aureole* in the *American Poetry Review*. Maso has an established reputation as a fiction writer, but with this book, she wanted to get the word out to poetry readers as well. And she wanted to do more for the book than her publisher was doing. Like many writers, Maso believes that her financial contributions toward promoting her work are a good investment—no different than an investment in a house or a car.

—J.S. 📖

Work with your publisher

Publishers are only too happy to have authors who are eager to promote themselves and their work. But when authors go off on their own without first speaking with their publicist, they may find themselves duplicating efforts, working at cross-purposes, and stepping on some very sensitive toes. Be smart: Meet with your publicist, and be sure to keep him or her continually apprised of your efforts.

Work with your agent

If you have an agent, use her or him! An agent's role is to represent your interests throughout the publishing process, not just when the book deal is being signed. Is your agent aware of and satisfied with the publication plans for your book? Who do they know who can help promote your work? If you have a new project in the works, when do they want to pitch it to the publisher?

Be mindful of timing

In today's book business, the unfortunate marketplace reality is that most booksellers will only keep hardcover books in stock for a few short months. Be mindful of this brief window of opportunity, and work aggressively with your publisher to keep your book alive throughout it. Then look ahead for ways of giving your book new life, such as submitting it for awards, printing a paperback edition, setting up additional public appearances, and so forth.

Final perspectives

Remember that regardless of how many copies your first book ultimately sells, it will move you ahead considerably in your craft. And when your second book comes out, you will have a new opportunity to sell your first book again.

Promotional Action Plan Worksheet

—Jason Shinder

Here is an outline of critical questions to ask your publisher as you assume responsibility for helping to promote your book and to maximize its readership and sales. As soon as a publisher has agreed to publish your book, you can begin collecting some of this information. In most cases, a promotional action plan should be in place six months before your book is scheduled to be published.

Catalogs

- ☐ Who is writing the catalog copy? What aspects of the book are they highlighting, and why?
- ☐ What is the deadline for catalog copy? Can I review the copy before the deadline?
- ☐ How much catalog space will my book receive? Will it include a photo of the cover? A photo of me?
- ☐ Will the copy include information about promotional plans, special sales offers, public events?
- ☐ When is the catalog being sent out and to whom?
- ☐ Can copies be sent to people on my mailing list?
- ☐ How many copies can I receive?

Cover Art and Copy

- ☐ Who is creating the cover art? Who is designing the cover? What aspects of the book are they highlighting, and why?
- ☐ What is the deadline for the final design?

📖 Will the cover be black-and-white, two-color, or four-color?

📖 Can I speak with the artist and/or designer?

📖 Can I review the cover before the deadline?

📖 Who is writing the cover copy? What is the deadline for the copy? Can I review the copy before the deadline?

Sales Meetings

📖 When will the book be introduced to the sales force and/or distributors? (Initial sales meetings are usually scheduled a season before the book is being published.)

📖 How will it be introduced? What will be the focus?

📖 Can I help out by speaking at a sales meeting or by securing advance comments on the book?

Special Sales

📖 What organizations might be interested in purchasing a quantity of books at a discount? (For instance, a book about the movies may be of interest at video stores and movie houses. A memoir about a swimmer may be of interest at health clubs and sporting goods stores.)

📖 Who will approach these organizations? When? How?

📖 Will a special sales package be developed?

Publicist

📖 Is a publicist being assigned to my book? When?

📖 Has the publicist read my book yet? Has he or she worked on similar books before?

📖 Can I meet with the publicist and review the promotional action plan? (If you are able to, consider hiring your own publicist. An independent publicist should be hired for a minimum of three months, beginning one month prior to publication. Be sure you and your publicist develop very specific objectives and strategies for achieving those objectives. Be sure you and your publicist work closely with your publisher. In some cases, hiring a publicist may help you leverage additional promotional support for your publisher. You may want to hire a publicist only under the condition that your publisher will then contribute to your promotional efforts.)

Blurbs

📖 Is the publisher soliciting blurbs for the book? When? 'From whom? (Most authors need at least two months to write a blurb. Give your publisher a list of people you think might comment on your book, and help contact those people you know.) What aspects of the book are they hoping the blurbs will address?

📖 What kinds of people are they approaching? Nationally celebrated writers? Regionally popular writers? Writers or experts associated with a specific subject or style?

Bound Galleys

📖 Are bound galleys being produced? When will they be ready? Will the galleys show the cover art? Will they include blurbs? How many copies are being printed? To whom are they being sent?

📖 Can copies be sent to people on my mailing list? (Develop a concise mailing list of key authors, book reviewers, and editors, especially those with whom you have some connection.)

📖 Will follow-up calls be made after the mailing?

📖 How many copies of the bound galleys can I receive?

Publication

📕 What is the bound book date? What is the official publication date? When will books arrive in stores? Are these dates firm, or is there a chance they will slip? Why?

📕 How many copies are being printed? If the publisher is printing hardcovers and paperbacks simultaneously, how many are being printed of each?

Sales

📕 How many copies has the book advanced (orders for the book placed prior to publication)?

📕 How many copies does the book need to sell to break even? By when?

📕 What will the book be priced at? (If the price of the book seems unusually high or low, ask the publisher to explain how they arrived at this price.)

Press Release

📕 Who is writing the press release?

📕 When is it being sent out? To whom?

📕 Can I review the copy before it is sent out?

📕 Will the release include blurbs? Cover art? An author photo?

📕 Are any special markets being targeted for the mailing?

📕 Will follow-up calls be made after the mailing?

📕 Will there be a special sales press release—one that offers a discount and includes an order form?

📕 Can I provide a mailing list?

📕 How many copies of the press release can I receive?

Press Kit

- Is a press kit being produced? When?
- What will the press kit include? (Press release, copy of book, author photo, special appeal letter?)
- Who will the press kits be sent to?
- Can I review the press kit before it is sent out?

Advertisements

- Will my book be advertised? Alone or with other books?
- When and where will the ads appear? How many ads will there be?
- Can I review the ads before they are finalized?
- If the publisher does not have a budget for ads, are they willing to split the costs with me? If I pay for running an ad, will the publisher design it for me? (Some small magazines will run book ads for free in exchange for offering the books at a special discount to its members or subscribers. Many magazines offer special ad rates to writers who are purchasing ad space for their own books.)

Postcards/Posters/Bookmarks

- Will the publisher be printing any promotional items to announce the book? When?
- How many are being printed and to whom will they be mailed?
- Can I review the items before they are printed?
- Will the items include blurbs? Cover art? Dates of upcoming events?
- If the publisher does not have a budget for promotional items, are they willing to split the costs with me?

Book Party

- Will the publisher be sponsoring a party for my book? When?
- Who will be invited? When will the invitations be mailed?

    📖 If the publisher does not have a budget for a book party, are they willing to split the costs with me?

Readings

    📖 Will the publisher be arranging readings for my book? When? Where?

    📖 Will I be reading alone or with other writers? Who?

    📖 How will the publisher promote these readings?

    📖 If I hire an outside events coordinator to arrange readings, will the publisher contribute to his or her fee? Will they promote the readings?

    📖 If I arrange readings on my own, will the publisher cover my travel expenses? Will they promote the readings?

    📖 Has the publisher confirmed that books will be available for sale at every reading?

Publicizing Your Novel

—Terry McMillan

Right after I learned that my publisher, Houghton Mifflin, wasn't going to take ads in the *New York Times* (among other places) for my first novel *Mama;* that they weren't going to be able to send me on the 20-city book tour I'd dreamed about; that my novel wouldn't form a pyramid in the (then) Scribner's window on Fifth Avenue in New York; that my chances of getting on *Good Morning America* and *The Oprah Winfrey Show* were slim to zero; and that the meager amount of money that had been allocated for publicity was too embarrassing to mention, I was disappointed and hurt, but more than anything, I felt I'd been misled by them. After all, hadn't my editor exclaimed his excitement over my book? And hadn't they sent me their booklet, "A Guide for Authors," telling me the various ways in which they would determine the most appropriate strategy for drawing attention to my book?

I found out that the most they were actually going to do was send out the standard media kit—a press release with my photo, a copy of the book, and any advance reviews—to reviewers and TV and radio producers. If they got a lead, they would follow it up with a phone call. More often than not, the people to whom they send the media kits already have a pile a mile high of just such kits, some of which never get opened, let alone read.

I learned quickly that this is standard operating procedure for most first novels, and even some second novels if the first one wasn't well received. Let me warn you now. Get used to hearing, "Don't expect much. This is just your literary debut." And get used to hearing, "Don't expect a review in the *New York Times Book Review* because chances are there won't be one. And if you get one, consider yourself lucky." And especially get used to hearing, "We can't. We wish we could, but we can't."

I had worked hard on my novel, and I wanted as many people as possible to know that it existed. I'd heard too many horror stories about first novels never being reviewed, never being available in bookstores. Most terrifying to me of all was the thought of being remaindered, reviewers panning my novel and thus, never selling enough copies of my book to see a royalty check. I didn't want to be one of those writers, and I also didn't want to spend another year as a freelance word processor for a law firm in Manhattan.

I didn't need long to realize that my publisher wasn't the only guilty one. Other friends whose first novels had also been accepted said, "My publisher's doing absolutely nothing to promote my book" and "My galleys were late and if I don't hear from the authors I've asked for blurbs in the next two weeks, the back of my book will be blank!" The question that came to my mind over and over was, "How can you expect to sell a product if no one's ever heard of it?"

If you happen to be one of the lucky ones and have published poetry or stories in all the right places, or established yourself writing nonfiction, or are "well-connected" (i.e., you know everybody who is anybody in the literary world), you might not have to be concerned about the attention your book is likely to get from your publisher. But if you're like me, and hundreds of other first novelists, who have few if any other publications to their credit and don't know anyone who may give them that fantastic blurb (three days before my deadline, of the 18 authors to whom I'd written, I received one blurb from Grace Paley, whom I'd never met), then you'll do well to do what I did: take matters into your own hands.

In July 1986 I found out just how little was going to be done to promote my book. My publication date was January 15, 1987. I had all kinds of books about all facets of writing, so I searched through them until I found one that dealt with promoting and publicizing books. Entitled *How to Get Happily Published,* it proved to be invaluable. A chapter called "Why and How to Be Your Own Best Sales Force" explained in detail the steps authors can take to drum up excitement, interest, and an audience for their books without feeling the least embarrassed. The book suggests that authors need not be intimidated by their publishers and that the best way to get them excited about your book is to "nag" them.

Let me say this now. If you have access to a computer, it'll make everything that much simpler, cheaper, and easier. Because I was a freelance word processor, I had access to one, but if you don't, there are many inexpensive word-processing services that can facilitate printing letters from multiple mailing lists. Your promotion and publicity campaign will be time consuming, so if you're not willing to sacrifice a few hours a day and some of your weekends, forget this notion. What will help is if you know an eager teenager, child, or lover who will help seal envelopes and even sign letters for you—or at least someone who'll do it for minimum wage! Most of my time was spent at the library, photocopying mailing lists, typing them into the computer, and merging the names to the letters I had written. (More about the letters follows.) How extensive your campaign becomes will determine how much time and money you'll spend. I sent out over 4,000 letters over a six-month period, and spent over $700. Most independent book publicists charge $3,000, and they basically end up doing the same thing you can do yourself.

The first thing I did was to tell my publicist (you will automatically be assigned a publicist by your publisher) that I was going to do everything I could to help promote my book; and that I would keep her apprised of my actions. She was delighted to hear this, as most publicists are, because it takes some of the burden of guilt off of them. So, during a heat wave in July, while all my friends were out sunbathing at the beach, I spent a week answering the questionnaire that all publishers send authors. *Take time to answer it,* because this may be the only opportunity you'll have to provide the publicity department with information that can help them zero in on your target audience. The more mailing lists and names of people you can give them, the less work you'll have to do in the long run. Included with the questionnaire will most likely be mailing labels on which the publishers asks you to provide names of people who you would like notified once your book is published. Not only did I go through my phone book, but also I picked names of authors, those I'd heard of and respected, from a listing in *A Directoy, of American Poets and Fiction Writers.* So what if E. L. Doctorow and Ann Beattie had never heard of me? By the time my book came out, they would.

Publishers periodically hold conferences with their sales representatives (the men and women who take your book around to the bookstores and try to get orders for it), at which they give a short synopsis of each of the books on the list for the upcoming season. You hope that the sales reps have read your book, that they like it and are excited about it, but you have no guarantee of this. Lots of times they haven't read it, even though at this meeting, they'll sit and listen to how the publisher wants to market each book. Editors never tell you all the details of this meeting, but if you can get on the good side of the sales reps your book will benefit. I got all their names and addresses (they live all over the United States because they work by regions), and I sent them all notes (on note cards), telling them that I hoped they liked my book and were excited by it.

I also told them how much I appreciated their efforts to secure a home in as many bookstores as possible for *Mama*. Although I never received any written responses, I was told by my editor and the publicity director how much the sales reps all appreciated my note.

I made up lists of my target audience. Because I'm black and a woman, I had to target groups right there. I spent much time in the library getting lists of all the black organizations in the United States. I also got a list of over 500 women's studies programs and a list of all black newspapers, magazines, and radio and TV programs. I knew I wanted all the black colleges and Afro-American studies programs to know about my novel, so I got listings of them too.

Since I had no guarantee that the sales reps would be enthusiastic about my book, I decided to write bookstores myself. Unenthusiastic sales reps can sometimes cause book buyers not to order your book, or encourage them to "wait and see." This usually means they'll wait to see what the prepublication reviewers, *Publishers Weekly, Kirkus Reviews, Library Journal*, and *Booklist,* have to say about your book before consulting the *American Book Trade Directory (ABTD),* which lists 25,500 bookstores, wholesalers, distributors, and bookstore chains (including the names of the buyers), alphabetically by state and city. I'm from Michigan, so I made a special effort to write down as many of the bookstores there as possible. Why? Because it's likely that the bulk of your initial sales will take place in the area you're from. Most of the bookstores are listed as "general," "antiquarian," "women's," Afro-American," etc., so that's how I came up with many of the stores to which I later wrote. After

I spent at least a hundred dimes photocopying these pages, I picked cities I knew had large populations of blacks. *Poets & Writers* also publishes a book entitled *Literary Bookstores: A Cross-Country Guide,* from which I made another list. (Some of them were in ABTD, but many of them weren't.) In total, I wrote letters to 1,010 bookstores.

If you belong to any organizations or have friends or relatives that do, try to get mailing lists from them. My sister worked at the Ford Motor Company; she told her supervisor about my novel, and in their Christmas newsletter was a half-page article about *Mama.* That newsletter reached over 2,500 people. If your book is about dogs, think of any and all organizations that deal with dogs. In your publisher's questionnaire you can provide the names of your local newspapers, TV and radio programs, auxiliary groups, churches, and especially your old high school and/or college. Both Detroit newspapers, as well as that city's slick monthly magazine, carried reviews and articles about me. My hometown newspaper actually had a full-color spread! The local bookstore couldn't keep *Mama* in stock.

The college audience is a big market, so I went to the back of *Webster's Dictionary,* checked off 260 colleges and universities, and plugged them into my computer. At these institutions, as well as at the black colleges, I included "variables" in my computer so I could write to different people at the same school. I wrote to the trade book buyer of the campus bookstore and also to the acquisitions librarian. Each person to whom I wrote was in charge of ordering books.

I know how valuable readings can be, and I wanted as many as I could get before and around my publication date. Most places that have a regular reading series planned at least six months to a year in advance. I had time. I made a list of all local places that had regularly scheduled readings. I used the New York City Poetry Calendar and *Author & Audience: A Readings and Workshops Guide,* which is published by Poets & Writers, Inc. This book lists universities and other places—by state and city— that have reading series, and it usually tells the honorarium. I ended up with a list of more than 200 places, to which, over a two-month period, I sent out the first twenty-five pages of my novel (by this time my book was in galley form). I ended up with over forty readings. Each time I got an invitation, I sent my publicist an updated itinerary so that she would have plenty of time to try to get press coverage before I arrived (she had agreed to do this when I told her I would get as many readings as I could). Some places already had their series planned, but others said they would keep me in mind for a future date.

Exactly what kind of letters did I write? Simple. The first paragraph told the name of my novel and who was publishing it in the United States and elsewhere. The second paragraph told why I was writing them; in hopes that they would consider ordering my book or adding it to their library, consider me for a reading or a lecture, consider using my book as a text in their class, or whatever. In this same paragraph I told them why I was writing to them directly became as a new novelist I was afraid my novel might not be widely distributed and I wanted them to know that I was doing all that I could to help generate an audience. (I received lots of letters from bookstores, thanking me for writing. Some even said how refreshing it was to receive a personal letter from the author, and in some cases, I was invited to bookstores for readings and autographings.) The third paragraph was my own synopsis of my book. In the fourth paragraph I thanked them for their time, interest, and consideration.

Because I had been living in Brooklyn, New York, for six years, I picked up copies of all the neighborhood throwaways (newspapers) and wrote them (at least three of which reviewed the book and interviewed me); I wrote the "People" page of the *Daily News* and got my picture in the Brooklyn section. Around my publication date, my three-year-old son and I spent days gallivanting around Brooklyn and Manhattan to bookstores to see if they had *Mama* on their shelves. The shocker was that most of them did, and when I told them I was the author all of them asked me to autograph the books!

To whom didn't I write? I didn't write to public librarians because the list was too massive, and I didn't know where to begin. I assumed libraries had their own method for ordering books. I did not write to a single reviewer, because I was told it was a waste of time. You can't force a reviewer to read your book, but you might want to write them if you know them personally.

So after doing all this, exactly what happened? The day before my publication date, I had sold out of my first printing. Six weeks later my book was in its third printing. I was a guest on seven television shows and six radio shows (some nationally syndicated), and was interviewed in approximately fourteen newspapers. *Mama* has been reviewed in more than thirty periodicals. I'm not sure how much, if any, of this good fortune has been due to all my efforts, but my editor and the publicity department seem to think they truly helped. All I know is if I hadn't done it, what would I have to compare it to? It was hard work, but it was worth every penny and every minute I spent. See for yourself.

AWARDS FOR PUBLISHED FIRST BOOKS

Name of Prize: Alden B. Dow Creativity Center Fellowships
Prize: $750
Open to: Open competition
Contact: Alden B. Dow Creativity Center Fellowships
 Northwood University
 Midland, MI 48640-2398
Categories: Novel-length fiction and short story, poetry, drama, screenplay, nonfiction, journalism, children's literature, Gay/Lesbian, religion, residency/colony.
Description: The Northwood Institute's Alden B. Dow Creativity Center Fellowships offer four fellowships each summer to individuals in any field or profession to pursue an innovative project or creative idea. It provides round-trip travel, room, board, and a $750 stipend. Project ideas should be new and have the potential for impact in their field. Send SASE for complete guidelines and rules.

Name of Prize: Arch and Bruce Brown Foundation Grants
Prize: $1,000
Open to: Open competition
Contact: Arch and Bruce Brown Foundation Grants
 PMB 503
 31855 Date Palm Drive #3
 Cathedral City, CA 92234
Categories: Novel-length fiction, drama, Gay/Lesbian.
Description: The Arch and Bruce Brown Foundation offers $1,000 grants for fiction that presents gay and lesbian lifestyle in a positive manner and is based on, or inspired by, history. Send SASE for complete guidelines, or e-mail to ArchWrite@aol.com.

Name of Prize: ArtsLink Collaborative Projects Prize
Prize: $10,000
Open to: U.S. citizens/permanent residents
Contact: Artslink Collaborative Projects
        CEC International Partners
        12 West 31st Street
        New York, NY 10001
Categories: Novel-length fiction and short story, poetry, translation.
Description: Artslink Collaborative Projects offers grants of $2,500 to $10,000 to enable creative artists, including writers and translators, to work with their counterparts in Central or Eastern Europe, the former Soviet Union, or the Baltics. Send SASE for complete guidelines and application, visit the Web site at *www.cecip.org*, or e-mail to artslink@cecip.org.

Name of Prize: Boston Book Review's Annual Fisk Fiction Prize
Prize: $1,000
Open to: Open competition
Contact: Kiril Alexandrov, President
        The Boston Book Review
        Fisk Fiction Prize
        30 Brattle Street, 4th Floor
        Cambridge, MA 01238
Categories: Novel-length fiction.
Description: This annual competition, sponsored by *The Boston Book Review*, offers $1,000 for a book of fiction published in the preceding year. The *BBR*'s editors compile a list of recommended titles, from which one judge chooses the winners. Publishers or authors may submit books of fiction published in the preceding year. Send SASE for complete guidelines, e-mail them at bbroinfo@ostonBookReview.com, or visit the Web site at *www.BostonBookReview.com*.

Name of Prize: Bunting Fellowship Program for Women
Prize: $40,000
Open to: Women Ph.D. scholars
Contact: Bunting Fellowship Coordinator
        Radcliffe College
        The Mary Ingraham Bunting Institute
        34 Concorde Avenue
        Cambridge, MA 02138
Categories: Novel-length fiction, short story, poetry, drama, nonfiction, women.
Description: The Mary Ingraham Bunting Institute at Radcliffe College is a multidisciplinary research center for women scholars, scientists, artists, and writers, and is one of the major fellowship programs for the support of women doing

advanced study in the United States. The Fellowship offers $40,000 for an 11-month appointment. Send SASE for complete guidelines.

Name of Prize: Chapter One Fiction Competition and Reading Series
Prize: $200
Open to: New York City residents over 18
Contact: Leslie Shipmen
       The Bronx Writers' Center
       2521 Glebe Ave.
       Bronx, NY 10461
Categories: Novel-length fiction
Description: The Chapter One Fiction Competition and Reading Series, held by the Bronx Writers' Center, a program of the Bronx Council on the Arts, seeks first chapters from published or unpublished novels, or works in progress. Writers must live in one of the five boroughs. No more than four selections will be made. Each one of these writers will receive a $200 honorarium and be invited to read the winning selection. For more information, including submission guidelines and deadlines, please contact them by mail, phone 718/409-1265, fax 718/409-1351, e-mail: wtrsctr@artswire.org, or visit the Web site at *www.bronxarts.org*.

Name of Prize: Fishtrap Fellowships
Prize: Varies
Open to: Open competition
Contact: Fellowship Director
       Fishtrap
       PO Box 38
       Enterprise, OR 97828
Categories: Novel-length fiction, short story, nonfiction, drama, poetry, screenplay.
Description: Fishtrap awards five fellowships to cover fees, food, and lodging for their annual Summer Writing Workshops and featured reading spot at the Summer Fishtrap Gathering in July. Send SASE for complete guidelines, or visit the Web site at *www.fishtrap.org*.

Name of Prize: Frances Shaw Fellowship for Older Women Writers
Prize: Varies
Open to: Women writers age 55 or older
Contact: Fellowship Director
       Frances Shaw Fellowship Committee
       Ragdale Foundation
       1260 North Green Bay Road
       Lake Forest, IL 60045

Categories: Fiction, novel and short story, poetry, drama, commercial nonfiction, women, residency/colony.

Description: The Ragdale Foundation offers residencies annually for women writers whose serious writing careers began after the age of 55. The person selected will be given round-trip transportation within the United States and a two-month residency at the Ragdale Foundation. She will have comfortable private living and working space, all her meals, other writers and artists to talk with, the support of the staff, and the use of all facilities of Ragdale, including its garden and the prairie and woods behind the house. Send SASE for complete guidelines and application form.

Name of Prize: Harold Morton Landon Translation Award
Prize: $1,000
Open to: U.S. citizens
Contact: The Harold Morton Landon Translation Award
The Academy of American Poets
584 Broadway, Suite 1208
New York, NY 10012-3250
Categories: Poetry translation.
Description: This $1,000 award recognizes a published translation of poetry from any language into English. Founded in 1976, the award was originally biennial. It has been given annually since 1984. A noted translator chooses the winning book. Books must be published in a standard edition (40 pages or more and 500 or more copies), and must consist primarily of poetry. Collaborations by two or more translators are eligible, but anthologies in which an editor has collected work by a number of translators will not be considered. Self-published books are not accepted. Translators must be living citizens of the United Sates. Send SASE for complete guidelines and information.

Name of Prize: Henry Hoyns Fellowships
Prize: Varies
Open to: M.F.A. candidates
Contact: Henry Hoyns Fellowship Director
Creative Writing Program
219 Bryan Hall
University of Virginia
Department of English
Charlottesville, VA 22903
Categories: Fiction, novel and short story, poetry.

Description: The Henry Hoyns Fellowship offers at least six fellowships that cover the cost of tuition for incoming students enrolled in the M.F.A. Creative Writing Program at the University of Virginia. Send SASE for complete guidelines and application forms.

_____

Name of Prize: Institute for Humane Studies Communicators Assistance Fund
Prize: $1,000
Open to: Open competition
Contact: IHS—Communicators Assistance Fund
       Institute for Humane Studies
       George Mason University
       4084 University Drive, Suite 101
       Fairfax, VA 22030-6812
Categories: Novel-length fiction, short story, screenplay, nonfiction, journalism.
Description: The Fund awards appropriate candidates who are pursuing nonacademic careers that involve the communication of ideas. Small grants help defray the expenses associated with such career opportunities. To qualify for consideration, applicant must be a young professional, college senior, or a graduate student pursuing a career in journalism, writing, film, publishing, or market-oriented public policy. Send SASE for complete guidelines.

_____

Name of Prize: Institute for Humane Studies Young Communicators Fellowships
Prize: $5,000
Open to: See description
Contact: Young Communicators Fellowships Coordinator
       Institute for Humane Studies
       George Mason University
       4084 University Drive, Suite 101
       Fairfax, VA 22030-6812
Categories: Novel-length fiction, short story, nonfiction, drama, screenplay, journalism.
Description: These fellowships offer grants up to $5,000 to advanced students and recent graduates pursuing nonacademic careers. To qualify for consideration, applicant must be a college junior or senior, a graduate student, or a recent graduate pursuing a career in journalism, writing, film, publishing, or market-oriented public policy. Send SASE for complete guidelines.

_____

Name of Prize: James Thurber Fiction-Writer-in-Residence Program
Prize: $5,000
Open to: Open competition
Contact: Michael J. Rosen, Literary Director
 The James Thurber Residency Program
 The Thurber House
 77 Jefferson Avenue
 Columbus, OH 43215
Categories: Novel-length fiction, short story, residency/colony.
Description: "The James Thurber Fiction-Writer-In-Residence will teach a fiction
 writing class in the Creative Writing Program at The Ohio State University and
 will offer one public reading sponsored by the Thurber House. The majority of
 time outside the two afternoons of teaching is reserved for the writer's own work-
 in-progress. Candidates should have published at least one book with a major
 publisher and should possess some experience in teaching. Send SASE for complete guidelines.

Name of Prize: Kosciuszko Foundation Scholarships and Grants
Prize: $1,500
Open to: U.S. citizens/permanent residents of Polish descent
Contact: Kosciuszko Foundation Scholarships and Grants Director
 Kosciuszko Foundation
 15 East 65th Street
 New York, NY 10021-6595
Categories: Fiction, novel and short story, nonfiction, poetry, drama, translation.
Description: The Kosciuszko Foundation offers scholarships and grants for appli-
 cants specializing in the Polish language, literature, and history for research and
 publication of scholarly books on topics pertaining to Polish history and culture.
 Send SASE for complete guidelines, deadlines, and required application forms.

Name of Prize: The Lenore Marshall Poetry Prize
Prize: $10,000
Open to: Poetry books published in previous year
Contact: The Lenore Marshall Poetry Prize
 The Academy of American Poets
 584 Broadway, Suite 1208
 New York, NY 10012-3250
Categories: Poetry.
Description: In 1994, the Academy was selected by the New Hope Foundation to
 administer the Lenore Marshall Poetry Prize in conjunction with the *Nation* maga-
 zine. Established in 1975, this $10,000 award recognizes the most outstanding book

of poetry published in the United States in the previous year. Past recipients include Philip Levine, Sterling A. Brown, Adrienne Rich, Thorn Gunn, W. S. Merwin, Marilyn Hacker, and Charles Wright. Submissions are accepted each year from April 1 to June 1. The Lenore Marshall Poetry Prize honors the memory of Lenore Marshall (1897-1971), a poet, novelist, essayist, and political activist. Send SASE for complete guidelines and information.

_____

Name of Prize: Midland Authors Award in Juvenile Fiction
Prize: $300
Open to: See description
Contact: Award Director
        S.M.A.
        PO Box 10419
        Chicago IL 61610-0419
Categories: Fiction, novel, short story, children's literature.
Description: The Society of Midland Authors offer a cash prize of $300 or more and a plaque, to be presented at the Society's annual Mid-May Awards Dinner, for the best book of juvenile fiction published during the calendar year by an author who lives in Illinois, Indiana, Iowa, Kansas, Michigan, Minnesota, Missouri, Nebraska, North Dakota, Ohio, South Dakota, or Wisconsin. Send SASE for complete guidelines and application forms.

_____

Name of Prize: Paul Bowles Graduate Fellowship in Fiction
Prize: $5,000
Open to: M.F.A. and Ph.D. students in fiction writing
Contact: Paul Bowles Graduate Fellowship in Fiction
        Georgia State University
        University Plaza
        Department of English
        Atlanta, GA 30303-3083
Categories: Novel-length fiction, short story.
Description: Georgia State University's Creative Writing Department offers this award of $5,000. To apply, you must be an M.F.A. or a Ph.D. student entering or studying at Georgia State University Creative Writing Program. Send SASE for complete guidelines.

_____

Name of Prize: Pearl Hogrefe Fellowship
Prize: $8,100
Open to: Open competition
Contact: Graduate Coordinator
Hogrefe Fellowship Committee
Iowa State University
Department of English
203 Ross Hall
Ames, IA 50011-1201
Categories: Fiction, novel and short story, poetry, commercial nonfiction, residency/colony.
Description: This fellowship is granted annually to support "graduate study toward a degree program that will involve an emphasis on creative writing. The major field for the degree need not be English. Fellowships are granted for a nine-month academic year...and carry a basic stipend of $900 per month." The candidate "must have submitted all materials required for admission to the Graduate College." Send SASE for complete guidelines and required application forms.

Name of Prize: The Raiziss/de Palchi Translation Award
Prize: $5,000
Open to: Living writers, publishers' nomination
Contact: The Raiziss/de Palchi Translation Award
The Academy of American Poets
584 Broadway, Suite 1208
New York, NY 10012-3250
Categories: Translation.
Description: Established in 1995, this award recognizes outstanding translations into English of modern Italian poetry through a $5,000 book prize and a $20,000 fellowship given in alternating years. The winner of the fellowship also receives a residency at the American Academy in Rome. The award was established by a bequest to the New York Community Trust by Sonia Raiziss Giop, a poet, translator, and longtime editor of the literary magazine *Chelsea.* To receive guidelines for either award, please send SASE and a note specifying "Fellowship" or "Book Prize" to the address above.

Name of Prize: Robie Macauley Fellowships
Prize: $1,000
Open to: Open competition
Contact: Robie Macauley Fellowships
        Ploughshares
        Emerson College
        100 Beacon Street
        Boston, MA 02116
Categories: Novel-length fiction, short story, nonfiction.
Description: The Annual Ploughshares International Fiction Writing Seminar at Kasteel Well, the Netherlands, offers a $1,000 and $500 fellowship. Winners will give a reading during the seminar. Submit a short story, memoir, or novel excerpt of less than 25 pages with an application. Send SASE for complete guidelines or e-mail to dgriffin@emerson.edu.

Name of Prize: Summerfield G. Roberts Award for Fiction
Prize: $2,500
Open to: U.S. citizens
Contact: Summerfield G. Roberts Award Director
        Sons of the Republic of Texas
        1717 8th Street
        Bay City, TX 77414
Categories: Fiction, novel and short story.
Description: Manuscripts representing Texas from 1836-1846, written or published during the year preceding the award, will be considered for the $2,500 annual prize. Novel, short story, or other fiction; poetry, biography; essay, or other non-fiction that will "encourage literary effort and research about historical events during the days of the Republic of Texas" will be considered. Five nonreturnable copies need to be submitted. Send SASE for guidelines.

Name of Prize: Wisconsin Institute for Creative Writing Fellowships
Prize: $20,000
Open to: See description
Contact: Wisconsin Institute for Creative Writing Director
        Wisconsin Institute for Creative Writing
        University of Wisconsin
        Department of English
        600 North Park Street
        Madison, WI 53706
Categories: Novel-length fiction, short story, poetry, residency/colony.
Description: Poets and fiction writers who have completed an M.A., M.F.A., or equivalent degree in creative writing, and have yet to publish a book, may apply for

residency at the Wisconsin Institute for Creative Writing and receive a $20,000 stipend. Send SASE for complete guidelines and application forms.

Awards for Published First Books by Size of Prize

Prize Name	Prize
Bunting Fellowship Program for Women	$40,000
Wisconsin Institute for Creative Writing Fellowships	$20,000
ArtsLink Collaborative Projects Prize	$10,000
The Lenore Marshall Poetry Prize	$10,000
Pearl Hogrefe Fellowship	$8,100
Institute for Humane Studies Young Communicators Fellowships	$5,000
James Thurber Fiction-Writer-in-Residence Program	$5,000
Paul Bowles Graduate Fellowships in Fiction	$5,000
The Raiziss/de Palchi Translation Award	$5,000
Summerfield G. Roberts Award for Fiction	$2,500
Kosciuszko Foundation Scholarships and Grants	$1,500
Arch and Bruce Brown Foundation Grants	$1,000
Boston Book Review's Annual Fisk Fiction Prize	$1,000
Harold Morton Landon Translation Award	$1,000
Institute for Humane Studies Communicators Assistance Fund	$1,000
Robie Macauley Fellowships	$1,000
Alden B. Dow Creativity Center Fellowships	$750
Midland Authors Award in Juvenile Fiction	$300
Chapter One Fiction Competition and Reading Series	$200/reading
Fishtrap Fellowship	Varies
Frances Shaw Fellowship for Older Women Writers	Varies
Henry Hoyns Fellowships	Varies

Awards for Published Books by Genre

Fiction

Alden B. Dow Creativity Center Fellowships
Arch and Bruce Brown Foundation Grants
ArtsLink Collaborative Projects Prize
Boston Book Review's Annual Fisk Fiction Prize
Bunting Fellowship Program for Women
Chapter One Fiction Competition and Reading Series
Fishtrap Fellowship Prize

Frances Shaw Fellowship for Older Women Writers
Henry Hoyns Fellowships
Institute for Humane Studies Communicators Assistance Fund
Institute for Humane Studies Young Communicators Fellowships
James Thurber Fiction Writer in Residence Program
Kosciuszko Foundation Scholarships and Grants
Midland Authors Award in Juvenile Fiction
Paul Bowles Graduate Fellowships in Fiction
Pearl Hogrefe Fellowship Prize
Robie Macauley Fellowships
Summerfield G. Roberts Award for Fiction Prize
Wisconsin Institute for Creative Writing Fellowships

Short Story (Short Fiction)

Alden B. Dow Creativity Center Fellowships
ArtsLink Collaborative Projects Prize
Bunting Fellowship Program for Women
Fishtrap Fellowship Prize
Frances Shaw Fellowship for Older Women Writers
Henry Hoyns Fellowships Prize
Institute for Humane Studies Communicators Assistance Fund
Institute for Humane Studies Young Communicators Fellowships
Midland Authors Award in Juvenile Fiction
Pearl Hogrefe Fellowship Prize
Robie Macauley Fellowships
Summerfield G. Roberts Award for Fiction Prize
Wisconsin Institute for Creative Writing Fellowships

Nonfiction

Alden B. Dow Creativity Center Fellowships
Bunting Fellowship Program for Women
Fishtrap Fellowship Prize
Frances Shaw Fellowship for Older Women Writers
Institute for Humane Studies Communicators Assistance Fund
Institute for Humane Studies Young Communicators Fellowships
Kosciuszko Foundation Scholarships and Grants Prize
Pearl Hogrefe Fellowship Prize
Robie Macauley Fellowships

Poetry

Alden B. Dow Creativity Center Fellowships
ArtsLink Collaborative Projects Prize
Bunting Fellowship Program for Women
Fishtrap Fellowship Prize
Frances Shaw Fellowship for Older Women Writers
Harold Morton Landon Translation Award
Henry Hoyns Fellowships
Kosciuszko Foundation Scholarships and Grants Prize
Pearl Hogrefe Fellowship Prize
The Lenore Marshall Poetry Prize
The Raiziss/de Palchi Translation Award
Wisconsin Institute for Creative Writing Fellowships

Children's Literature

Alden B. Dow Creativity Center Fellowships
Midland Authors Award in Juvenile Fiction

Drama

Alden B. Dow Creativity Center Fellowships
Arch and Bruce Brown Foundation Grants
Bunting Fellowship Program for Women
Fishtrap Fellowship Prize
Frances Shaw Fellowship for Older Women Writers
Institute for Human Studies Young Communicators Fellowships Prize
Kosciuszko Foundation Scholarships and Grants Prize

Screenplay

Alden B. Dow Creativity Center Fellowships
Fishtrap Fellowship Prize
Institute for Humane Studies Communicators Assistance Fund
Institute for Humane Studies Young Communicators Fellowships Prize

Residency/Colony

Alden B. Dow Creativity Center Fellowships
Frances Shaw Fellowship for Older Women Writers
James Thurber Fiction-Writer-in-Residence Program
Pearl Hogrefe Fellowship Prize
Wisconsin Institute for Creative Writing Fellowships

Translation

ArtsLink Collaborative Projects Prize
Kosciuszko Foundation Scholarships and Grants
The Raiziss/de Palchi Translation Award

FIRST BOOK AMERICAN CLASSICS

Claude McKay

Songs of Jamaica
London: Jamaica Agency, 1912
Schomburg Center for Research in Black Culture

In 1912, Claude McKay (1889-1948) left his home in Jamaica for the United States and the famous Tuskagee Institute, to find himself and a larger audience for his poetry. "I had read my dialect poems before many of these poetry societies before and the members used to say 'Well, he's very nice and pretty, you know, but he's not a real poet as Browning and Byron and Tennyson are poets.' I used to think I would show them something. Someday I would write poetry in straight English and amaze and confound them." *Songs of Jamaica* was, it turned out, McKay's farewell to his native land. Although he loved Jamaica passionately, he was to return to it only in his poetry. McKay stayed only a year at Tuskagee before he left for Kansas State College; he then left his studies altogether for radical New York in 1914, near the beginning of the New Negro movement. He spent 1920 in London, and in 1922 he was feted in the Soviet Union. He later traveled for 12 years through France, Germany, Spain, and North Africa, returning to Harlem in 1934. He died in 1948, after converting to Catholicism and working for the poor of Harlem in the Catholic Friendship House.

In Songs of Jamaica and its companion, *Constab Ballads,* McKay creates authentic portraits of Jamaican life, particularly through his use of dialect; McKay's books are free, as James Weldon Johnson said, "of both the Minstrel and the Plantation traditions, free from exaggerated sweetness and wholesomeness." Although he rarely used dialect after he left

Jamaica, the lessons he learned in craft and expression were never forgotten. His later books included poetry, novels, short stories, nonfiction, and autobiography.

From the beginning, McKay confronted prejudice and bigotry head-on with courage and poise. His most famous poem, "If We Must Die," written in response to lynchings and massacres of black Americans that occurred in the Red Summer of 1911, was read before Parliament by Winston Churchill for inspiration in the worst days of World War II.

Hilda Doolittle (H.D.)

Sea Garden
London: Constable, 1916

In the fourth issue (January 1913) of Harriet Monroe's new *Poetry, a magazine of verse* appeared three poems entitled as a group "Verses, Translations and Reflections from the Anthology" that were attributed to a poet identified only as "H.D. Imagiste." Two of these poems, augmented by 26 others, were published in 1916 as *Sea Garden,* the first publication of the newly anointed American poet Hilda Doolittle of Bethlehem, Pennsylvania, who had followed her fiance, the irrepressible, green-eyed, red-haired Ezra Pound, to London in 1911. The poet herself, nicknamed Dryad by Pound, credited the young poetry impresario with the publication of her new poems, describing the fateful moment in the British Museum tea room when he "scrawled 'H.D. Imagiste' at the bottom of the page," before sending them off to Chicago and Harriet Monroe. In literary legend, this moment is often considered the birth of the movement of imagism, which flourished briefly in London among the American expatriate writers who gathered there before World War I, and provided the break from Victorianism and the past needed for the beginning of literary modernism.

H.D.'s early poems are the quintessential imagist poems: spare, powerful, and sharp presentations of feeling embodied in natural images of surpassing clarity. H.D. herself applied the lessons of imagism to her great modernist *Trilogy,* published in Oxford during World War II as three booklets, *The Walls Do Not Fall* (1944), *Tribute to the Angels* (1945), and *The Flowering of the Rod* (1946). These works, and her psychoanalytic sessions and correspondence with Freud, provided a breakthrough for H.D., whose later work in both poetry and prose differed from her earlier "imagist" poems in length, in complexity, and in their more open personal nature, as well as in their expanding, epic vision of the world. About the early poems in this book, which include those for which she is best known— "Orchard," "Heat," "The Helmsman," "Sea Rose," and "Pear Tree"— H.D. wrote: "It is nostalgia for a lost land. I call it Hellas. I might psychologically just as well have listed the Casco Bay off the coast of Maine."

Edna St. Vincent Millay

Renascence and Other Poems
New York: Mitchell Kennerly, 1917
Estate of Carter Burden

One of the most famous poems of the early twentieth century, "Renascence" changed the life of its young author, who was to become in the public's eye, for a time, the absolute epitome of the poet. Edna St. Vincent Millay (1892-1950) had been pushed by her mother to enter a national poetry contest sponsored by the *Lyric Year* magazine. "Renascence," a long meditative poem concerned with the author's near death experience as a child, won acclaim if not first prize. The occasion caused a small literary scandal, as the editor of the volume in which her poem appeared had enthusiastically informed Millay that her poem was certain to take first prize of $500, only to have the selection committee opt to give the prizes to three more conventional, established poets. In the hearts of readers and critics, however, the true winner was Millay. The poet, identified only as "E. Vincent Millay," turned out to be an ethereal, low-voiced 20-year-old woman with flowing red hair. When she recited "Renascence" in public a few months later, an astounded stranger offered her a college scholarship. She entered Vassar College and became its most famous graduate. Her first book, *Renascence and Other Poems*, was published by Mitchell Kennerly in 1917, in black-ribbed cloth. A special limited edition, printed on Vellum and bound in white, was issued in only 17 copies. Only three of these special copies were sold; the other 14 were given as gifts by Kennerly, who kept them in his desk drawer for years.

Thomas Wolfe

The Crisis in Industry
Chapel Hill: Published by the University of North Carolina, 1919

Thomas Wolfe's (1900-1938) first year at the University of North Carolina was miserable: He wanted to attend Princeton or the University of Virginia, but his father would only pay for UNC, whose law school he wanted Wolfe to attend. But he threw himself into campus life beginning in his sophomore year, writing at least two one-act plays and contributing to the *Carolina Magazine* and *Tar Heel,* which he also edited. In his junior year, his essay on the resolution of labor disagreements won the Worth Prize from the Department of Philosophy; his adviser justified the award as acceptable "If philosophy could throw any light on the problems of labor." Published by the university in an edition of 200 copies, the essay became his first book publication.

Ernest Hemingway

Three Stories and Ten Poems
Paris: Contact Editions, 1923
Rare Books Division

Ernest Hemingway (1899-1961) came to Paris with his new wife, Hadley Richardson, in December 1921, and quickly made friends with Gertrude Stein, who later reviewed his first book, *Three Stories and Ten Poems*, in the *Paris Tribune* of November 27, 1923: "So far so good, further than that, and as far as that...I should say that Hemingway should stick to poetry and intelligence and eschew the hotter emotions...." Hemingway's signature style was probably developed from Stein, though he vehemently denied it. The two were to quarrel, attacking each other in the *Autobiography of Alice B. Toklas* and *A Moveable Feast.*

In July 1923, 300 copies of *Three Stories and Ten Poems* were printed in Dijon by Maurice Darantiere, who had the previous year printed James Joyce's *Ulysses.* The publisher was the American émigré Robert McAlmon, who was married to the novelist Bryher (Winifred Ellerman), and traveling with her and the poet and novelist H.D. Spending some of Ellerman's money but exercising his own exquisite taste, he set up Contact Editions, headquartering at Sylvia Beach's Shakespeare & Company Books, 12 rue de L'Odeon, in Paris.

First published in this volume, "Up in Michigan" was the only manuscript to survive a theft from Hemingway's wife in the Gare de Lyon of a valise containing everything he had written up to that point: The manuscript of "Up in Michigan" had fortunately been left in a drawer. "Out of Season" was written later, and six of the poems and "My Old Man" were already at their respective serial publishers *(Poetry* magazine and *Best Short Stories).* Along with four previously unpublished poems, they made up Hemingway's first book.

William Faulkner

The Marble Faun
Boston: The Four Seas Company, 1924

William Faulkner (1897-1962) often referred to himself as a "failed poet." At the beginning of his career, he pursued his failure with a single-minded dedication that alarmed some of his relatives, who shook their heads as he padded about Oxford, Mississippi, in bare feet and drifted from job to job. From his teens until well into his twenties, Faulkner wrote hundreds of poems, laboriously reworking many of them; forged poetic sequences inspired by Conrad Aiken's "verse symphonies"; devoured Eliot and parodied him ("Shall I walk, then, through a corridor of profundities"); and produced hand-made books in which his often feverish poems throbbed between hand-painted watercolor boards. Faulkner's first appearance in print was in the August 6, 1919, issue of *The New Republic,* which paid $15 for "L'apresmidi d'un faune" (title from Mallarme). The magazine rejected another handful of his poems, so Faulkner, as a joke, typed up Coleridge's "Kubla Khan" and submitted it. This time Faulkner received some feedback from the editor: "We like your poem, Mr. Coleridge, but we don't think it gets anywhere much." Thirteen of Faulkner's poems and some criticism appeared in *The Mississippian,* the student paper at the University of Mississippi, where he had enrolled in 1919 after very brief service in the Royal Air Force-Canada in World War I.

The Marble Faun, whose 19 interlocking poems create a pastoral fantasy out of the voices of the nymphs and shepherds, was published in 1924. The Four Seas Company was a "subsidy" or vanity book publisher, which also published Stephen Vincent Benet's first book, *Five Men and Pompey,* as well as books by Williams Carlos Williams, Gertrude Stein, Conrad Aiken, H.L Mencken, and H.D. Although the records are not clear, from a variety of sources it appears that only 500 copies of this volume were printed and that 50 to 60 of them were given as gifts to people in and around Oxford. Some copies, at least 20, were destroyed in the fire that gutted the house and collection of Faulkner's mentor Phil Stone, who had paid for either half or all of the publication (it's not clear whether Faulkner contributed).

Countee Cullen

Color
New York: Harper Brothers, 1925

In 1925, Harvard University graduate student Countee Cullen (1903-1946) published his first book *Color,* and he published it with a major American publisher. That same year, his poem "To One Who Say Me Nay" took second prize in the annual literary contest run by *Opportunity: The Journal of Negro Life.* One of the few black students at New York's academically stringent DeWitt Clinton High School, from which James Baldwin later graduated, Cullen had been a frequent contributor of poems to *Magpie,* the school literary magazine. While at New York University, he published his work in national literary magazines such as *Poetry* and *Harper's.* His second book, *Copper Sun*, was published just two years after his first, and other prizes were showered on him, including a Guggenheim grant to study in Europe. In 1928 he married the daughter of W. E .B. DuBois in a huge, well-publicized ceremony (Langston Hughes was an usher). Nevertheless, in May 1926, racist practices still stopped him from reading from his poetry in Baltimore's Emerson Hotel, to which he had been invited by the Baltimore Civic Club.

Cullen published three more books of poetry, an autobiographical novel, two children's books, and an important anthology of black poetry, *Caroling Dusk* (1927). An intense Francophile, he spent long periods in Paris and taught French at a New York City junior high school. The New York Public Library's 135th Street branch was named in his honor after his sudden death of uremic poisoning in 1946.

Hart Crane

White Buildings
New York: Boni & Live-right, 1926

When Crane submitted the manuscript of *White Buildings* to the publisher Thomas Seltzer in May 1925, he sent the following cost estimate from the Polytype Press at 38 West 8th Street (where designer/ printer Samuel Jacobs had done e. e. cummings's *Tulips and Chimneys,* which Crane admired). The estimate was for an edition of 500 copies, the book to be "admirable had every detail." Jacobs had agreed to donate the composition costs:

500 copies—White Buildings—64pp.

Stock (Warren's Oldstyle)	$17.00
Makeup (Coy Pelley Press)	16.00
Lockup and Press work	40.00
Casing and Shipping	2.00
Binding (@25 cents per copy)	125.00
Total	$200.00

The book was finally published not by Seltzer, but by Boni and Liveright, where Crane's friend Waldo Frank, to whom the book was dedicated, had placed it. The foreword to the volume was written (and signed) by Allen Tate, who had offered to have it printed under Eugene O'Neill's name, since the publishers had agreed to accept the book only if O'Neill would write a preface (they published it anyway). For the younger poet, who did not finish high school and was largely self-educated, it must have been like first love, the "realization of one's dreams in flesh, form, laughter and intelligence."

Wallace Stevens

Harmonium
New York: Alfred A. Knopf, 1931

Hammonturn was published in 1923, a year after Joyce's *Ulysses* and Eliot's *The Waste Land.* It was mostly ignored and remaindered; there were three different bindings—checkered, striped, and plain blue—and of the plain blue, for example, 715 of the 1,500 copies were remaindered. For another five or six years, Stevens wrote little poetry, devoting himself instead to his newly born daughter and to consolidating his career in insurance law (he became an expert on surety bonds). Despite the remaindering of the first edition, Knopf reprinted *Harmonium* in 1931, in response to pressure from other poets and literary people. Stevens added 14 poems and removed three. Even today, "The Comedian as the Letter C," the long poem from *Harmonium,* can be read as a summary of Stevens's poetic life up to the publication of *Harmonium,* and a prophesy for the future: "In the presto of the morning, Crispin trod/Each day, still curious, but in a round/Less prickly and much more condign than that/He once thought necessary." He went on to write many more fine poems and many long ones, such as "The Man with the Blue Guitar," and to compose several philosophical essays on poetry.

Stevens went every year to Florida, escaping from his hibernation in the cold north of Hartford. He loved France and the French language, but visited Europe only in his imagination and poetry. As a young man, Stevens had been fond of hikes, of long walks, murmuring poetry for companionship; he once walked from New York City to Paterson, New Jersey, and back in an afternoon. Until his retirement from Hartford Accident and Indemnity at age 70, he continued to walk to work every day across Elizabeth Park in Hartford, composing his magnificent poems.

Eudora Welty

The Key with a note on the Author and her work by Katherine
Anne Porter from Miss Welty's forthcoming *A Curtain of Green*
Garden City, NY: Doubleday, Doran, 1941

Katherine Anne Porter (acting as an agent for English novelist Ford Maddox Ford) had, in 1938, written to Welty of her admiration of her stories. Ford tried to find an English publisher for a collection, but died shortly after Porter had transferred the Welty stories to him. Meanwhile, Welty's agent, Diarmuid Russell, prodded by Porter, had placed most of her stories in magazines such as *Harper's Bazaar.* Doubleday then agreed to publish the book, with Porter's introduction. *A Curtain of Green* was, however, preceded by this much rarer, glossy pamphlet, used as an advertising or promotional piece for booksellers and reviewers. This pamphlet prints "The Key," a story from *A Curtain of Green,* and is Welty's first "publication." About her new friend's future, Porter was to say, "My money is on her nose for the next race."

Jack Kerouac

The Town and the City
New York: Harcourt, Brace & Company, 1950

Jean-Louis Lebris de Kerouac (1922-1969) began to outline in his mind the novel that was to become *The Town and the City* in December 1945 when he was hospitalized for phlebitis, caused by Benzedrine abuse. At his mother's apartment near the Cross Bay Boulevard in Ozone Park, Queens, he began the actual writing of the novel after his father's death in 1946. His composition was interrupted by a life-changing meeting with Neal Cassady and a cross-country trip full of adventures, some of which would appear in his most famous novel, *On the Road* (1957). *The Town and the City* is a thinly veiled autobiography in which Kerouac romanticizes his youth in Lowell, Massachusetts, combining it with the family situation of his friends in the Greek-American Sampas family. Mostly completed in December 1948, the novel was rejected by Scribners, Little, Brown, and Putnam's before it was eventually published by Harcourt, Brace in 1950. Kerouac and his first book had been recommended to the young editor Robert Girouxby by the eminent Columbia scholar Mark Van Doren. Kerouac had prompted Van Doren with the Zen parable: "Do what you will when you think of it, at once."

Part
7

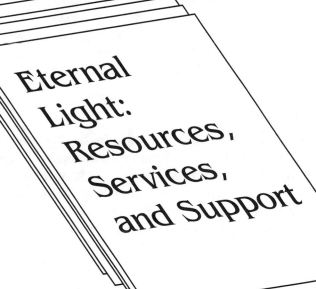

Eternal
Light:
Resources,
Services,
and Support

Introduction

—*Ruth Greenstein*

I am always surprised at how many writers make the mistake of approaching a publishing company without having first done their homework. Too often the publisher is asked to play the role of librarian, teacher, and adviser, referring such writers to resources that should already be familiar to them. No matter what part of the country you live in, there are organizations, publications, and computer-based resources that are indispensable to the serious professional. Writing is a lonely business; there's no reason to make it lonelier still by working in a vacuum. Here is a brief overview of the resources listed in this section:

Organizations

State and regional arts organizations, funded by your tax dollars, are a conduit of information to the local arts community. They are excellent sources for up-to-date information on awards, grants, workshops, and programs of interest to writers. Why not give your local arts council a call and see what they have to offer? Professional organizations, generally funded by dues-paying members, are good places to network with other writers working in your area of interest. Their offerings may include job banks, educational events, even group medical plans.

Publications

There are a vast array of books, directories, and periodicals that writers can turn to for information on how to write a good book, how to find a literary agent, and how to get published. Your local librarian should be able to point you toward those publications that will be most helpful to you. Have a look at a few trade magazines to learn more about how the publishing business works, to keep abreast of industry changes, and to find out what kinds of books are being published—and by whom.

Web sites

For all writers, but especially those who do not have ready access to traditional resources, the Internet is a godsend. Web sites offer many of the above resources in electronic form, and much more. In addition to being a superb research tool, the Web is also a great place to publicize your work. Check it out!

WHAT YOU'VE HEARD IS TRUE

There's no place like home

Often, everything you need to get your first book published can be found right in your own neighborhood. If it's not, be creative. For instance, if there are no writer's workshops offered in your community, you can start a home workshop. Gather several local writers together and split the cost of hiring a professional writer or editor to lead a series of discussions at one of your homes. If the professional cannot come to one of your homes, perhaps he or she can work with you through a regular mail or e-mail correspondence program. In rural areas and other communities that do not offer writer's workshops, home workshops are an increasingly popular option.

—J.S. 📖

ORGANIZATIONS

State and Regional Organizations

NATIONAL ASSEMBLY OF STATE ARTS AGENCIES
1029 Vermont Avenue, NW, 2nd Floor
Washington, DC 20005
202-347-6352; Fax: 202-737-0526; TDD: 202-347-5948
e-mail: nasaa@nasaa-arts.org
www.nasaa-arts.org

NATIONAL ENDOWMENT FOR THE ARTS
1100 Pennsylvania Avenue, NW
Washington, DC 20506
202-682-5400
arts.endow.gov

ALABAMA STATE COUNCIL ON THE ARTS
201 Monroe Street
Montgomery, AL 36130-1800
334-242-4076; Fax: 334-240-3269
www.arts.state.al.us/
Executive Director: Al Head; Chair: Lydia Daniel

ALASKA STATE COUNCIL ON THE ARTS
411 West 4th Avenue, Suite 1E
Anchorage, AL 99501-2343
907-269-6610; Fax: 907-269-6601
e-mail: asca@alaska.net
www.aksca.net

ARKANSAS ARTS COUNCIL
1500 Tower Building
323 Center Street
Little Rock, AR 72201
501-324-9766; Fax: 501-324-9154
e-mail: info@dah.state.ar.us
www.heritage.state.ar.us/aac/
Executive Director: Jim Mitchell; Chair: Dick Trammel

ARIZONA COMMISSION ON THE ARTS
417 West Roosevelt Street
602-255-5882; Fax: 602-256-0282
e-mail: geneml@ArizonaArts.org
az.arts.asu.edu/artscomm/
Executive Director: Shelley Cohn; Chair: Jane Jozoff

ARTS MIDWEST (IL, IN, IA, MI, MN, ND, OH, SD, WI)
528 Hennepin Avenue, Suite 310
Minneapolis, MN 55403
651-341-0755; Fax: 651-341-0902
e-mail: info@artsmidwest.org
www.artsmidwest.org/
Executive Director: David Fraher (david@artsmidwest.org); Chair: Barbara Robinson

CALIFORNIA ARTS COUNCIL
1300 1st Street, Suite 930
Sacramento, CA 95814
916-322-6555; Fax: 916-322-6575
e-mail: cab@two.com
www.cac.ca.gov/
Executive Director: Barbara Pieper; Chair: Steven J. Fogel

COLORADO COUNCIL ON THE ARTS
750 Pennsylvania Street
Denver, CO 80203
303-894-2617; Fax: 303-894-2615
e-mail: coloarts@artswire.org
www.coloarts.state.co.us/
Executive Director: Fran Holden; Chair: Donald K. Bain

CONNECTICUT COMMISSION ON THE ARTS
One Financial Plaza, 755 Main Street
Hartford, CT 06103
860-566-4770; Fax: 860-566-6462
www.ctarts.org
Executive Director: John Ostrout; Chair: Michael Price

GEORGIA COUNCIL FOR THE ARTS
260 14th Street, NW, Suite 401
Atlanta, GA 30318
404-651-7920; Fax: 404-651-7922
e-mail: info@arts-ga.com
www.ganet.org/georgia-arts/
Interim Executive Director: Rick George; Chair: Ruth Bmeewell

STATE FOUNDATION ON CULTURE AND THE ARTS (HAWAII)
44 Merchant Street
Honolulu, HI 96813
808-586-0300; Fax: 808-586-0308
e-mail: sfca@sfca.state.hi.us
www.state.hi.us/sfca/

IDAHO COMMISSION ON THE ARTS
PO Box 83720
Boise, ID 83720-0008
208-334-2119; Fax: 208-334-2488
e-mail: FHebert@ica.state.id.us
www.state.id.us/arts/
Executive Director: Frederick J. Hebert; Executive Director Chair: James P. Mertz

ILLINOIS ARTS COUNCIL
100 West Randolph Street, Suite 10-500
Chicago, IL 60601
312-814-6750; Fax: 312-814-1471
e-mail: ilarts@state.il.us
www.state.il.us/agency/iac/
Executive Director: Rhoda Pierce; Chair: Shirley Madigan

INDIANA ARTS COMMISSION
402 W. Washington Street, Room W072
Indianapolis, IN 46204
317-232-1268; Fax: 317-232-5595
e-mail: InArtsComm@aol.com
www.ai.org/iac/
Executive Director: Dorothy Ilgen; Chair: Sandra Neale

IOWA ARTS COUNCIL
Capitol Complex, 600 E. Locust
Des Moines, IA 50319
515-281-4451; Fax: 515-242-6498
www.state.ia.us/government/dca/iac/
Executive Director: Doug Larche; Chair: Phyllis Otto

KANSAS ARTS COMMISSION
Jayhawk Tower
700 SW Jackson, Suite 1004
Topeka, KS 66603-3761
785-296-3335; Fax: 785-296-4989
e-mail: KAC@arts.state.ks.us
arts.state.ks.us/
Executive Director: David Wilson; President: Martin W. Bauer

KENTUCKY ARTS COUNCIL
300 West Broadway
Frankfort, KY 40601-1950
502-564-3757; 888-833-2787; Fax: 502-564-2839
e-mail: kyarts@mail.state.ky.us
www.kyarts.org/
Executive Director: Gerri Combs; Chair: William Francis

LOUISIANA COMMISSION OF THE ARTS
PO Box 44247
Baton Rouge, LA 70804
225-342-8180; Fax: 225-342-8173
e-mail: arts@crt.state.la.us
www.crt.state.la.us/crt./ocd/doapage/doapage.htm
Executive Director: James Borders; Chair: Dan Henderson

MAINE ARTS COMMISSION
55 Capitol Street, State House Station 25
Augusta, ME 04333
207-287-2724; Fax: 207-287-2335
www.mainearts.com
Executive Director: Alden C. Wilson; Chair: Christopher B. Crosman; Communications Coordinator: Hilary M. Nangle

MARYLAND STATE ARTS COUNCIL
175 W. Ostend Street, Suite E
Baltimore MD 21230
410-767-6555; Fax: 410-333-1062
e-mail: tbamett@mdbusiness.state.md.us
www.msac.org
Executive Director: James Backas; Chair: Ardath M. Cade

MASSACHUSETTS CULTURAL COUNCIL
120 Boylston Street, 2nd Floor
Boston, MA 02116-4600
617-727-3668; Fax: 617-727-0044
www.masscultumlcouncil.org
Executive Director: Mary Kelley

MICHIGAN COUNCIL FOR ARTS & CULTURAL AFFAIRS
G. Merman Williams Building, 3rd Floor
525 West Ottawa, PO Box 30705
Lansing, MI 48909-8205
517-241-4011; Fax: 517-241-3979
e-mail: mcacal@artswire.org
www.commerce.state.mi.us/arts
Executive Director: Betty Boone

MID-AMERICA ARTS ALLIANCE (AR, KS, MO, NE, OK, TX)
912 Baltimore Avenue, Suite 700
Kansas City, MO 64105
816-421-1388; Fax: 816-421-3918
www.maaa.org
Executive Director: Henry Moran (henry@maaa.org); Chair: Mr. Wallace Richardson

MID-ATLANTIC ARTS FOUNDATION (DE, DC, MD, NJ, NY, PA, VI, VA, WV)
22 Light Street, Suite 300
Baltimore, MD 21202
410-539-6656; Fax: 410-837-5517
e-mail: maas@midarts.usa.com
www.midatlanticarts.org/
Executive Director: Alan W. Cooper (Alan@midatlanticarts.org);
   Chair: Lakin Ray Cook

MINNESOTA STATE ARTS BOARD
Park Square Court
400 Sibley Street, Suite 200
St. Paul, MN 55102
651-215-1600; Fax: 651-215-1602
e-mail: msab@state.mn.us
www.arts.state.mn.us
Executive Director: Robert Booker

MISSOURI ARTS COUNCIL
111 North 7th Street, Suite 105
St. Louis, MO 63101
314-340-6845; Fax: 314-340-7215
e-mail: mac@artswire.org
www.ecodev.state.mo.us/moartscouncil
Executive Director: Flora Maria Garcia; Chair: Karen K. Holland

MISSISSIPPI ARTS COMMISSION
239 North Lamar Street, 2nd Floor
Jackson, MS 39201
601-359-6030 or 6040; Fax: 601-359-6008
e-mail: msartcom@artswire.org
www.arts.state.ms.us
Executive Director: Betsy Bradley

MONTANA ARTS COUNCIL
City County Building
316 North Park Avenue, Room 252
Helena, MT 59620-2201
406-444-6430; Fax: 406-444-6548
e-mail: mac@state.mt.us
www.art.state.mt.us
Executive Director: Arlynn Fishbaugh; Chair: Bill Frazier;
   Communications Director: Barbara Koostra

NEBRASKA ARTS COUNCIL
Joslyn Castle Carriage House
3838 Davenport
Omaha, NE 68131-2329
402-595-2122; Fax: 402-595-2334
e-mail: nacart@synergy.net
www.gps.k12.ne.us/nac_web_site/nac.htm
Executive Director: Jennifer S. Clare; Interim Chair: Terry Ferguson

NEW YORK STATE COUNCIL ON THE ARTS
915 Broadway, 8th Floor
New York, NY 10010
212-387-7000; Fax: 212-387-7164
www.nysca.org
Executive Director: Nicolette B. Clarke; Chair: Richard J. Schwartz

NEVADA ARTS COUNCIL
Capitol Complex, 602 North Curry Street
Carson City, NV 89703
775-687-6680; Fax: 775-687-6688
dmla.clan.lib.nv.us/docs/arts
Executive Director: Susan Boskoff (seboskof@clan.lib.nv.us); Chair: Kathie Bartlett

NEW ENGLAND FOUNDATION FOR THE ARTS (CT, ME, MA, NH, RI, VT)
330 Congress Street, 6th Floor
Boston, MA 02210-1216
617-951-0010; Fax: 617-951-0016
e-mail: info@nefa.org
www.nefa.org/index.html
Executive Director: Samuel A. Miller (smiller@nefa.org); Chair: John Plukas

NEW HAMPSHIRE STATE COUNCIL ON THE ARTS
40 North Main Street, Phoenix Hall
Concord, NH 03301
603-271-2789; Fax: 603-271-3584
www.state.nh.us/nharts/
Executive Director: Rebecca Lawrence (rlawnrence@nharts.state.nh.us);
    Chair: M. Christine Dwyer (cdwyer@rmcres.com)

NEW JERSEY STATE COUNCIL ON THE ARTS
PO Box 306
Trenton, NJ 08625-0306
609-292-6130; Fax: 609-989-1440
www.njartscouncil.org
Executive Director: Barbara Russo (barbara@arts.sos.state.nj.us); Chair: Dr. Penelope
E. Lattimer (plattimer@nbps.kl2.nj.us); Director of Communications: Pamela
Pruitt (pamela@arts.sos.state.nj.us)

NEW MEXICO ARTS
228 East Palace Avenue
Santa Fe, NM 87501
505-827-6490; Fax: 505-827-6043
www.artsnet.org/mna
Executive Director: Margaret Brommelsiek; Chair: Ramona Sakiestewa

NORTH CAROLINA ARTS COUNCIL
Department of Cultural Resources
Raleigh, NC 27699-4632
919-733-2821; Fax: 919-733-4834
www.ncarts.org/home.htlnl
Executive Director: Mary Regan (mregan@ncacmail.dcr.state.nc.us);
Chair: Margaret S. "Tog" Newman (tognewlnan@aol.com)

NORTH DAKOTA COUNCIL ON THE ARTS
418 East Broadway, Suite 70
Bismarck, ND 58501-4086
701-328-3954; Fax: 701-328-3963
e-mail: comserv@pioneer.state.nd.us
www.state.nd.us/arts/
Executive Director: Daphne Ghorbani (dghorb.an@state.nd.us); Chair: David Trottier

OHIO ARTS COUNCIL
727 East Main Street
Columbus, OH 43205
614-466-2613; Fax: 614-466-4494
www.oac.state.oh.us/
Executive Director: Wayne Lawson (wlawson@oac.state.oh.us);
Chair: Barbara Robinson

OKLAHOMA ARTS COUNCIL
Jim Thorpe Building
PO Box 52001-2001
Oklahoma City, OK 73152-2001
405-521-2931; Fax: 405-521-6418
e-mail: okarts@arts.state.ok.us
www.oklaosf.state.ok.us/~arts/
Executive Director: Betty Price; Chair: Linch S. Frazier

OREGON ARTS COMMISSION
775 Summer Street, NE
Salem, OR 97310
503-986-0088; Fax: 503-986-0260
e-mail: Oregon.ArtsComm@State.OR.US
art.econ.state.or.us/
Executive Director: Christine D'Arcy (christine.t.darcy@state.or.us);
    Chair: Mike Lindberg

PENNSYLVANIA COUNCIL ON THE ARTS
216 Finance Building
Harrisburg, PA 17120
717-787-6883; Fax: 717-783-2538
artsnet.heinz.cmu.edu/pca/
Executive Director: Philip Horn (phornstate.pa.us)

RHODE ISLAND STATE COUNCIL ON THE ARTS
95 Cedar Street, Suite 103
Providence, RI 02903-1034
401-222-3883; Fax: 401-521-1351
e-mail: info@risca.state.ri.us
www.risca.state.ri.us/
Executive Director: Randall Rosenbaum (randy@risca.state.ri.us);
    Chair: Thomas J. Reilly, Jr.

SOUTH CAROLINA ARTS COMMISSION
1800 Gervais Street
Columbia, SC 29201
803-734-8696; Fax: 803-734-8526
www.state.sc.us/arts
Executive Director: Suzette Surkamer; Chair: Patricia E. Wilson

SOUTH DAKOTA ARTS COUNCIL
Office of the Arts
800 Governors Drive
Pierre, SD 57501-2294
605-773-3131; Fax: 605-773-6962
e-mail: sdac@stlib.state.sd.us
www.state.sd.us/state/executive/deca/sdarts/sdarts.htm
Executive Director: Dennis Holub (dennish@stlib.state.sd.us);
    Chair: Terry Anderson

SOUTHERN ARTS FEDERATION (AL, FL, GA, KY, LA, MS, NC, SC, TN)
1401 Peachtree Street, Suite 460
Atlanta, GA 30309
404-874-7244; Fax: 404-873-2148
e-mail: saf@southarts.org
www.southarts.org/
Executive Director: Jeffrey Kesper (jkesper@southarts.org); Chair: Jeffrey Dunn

TENNESSEE ARTS COMMISSION
Citizens Plaza, 401 Charlotte Avenue
Nashville, TN 37243-0780
615-741-1701; Fax: 615-741-8559
www.arts.state.tn.us/
Executive Director: Rich Boyd (rboyd@mail.state.tn.us);Chair: Howard W. Hemdon

TEXAS COMMISSION ON THE ARTS
PO Box 13406, Capitol Station
Austin, TX 78711
512-463-5535; Fax: 512-475-2699
e-mail: front.desk@arts.state.tx.us
www.arts.state.tx.us/
Executive Director: John Paul Batiste (jbatiste@arts.state.tx.us); Chair: Connie Ware

UTAH ARTS COUNCIL
617 E. South Temple Street
Salt Lake City, UT 84102
801-236-7555; Fax: 801-236-7556
www.dced.state.ut.us/arts
Executive Director: Bonnie Stephens (bstephen@arts.state.ut.us);
    Chair: Sam Lee Gibb

VERMONT ARTS COUNCIL
136 State Street, Drawer 33
Montpelier, VT 05633-6001
802-828-3291; Fax: 802-828-3363
e-mail: info@arts.vca.state.vt.us
www.state.vt.us/vermont-arts
Executive Director: Alexander L. Aldrich (aaldrich@arts.vca.state.vt.us); Co-chairs: David Binch (binhar@vbimail.champlain.ed); and Linda Rubinstein (lindar@sover.net)

VIRGINIA COMMISSION FOR THE ARTS
223 Governor Street, 2nd Floor
Richmond, VA 23219
804-225-3132; Fax: 804-225-4327
e-mail: vacomm@artswire.org
www.artswire.org/~vacomm
Executive Director: Peggy Baggett (pbaggett.arts@state.va.us); Chair: Thomas S. Gay

WASHINGTON STATE ARTS COMMISSION
234 E 8th Avenue
P O Box 42675
Olympia, WA 98504-2675
360-753-3860; Fax: 360-586-5351
www.wa.gov/art
Executive Director: Kristin Tucker; Chair: Dan Harpole

WEST VIRGINIA COMMISSION ON THE ARTS
1900 Kanawha Boulevard East
Charleston, WV 25305
304-558-0240; Fax: 304-558-2779
www.wvculture.org
Executive Director: Richard Ressmeyer (ressmeyr@wvnet.edu); Chair: William Davis

WESTERN STATES ARTS FEDERATION (AK, AZ, CA, CO, HI, ID, MT, NM, NV, OR, UT, WA, WY)
1543 Champa, Suite 220
Denver, CO 80202
303-629-1166; Fax: 303-629-9717
e-mail: staff@westaf.org
www.westaf.org
Executive Director: Anthony Radich (anthony.radich@westaf.org); Chair: Larry Williams

WISCONSIN ARTS BOARD
101 East Wilson Street, 1st Floor
Madison, WI 53702
608-266-O190; Fax: 608-267-0380
e-mail: rtertin@arts.state.wi.us
www.ans.state.wi.us
Executive Director: George Tzougros (gtzougro@arts.state.wi.us);
    Chair: Kathryn Burke

WYOMING ARTS COUNCIL
2320 Capitol Avenue
Cheyenne, WY 82002
307-777-7742; Fax: 307-777-5499
e-mail: wyoarts@artswire
commerce.state.wy.us/cr/arts/index.htm
Executive Director: John G. Coe (jcoe@missc.state.wy.us); Chair: Brent R. Boehme

U.S. Territories (Non-State) Organizations

AMERICAN SAMOA COUNCIL ON CULTURE, ARTS, AND HUMANITIES
PO Box 1540
Office of the Governor
Pago Pago, AS 96799
684-633-4347; Fax: 684-633-2059
www.nasaa-arts.org/new/nasaa/gateway/AS.html
Governor: Tauese P. Sunia; Executive Director: Ms. Le'ala E. Pili;
    Chair: Mr. Simone Lauti

**DISTRICT OF COLUMBIA (DC) COMMISSION ON THE ARTS
    AND HUMANITIES**
410 Eighth Street, NW, Fifth Floor
Washington, DC 20004
202-724-5613; Fax: 202-727-4135
e-mail: dccah@erols.com
www.capaccess.org/dccah
Executive Director: Anthony Gittens; Chair: Dorothy McSweeny

GUAM COUNCIL ON THE ARTS & HUMANITIES AGENCY
PO Box 2950
Agana, GU 96910
671-475-CAHA 2242/3-; Fax: 671-472-ART1 2781-
e-mail: Kaha1@kuentos.guam.net
www.nasaa-arts.org/new/nasaa/gateway/Guam.html
Executive Director: Deborah Bordallo; Chair: Anthony C. Corn

COMMONWEALTH COUNCIL FOR ARTS AND CULTURE
(Northern Mariana Islands)
PO Box 5553, CHRB
Saipan, MP 96950
670-322-9982 or 9983; Fax: 670-322-9028
e-mail: galaidi@gtepacifica.net
www.nasaa-arts.org/new/nasaa/gateway/NorthemM.html
Executive Director: Robert Hunter

CONSORTIUM FOR PACIFIC ARTS & CULTURES (AS, CM, GU)
1580 Makaloa Street, Suite 930
Honolulu, HI 96814-3220
808-946-7381; Fax: 808-955-2722
e-mail: epac@pixi.com
www.nasaa-arts.org/new/nas aa/gateway/CPAC.html
Executive Director: Epi Enari; Acting Chair: Anthony Com CH (Guam)

INSTITUTE OF PUERTO RICAN CULTURE
PO Box 9024184
San Juan, PR 00902-4i84
787-725-5137; Fax: 787-724-8393
www.nasaa-arts.org/new/nasaa/gateway/PR.html
Executive Director: Dr. Jose Ramon de la Torte; President: Dr. Gonzalo Cordova

VIRGIN ISLANDS COUNCIL ON THE ARTS
PO Box 103
St. Thomas, VI 00802
340-774-5984; Fax: 340-774-6206
e-mail: vicouncil@islands.vi
www.nasaa-arts.org/new/nasaa/gateway/VI.html
Governor: Charles W. Tumbull; Executive Director: John Jowers; Acting Chair:
    Rosary Harper

Key Service Organizations

American Book Producers Association
160 Fifth Avenue, Suite 652
New York, NY 10010
212-645-2368; 1-800 209-4575; Fax: 212-989-7542
e-mail: abpahdq@ibm.net

Associated Writing Programs
George Mason University
Tallwood House
MS-1E3
Fairfax, VA 22030
703-993-4301; Fax: 703-993-4302
www.awpwriter.org
AWP offers its members career placement services, an online conferencing system, job listings for writers, and an annual conference. *The Writer's Chronicle* is the official magazine of the AWP, which offers articles on writing, the industry, writing programs, and more.

Council of Literary Magazines & Presses
154 Christopher Street, Suite 3-C
New York, NY 10014-2839
212-741-9110; Fax: 212-741-9112
CLMPNYC@aol.com
www.litline.org/html/clmp.html

Dial-a-Writer Referral Service
1501 Broadway, Suite 302
New York, NY 10036
212-398-1934
A service of The American Society of Journalists and Authors, Dial-a-Writer connects ASJA members to clients seeking specialists in articles, books, videos, brochures, editing, ghostwriting, proposals, newsletters, texts, photojournalism, public relations, speechwriting, advertising, and corporate communications.

Editorial Experts
66 Canal Center Plaza, Suite 200
Alexandria, VA 22314
703-683-0683; Fax: 703-683-4915
e-mail: info@eeicommunications.com
www.eeicommunications.com/
A publications consulting company that provides writers, editors, proofreaders, and word and data processing for its clients. Editorial Experts also has an informative newsletter, *The Editorial Eye*.

Editorial Freelancers Association
71 West 23rd Street, Suite 1504
New York,. NY 10010
212-929-5400; Fax: 212-929-5439
Members have access to information about job opportunities through a telephone bulletin board. The EFA also offers a newsletter, a directory, and insurance at group rates, plus educational and supportive meetings.

The Foundation Center (NY)
79 Fifth Avenue/16th Street
New York, NY 10003-3076
212-620-4230; Fax: 212-807-3677
With national offices in New York and Washington, field offices in San Francisco and Cleveland, and cooperating collections in libraries throughout the United States and abroad, the Foundation Center is a splendid source of information about thousands of foundations that offer grants to individuals and groups.

The Foundation Center (GA)
50 Hurt Plaza, Suite 150
Atlanta, GA 30303
404-880-0094; Fax: 404 880-0097
fdncenter.org/aflantafmdex.html

The Foundation Center (DC)
1001 Connecticut Avenue at K Street, Suite #938
Washington, DC 20036
202-331-1400; Fax: 202 331-1739
fdncenter.org/washington/index.html

The Foundation Center (CA)
312 Sutter Street, #606
San Francisco, CA 94108-4314
415-397-0902; Fax: 415-397-7670
fdncenter.org/sanfrancisco/index.html

The Foundation Center (OH)
1422 Euclid Avenue Suite 1356
Cleveland, OH 44115-2001
216-861-1933; Fax: 216-861-1936
fdncenter.org/cleveland/index.html

International Association of Business Communicators
One Hallidie Plaza, Suite 600
San Francisco, CA 94102
415-544-4700; Fax: 415-544-4747
service_centre@iabc.com
www.iabc.com

Poets & Writers Inc.
72 Spring Street
New York, NY 10012
212-226-3686; Fax: 212-226-3963
e-mail: pwsubs@pw.org
www.pw.org
Through their publications and referral services, Poets & Writers can boost the income as well as the spirits of people who write fiction, poetry, and nonfiction.

U.S. Government

Federal agencies engaged in all sorts of activities. Education, commerce, agriculture, defense, and so forth—have libraries and issue press releases about where funds are going and what they've been earmarked for. There's grist for sales and promotion plans when and if money is allocated to a particular region for study of the particular subject you've written about, so ask to be put on the mailing lists of agencies whose bailiwicks are relevant to your writing/publishing efforts. And, find out if they have special-interest libraries that might buy your book.

Volunteer Lawyers for The Arts
One East 53rd Street
New York, NY 10022
212-319-ARTS; Fax: 212-752-6575
www.vlany.org

Founded in New York to provide legal services for artists who can't afford lawyers' fees. Volunteer Lawyers for the Arts has affiliates across the country: in California (San Francisco, Los Angeles, and La.loUa); Colorado (Denver); Connecticut (Hartford); the District of Columbia; Florida (Clearwater, Fort Lauderdale, Miami, and Tallahassee); Georgia (Atlanta); Illinois (Chicago); Iowa (Cedar Rapids and Dubuque); Kentucky (Lexington and Louisville); Louisiana (New Orleans); Maine (Augusta); Maryland (Baltimore); Massachusetts (Amherst and Boston); Minnesota (Minneapolis); Missouri (St. Louis); Montana (Missoula); New Jersey (Trenton); New York (Albany, Buffalo, Huntington, and Poughkeepsie, as well as New York City); North Carolina (Raleigh); Ohio (Cleveland and Toledo); Oklahoma (Oklahoma City); Pennsylvania (Philadelphia); Rhode Island (Narragansett); South Carolina (Greenville); Tennessee (Nashville); Texas (Austin and Houston); Utah (Salt Lake City); and Washington (Seattle). And there's an office in Toronto, too. Write or call the affiliate nearest you to find out about services and costs, or send $10 to the New York City office for the group's directory.

The Association for Women in Communications
1244 Ritchie Highway, Suite 6
Arnold, MD 21012
410-544-7442; Fax: 410-544-4640
www.womcom.org

Job hotlines and programs that hone professional skills are just two of the benefits Women in Communications offers members. Contact the national headquarters for information on nearby chapters.

Organizations That Offer Group Health Insurance

American Society of Journalists and Authors
1501 Broadway, Suite 302
New York, NY 10036
212-997-0947; Fax: 212 768-7414
www.asja.org

The Authors Guild, Inc.
330 West 42nd Street, 29th Floor
New York, NY 10036
212-564-5904; Fax: 212-564-5363
e-mail: staff@authorsguild.org
www.authorsguild.org

Editorial Freelancers Association
71 West 23rd Street, Suite 1504
New York, NY 10010
212-929-5400; Fax: 212-929-5439
e-mail: info@the-efa.org
www.the-efa.org

International Women's Writing Guild
PO Box 810, Gracie Station
New York, NY 10028-0082
212-737-7536; Fax: 212-737-9469
www.iwwg.com

Mystery Writers of America, Inc.
17 E. 47th St., 6th floor
New York, NY 10017
212-888-8171; Fax: 212 888-8107
e-mail: mwa-org@earthllnk.net
www.mysterywriters.net/index.htm

National Writers Union
113 University Plaza, 6th Floor
New York, NY 10003
212-254-0279; Fax: 212-254-0673
e-mail: nwu@nwu.org
www.nwu.org

PEN American Center
568 Broadway, Suite 401
New York, NY 10012
212-334-1660; Fax: 212-334-2181
e-mail: pen@pen.org
www.pen.org/index.html

Society of Children's Book Writers and Illustrators
8271 Beverly Blvd.
Los Angeles, CA 90048
323-782-1010; Fax: 323-782-1892
e-mail: membership@scbwi.org
www.scbwi.org/

United States Federation of Small Businesses
249 Green Street
Schenectady, NY 12305
800-637-3331; Fax: 888-568-3823
www.usfsb.com/

Other Professional Organizations

The Academy of American Poets
584 Broadway, Suite 1208
New York, NY 10012
212-274-0343; Fax: 212-274-9427
e-mail: acedemy@dti.net
www.poets.org

American Academy of Arts & Sciences
Nortons Woods
136 Irving Street
Cambridge, MA 02138
617-576-5000; Fax: 617-576-5050

American Association of Advertising Agencies
405 Lexington Avenue, 18th Floor
New York, NY 10174-1801
212-682-2500; Fax: 212-682-8391

American Book Producers Association
160 Fifth Avenue, Suite 652
New York, NY 10010
212-645-2368; 1-800-209-4575; Fax: 212-989-7542
e-mail: abpahdq@ibm.net

American Booksellers Association
828 Broadway
Tarrytown, NY 10591
914-591-2665; Fax: 914-591-2720
e-mail: editorial@bookweb.org

American International Book Development Council
1319 18th Street NW
Washington, DC 20036
202-296-6267; Fax: 202-296-5149

American Literary Council
680 Fort Washington Avenue
New York, NY 10040
212-781-0099 voice and fax
e-mail: amspell@aol.com

American Literary Translators Association
Affiliate of University of Texas, Dallas
Box 830688
Richardson, TX 75083-0688
972-883-2093; Fax: 972-883-6303
ert@udallas.edu
www.utdallas.edu/research/cts

American Management Association International
1601 Broadway
New York, NY 10019-7420
212-586-8100; Fax: 212-903-8168

American Marketing Association
311 South Wacker Drive, Suite 5800
Chicago, IL 60606-6622
312-542-9000; 1-800-262-1150
e-mail: info@ama.org
www.ama.org

American Medical Association
515 N. State Street
Chicago, IL 60610
312-464-5000; Fax: 312-464-4184
www.ama-assn.org

American Medical Publishers Association
14 Fort Hill Road
Huntington, NY 11743
516-432-0075; Fax: 516-432-0075
e-mail: Urudansky-ampa@msn.com
www.am-pa.com

American Medical Writers Association
40 W. Gude Drive
Rockville, MD 20850-1192
301-294-5303; Fax: 301-294-9006

American Psychological Association
750 First Street NE
Washington, DC 20002-4242
202-336-5500; 1-800-374-2721; Fax: 202-336-5620
e-mail: order@apa.org

American Society of Composers, Authors, & Publishers
One Lincoln Plaza
New York, NY 10023
212-621-6000; 1-800-952-7227; Fax: 212-724-9064
www.ascap.com

American Society of Indexers, Inc.
PO Box 39366
Phoenix, AZ 85069
623-979-5514; Fax: 623-530-4088
e-mail: info@asindexing.org
www.asindexing.org

American Society of Journalists & Authors
1501 Broadway, Suite 302
New York, NY 10036
212-997-0947; Fax: 212-768-7414
e-mail: asja@compuserve.com

American Society of Magazine Editors
919 Third Avenue
New York, NY 10022
212-872-3700; Fax: 212-906-0128

American Translators Association
225 Reinekers Lane, Suite 590
Alexandria, VA 22314
703-683-6100; Fax: 703-683-6122
www.atanet.org

Antiquarian Booksellers' Association Of America
20 W. 44th Street, 4th Floor
New York, NY 10036
212-944-8291; Fax: 212-944-8293
e-mail: abaa@panix.com
www.abaa-booknet.com

Associated Business Writers of America, Inc.
4130 South Peoria Street, Suite 295
Aurora, CO 80014
303-841-0246; Fax: 303-751-8953
e-mail: sandtwrtr@aol.com
www.nationalwriters.com

Associated Collegiate Press
2221 University Avenue SE, Suite 121
Minneapolis, MN 55414
612-625-8335

Associated Writing Programs
George Mason University
Tallwood House
MS-1E3
Fairfax, VA 22030
703-993-4301; Fax: 703-993-4302

Association of American Publishers, Inc.
71 Fifth Avenue, 2nd Floor
New York, NY 10003-3004
212-255-0200; Fax: 212-255-7007
www.publishers.org

Association of American University Presses
71 West 23rd Street, Suite 901
New York, NY 10010
212-989-1010; Fax: 212-989-0275
e-mail: aaupny@aol.com
aaup.uchicago.edu/aaup-home.html

Association of Authors' Representatives, Inc.
10 Aston Place, 3rd Floor
New York, NY 10003
212-353-3709
www.aar-online.org

Association of Canadian Publishers
110 Elington Avenue West, Suite 403
Toronto, ON M4R 1A3 Canada
416-487-6116; Fax: 416-487-8815

Association of College & University Presses
Penn State University
101 Business Services Bldg.
University Park, PA 16802
814-865-7544; Fax: 814-865-3386

The Association of Direct Marketing Agencies
PO Box 3139, Grand Central Station
New York, NY 10163-3139
212-644-8085; Fax: 212-6842-0270
e-mail: jwpgroup@aol.com
www.adma.org

Association of Graphic Communication
330 Seventh Avenue
New York, NY 10001-5010
212-279-2100; Fax: 212-279-5381
e-mail: bdage@june.com
www.agcomm.org

Association of Jewish Book Publishers
c/o Jewish Lights Publishing
Sunset Farm Offices
Woodstock, VT 05091
802-457-4000; Fax: 802-457-4004

Association of Jewish Libraries (AJL)
15 East 26th Street, Room 1034
New York, NY 10010-1597
212-725-5359; Fax: 212-678-8998
www.jewishlibraries.org

Authors Guild
330 West 42nd Street
New York, NY 10036
212-563-5904; Fax: 212-564-8363
e-mail: staff@anthorsguild.org
www.authorsguild.org

The Authors League Fund
330 West 42nd Street
New York, NY 10036
212-268-1208; Fax: 212-569-5363

The Authors League of America, Inc.
330 West 42nd Street
New York, NY 10036
212-564-8350; Fax: 212-564-8363

The Authors Registry, Inc.
330 West 42nd Street
New York, NY 10036
212-563-6920; Fax: 212 564-5363
e-mail: staff@authorsregistry.org

Book Industry Study Group, Inc.
160 Fifth Avenue
New York, NY 10010
212-929-1393; Fax: 212-989-7542
www.bisg.org

Book Manufacturers Institute, Inc. (BMI)
65 William Street, Suite 300
Wellesley, MA 02481-3800
781-239-0103; Fax: 781-239-0106

Book Publicists of Southern California
6464 Sunset Blvd., Room 580
Hollywood, CA 90028
323-461-3921; Fax: 323-461-0917

Brooklyn Writers Club
PO Box 184, Bath Beach Station
Brooklyn, NY 11214-0814
718-837-3484

Catholic Book Publishers Association
2 Park Avenue
Manhasset, NY 11030
516-869-0122; Fax: 516-627-1381
e-mail: cbpal@aol.com
www.cbpa.org

Center for Book Arts
626 Broadway, 5th floor
New York, NY 10012
212-460-9768; Fax: 212-673-4635

Christian Writers Guild
65287 Fern Street
Hume, CA 93628
559-335-2333; Fax: 559-335-2770

Copywriter's Council of America (CCA)
PO Box 102
Middle Island, NY 11953-0102
516-924-8555; Fax: 516-924-3890

Council of Literary Magazines & Presses
154 Christopher Street, Suite 3-C
New York, NY 10014-2839
212-741-9110; Fax: 212-741-9112

Digital Printing & Imaging Association
10015 Main Street
Fairfax, VA 22031-3489
703-385-1339; Fax: 703-359-1336
e-mail: dpi@dpia.org
www.dpia.org

Editorial Freelancers Association
71 West 23rd Street, Suite 1504
New York, NY 10010
212-929-5400; Fax: 212-929-5439

EdPress: The Association of Educational Publishers
c/o Rowan University
201 Mullica Hill Road
Glassboro, NJ 08028-1701
856-256-4610; Fax: 856-256-4561
e-mail: edpress@aol.com
www.edpress.com

Education Writers Association
1331 "H" Street NW, Suite 307
Washington, DC 20005
202-637-9700; Fax: 202-637-9707
e-mail: ewa@ceosslink.net
www.ewa.org

Freelance Editorial Association
PO Box 380835
Cambridge, MA 02238-0835
617-576-8979
e-mail: freelance@tiac.net

Garden Writers Association of America
10210 Leatherleaf Court
Marmassas, VA 20111
703-257-1032; Fax: 703-257-0213

Horror Writers Association
PO Box 50577
Palo Alto, CA 94303
e-mail: hwa@horror.org

Inter-American Press Association
2911 NW 39th Street
Miami, FL 33142
305-634-2465; Fax: 305-634-2272

International Association of Business Communicators
One Hallidie Plaza, Suite 600
San Francisco, CA 94102
415-544-4700; Fax: 415-544-4747
e-mail: service_centre@iabc.com
www.iabc.com

International Food, Wine & Travel Writers Association
PO Box 8429
Calabasas, CA 91372-8249
562-433-5969; Fax: 562-438-6384

International Publishing Management Association
1205 College Street
Liberty, MO 64068-3733
816-781-1111; Fax: 816-781-2790
e-mail: ipmainfo@ipma.org
www.ipma.org

The International Women's Writing Guild
Box 810, Gracie Station
New York, NY 10028-0082
212-737-7536; Fax: 212-737-9469
e-mail: iwwg@iwwg.org
www.iwwg.org

Magazine Publishers of America
919 Third Avenue, 22nd Floor
New York, NY 10022
212-872-3700; Fax: 212-888-4217

Modern Language Association of America
10 Astor Place
New York, NY 10003-6981
212-475-9000; Fax: 212-477-9863
e-mail: convention@mla.org

Motion Picture Association of America
1600 "I" Street NW
Washington, DC 20006
202-293-1966; Fax: 202-293-7646

Multicultural Publishing & Education Catalog
177 S. Kihei Rd.
Kihei, Maui, HI 96753
e-mail: mpec@aol.com

National Association of Independent Publishers
PO Box 430
Highland City, FL 33846-0430
941-648-4420
e-mail: naip@aol.com

National Coalition Against Censorship
275 Seventh Avenue, 9th Floor
New York, NY 10001
212-807-6222; Fax: 212-807-6245
e-mail: ncac@ncac.org
www.ncac.org

National Conference of Editorial Writers
6223 Executive Boulevard
Rockville, MD 20852
301-984-3015; Fax: 301-231-0026
e-mail: ncewhqs@erols.com
www.ncew.org

National Writers Association
3140 Peoria, Suite 295
Aurora, CO 80014
303-841-0246; Fax: 303-751-8593
e-mail: sandywrter@aol.com
www.nationalwriters.com

National Writers Union
113 University Place, 6th Floor
New York, NY 10003-4527
212-254-0279; Fax: 212-254-0673
e-mail: nwu@nwu.org
www.nwu.org

New England Poetry Club
2 Farrar Street
Cambridge, MA 02138

The Newsletter Publishers Association
1501 Wilson Blvd., Suite 509
Arlington, VA 22209
703-527-2333; Fax: 703-841-0629

PEN American Center
568 Broadway, Suite 401
New York, NY 10012
212-334-1660; Fax: 212-334-2181
e-mail: pen@pen.org
www.pen.org

Poetry Society of America
15 Gramercy Park
New York, NY 10003
212-254-9628; Fax: 212-673-2352
e-mail: poetrysocy@aol.com
www.poetrysociety.org

Poets & Writers, Inc.
72 Spring Street
New York, NY 10012
212-226-3686; Fax: 212-226-3963
e-mail: pwsubs@pw.org
www.pw.org

Printing Industries of America, Inc.
100 Dangerfield Road
Alexandria, VA 22314
703-519-8100; Fax: 703-548-3227

Public Relations Society of America
33 Irving Place
New York, NY 10003
212-995:2230; Fax: 212-995-0757

Publishers Information Bureau
919 Third Avenue, 22nd Floor
New York, NY 10022
212-872-3700; Fax: 212-888-4217

Publishers Marketing Association
627 Aviation Way
Manhattan Beach, CA 90266
310-372-2732; Fax: 310-374-3342
e-mail: pmaonline@aol.com

Reporters Committee for Freedom of the Press
1815 North Fort Meyer Drive
Arlington, VA 22209-1817
703-807-2100; 1-800-336-4243; Fax: 703-807-2109
e-mail: rcfp@rcfp.org
www.rcfp.org/rcfp

Romance Writers of America
3707 FM 1960 West, Suite 555
Houston, TX 77068
281-440-6885; Fax: 281-440-7510
e-mail: info@rwanational.com
www.rwanational.com

Science Fiction & Fantasy Writers of America
PO Box 171
Unity, ME 04988-0171
207-861-8078 (voice & fax)
e-mail: execdir@sfwa.org
www.sfwa.org

Small Press Center
20 West 44th Street
New York, NY 10036
212-764-7021; Fax: 212-354-5365
e-mail: smallpress@aol.com
www.smallpress.org

Small Publishers Association of North America
425 Cedar Street
Buena Vista, CO 81211
719-395-4790; Fax: 719-395-8374
e-mail: span@spamaet.org
www.spannet.org

Society for Scholarly Publishing
10200 West 44th Avenue, Suite 304
Wheat Ridge, CO 80033
303-422-3914; Fax: 303-422-8894
e-mail: ssp@resourcenter.com
www.sspnet.org

Society of American Business Editors & Writers
University of Missouri
School of Journalism
176 Gannett Hall
Columbia, MO 65211
573-882-7862; Fax: 573-884-1372
www.sabew.org

Society of American Travel Writers
4101 Lake Boone Trail, Suite 201
Raleigh, NC 27607
919-787-5181; Fax: 919-787-4916

Society of Children's Book Writers & Illustrators
8271 Beverly Boulevard
Los Angeles, CA 90048
323-782-1010; Fax: 323-782-1892
e-mail: scbwi@juno.com
www.scbwi.org

Society of Illustrators
128 East 63rd Street
New York, NY 10021-7303
212-838-2560; Fax: 212-838-2561
e-mail: terry@societyillustrators.org
www.societyillustrators.org

Society of National Association Publishers
1550 Tysons Boulevard, Suite 200
McLean, VA 22102
703-506-3285; Fax: 703-506-3266
www.snaponline.org

The Society of Professional Journalists
PO Box 77
Greencastle, IN 46135
765-653-3333; Fax: 765-653-4631
e-mail: spj@spjhq.org
www.spjhq.org

Special Libraries Association
1700 18th Street NW
Washington, DC 20009-2508
202-234-4700; Fax: 202-265-9317
e-mail: sla@sla.org
www.sla.org

United States Ski Writers Association
7 Kensington Road
Glens Falls, NY 12801
518-793-1201; Fax: 518-792-0648
e-mail: cigar83@aol.com

U.S. Board on Books For Young People
c/o IRA
Box 8139800
Birksdale Road
Newark, DE 19714
302-731-1600; Fax: 302-731-1057
e-mail: acutts@reading.org
www.usbby.org

Web Printing Association 100
Daingerfield Road
Alexandria, VA 223-14
703-519-8140; Fax: 703-519-7109
e-mail: tbasore@printing.org
www.priiating.org

Western Writers of America Inc.
1012 Fair Street
Franklin, IN 37064
615-791-1444; Fax: 615-791-1444
e-mail: tncrutch@aol.com

Women in Scholarly Publishing
c/o University of Georgia Press
330 Research Drive
Athens, GA 30602-4901
706-369-6158; Fax: 706-369-6131

Women Who Write
PO Box 652
Madison, NJ 07940
973-731-2841

Women's National Book Association, Inc.
160 Fifth Avenue
New York, NY 10010
212-675-7805; Fax: 212 989-7542
e-mail: skpassoc@cwixmail.com
www.bookb-77.com/wnba/htm

Writer's Guild of America
7000 West Third Street
Los Angeles, CA 90048
323-951-4000; Fax: 323-782-4800
www.wga.org

Writers-in-Exile, American Branch
42 Derby Avenue
Orange, CT 06477
203-397-1479; Fax: 203-737-4233
e-mail: gyorgyey@ct2.nai.net

PUBLICATIONS

Suggested Periodical Reading

Atlantic Unbound/The Atlantic Monthly
PO Box 52661
Boulder, CO 80322
800-234-2411
e-mail: web@theatlantic.com
www.theatlantic.com

Book: The Magazine for the Reading Life
84 Summit Ave.
Summit, NJ 07901
908-522-0300; Fax: 908-522-3104
e-mail: foss@pcc.net
www.bookmagazine.com

Boston Review
Boston Review
E53-407 MIT
Cambridge, MA 02139
617-252-1792
e-mail: rmitchel@mit.edu
foostonreview.mit.edu

Folio Magazine
PO Box 10571
Riverton, NJ 08076-0571
203-358-9900; Fax: 203-358-5812
www.foliomag.com

Booklist
434 W. Downer Place
Aurora, IL 60506
630-892-7465; 1-800-545-2433, ext. 5716
pfoley@ala.org
www.ala.org/booklist/

Book Page
ProMotion, Inc.
2143 Belcourt Avenue
Nashville, TN 37212
615-292-8926, ext. 34; Fax: 615-292-8249
e-mail: elizabeth@bookpage.com
www.bookpage.com

ProMotion, Inc.
2143 Belcourt Avenue
Nashville, TN 37212
615-292-8926, ext. 15; Fax: 615-292-8249
e-mail: julia@bookpage.com

BookSelling This Week
American Booksellers Association
828 South Broadway
Tarrytown, NY 10591
800-637-0037; Fax: 914-591-2720
e-mail: info@members.bookweb.org
www.ambook.org/news/btw/

Book Tech
215-238-5443; Fax: 215-238-5217
www.booktechmag.com

Cole Group
News about Newspapers, Technology, Journalism, and Publishing
The Cole Group
PO Box 3426
Daly City, CA 94015-0426 USA
650-994-2100; Fax: 650-994-2108
e-mail: info@colegroup.com
www.colegroup.com

Columbia Journalism Review
Journalism Building, Columbia University
2950 Broadway
New York, NY 10027
212-854-3958
e-mail: cjr@columbia.edu
www.cjr.org

Editor & Publisher
Editor & Publisher Co.
11 West 19th Street
New York, NY 10011-4234
212-675-4380; Fax: 212-929-1894
e-mail: edpub@mediainfo.com
www.mediainfo.com

Copy Editor
PO Box 230604
Ansonia Station
New York, NY 10023-0604
www.copyeditor.com

The Editorial Eye
66 Canal Center Plaza, Suite 200,
Alexandria, VA 22314-5507
703-683-0683; Fax: 703-683-4915
e-mail: webmaster@eeicom.com
www.eei-alex.core/eye/

Fact Sheet 5
PO Box 170099
San Fransisco, CA 94117
www.factsheet5.com

Granta
Granm Books
2-3 Hanover Yard, Noel Road,
London N1 8BE, UK
Tel: +44 (0) 207 704 9770; Fax: +44 (0) 207 354 3469
e-mail: hu£o@granm.com
granta.nybooks.com

Hungry Mind Review
Hungry Mind Review
1648 Grand Avenue
St. Paul, MN 55105
www.book'wh'e.com/hmr/

Locus Magazine
Science Fiction News, Reviews, Resources
www.locusmag.com

Locus Publications
PO Box 13305
Oakland, CA 94661
510-339-9198; Fax: 510-339-8144
www.bookwire.com/hmr/

Mediaweek
Adweek Magazines
1515 Broadway, 12th Floor
New York, NY 10036
212-536-6534; Fax: 212-536-5353
www.mediaweek.com

The Missouri Review
1507 E. Broadway
Hillcrest Hall
University of Missouri Columbia, MO 65211
e-mail: MR@xniss ourireview.org
www.missourireview.org

The New York Review of Books
1755 Broadway, 5th Floor
New York, NY 10019-3780
800-829-5088; Fax: 212-333-5374
www.nybooks.com

Poets & Writers
72 Spring Street
New York, NY 10012
212-226-3586; Fax: 212-226-3962
e-mail: poet@kable.com
www.pw.org

Presstime
1921 Gallows Road, Suite 600
Vienna, VA 22182-3900
703-902-1642; Fax: 703-902-1616
www.naa.org/presstime/

PRINT—America's Graphic Design Magazine
PRINT Magazine
3200 Tower Oaks Blvd.
Rockville, MD 20852
Fax: 301-984-3203
www.printmag.com

Publishers Marketing Association
627 Aviation Way
Manhattan Beach, CA 90266
310-372-2732; Fax: 310-374-3342
e-mail: infoa@pma-online.org
www.pma-online.org/news.html

Publisher's Weekly
PO Box 16178
North Hollywood, CA 91615-6178
800-278-2991; Fax: 818-487-4550
e-mail: pw@bookwire.com
www.publishersweekly.com

Publishing & Production Executive
Fax: 215-238-5217
e-mail: gldrby@napco.com
www.ppe-online.com

Ploughshares
100 Beacon Street
Boston, MA 02116
617 824-8500
e-mail: pshares@emerson.edu
www.emerson.edu/ploughshares/

The Zuzu's Petals Literary Resource
PO Box 4853
Ithaca, NY 14852
e-mail: info@zuzu.com
www.zuzu.com

Poet Band Co.
PO Box 2648
Newport News, VA 23609

Poet Magazine
PO Box 54947
Oklahoma City, OK 73154

Poet's Fantasy
227 Hatten Avenue
Rice Lake, WI 54868

Poet's Newsletter
609C Idlewild Circle
Birmingham, AL 35205

Poet's Study Club
826 South Center Street
Terre Haute, IN 47807

Poetry Magazine
PO Box 54947
Oklahoma City, OK 73154

Poetry Plus Magazine
State Street Box 52
Pulaski, IL 62976

Poets & Writers Magazine
72 Spring Street
New York, NY 10012

RE:Vision
PO Box 14067
Sarasota, FL 34278

Rhyme Time Poetry
PO Box 2907
Decatur, IL 62526

Stapes
41 Lehigh Street
Williston Park, NY 11596

Scavenger's Newsletter
519 Ellinwood
Osage City, KS 66523

Strophes
R Rte. 3, Box 348
Alexandria, IN 46001

Story
F&W Publications, Inc.
1507 Dana Avenue
Cincinnati, OH 45212

Wordweavers
2112 Arbor Drive
Shrewsbury, MA 01545

Write Now!
Right Here Publications
PO Box 1014
Huntington, IN 46750

The Writer
120 Boylston Street
Boston, MA 02116

Writer's Alliance
Box 2014
Setauket, NY 11733

Writer's Connection
160 Sunnyvale Road, Suite 180
Cupertino, CA 95014

Writer's Exchange
PO Box 394
Society Hill, SC 29593

Writer's Guidelines
PO Box 608
Pittsburg, MO 65724

Writer's Haven
PO Box 413
Joaquin, TX 75954

Writer's Journal
Minnesota Ink, Inc.
27 Empire Drive
St. Paul, MN 55103

Writer's Keeper
PO Box 620
Orem, UT 84059

Writer's Nook News
38114 Third Street, Suite 181
Willoughby, OH 44094

Writer's Open Forum
Box 516
Tracyton, WA 98393

Writer's World
204 E. 19th Street
Big Stone Gap, VA 24219

American Writer: Journal of the American Writer's Union
873 Broadway #203
New York, NY 10003

Anterior Monthly Review
7735 Brand Avenue
St. Louis, MO 63135

Byline Magazine
PO Box 130596
Edmond, OK 73013

Family Earth
129 West Lincoln Avenue
Gettysburg, PA 17325

Felicity
NCR 13 Box 21AA
Attemas, PA 17211

Fiction Writer
84208 Charter Club Circle
Ft. Myers, FL 33919

Final Draft
PO Box 28324
Jacksonville, FL 32226

Gila Queen's Guide to the Markets
PO Box 97
Newton, NJ 07860

Gotta Write Network
612 Cobblestone Circle
Glenview, IL 60025

Housewife Writer's Forum
PO Box 780
Lyman, WY 82937

HWUP! The Wordshop for Poets
PO Box 13743
Tallahassee, FL 32317

Letter Ex: Chicago's Poetry Newsletter
PO Box 476917
Chicago, IL 60647

Literary Markets
4340 Coldfall Road
Richmond, BC CANADA

Little Handbook of Literary Events
Columbus Literary Gazette
PO Box 141418
Columbus, OH 43214

Minnesota Literature Newsletter
1 Nord Circle
St. Paul, MN 55127

Muse Portfolio
25 Tannery Road Box 8
Westfield, MA 01085

New Writer's Magazine
Sarasota Bay Publishing
PO Box 5976
Sarasota, FL 34277

Northwoods Journal
PO Box 298
Thomaston, ME 04861

Our Write Mind
3260 Keith Bridge Road Suite 131
Cuming, GA 30130

Self-Publishing Resources

**The Complete Guide to Self-Publishing: Everything You Need to Know to Write,
    Publish, Promote and Sell Your Own Book**
by Tom Ross, Marilyn J. Ross
Writer's Digest Books
1507 Dana Avenue
Cincinnati, OH 45207
513-531-2222; Fax: 513-531-4744

A Simple Guide to Self-Publishing: A Step-by-Step Handbook to Prepare, Print, Distribute & Promote Your Own Book - 3rd edition
by Mark Ortman
Wise Owl Books
PO Box 29205
Bellingham, WA 98228
360-671-5858
e-mail: publish@wiseowlbooks.com

The Complete Self-Publishing Handbook
by David M. Brownstone, Irene M. Franek Plume
375 Hudson Street
New York, NY 10014
212-366-2000

Business and Legal Forms for Authors and Self-Publishers
by Tad Crawford
Allworth Press
10 East 23rd Street, Suite 210
New York, NY, 10010
212-777-8395

The Economical Guide to Self-Publishing : How to Produce and Market Your Book on a Budget
by Linda Foster Radke, Mary E. Hawkins (Editor)
Five Star Publications
PO Box 6698
Chandler, AZ 85246-6698
480-940-8182

A Guide to Successful Self-Publishing
by Stephen Wagner
Prentice Hall Direct
240 Frisch Court
Paramus, NJ 07652
201-909-6200

How to Make Money Publishing from Home: Everything You Need to Know to Successfully Publish Books, Newsletters, Greeting Cards, Zines, and Software
by Lisa Shaw
Prima Publishing
3000 Lava Ridge Court
Roseville, CA 95661
916-787-7000; Fax: 916-787-7001
e-mail: sales@primapub.com

How to Publish, Promote, and Sell Your Own Book
by Robert Lawrence Holt
St. Martin's Press
175 Fifth Avenue
New York, NY 10010
212-674-5151

How You Can Become a Successful Self-Publisher in America and Elsewhere
by Paul Chika Emekwulu
Novelty Books
PO Box 2482
Norman, OK 73070
Tel/Fax: 405-447-9019
e-mail: novelty@telepath.com

The Publish It Yourself Handbook (25th Anniversary Edition)
by Bill Henderson (Introduction)
W.W. Norton & Co.
500 Fifth Avenue
New York, NY 10110
212-354-5500

Publish Your Own Novel
by Connie Shelton, Lee Ellison (Editor)
Intrigue Press
PO Box 27553
Philadelphia, PA 19118
800-996-9783

The Self-Publisher's Writing Journal
by Lia Relova
Pumpkin Enterprises
12 Packet Road
Palos Verdes, CA 90275
e-mail: princesslia@hotmail.com

The Self-Publishing Manual: How to Write, Print & Sell Your Own Book
by Dan Poynter
Para Publishing
PO Box 8206-240
Santa Barbara, CA 93118-8206
805-968-7277; Fax: 805-968-1379
e-mail: DanPoynter@aol.com (75031.3534@compuserve.com)

Smart Self-Publishing: An Author's Guide to Producing a Marketable Book
by Linda G. Salisbury
Tabby House
4429 Shady Lane
Charlotte Harbor, FL 33980-3024
941-629-7646; Fax: 941-629-4270

The Woman's Guide to Self-Publishing
by Donna M. Murphy
Irie Publishing
301 Boardwalk Drive
PO Box 273123
Fort Collins, CO 80527-3123
970-482-4402; Fax: 970-482-4402
e-mail: iriepub@verinet.com

The Art of Self-Publishing
by Bonnie Stahlman Speer
Reliance Press
60-64 Hardinge Street
Denillquin NSW 2710
e-mail: reliance@reliancepress.com.au

Book Production: Composition, Layout, Editing & Design. Getting it Ready for Printing
by Dan Poynter
Para Publishing
PO Box 8206-240
Santa Barbara, CA 93118-8206
805-968-7277; Fax: 805 968-1379
e-mail: DanPoynter@aol.com (75031.3534@compuserve.com)

Suggested Books and Directories

1001 Ways to Market Your Books : For Authors and Publishers : Includes over 1000 Proven Marketing Tips Just for Authors
by John Kremer
Open Horizons
PO Box 205
Fairfield, IA 52556

Publish to Win: Smart Strategies to Sell More Books
by Jerrold R. Jenkins, Anne M. Stanton
Rhodes & Easton
35 Clark Hill Road
Prospect, CT 06712-1011
203-758-3661; Fax: 603-853-5420
e-mail: biopub@aol.com

The Art and Science of Book Publishing
by Herbert S., Jr. Bailey
Ohio University Press
Scott Quadrangle
Athens, Ohio 45701

Making It in Book Publishing
by Leonard Mogel
IDG Books Worldwide, Inc.
919 E. Hillsdale Blvd., Suite 400
Foster City, CA 94404-2112
800-762-2974

1,818 Ways to Write Better & Get Published
by Scott Edelstein
Writer's Digest Books
1507 Dana Avenue
Cincinnati, OH 45207
513-531-2222; Fax: 531-531-4744

Breaking into Print : How to Write and Publish Your First Book
by Jane L. Evanson, Luanne Dowling
Kendall/Hunt Publishing Company
4050 Westmark Drive, PO Box 1840
Dubuque, Iowa 52004-1840
319-589-1000; 1-800-228-0810

Exports/Foreign Rights, Selling U.S. Books Abroad
by Dan Poynter
Para Publishing
PO Box 8206-240
Santa Barbara, CA 93118-8206
805-968-7277; Fax: 805-968-1379
e-mail: DanPoynter@aol.com (75031.3534@compuserve.com)

**This Business of Books : A Complete Overview of the Industry from Concept Through
   Sales**
by Claudia Suzanne, Carol Amato (Editor), Thelma Sansoucie (Editor)
Wambtac
17300 17th Street, #J276
Tustin, CA 92780
714-954-580; 1-800-641-3936; Fax: 714-954-0793
e-mail: bookdoc@wambtac

2000 Poet's Market : 1,800 Places to Publish Your Poetry (Poet's Market, 2000)
by Chantelle Bentley (Editor)
Writer's Digest Books
1507 Dana Avenue
Cincinnati, OH 45207
513-531-2222; Fax: 513-531-4744

**2000 Writer's Market: 8,000 Editors Who Buy What You Write (Writers
   Market 2000)**
by Kirsten Holm (Editor), Donya Dickerson (Editor)
Writers Digest Books
1507 Dana Avenue
Cincinnati, OH 45207
513-531-2222; Fax: 513-531-4744
Electronic version also available

**The Prepublishing Handbook: What You Should Know Before You Publish Your
   First Book**
by Patricia J. Bell
Cats Paw Press
9561 Woodedge Circle
Eden Prairie, MN 55347
952-941-5053; Fax: 952-941-4759
e-mail: eatspawpre@aol.com

Write the Perfect Book Proposal: 10 Proposals That Sold and Why
by Jeff Herman, Deborah M. Adams
John Wiley & Sons
605 Third Avenue
New York, NY 10158-0012
212-850-6000; Fax: 212-850-6088
e-mail: info@wiley.com

From Book Idea to Bestseller : What You Absolutely, Positively Must Know to Make Your Book a Success
by Michael Snell, Kim Baker (Contributor), Sunny Baker (Contributor)
Prima Publishing
3000 Lava Ridge Ct.
Roseville, CA 95661
916-787-7000; Fax: 916-787-7001
e-mail: sales@primapub.com

The Shortest Distance Between You and a Published Book
by Susan Page
Broadway Books

The Complete Idiot's Guide to Getting Published
by Sheree Bykofsky, Jennifer Basye, Sander MacMillan
201 West 103rd Street
Indianapolis, IN 46290
317-581-3500

30 Steps to Becoming a Writer : And Getting Published : The Complete Starter Kit for Aspiring Writers
by Scott Edelstein
Writer's Digest Books
1507 Dana Avenue
Cincinnati, OH 45207
513-531-2222; Fax: 513-531-4744

The Art and Science of Book Publishing
by Herbert S., Jr. Bailey
Ohio University Press
Scott Quadrangle
Athens, Ohio 45701

An Author's Guide to Publishing
by Michael Legat
Robert Hale, Ltd.
Clerkenwell House 45-47
Clerkenwell Green, London
EC1R 0HT ENGLAND 0171 251 2661

Book Editors Talk to Writers
by Judy Mandell
John Wiley & Sons
605 Third Avenue
New York, NY 10158-0012
212-850-6000; Fax: 212-850-6088
e-mail: info@wiley.com

Book Promotion for Virgins: Answers to a New Author's Questions About Marketing and Publicity
by Loma Tedder
Spilled Candy Publications
PO Box 5202
Niceville, FL 32578-5202
850-897-4644
e-mail: orders@spilledcandy.com

Book Publishing: The Basic Introduction
by John P. Dessauer
Continuum Publishing Group
370 Lexington Avenue
New York, NY 10017
212-353-5858

The Career Novelist: A Literary Agent Offers Strategies for Success
by Donald Maass
Heinemann
22 Salmon Street
PORT MELBOURNE
VIC 3207 Australia
e-mail: customer@hi.com.au

The Case of Peter Rabbit: Changing Conditions of Literature for Children
by Margaret MaeKey
Garland Publishing
29 W. 35th Street
New York, New York 10001-2299
212-216-7800; Fax: 212-564-7854
e-mail: info@taylorandfrancis.com

Children's Writer's & Illustrator's Market, 2000: 800 Editors & Art Directors Who Buy Your Writing & Illustrations
by Alice Pope (Editor)
Writer's Digest Books
1507 Dana Avenue
Cincinnati, OH 45207
513-531-2222; Fax: 513-531-4744

The Complete Guide to Writer's Groups, Conferences, and Workshops
by Eileen Malone
John Wiley & Sons
605 Third Avenue
New York, NY 10158-0012
212-850-6000; Fax: 212-850-6088
e-mail: info@wiley.com

The Complete Guide to Writing Fiction and Nonfiction—And Getting It Published
by Patricia Kubis, Robert Howland
Prentice Hall Direct
240 Frisch Court
Paramus, NJ 07652
201-909-6200

A Complete Guide to Writing for Publication
by Susan Titus Osborn (Editor)
ACW Press
5501 N. 7th Ave., # 502
Phoenix, AZ 85013
877-868-9673
e-mail: editor@acwprcss.com

The Complete Idiot's Guide to Getting Your Romance Published
by Julie Beard
Alpha Books
4500 E. Speedway, Suite 31
Tucson, AZ 85712
800-528-3494; Fax: 800-770-4329

The Copyright Permission and Libel Handbook : A Step-By-Step Guide for Writers, Editors, and Publishers
by Lloyd J. Jassin, Steve C. Schecter
John Wiley & Sons
605 Third Avenue
New York, NY 10158-0012
212-850-6000; Fax: 212 850-6088
e-mail: info@wiley.com

Desktop Publishing & Design for Dummies
by Roger C. Parker
IDG Books Worldwide, Inc.
919 E. Hillsdale Blvd., Suite 400
Foster City, CA 94404-2112
800-762-2974

Formatting & Submitting Your Manuscript (Writer's Market Library Series)
by Jack Neff
Writer's Digest Books
1507 Dana Avenue
Cincinnati, OH 45207
513-531-2222; Fax: 513-531-4744

From Pen to Print : The Secrets of Getting Published Successfully
by Ellen M. Kozak
Henry Holt
115 West 18th Street
New York, NY 10011
212-886-9200; Fax: 212-633-0748
e-mail: publicity@hholt.com

Get Published: Top Magazine Editors Tell You How
by Diane Gage
Henry Holt
115 West 18th Street
New York, NY 10011
212-886-9200; Fax: 212-633-0748
e-mail: publicity@hholt.com

How to Be Your Own Literary Agent: The Business of Getting a Book Published
by Richard Curtis
Houghton Mifflin Co.
222 Berkeley Street
Boston, MA 02116-3764
617-351-5000

How to Get Happily Published (5th Ed.)
by Judith Appelbaum
HarperCollins
10 East 53rd Street
New York, NY 10022-5299
212-207-7000

How to Publish, Promote, and Sell Your Own Book
by Robert Lawrence Holt
St. Martin's Press
175 Fifth Avenue
New York, NY 10010
212-674-5151

How to Write & Sell Your First Novel
by Oscar Collier
Writer's Digest Books
1507 Dana Avenue
Cincinnati, OH 45207
513-531-2222; Fax: 513-531-4744

How to Write Irresistible Query Letters
by Lisa Collier Cool
Writers Digest Books
1507 Dana Avenue
Cincinnati, OH 45207
513-531-2222; Fax: 513-531-4744

How to Write What You Want and Sell What You Write
by Skip Press
Career Press
3 Tice Road
PO Box 687
Franklin Lakes, NJ 07417
201-848-0310

In the Company of Writers: A Life in Publishing
by Charles Scribner
Scribner
1230 Avenue of the Americas
New York, NY 10020
212-698-7000

The Insider's Guide to Getting an Agent
by Lori Perkins
Writer's Digest Books
1507 Dana Avenue
Cincinnati, OH 45207
513-531-2222; Fax: 513-531-4744

The Joy of Publishing
by Nat G. Bodian
Open Horizons
PO Box 205
Fairfield, IA 52556

Literary Agents: A Writer's Introduction
by John F. Baker
IDG Books Worldwide, Inc.
919 E. Hillsdale Blvd., Suite 400
Foster City, CA 94404-2112
800-762-2974

Marketing Strategies for Writers
by Michael H. Sedge
Ilworth Press
10 East 23rd Street, Suite 210
New York, NY 10010
212-777-8395

Merriam-Webster's Manual for Writers and Editors
Merriam Webster
47 Federal Street
PO Box 281
Springfield, MA 01102
413-734-3134; Fax: 413-731-5979
e-mail: mwsales@m-w.com

Negotiating a Book Contract : A Guide for Authors, Agents and Lawyers
by Mark L. Levine
Moyer Bell Ltd
Kymbolde Way
Wakefield, RI 02879
401-789-0074; 1-888-789-1945; Fax: 401-789-3793
e-mail: sales@moyerbell.com

Novel & Short Story Writer's Market, 2000: 2,000 Places to Sell Your Fiction (Novel and Short Story Writer's Market, 2000)
by Barbara Kuroff (Editor), Tricia Waddell (Editor)
Writer's Digest Books
1507 Dana Avenue
Cincinnati, OH 45207
513-531-2222; Fax: 513-531-4744

Poet Power! The Practical Poet's Complete Guide to Getting Published (and Self-Published)
by Thomas A. Williams
Venture Press
PO Box 1582
Davis, CA 95617-1582
530-756-2309; Fax: 530-756-4790
e-mail: wmaster@ggweb.com

Secrets of a Freelance Writer: How to Make $85,000 a Year
by Robert W. Bly
Henry Holt
115 West 18th Street
New York, NY 10011
212-886-9200; Fax: 212-633-0748
e-mail: publicity@hholt.com

This Business of Publishing: An Insider's View of Current Trends and Tactics
by Richard Curtis
Allworth Press
10 East 23rd Street, Suite 210
New York, NY 10010
212-777-8395

Writer's Guide to Book Editors, Publishers, and Literary Agents, 2000-2001 : Who They Are! What They Want! and How to Win Them Over!
by Jeff Herman
Prima Publishing
3000 Lava Ridge Ct.
Roseville, CA 95661
916-787-7000; Fax: 916-787-7001
e-mail: sales@primapub.com

A Writer's Guide to Overcoming Rejection: A Practical Sales Course for the As Yet Unpublished
by Edward Baker
Summerdale Publishing Ltd.

Writer's International Guide to Book Editors, Publishers, and Literary Agents: Make the Whole English-Speaking Publishing World Yours with This One-of-a-Kind Guide
by Jeff Herman
Prima Publishing
3000 Lava Ridge Ct.
Roseville, CA 95661
916 787-7000; Fax: 916-787-7001
e-mail: sales@primapub.com

The Writer's Legal Guide (2nd Ed)
by Tad Crawford, Tony Lyons
Allworth Press
10 East 23rd Street, Suite 210
New York, NY, 10010
212-777-8395

You Can Make It Big Writing Books: A Top Agent Shows How to Develop a Millon-Dollar Bestseller
by Jeff Herman, Deborah Levine Herman, Julia DeVillers
Prima Publishing
3000 Lava Ridge Ct.
Roseville, CA 95661
916-787-7000; Fax: 916-787-7001
e-mail: sales@primapub.com

The Author's Guide to Marketing Your Book: From Start to Success, for Writers and Publishers
by Don Best, Peter Goodman
Stone Bridge Press
PO Box 8208
Berkeley, CA 94707
800-947-7271; Fax: 510-524-8711
e-mail: sbporter@,stonebridge.com

The Complete Guide to Book Publicity
by Jodie Blanco
Allworth Press
10 East 23rd Street, Suite 210
New York, NY, 10010
212-777-8395

The Directory of Poetry Publishers : 1999-2000 (Directory of Poetry Publishers, 15th Ed)
by Len Fulton (Editor)
Dustbooks
PO Box 100
Paradise, CA 95967
530-877-6110; 1-800-477-6110; Fax: 530-877-0222

Directory of Small Press/Magazine Editors & Publishers 1999-2000: Press Editors & Publishers
by Len Fulton (Editor)
Dustbooks
PO Box 100
Paradise, CA 95967
530-877-6110; 1-800-477-6110; Fax: 530-877-0222

The Editors Speak: 500 Top Book Editors Tell You Who They Are, What They Want, and How to Win Them Over
by Jeff Herman
Career Press
3 Tice Road
PO Box 687
Franklin Lakes, NJ 07417
201-848-0310

Getting Your Book Published for Dummies
by Sarah Parsons Zackheim
IDG Books Worldwide, Inc.
919 E. Hillsdale Blvd., Suite 400
Foster City, CA 94404-2112
800-762-2974

Getting Your Manuscript Sold: Surefire Writing and Selling Strategies That Will Get Your Book Published
by Cynthia Sterling, M. G. Davidson
Empire Publishing Service
PO Box 717
Madison, NC 27025-0717
336-427-5850; Fax: 336-427-7372

What Book Publishers Won't Tell You : A Literary Agent's Guide to the Secrets of Getting Published
by Bill Adler
Citadel Press
3300 Business Drive
Sacramento, CA 95820
916-456-6000; Fax: 916-732-2070

The Writer's Market Companion
by Joe Feiertag, Mary Carmen Cupito
Writer's Digest Books
1507 Dana Avenue
Cincinnati, OH 45207
513-531-2222; Fax: 513-531-4744

WEB SITES OF INTEREST

Publishing and Writing Resources

ACQWeb
www.library.vanderbilt.edu/law/acqs.acqs.html
The site is the "gathering place for librarians and other professionals interested in acquisitions and collection development." The site provides a directory of publishers and vendors and "Web News for Acquiring Minds."

American Booksellers Association
www.bookweb.org
The American Booksellers Association is a trade association representing independent bookstores nationwide. The site links members to recent articles about the industry and features Idea Exchange discussion forums.

Associated Writing Programs
www.awpwriter.org
The AWP Web site features select articles from the current issue of the Chronical, information about their award series, career advice, as well as a listing of many literary sites on the Internet. In addition to these resources, their conference information, current literary news, advertising information, editorial guidelines, and membership information is all available online.

Association of American Publishers, Inc.
www.publishers.org/home/index.htm
The Association of American Publishers "is the principal trade association of the book publishing industry." The site includes information and registration for annual meetings and conferences, industry news, info about book publishing, industry stats and issues, and copyright data.

Association of Author's Representatives, Inc.
www.bookwire.com/aar
The Association of Author's Representatives, Inc. is "an organization of independent literary and dramatic agents." It is a member-only site that offers information about finding an agent, Internet links, a newsletter, and a canon of ethics.

The Author's Guild
www.authorsguild.org/
For more than 80 years the Guild has been the authoritative voice of American writers...its strength is the foundation of the U.S. literary community. This site features contract advice, a legal search, information on electronic rights and how to join the organization, a bulletin index, publishers row, a listing of board members, and current articles regarding the publishing field. There is also a link for Back-in-print.com, an online bookstore featuring out-of-print editions made available by their authors.

Authorlink
www.authorlink.com
This information service for editors, literary agents, and writers boasts more than 165,000 loyal readers per year. Features include a "Manuscript Showcase" that contains 500+ ready to publish, evaluated manuscripts.

The Authors Registry
www.webcom.com/registry/authordir.html
The Authors Registry is an extensive directory of authors with contact addresses, phone numbers, fax numbers, and e-mail addresses. Authors are free to list the contact information of their choice in this searchable database. This site contains instructions for accessing the registry.

@writers: For Writers on the Internet
www.geocities.com/Athens/Acropolis/6608
The @writers site includes information about markets, links to a myriad of Internet resources, and reviews of writing-related books. It also provides a technical Q&A section to answer questions about hardware, software, and the Internet. Also available is a chat room and monthly newsletter subscription.

Aylad's Creative Writing Group
www.publication.com/aylad
This site provides a forum for "people to get their work read and critiqued by fellow writers in a friendly atmosphere." The service is free and all writing forms are welcome. The site includes links to other resources for writers.

The Book Report
www.bookwire.com/tbr/
The Book Report is "where readers meet readers and readers meet writers." It is a conversational site where visitors may talk about a book they have recently read or get tips on great new books from other visitors. The site also includes book reviews and transcriptions of an exclusive chat with authors.

Booklist
www.ala.org/booklist/index.html
Booklist is a "digital counterpart of the American Library Association's *Booklist* magazine." In the site is a current selection of reviews, feature articles, and a searchable cumulative index. Review topics include books for youth, adult books, media, and reference materials. The site also includes press releases, the best books list, and subscription information.

Booknotes
www.booknotes.org/right.htm
Based on the book and television program, "Booknotes" on C-SPAN, this site allows one to learn about the authors who have appeared on the program, read transcripts from the program, watch RealVideo clips from authors who were featured in this book, preview the upcoming "Booknotes" schedule, listen to recent "Booknotes" programs in their entirety in RealAudio, and learn about the publishing industry in general. The site also features message boards, a link to the C-SPAN bookstore, and message boards.

Bookreporter
www.bookreporter.com/brc/index.asp
Bookreporter is a site that offers book reviews and a perspectives section that deals with topics such as when a book becomes a movie. It features a daily quote by a famous author.

Booktalk
www.booktalk.com
This site is a publishing insider's page where you'll find out who's hot and what's up. It features links to get in touch with authors, agents, and publishers, as well as a slush pile and bookstores.

BookWire
www.bookwire.com
Partners with *Publishers Weekly, Literary Market Place* and the *Library Journal* among others, BookWire is a site that offers book industry news, reviews, original fiction, author interviews, and guides to literary events. The site includes publicity and marketing opportunities for publishers, authors, booksellers, and publicists, and it includes a list of the latest BookWire press releases.

BookZone
www.bookzone.com
Articles on writing, marketing, business, and legal issues for publishing professionals. Forums, publishing news, online subscriptions to journals "at the guaranteed lowest prices on the Web." For design, development, e-commerce solutions, promotion and exposure, BookZone is the busiest and best Web host for publishers, authors, and other publishing professionals.

The Children's Book Council
www.cbcbooks.org
"CBC Online is the Web site of the Children's Book Council—encouraging reading since 1945." It provides a listing of articles geared toward publishers, teachers, librarians, booksellers, parents, authors, and illustrators—all those interested in the children's book field.

Critique Partner Connections
members.tripod.com/%7EPetalsofLife/cpc.html
Users of Critique Partner Connections pay a one-time fee of $15 to be matched with a fellow writer for the purpose of critiquing one another's work. Maintainers of this site strive to match people with similar interests and critique styles.

The Eclectic Writer
www.eclectics.com/writing/writing.html
This site in an information source for those interested in crime, romance, horror, children's, technical, screen, science fiction, fantasy, mystery, and poetry writing. It features articles, a fiction writers character chart, resources by genre, reference materials, research, general writing resources, online magazines and journals, writing scares, awards, and a writing related fun page.

The Editor's Pen
www.pathway.net/dwlacey/default.htm#begin
The Editor's Pen site exists to connect "sites for and about writer, editors, and indexers." It includes links to lists of freelancers and online dictionaries. Other interesting links include an "Edit challenge" and "Quotable words of editorial wisdom."

The Editorial Eye
www.eei-alex.com
The Editorial Eye Web site consists of a sampler of articles originally printed in the newsletter by the same name. The articles discuss techniques for writing, editing, design, and typography, as well as information on industry trends and employment. The Eye has been providing information to publications professionals for 18 years.

Encyclopedia Britannica
www.eb.com
This service is subscription based and allows the user to search the Encyclopedia Britannica. New users can try a "sample search."

Forwriters.com
www.forwriters.com
This "mega-site" provides numerous links to writing resources of all kinds. It lists conferences, markets, agents, commercial services, and more. The "What's New" feature allows the user to peruse what links have recently been added under the various categories.

Granta
www.granta.com
The Granta Web site offers information about the most current issue of this highly regarded literary journal. The introduction is an explanation and background information about the issue around which the issue is based. The contents of the issue are listed and visitors to the site may read a sample from the issue as well as obtain subscription and ordering information. It also offers similar information about back issues and a readers' survey.

Hungry Mind Review
www.bookwire.com/hmr
The Hungry Mind Review is a national magazine that presents essays, author interviews, children's book reviews, nonfiction reviews, a section on poetics and poetry reviews. Hungry Mind Review is also offered in print version where each issue is built around a particular theme.

Indispensable Writing Resources
www.stetson.edu/~rhansen/writweb.html
Indispensable Writing Resources is a site that offers a categorized listing of Internet writing resources. Categories include online writing labs and centers, general writing/grammar, subject-specific writing, and a miscellaneous collection of writers' resources. It is a searchable site that offers a writing and style library as well as reference material.

Inkspot
www.inkspot.com
Inskspot provides articles, how-to tips, market information, and networking opportunities. Special features include a FAQ for beginners, classifieds, and a section for young writers. Information is sorted by genre.

The Inkwell Writers Connection
home.earthlink.net/ ~ natura/
"The Inkwell is a place for writers to connect. This site has Private Writers Workshops, a survey form, guest book, online magazine, online newsletter, and a link to the Inkwell Message Boards." The site also features links for Inkwell "New Era Novels," games, a message forum, a workshop inquiry form, writers private critique groups, a workshop hostess page, and background music.

Inner Circle
www.geocities.com/SoHo/Lofts/1498/circlefaq.htm
The Fictech Inner Circle was started in April 1997 as "a means for writers—especially new and unpublished writers—to correspond through e-mail with others of similar interest." Membership is free and provides the opportunity—to communicate with over 1,500 writers from around the globe.

International Online Writers Association
www.best.com/ ~ kali/iowa/iowa/section-a1.html
IOWA's purpose is to "offer help and services to writers around the world through shared ideas, workshops, critiques, and professional advice." Services include real-time monthly workshops, real-time weekly critiques, and periodic round robins. The site also includes a library of essays, poems, short stories, and novel chapters.

Internet Writing Workshop
www.geocities.com/ ~ lkaus/workshop/index.html
The Internet Writing Workshop exists to "create an environment where works in progress can be passed around and critiqued, to help us improve these works and to improve as writers," as well as to provide support for writers. The service is membership-based and includes a variety of genres.

Library Journal Digital
www.bookwire.com/ljdigital/
Library Journal Digital is a site that offers articles about news in the publishing industry, editorials, a calendar of events, video reviews, audiobook reviews, bestseller news, and a job search section.

Literary Market Place
lmp.bookwire.com/
The Literary Market Place Web site offers information about publishers, which are categorized by US book publishers, Canadian book publishers and small presses, as well as literary agents including illustration and lecture agents. The site also offers trade services and resources.

Local Writers Workshop
members.tripod.com ~ lww_2/introduction.htm
The Local Writers Workshop is an Internet forum for works in progress, especially those "in the early stages of revision." The creators of this membership-based site pride themselves on its community ethic.

Midwest Book Review
www.execpc.com/ ~ mbr/bookwatch/mbr/pubinfo.html
Responsible for "Bookwatch," a weekly television program that reviews books, videos, music, CD-ROMs, and computer software, as well as five monthly newsletters for community and academic library systems, and much more. The *Midwest Book Review* was founded in 1980. This site features its reviews.

MISC.WRITING
www.scalar.com/mw
"Misc.writing is a Use Net newsgroup that provides a forum for discussion of writing in all its forms—scholarly, technical, journalistic, and mere day-to-day communication." Web site resources include a writer's bookstore and market information.

The National Writers Union
www.nwu.org/nwuinfl/htm
The National Writers Union is the trade union for freelance writers of all genres. The Web site provides links to various services of the Union including grievance resolution, insurance, job information, and databases.

The Novel Workshop
www.ameritech.net/users/novelshop/index.html
The Novel Workshop is an "online writer's colony; a place where writers—from novice to professional—gather to critique, advise, and encourage each other." The site provides links to other resources for writers and a list of suggested books.

Painted Rock
www.paintedrock.com/memvis/memvis1.htm
"Painted Rock provides services to non-published writers, published writers, and readers." Free features on the site include information on a free 12-week Artist's Way program, message boards, goal writing groups, writing topics, a book discussion group, a research listserv, and "The Rock" online magazine. In addition to their free services, the site offers paid online writing classes, a subscription-based newsletter, and two bookstores, as well as advertising, promotion for authors, and Web site hosting and design.

Para Publishing

www.parapublishing.com/cgi-bin/WebObjects?welcome=publisher-visitor
The Para Publishing Book Publishing Resources page offers "the industry's largest resources/publications guide," a customized book writing/publishing/promoting information kit, as well as current and back issues of their newsletter. The site also includes research links, a listing of suppliers, and mailing lists.

PEN American Center

www.pen.org
PEN is an International "membership organization of prominent literary writers and editors. As a major voice of the literary community, the organization seeks to defend the freedom of expression wherever it may be threatened, and to promote and encourage the recognition and reading of contemporary literature." The site links to information about several PEN sponsored initiatives, including Literary Awards.

Publishers Weekly Online

www.bookwire.com/pw/pw.html
Publishers Weekly Online offers news about the writing industry in general as well as special features about reading and writing in general and genre writing. The site also includes news on children's books, bookselling, interviews, international book industry news, and industry updates.

Pure Fiction

www.purefiction.com/start.htm
Based in London and New York, Pure Fiction is a Web site "for anyone who loves to read—or aspires to write—best-selling fiction." The site includes reviews, previews, writing advice, an online bookshop, a writers' showcase, Internet links, and more. They also offer a mailing list.

R.R. Bowker

www.bowker.com
R.R. Bowker is a site that offers a listing of books in print on the Web, books out of print, an online directory of the book publishing industry, a data collection center for R.R. Bowker publications, and a directory of vendors to the publishing community.

ReadersNdex

www.ReadersNdex.com
ReadersNdex is a searchable site designed to give "access to the most up-to-date information about your favorite authors and titles, regardless of publisher affiliation." Books on ReadersNdex are cross-referenced by author, title, subject, and publisher, and may be purchased through the bookstore, the Tattered Cover, or from the publisher. The Bookshelf section is designed for browsing the available books. The site also includes a Reading Room where magazines and reviews may be read; links to the Web sites of participating publishers; and the searchable index of books.

Reference Shelf
Alabanza.com/kabacoff/Inter-Links/reference.html
The Reference Shelf site provides quick access to words, facts, and figures useful when writing and fact-checking. A special "words" section features dictionaries, acronym finders, and links to computer-jargon.

Sensible Solutions for Getting Happily Published
www.happilypublished.com
This site is "designed to help writers, publishers, self-publishers, and everyone else who cares about reaching readers, including editors, agents, booksellers, reviewers, industry observers, and talk show hosts.., and aims to help books get into the hands of the people they were written for." It includes information about finding a publisher, ways for publishers to raise revenues, the self-publishing option, how to boost a book's sales, and sensible solutions for reaching readers.

SharpWriter.Com
www.sharpwriter.com
SharpWriter.Com is a practical resources page for writers of all types—a "writer's handy virtual desktop." Reference materials include style sheets, dictionaries, quotations, and job information. The "Office Peacemaker" offers to resolve grammar disputes in the workplace

Shaw Guides: Writer's Conferences
www.shawguides.com
The Shaw Site for Writers Conferences allows the user to search for information about 400 conference and workshops worldwide. An e-mail service can be used to get updates about conferences that meet user criteria for dates, topics, and locations. Other resources include "Quick Tips," links to organizations, and information about residencies and retreats.

Small Publishers of North America
www.spannet.org/home.htm
Small Publishers of North America is a site for "independent presses, self-publishers, and savvy authors who realize if their books are to be successful, they must make them so." The site offers pages for "fun, facts, and financial gain." They offer a newsletter.

United States Copyright Office
lcweb.loc.gov.copyright
The United States Copyright Office site allows the user to find valuable information about copyright procedures and other basics. In addition, the user can download publications and forms and link to information about International copyright.

A Web of On-Line Dictionaries
www.facstaf.bucknell.edu/rbeard/diction.html
This index of online dictionaries includes 165 different languages and gives preference to free resources. A new feature allows the user to translate words from any European language to any other.

Webster Dictionary
www.m-w.com/netdict.htm
Like its paper counterpart, this Web-based dictionary provides definition to words and phrases sought by users. For word lovers, features like "Word of the Day" and "Word Game of the Day" are included as well.

The WELL
www.well.com
The WELL (Whole Earth 'Lectronic Link) is an online gathering place that its creators call a "literate watering hole for thinkers from all walks of life."

Women Who Write
memers.aol.com/jfavetti/womenww/www.html
Women Who Write is a "collage of women based all over the United States with a passion for writing." The site provides useful links and a large dose of encouragement to women writers of all experience levels.

The Write Page
www.writepage.com
The Write Page is "an online newsletter with over 300 pages of author and book information for readers and how-to information for writers of genre fiction." Genres that the site deals with include science fiction, romance, historical novels, murder mysteries, techno thrillers, and also children's, young adult, non-fiction, poetry, and small press publications. Articles grapple with issues such as how to write and get published, research, tools of the trade, and listings of conferences and contests.

Write Page Author Listing Information
www.writepage.com/pageinfo.htm
This site offers authors a chance to create their own Web sites with the help of Callie Goble. It answers many of the questions that one might have about such an enterprise like "How long CAN my page be?"; "How long does it take to get listed?"; "What sort of exposure will my books get?"; "What does the competition charge?"; and much more.

WriteLinks
www.writelink.com/
The site provides an army of services including workshops, personalized tutoring, and critique groups. "WriteLinks is designed to be of value to all writers, regardless of their experience, genre, or focus."

The Writer's Retreat
wysiwyg://151/http://www.angelfire.com/va/dmsforever/index.html
The objectives of The Writer's Retreat are "to provide a meeting place for writers everywhere, to provide market information, to list relevant Internet links, to list inspirational and motivational information and quotations for writers of all races, creeds, and backgrounds, and to have and provide fun while doing it!"

Writer's Toolbox
www.geocities.com/Athens/6346/body.htrnl
The site contains a "diverse and ever-growing collection of Internet resources for writers." The resources are categorized for many types of writers from technical writers and public relations professionals to fiction and drama writers. The site also includes links to software for writers and business resources.

The Writers Center
www.writer.org/aboutwc.htm
The Writers Center is a Maryland-based nonprofit that "encourages the creation and distribution of contemporary literature." On the Web site, they provide information on their 200+ yearly workshops and links to their publication Poet Lore and Writer's Carousel.

Writers Club
www.writersclub.com
Writers Club is a site that aims to provide "services and information to support, educate, and encourage writers in both their professional and personal lives." The site offers publishing and agent information, industry newsletters, articles on writing, and a mentor program. It also offers author interviews and message boards.

Writers Guild of America West
www.wga.org/manual/index.hml
The WGA West site provides information about the Guild and its services, such as script registration. Other links to writing resources are provided as well.

Writers Net
www.writers.net
Writes Net is a site that "helps build relationships between writers, publishers, editors, and literary agents." It consists of two main sections, The Internet Directory of Published Writers, which includes a list of published works and a biographical statement, and The Internet Directory of Literary Agents, which lists areas of specialization and a description of the agency. Both are searchable and include contact information. It is a free service that hopes to "become an important, comprehensive matchmaking resource for writers, editors, publishers, and literary agents on the Internet."

Writers on the Net
www.writers.com
"Writers on the Net is a group of published writers and experienced writing teachers building an online community and resource for writers and aspiring writers." A subscription to the mail list provides a description and schedule of classes provided by the site and a monthly newsletter.

Writers Write ®
www.writerswrite.com
This "mega-site" provides a myriad of resources including a searchable database of online and print publications in need of submissions. The Writers Write® chatroom is open 24 hours for live discussion.

The Writers' BBS
www.writers-bbs.com/home/shtml
The Writers' BBS is intended for "authors, poets, journalists, and readers" and highlights writers' chat rooms, discussion forums, and an e-zine for beginning writers called "Fish Eggs for The Soul." It also includes games, personal ads, copyright information, mailing lists, Internet links, an adults-only section, and the online King James Bible.

Writers' Exchange
writerexchange.miningco.com
Writers' Exchange offers links on various topics from agents to humor, to writers' resources, as well as interviews, information about upcoming writing conferences, writing classes, information about markets, bulletin boards, chat rooms, newsletters, and opportunities to shop in their bookstore, video store, and marketplace.

The Writers' Pen
members.xoom.com/WritersPen/index.html
The Writers' Pen began with a weekly chat meeting and has evolved into its own chat room. It features a roster of its members, chat rooms, links to other Web sites, and opportunities to read their newsletter or shop their bookstore.

WritersNet
www.writers.net/about_body.html
This Web site "helps build relationships between writers, publishers, editors, and literary agents." Currently there are two searchable directories associated with the free service, The Internet Directory of Published Writers and The Internet Directory of Literary Agents.

Writerspace
www.writerspace.com
"Writerspace specializes in the design and hosting of Web sites for authors. We also provide Web services for those who may already have Web sites but wish to include more interactivity in the way of bulletin boards, chat rooms, contests, and e-mail newsletters." The site also features an author spotlight, contests, workshops, mailing lists, bulletin boards, chat rooms, romance links, a guest book, and information on adding your link, Web design, Web hosting, their clients, and rates.

The Zuzu's Petals Literary Resource
www.zuzu.com
The Zuzu's Petals Literary Resource is a site that focuses on a comprehensive list of writers' resource links and information. It includes a bookstore, discussion forums, its literary magazine, *Zuzu's Petals Quarterly Online*, art news that reports on news in the literary world, and contests.

1001 Ways to Market Your Books
www.bookmarket.com/1001bio.html
1001 Ways to Market Your Book is a site that offers a book marketing newsletter, consulting services, and book marketing updates. Other topics include success letters, author biographies, sample chapters, and tables of contents.

Poetry Resources

Atlantic Unbound Poetry Pages
www.theatlantic.com/atlantic/atlweb/poetry/poetpage.htm
The Atlantic Unbound Poetry Pages are presented by the *Atlantic Monthly*, a literary magazine. The Web site offers reviews of new poetry, a discussion forum, the Audible Anthology (a collection of poetry sound files), poetry articles, links, and poetry from the *Atlantic Monthly* online e-zine. It is a searchable site and offers poetry and literature links.

Electronic Poetry Center
Wings.buffalo.edu/epc/
There are perhaps more poetry Web sites online than any other literary genre, so picking one representative site is really quite pointless. But we do recommend the Electronic Poetry Center at the University of New York at Buffalo, which is the heart of the contemporary poetry community online, having been around since the early days of gopher space, practically the dark ages in computer time. Of particular note is the active and well-respected poetics mailing list, the large collection of audio files, and extensive listing of small press poetry publishers.

Inkspot Resources for Poets
www.inkspot.com/genres/poetry.html
Inkspot Resources for poets offers many Interact poetry links, a poets' chat forum, contests, general resources such as a glossary of poetic terms, mailing lists, courses available, critique groups and workshops for poets, and articles and essays on writing poetry.

The International Library of Poetry
www.poetry.com/nlp/nlp.stm
The International Library of Poetry Web site offers information about their writing competitions, which focus on "awarding large prizes to poets who have never before won any type of writing competition." The site also includes Internet links, a list of past winners, anthologies of winning poems, and chat rooms.

National Poetry Association
www.nationalpoetry.org
The National Poetry Association Web site, supported in part by Grants for the Arts and Maya Angelou, offers an online poetry journal called Poetry USA, and aims to "promote poets and poetry to wider audiences by all possible means, serving both the literary community and the general public." The site is dedicated to the memory of William Burroughs, Allen Ginsberg, and Denise Levertov. It includes information about the National Poetry Association's current projects and offers contests for poets.

Perihelion Round Table Discussions
www.webdelsol.com/Perihelion/p-discussion3.htm
The Perihelion Round Table discussions is a site that brings the thoughts of established poets and editors on issues of the Internet and its effect on poetry and the writing of poetry. There is also a discussion area where readers and visitors may add their insight to the discussions.

Poetry from the Mining Co.
poetry.miningco.com
Poetry from the Mining Co. offers links to such poetry resources as online contests and workshops, magazines and anthologies, poets from the classical period to the 20th century, multilingual and poetry translations, festivals and live poetry events, audio poetry archives, publishers and online catalogs. The site offers a poetry newsletter, bulletin board, chat, bookstore, and "gossip on the poetry word circuit." It also includes "an alphabetical listing and links to online publications, anthologies, and the online sites of print poetry magazines."

Poets & Writers
www.pw.org
Poets & Writers is an online resource for creative writers that includes publishing advice, message forums, contests, a directory of writers, literary links, information on grants and awards, news from the writing world, trivia, and workshops.

Poetry Society of America
www.poetrysociety.org
The Poetry Society of America Web site includes information about the newest developments in the Poetry in Motion project, which posts poetry to seven million subway and bus riders in New York City, Chicago, Baltimore, Portland, and Boston. It also includes news about poetry awards, seminars, the tributes in libraries program, poetry in public program and poetry festivals.

Screenwriting Resources

Hollywood Scriptwriter
www.hollywoodscriptwriter.com/about/tr.html
Hollywood Scriptwriters is an international newsletter that offers articles on craft and business "to give screenwriters the information they need to work at their careers." The site includes low-budget and indie markets available for finished screenplays, as well as a listing of agencies who are currently accepting submissions from readers of *Hollywood Scriptwriter*. According to *Hollywood Scriptwriter*, "people like Harold Ramis, Francis Ford Coppola ,and Larry Gelbart have generously given of their time, knowledge and experiences to share with our readers."

Screaming in the Celluloid Jungle
wysiwyg://37/http://38.201.147.161/index.html
Screaming in the Celluloid Jungle is a screenwriting site that offers message boards, script sales archives, industry news, box office stats, and a writer's forum. Other topics include agents, production companies, a glossary of screenwriting and production terms, articles, producing and directing.

The Screenwriter's Home Page
home.earthlink.net/ ~ scribbler
The Screenwriter's Home Page offers "articles and interviews by people who work, day in and day out, in the movie business." Its aim is to help "not only with writing, but with the reality of the entertainment world." It includes agent listings, best ways to have your script rejected, professionals' thoughts on screenwriting, and industry news.

Screenwriter's Resource Center
www.screenwriting.com
The Screenwriters Resource Center aims to "provide links to products and services for Screenwriters, compiled by the staff at the National Creative Registry TM." It includes links to many screenwriting sites, and offers advice and copyright words of warning for writers posting original work on the Internet.

Screenwriter's Utopia
www.screenwritersutopia.com
Screenwriter's Utopia includes "helpful hints for getting screenplays produced, script development services, and contest information." The site includes a screenwriters' work station, tool kit, agent listings, and creative screenwriting magazines. Interviews with the screenwriters of *Sleepless in Seattle*, *Blade*, and *The Crow*, and *City of Angels* are featured, and other interviews archived. The site also includes chat rooms, message boards, a writer's directory, and a free newsletter.

Screenwriters & Playwrights Home Page
www.teleport.com/ ~ cdeemer/scrwriter.html
The Screenwriters & Playwrights Home Page "is designed to meet the special needs of screenwriters and playwrights." Features of the site include screenwriting basics, marketing tips, screenplay formats, agent listings, pitches and query letters, producer listings, writing for actors, and tips from pros. It also offers a free newsletter and Internet resources.

Horror Resources

Classic Horror and Fantasy Page
home6.swipnet.se/ ~ w-60478
The Classic horror and Fantasy Page aims to "collect links to every work of classic horror and fantasy fiction available on the Internet. The main purpose of this page is not to display the works themselves, but rather to direct the reader to other sites where the works are housed." Some of the authors and works that the site includes are Sir Richard Burton, *The Arabian Nights* 1850 (translation), Johann Wolfgang von Goethe, *Faust* 1808, and Edgar Allan Poe's collected works.

Dark Echo Horror
www.darkecho.com/darkecho/index.html
Dark Echo horror features interviews, reviews, a writers workshop, dark links, and a newsletter. Articles relate to topics such as the perception and psychology of the horror writer, the "best" horror, and reviews of dark erotica. The site also offers information and links to fantasy writing.

Horror Writers Association
www.horror.org/
The Horror Writers Association (HWA) was formed to "bring writers and others with a professional interest in horror together, and to foster a greater appreciation of dark fiction in general." Bestower of the Bram Stoker Awards, HWA offers a newsletter, late-breaking market news, informational e-mail bulletins, writers' groups, agents FAQ, links.

HorrorNet
www.horrornet.com/
HorrorNet was created "purely as a way of giving horror fiction a well-needed boost of exposure. My goal here is to provide the most comprehensive Web site for lovers of horror and suspense fiction." The site includes new book releases, events, message boards, chat, links, articles, interviews, book reviews, and original fiction.

Masters of Terror
members.aol.com/andyfair/mot.html
Masters of Terror offers information about horror fiction, book reviews, new authors, horror movies, author message boards, HorrorNet chat room, and a reference guide and critique of horror fiction that features some 500 authors and 2,500 novels. The site also includes exclusive author interviews, book and chapbook reviews, and horror news.

Children's Literature Resources

Children's Writing Resource Center
www.write4kids.com
"Whether you're published, a beginner, or just someone who's always dreamed of writing for kids," here you'll find a free library of how-to information, opportunities to chat with other children's writers and illustrators, links to research databases, articles, tips for beginners, secrets for success as a children's writer, message boards, a children's writing survey, ask questions of known authors, and register in their guestbook to receive free e-mail updates filled with news and tips. The site also features a listing of favorite books, Newberry Medal Winners, Caldecott Award Winners, current bestsellers, and a link to their own children's bookshop.

Funding

The Art Deadline
custwww.xensei.com/adl
The Art Deadline is a "monthly newsletter providing information about exhibitions and competitions, call for entries/proposals/papers, poetry and other writing contests, jobs, internships, scholarships, residencies, fellowships, casting calls, auditions, tryouts, grants, festivals, funding, financial aid, and other opportunities for artists, art educators, and art students of all ages. Some events take place on the Internet."

The At-A-Glance Guide to Grants
www.adjunctadvocate.com/nafggrant.html
The At-A-Glance Guide to Grants offers information about grants, including a glossary of terms in grant forms, sample contracts, links to grant-related sites, a database of funding opportunities, and related agencies, foundations and organizations. The site also includes a tutorial section that includes information about how to write a proposal, how to win a grant.

The Authors Registry
www.webcom.com/registry/authordir.html
Musicians have ASCAP and BMI, now writers have The Authors Registry. Formed in 1996, this not-for-profit organization collects fees and royalties from publishers and distributes them to authors whose works are being used. The registry also acts as a non-exclusive licenser of author-controlled rights. Log on to their site and search an extensive author directory or add your own name.

The Foundation Center
www.fdncenter.org
The Foundation Center Web site is dedicated to assisting writers in finding grants. They offer "over 200 cooperating sites available in cities throughout the U.S. Of particular note is their large online library with a wonderful interactive orientation to grant-seeking. You'll even find application forms for several funding sources here."

National Writers Union
www.nwu.org
"The union for freelance writers working in U.S. markets...We are a modern, innovative union offering grievance resolution, industry campaigns, contract advice, health and dental plans, member education, job banks, networking, social events, and much more."

Western States Arts Federation
www.westaf.org
The WSAF is a "non-profit arts service organization dedicated to the creative advancement and preservation of the arts. Focused on serving the state arts agencies, arts organizations, and artists of the West, WSAF fulfills its mission by engaging in innovative approaches to the provision of programs and services, and focuses its efforts on strengthening the financial, organizational, and policy infrastructure of the arts in the West."

Canadian Resources

The Association of Canadian Publishers
www.digitalbookworld.com/ACP/welcomeinfo.html
The Association of Canadian Publishers represents more than 135 Canadian-owned book publishers and members of the literary, general trade, education; and scholarly sectors. Through all its activities, the ACP encourages the writing, publishing, distribution, and promotion of Canadian books. The mission is to support the development of a strong, independent and vibrant Canadian-owned publishing industry.

Canadian Authors Association
www.canauthors.org/homepage.html
The Canadian Authors Association is Canada's national writing organization. The Canadian Authors Association home page includes a series of pages describing the activities of the association at the national level. Canadian Author - On-Line Edition is the electronic version of Canada's national writing magazine. The CAA Victoria & Islands Branch home page lists the activities of 15 CAA branches in cities across Canada. The CAA Writing Links Index Page offers a very well organized list of Internet links sorted by genre.

Canadian Book Review Annual
www.interlog.com/ ~ cbra/
The Canadian Book Review Annual is "the most comprehensive collection of authoritative reviews of English-language trade, scholarly, and reference books published in Canada each year." Since 1975 it has reviewed more than 23,000 Canadian books.

Canadian Children's Books Centre
www3.sympatico.ca/ccbc/mainpage.htm
The Canadian children's Book Centre "helps the creative talent of Canada—the writers, the illustrators—reach the people who count; the readers. An investment in The Canadian Children's Book Centre is an investment in your child's future as a Canadian." The site includes biographies and bibliographies of touring authors and illustrators.

Canadian Children's Literature Review
www.interlog.com/ ~ cbra/CCLR/home.html
The Canadian Children's Literature Review is a wonderful resource for parents, students, librarians, teachers and booksellers. It includes a useful consumer guide and is helpful in identifying resources for students.

Canadian Poetry Association
www.mirror.org/groups/cpa/
The aims of the Canadian Poetry Association are to promote the reading, writing, publishing, and preservation of poetry in Canada through the individual efforts of members; to promote communication among poets, publishers, and the general public; to encourage leadership and participation from members; and to encourage the formation and development of autonomous local chapters.

Canadian Society of Children's Authors, Illustrators and Performers
La société canadienne des auteurs, illustrateurs, et artistes pour enfants
www.interlog.com/~canscaip/
Canadian Society of Children's Authors, Illustrators and Performers (CANSCAIP) is a group of professionals in the field of children's culture. CANSCAIP is instrumental in the support and promotion of children's literature through newsletters, workshops, meetings and other programs for authors, parents, teachers, librarians and publishers. It includes Internet links.

Citation
www.harbour.sfu.ca/ccsp/citation/
Citation is a source of information for Canadians and Canadian publishers looking for information about publishing on the Internet, doing business on the Internet, or publishing for the Internet. Included are lists of publishers, booksellers, libraries, literary magazines, and other related international Web sites.

The Crime Writers of Canada
www.swifty.com/cwc/cwchome.htm
The Crime Writers of Canada pages are intended to offer news and information about members and their books. It includes award lists, directories of members' works, mystery links, and the Crime Writers of Canada cookbook.

Federation of British Columbia Writers
www.swifty.com/bcwa/index.htm
The Federation of British Columbia Writers seeks to serve the needs of established and emerging writers. The Federation helps to improve working conditions and expand support programs for writers. They provide members with up-to-date information that helps locate larger audiences.

Forthcoming Books
www.nlc-bnc.ca/forthbks/efbintro.htm
Forthcoming Books lists titles processed by the National Library of Canada's Canadian Cataloging in Publication (CIP) program. 1600 publishers participate in the Canadian CIP program. The entries are listed alphabetically.

Manitoba Writers' Guild, Inc.
www.mbwriter.mb.ca
The Manitoba Writers' Guild aims to promote the art in all its forms in Manitoba. They offer a manuscript reading service, bulletin boards, and literary awards.

Shiba Hill
members.tripod.com/ ~ ShibaHill
Shiba Hill is an "authors cooperative," a place where authors can showcase their works for potential agents and/or publishers. Shiba Hill is not an agent or publisher, rather it strives to help other writers. The site includes the H.E.L.P. Fund Bookstore, which consists of signed books by authors including Raymond E. Feist, Stephen G. Esrati, and Irene Holstein, William Quick, and Jack Mingo. It has a comprehensive list of Internet links to writing organizations, literary agent information, research links, and other writing links.

Wordwrights Canada
home.ican.net ~ susioan
Wordwrights Canada is an editing and author service for those who strive for a high professional standard in their fiction, nonfiction, and poetry. Founded on a belief in the power and integrity of language, Wordwrights Canada has made its aim "The right words in the best places." They offer handbooks for writers, writing contests, editing services, educational services and Internet links.

Writer's Block
www.niva.com/writblok
Writer's Block is a "creative reference for today's writers." It is a connection to professional writers and editors, and the secrets that have made them among the best in their field. Some issues that it deals with are electronic publishing and intellectual property law, a hypothesis about the replacement of words with video images, and a musing about the little words that pervade language.

Writers' Federation of New Brunswick
www.sjfn.nb.ca/Community_Hall/w/Writers_Federation_NB/index.htm
The Writers' Federation of New Brunswick is a community of writers, both emerging and established who strive to develop the craft of writing and who work to promote and encourage the literary arts in New Brunswick. It includes events, a literary competition, and Internet links.

Writers' Federation of Nova Scotia
www.chebucto.ns.ca/Culture/WFNS/index.html
The Writers' Federation of Nova Scotia aims to foster creative writing and the profession of writing in Nova Scotia; to provide advice and assistance to writers at all stages of their careers; to encourage greater public recognition of Nova Scotian writers and

their achievements; and to enhance the literary arts in our regional and national culture. It includes online markets and resources, information about Nova Scotian writers, competitions, newsletters and workshops.

The Writers Guild of Alberta
www.writersguild.ab.ca/
The Writers Guild of Alberta is a community of writers that exists to support, encourage, and promote writers and writing; to safeguard the freedom to write and read; and to advocate for the well-being of writers. They list Canadian author readings, writers-in-residence programs, and plan to establish an e-mail database for timely announcements.

Writers Guild of Canada
home.ican.net/ ~ wgc/One_Sheet.html
The Writers Guild of Canada is an organization of freelance writers working in film, television, and radio production in Canada. It administers, negotiates and enforces collective agreements that set out minimum rates, terms and conditions of work in the Guild's jurisdiction (all English-language production in Canada). The Guild helps resolve disputes regarding work conditions, writing credits, contracts, and collections.

The Writers' Union of Canada
www.swifty.com/twuc/
The Writers' Union of Canada is a national organization of professional writers of books for the general public. The Union works to advance conditions for all writers, to unite writers for the advancement of their common interest, and to foster writing in Canada. The site includes a resource guide for writers called Dear Writer, competitions and awards, technical publications, manuscript evaluation services, and guidelines for hosting a successful signing.

INDEX

D

E

F

G

H

I

K

L

ABOUT THE EDITORS

Jason Shinder, founding editor of *Get Your First Book Published* (previously *The First Book Market*), is the author of the poetry books *Every Room We Ever Slept In* and *Among Women* (Graywolf Press). He has edited several anthologies, including, most recently, *Tales From the Couch: Writer on Therapy* (HarperCollins) and *Best American Movie Writing* (St. Martin's Press), of which he is the series editor. He teaches in the graduate writing programs at Bennington College and the New School University. Founder and director of the YMCA National Writer's Voice, he is also the director of The Writing Program at Sundance Institute.

Amy Holman directs the Literary Horizons program at Poets & Writers, Inc. where she co-founded The Publishing Seminars in 1995. She speaks at bookstores, literary centers, and writers conferences nationwide and has written book reviews and articles on publishing issues for *The Cortland Review, Frigate, Poets & Writers Magazine, Poets & Writers Online, SideRoad, A View From The Loft,* and *Poet's Market* (Writer's Digest Books, 1995). Her own poetry and prose has been published in chapbooks, including *Dwelling With Fire* (Linear Arts, 1997), finalist in Glimmer Train and Alligator Juniper contests, and published in the anthologies, *The Best American Poetry* (Scribner, 1999), *The Second Word Thursdays Anthology* (Bright Hill Press, 1999), *Poets On The Line* (online), and *The History of Panty Hose in America* (Espresso Press, 1999). Poems have appeared in *Poet Lore, CrossConnect, Literal Latte, Failbetter, Aileron, 4th Street, The Metropolitan Review, Mystic River Review* and *Clean Sheets*. She was Associate Editor for *The First Book Market*.

Jeff Herman is president of The Jeff Herman Literary Agency, and author of several books, including *The Writer's Guide to Book Editors, Publishers, and Literary Agents,* and *Write the Perfect Book Proposal.* His Web site address is www.Jeffherman.com.